I, Magdalena

©2022, M P Sherman

ISBN: 978-1-66782-453-6
ISBN eBook: 978-1-66782-454-3

I,

Magdalena

MP SHERMAN

⋆ ONE ⋆

WERE MY STORY not written by men, it would be a more honest tale. For women have a greater understanding of the road set before us. They would have greater empathy for the circumstances of my life and appreciate the choices I was forced to make. The legend of my life was made by men who never knew me, or if I existed, and was brought to lore hundreds of years after I walked this earth. Who I was, how, or if, I came to my situation, never concerned them; they simply made an assumption of my character. It is easy to accept and hold stories as they are told, without evidence or inquiry because they fit the narrative we want to believe. To those scribes, I was an inconsequential and meaningless woman, obscure and useful only in illustrating that a great man saved a worthless sinner. That he was good is without question. That I lacked morality, I must leave for you to decide. But, as is true for us all, there was more to my life than one moment.

I was a girl searching for justice and truth, but in my world, I was merely a woman. I had no rights, and any independent thought was to be denied, forbidden, or silenced. Movement and freedom meant more to me than norms and customs. Light, sound, and art spoke to my soul, and the natural earth and stars were my only genuine comfort.

My society refused to see or understand me, but somehow, and for some unknown reason, the heavens did.

My story really began on the worst day of my mother's young life. On that fateful morning, stumbling up a steep incline, her heart and lungs pounding with panic, she ran searching for her mother. Though thin and underfed, my mother was born to the land and its hardships, and was strong for her size. At any other time, she would have taken the hill in stride, but in those moments, fear weakened her. Gifted with intuition from an early age, she could read people as few did. For days, the stark change in her mother's appearance had alarmed her. The permanent, sorrowful scowl etched on her mother's face had softened into an eerie resolve. The elder's eyes had grown vacant, and she moved as if a shadow no longer connected to a body. When her mother failed to appear at the hearth, the child knew something was wrong.

The desert wind whipped my mother's face while she shivered from the chill that ran through her. As she willed herself up the gravel path, it was futile denying what she knew to be true, but she was always one to hope. Clutching her heart, she peered over the cliff. At the ragged bottom lay scattered bones of unsuspecting animals who, while grazing on the rich grass at the cliff's edge, slipped on the unsettled shale and fell to an untimely death below. On top of those remains, fresh and covered with her single, tattered cloak, lay the broken and dead form that had once been her mother.

The child laid there for hours, traumatized and without expression, abandoned to a desolate world her parent found too painful to endure. Fear, sorrow, and failure overwhelmed her. It would have been easy to fling herself over the brink to join her mother, but she could not find the will to do it. As night closed its grip on her numb form, my mother pulled herself up, picked out two small rocks, and put them in her pocket. These stones would be her only inheritance from a mother she had tried so hard to love but never reached. Cold tears finally fell down her cheeks. With one last look at the woman lying on the jagged rocks below her, Rachel made a vow.

"I will not follow you. I will create the happiness you could never know."

*   *   *

That was all I knew of my grandmother; there had been a terrible accident at the cliff, and my mother did not care to discuss it. But the mystery of it spoke to the misery I carried in my heart; grief about life I did not fully understand. It had something to do with whatever drove my grandmother off that cliff, for eventually, I realized she had taken her own life. I wanted to know why. I felt entitled to the truth. It had as much to do with me as anything did. Although I asked countless questions, I received few satisfying answers. In my determination, I eavesdropped on every scrap of gossip around me while closely observing and analyzing everyone I encountered. I tried desperately to understand how to navigate this life I found so unfair. And yet, I must admit, I was undeniably judgmental of my observations, in no way a clear path for the discovery of truth. As I searched for equity I was sure did not exist, my mother wrapped me in the love she had never known. She tried to protect me and soften the reality of life by creating a world of song, dance, and art.

Yet, with my continued eavesdropping, I learned I was right about life not being just, not for me or any girl, and it got worse the older we became. Such was life in our discordant era of war and occupation, and apparently, I was expected to accept it. But there was more to it than that. While the Romans ruled the countryside and the priests dominated our lives, our frustrated and angry husbands and fathers had dominion over us. Even in the best of situations, they took this power to heart. None of it felt right to me, and while most knew better than to question it, I felt the need to resist. I listened to the music my mother heard, and I tried to find peace in the world of imagination she created for me. But we were different from each other, Mother and me. She was a gentle spirit who found joy and carried her songs within her, and I resented having to keep them hidden.

One day, sitting at the well with Mother and the other women, listening attentively to the lively gossip around me, a woman approached us. She was clutching her chest and wringing her hands in desperation.

"Oh, Rachel," she uttered to my mother. "My Lena has been promised by my husband to the widower Aaron. She is too young, and has cried endlessly for days. She will not eat, and cannot sleep. I don't know what to do."

"But he is three times her age," Mother responded. "Can you not talk him out of this? She is not yet twelve." Mother had a worried look. All the women came to her, for she had a way about her that set people at ease.

"His mind is made, there is no talking," the woman lamented, and began to weep with an anguish that would move even the coldest heart.

Mother had no answer for her, none that would ease her pain.

"I am so deeply sorry," was all Mother could say, and she held the woman close as if to absorb her pain. "Let us hope he will be gentle with her. She will find her way. I do not know the man, but maybe he is kind." Even at a very young age, I knew that was as improbable a chance as any.

I watched the two women, knowing what I had to do. At that moment, I instinctively understood I needed to make myself as undesirable as possible to assure that no one would ever want to marry me.

I had seen and heard enough to know that girlish dreams of romance did not last long. Those fantasies faded quickly as the girls settled into marriages with men they hoped to love, but rarely did. This was the main topic of discussion and gossip among the girls older than me. Without voice or consent, they were most often fated to subservient, often brutal lives, complaining only among themselves until their use was over. Or live a withering existence with an unpleasant man they could never love. That would include me soon enough, and I needed to avoid it.

So, at that moment, I became mute, refusing to speak to any adult outside my home. I pretended I had no tongue. I felt repulsed by every man I saw anyway, not because of how they looked, but because they made me feel worthless and insignificant—and because their attention threatened me. Tempted to spit at their feet and run, I held myself, knowing that would get me nothing but punished. The thought of making myself unappealing felt ingenious.

My pretense made me happy. Except for the gossip at the well, which I relished enthusiastically, most of what people had to say was senseless chatter anyway, and I had no desire to participate in the exchange. As I knew I could not spit at or kick anyone without significant castigation, it seemed the perfect plan. I pretended I was unable to hear what they were saying. I gave no response when they spoke, and practiced confused looks and curious expressions to perfection, thinking myself brilliant. They had no idea what was wrong with me, nor did they care, so they quickly overlooked me, giving me exactly what I wanted; invisibility. The game pleased me greatly, as I desperately wanted separation from them and their rules and obligations. I built an emotional wall around myself, for it seemed my only defense against being taken from my beloved mother and given to an old and angry man I already knew I hated. My mother, most likely understanding me better than I could have imagined, never discussed my behavior. I like to believe she also hoped it would delay the day I left her. As I fought against my inevitable misery, she was my invariable ally.

In so many ways, I was a troubled child. I worried about myself, mostly, but had no clear idea why. Hopelessness and despair closed the air around me after I heard stories of hardships and cruelty from the women at the well. Because I did not speak or interact, the women quickly forgot about me. They felt free to discuss matters more openly and share even their most sordid gossip around me. I was horrified by most of it, although I could never let it show on my face. That would give my ruse away, so I perfected an ignorant, expressionless look that fooled everyone and caused me great pride. Being a self-concerned child, I asked too many questions after these visits that my mother had not the heart to answer, interrogating her over conversations I overheard, begging to know more. I argued against her diluted versions, feeling my need to know stood above everything else, oblivious to her feelings and considerations. She avoided my questions skillfully, giving me songs and stories in their place, hoping to guide better thoughts for the daughter of her heart. I was too self-absorbed at the time to recognize and respect the shadow that life cast on my own mother's heart, for she hid it all too well.

She was an uncommonly beautiful woman who held a sense of joy about her that was not of this world. Since that fateful day at the cliff's edge, she had carefully curated an inner life that was aesthetically rich and delightful. I believe now that however physically pleasing she was, her soul held a beauty the outer world could not fully comprehend. The smell of her was sweet and fresh, like the wash of clear air that hung about the moving stream. Only in years to come would I recognize it as the scent of pure love. Other women in our village were also attractive, but they all looked alike to me. And life quickly wore them down into weary and worn women, at least in appearance. Smiles were rare among the ones I knew. But Mother was different. Her eyes shone with the light of a hundred lamps, holding the pure illumination of creative thought and unconditional love within them. Gracing those brilliant, smiling eyes was a slender nose of perfect length and a rich and generous mouth. Shiny, thick hair, the color of chestnuts sold in winter, hung down on lean, graceful shoulders whenever it dared escape the scarf she used to cover it. She walked with a long, easy stride that transported her with a rhythm of purpose and grace, as if the very ground felt the favor of holding her. Perhaps that is just how my heart recalls it, but prejudiced or not, I noticed that everyone was drawn to her. Faces usually set in a deep downturned frown that had not known a smile in too many years brightened when her gaze met theirs. I didn't miss this even at an early age. Children skipped after her, knowing they were seen and valued in ways they knew nowhere else. But men, too, were drawn to her, some kindly and some with darkness in their eyes and hearts, and these men made my skin crawl as we passed them.

As much as I sought to alienate people in general, I had one true friend. We met by the well while our mothers made their trades. We were kindred spirits, she and I. Instantly, without word or discussion, I knew she worried about things as I did, and we quickly formed an alliance. I spoke only to her, and only in whispered tones when no one else could hear. She delighted in my deception, finding my act one of courage and ingenuity, and we held a secret pact to never break it. She owned cloth dolls made of old rags, and I owned two carved animals my father had made at times when he felt kindly toward me. These moments were rare. He resented me from the first moment he laid eyes on me, for I had committed the ultimate sin in his eyes. I was not a son.

I remember the evening that my father handed the carved horses to me. He had been whittling away for weeks, a way of relaxing in the evening while waiting to be served his meal. I became very curious as I realized what he was making, but of course, I would not dare to ask him. I was not to speak to him unless allowed. But I loved animals, and his carvings were becoming quite intriguing. Looking back, I realize he made them for his pleasure, not mine, but once finished, the only obvious thing was to hand them to the nearest child. He had no other children. I was the only one, another offense for which I apparently would never be forgiven. Still, he handed me the carved horses.

"Here, Magdalena," he said blandly, offering them to me.

I put out my hands to take them, delight in my eyes, but the situation confused me. I was not used to gifts or thoughtfulness from my father, and I was unsure how to respond. I stared at him and could not speak, having no idea how to address him. If there had been any kindness behind his gift, it dissipated quickly. He heard too many disparaging remarks throughout our town regarding my strange behavior. In anger, he pushed me away dismissively.

"Get out of my way, Girl. Go on," he shouted angrily, and brushed me away with his hand, forcing the horses from my grip.

My father, most unfortunately, was a man of little consequence for the successful merchants in our town; a tragedy since his greatest desire was to win their favor. My behavior as a child who could not or would not speak embarrassed him. He felt diminished by it. I had failed him by not being a son, and I seriously disappointed him as a daughter.

Still, I treasured those wooden animals. They were my only playthings, and they meant the world to me. Mother was generous with her affection toward him when she saw my happiness. But it did not last long, for he knew I was the one who held her heart, putting the bitter taste of jealousy in him as well. He resented my very presence. I was of use only for the work I did.

On reflection, I think my father loved my mother more than he understood or could manage. Her good nature was infectious, and even though he could respond in kind for moments at a time, it seemed he could not scale the stone wall blocking his heart. He was too emotionally handicapped and stubborn to love fully, so his emotions often confused and frustrated him.

Occasionally, Mother would leave me at the well under the protection of women she knew and allow me to play with my friend while she finished her trade. We would tie my friend's cloth dolls on the backs of my wooden horses and have them ride with abandon around the base of the well. I was daring in their pursuits, as my friend giggled riotously at their bravery, especially when one might take a mighty leap into the well itself. Hardly noticed by the adults and easily ignored, I heard a great many things that helped me put the pieces of my family's story together. While my mother was not one to speak ill of anyone, the other women were certainly not hindered by such concerns.

I heard my father's father had been a harsh and cruel man, one who beat his wife and showed little respect for anything feminine. I began to understand how that wall around Father's heart came to be. Always sensing his happiness in Mother's presence, I could feel the warmth and light leave the room when she was no longer in it. He rarely showed any overt affection, probably fearing it would make him look weak. That would be more than he could bear. There were very few loving words or gentle gestures, despite her genuinely giving nature. Although he did not spare his hand against me, I never saw him raise it against her, something I would never have tolerated.

In time, I gained an understanding of my father's early life, as the women loved to tell their stories. His father was born to nothing. Through mere luck and inheritance, he became the owner of a single olive grove. My grandfather worked it poorly but managed to keep the trees producing until his death. Inheriting the land made my father a bit better than poor-born, but hardly well-born or of the rising merchant class. Being my grandfather's only son, the land came to him long before I was born. These stories explained numerous things even to my young mind. Although the women embellished the tales with much color and enthusiasm, I recognized the threads of truth that ran through them, and I put the pieces together.

The women at the well believed it to be absolute truth that my mother, with her considerable talents, was the driving force behind any success my father gained. With sales of her ingenious creations, he added hectares of land and planted more orchards. Mother discovered clever ways to use his oil to make highly coveted goods for trade. Her endless creativity transformed what could be endless, repetitive, menial despair into fulfilling works of art. She was brilliant at it. Over the years, Father bought a press, so she could make the oil herself rather than sell the olives directly to the merchants. Eventually, he added a herd of sheep and Mother perfected her skills at the loom. She made their income and reputation grow, not him, but he could never see it. That would have destroyed him. Eventually, he was able to hire a few less fortunate men to work in his orchards, giving him more prestige as a landowner. It did him little good, however, for he never gained the respect he felt he deserved from the merchants, who increased their wealth on the back of his hard work. To them, he was a poor-born man working the dirt. They saw him trying to gain wealth and influence, and they felt only contempt for him. He was not the kind of man they cared to be around. He was not charming or witty, and would not throw his hard-earned money about for their pleasure. They viewed him as a commodity only, and of little other interest. And it seemed many of the women agreed with this assessment.

* * *

One evening, while carrying hot tea to Father, I stumbled and spilled it on his lap. I was but four or five at the time.

"Stupid girl!" he shouted, and slapped my face so hard I fell backward over a chair and into the wall behind me.

Mother seized with anger, but she held her temper, a discipline I should have learned but never did. She knew if she interfered, he would hit me harder.

"You are a mean and horrible man!" I cried. "I want you to drown in tea."

It was a mistake I should not have made, but I did anyway. I was like that, and it never served me well.

"Wretched girl!" he shouted, his face red with anger, and he struck me again. Blood poured from my nose and would not stop. Mother, incensed, grabbed me and hurriedly carried me out of the house as if to take care of the problem once and for all.

"Rachel" Father demanded, in a threatening, commanding tone, but she did not turn around. She moved with a calm assurance that let him believe he was still in control. He thought she was removing me for his comfort, not mine.

She carried me quickly along the worn path to our favorite spot, the stream where we took refuge on hot afternoons. We often did our wash higher up the hill and rested in the shade of the olive trees while we waited for our laundry to dry. The stream was our sanctuary, where we could be our truest selves without rules and judgement and eyes upon us.

I can still feel the warm breeze against my wet cheeks as she settled me into her lap and held her scarf against my nose to slow the blood loss. Only there, in closeness to her, did I feel safe or under-stood. Only she could calm the storms that raged so often within my young soul. She tilted my head and pointed her slender finger into the night sky.

"Do you see those two special stars, Magdalena?" she asked, distracting me from my hurt and anger. I nodded as she continued. "One rules music and the other dance. Only once in a very great while do they choose a child as their own."

As she helped me see beyond my misery, I became instantly fasci-nated that such things might exist.

"They leapt high in the sky and danced across the moon at the very moment you were born. They gave their gifts to you that night," she continued, in her conspiratorial way.

How important I suddenly felt. I looked from her to the stars and back again, forgetting the blood or the injury to my pride.

"Me?" I asked, mesmerized.

"Yes," she answered, assuredly. "They claimed you as their own and set a destiny before you. The entire sky lit up, and there was sound so rare and beautiful, that it could only be heard by those with ears tuned to music." She was enjoying herself as she wove her tale. "They promised to watch over you as long as the sky and stars exist. Do not worry about things of this small life, Magdalena, for you belong to the heavens themselves."

She reached deep into her robe, finding her secret hidden pocket, and pulled out two small stones. I had no idea then that these were the stones taken from the site of her mother's fall, pebbles she had kept close to her all these years. I looked at them and wondered what they could mean.

"Magdalena, these stones are special. They look ordinary, like any uninteresting rock one might find, but they are far from it. They are magic stones, fragments of your stars, sent to advise you that what might look ordinary on the outside can hold a world of mystery and potential to those who understand it; like you, my sweet child. Maybe some will not recognize your beauty and nature, but that does not negate it. This is to remind you always to believe in yourself and your gifts. I will hold one, and you keep the other, and we will be joined and guided throughout our lives, even when you grow up and live apart from me. They will connect us no matter what life brings our way."

I took the small, gray, irregular stone, and it looked to me like the most precious jewel ever created. It was something she and I alone would share; a piece of the heavens, a fragment of the stars, a secret for the two of us.

Her words more than soothed me. They gave me entry to her mind. While she could calm turbulent waters with creative thought, she understood I swam against the current, so she offered me the life of imagination. And I believed in it and her completely. It became our story, the one we told when the two of us were alone or when I felt life closing in on me. We needed to be clandestine in our telling. Our world did not tolerate silly girls and women, and stories of magic rocks and dancing stars might be thought heresy by some. Still, I begged to hear them as often as possible, and they grew more wonderful with each telling.

"Please, please tell my story," I begged, when life's inequities weighed on me. And she would, so I could take them with me into dreams at night, celestial bandits stealing all mundanity from my life and claiming me as their own. They promised a life that did not then exist and a vision I could dream of owning.

My stars became my weapons against misery. When I slept, I floated in colored skies and danced among the clouds. But when I was awake, I was forced to subdue my true nature and know my place, a place I resented, and that fit me poorly.

On the day of my grandmother's death, when my mother vowed she would not live without knowing a single day of joy, she knew she had to create it within herself. She would not find it anywhere else. She wanted desperately to teach me how to do the same, but now I understand the fear that always lived in the back of her mind. What if I was like my grandmother?

But for my mother's influence, life could have destroyed me long before I came of age. On appearance, she managed to be a dutiful, devout, and subservient woman, while within, she was vibrantly alive with beauty and curious thought. With her artist's imagination, she moved with intention, adroitly transforming each tedious task into fine art that pleased her senses. Mundane duties became creative escapes. She saw color as few could, celebrating and delighting in the varied richness of the natural world. She could sit in nature and feel the abundance of life's bounty wash through her soul. She found joy in the sacred melody of the birds' songs, the rhythms of the earth, and the silent clouds that danced so elegantly above her. When she had me and became a mother, her life changed in ways she never imagined. She finally knew love. Her mother had been emotionally absent from the start of her life. Her father had little regard for women, was harsh and demanding, and barely gave a thought to his wife's demise. For the right price, she was given in marriage to a man she could only be relieved to tolerate; hardly the picture of love. But motherhood brought a dimension to her life that seemed miraculous.

* * *

One hot summer afternoon, after finishing the morning chores, we had the luxury of waiting at the stream for our wash to dry. We rested lazily in the shade by our stream, enjoying our rare moments of relaxation. The slow-moving water rippled over the round, worn stones, creating a lulling, hypnotic rhythm. The freshness of the water against the lush banks lifted the loveliest scent to our noses. The stream was our sanctuary; a creative, peaceful world of our own making. Falling into the surrounding sounds, Mother began to sing a song she had never sung before, a mystery to me even then. Inspired, I ran hypnotically about the field, brushing my arms in large strokes across the sky pretending to heave colors onto the cliffs and throwing my stars into the heavens. I jumped high, twirled and rolled, pretending my stars were commanding my dance, dictating my courageous leaps, and favoring me above all others.

Mother laughed, I thought at the magnificence and power of my performance, but now I see it was because I took myself and my story so seriously.

"My little pagan child," she mused, the loveliest smile lightly upturning her full lips.

I cocked my head curiously and thought about this for a moment. I thought my dance had been extraordinarily inspired by the heavens, dictated by magical stars. Was she not taking this seriously?

"What is a pagan?" I asked, defensively.

"That is hard to explain," she answered, even more amused. "Certainly, they are free to act as boldly as they wish. They love music and dance. It is said that pagans are godless creatures, but then who is to say anyone's belief is wrong?"

"Godless?" I questioned, and I could not picture the meaning of this in any way.

"I sometimes think we need to judge the beliefs of others, so we can feel more assured of our own," she continued, "but the name belongs to those who believe and act differently from us." She was speaking more to herself than to me as she continued. "I think most people believe a pagan is someone without a belief in God, or maybe people who do not conform to the rules others would have them obey. Many think of them as evil." She looked away thoughtfully. "Perhaps they just celebrate the only lives they know."

"But we celebrate when we dance and sing," I stubbornly continued.

"Yes, Magdalena, that is why I teased you, but that is for the two of us only. We must also live the life we were born to."

My eyes narrowed, and I pursed my mouth in serious thought, at which she laughed again. So little made sense to me then. Only now do I fully understand how deeply she wished to be as free of oppression as I. I could not grasp it at the time, but she was explaining humanity to me in a way I would have to discover for myself. Having no understanding of what a pagan was, I found her hidden smiles and thoughts of being free of rules and obligations fascinating. I loved that Mother and I could share our secrets and that she was not filled with judgement and condemnation as so many were. Had I been born to anyone else, I would have had my independence beaten out of me early. Most likely, I would have flung myself over the closest cliff at an even younger age than my grandmother. From that day on, I associated the word pagan with Mother's ethereal voice, dancing, and freedom of spirit. It was clear I needed to hide my proclivities from others, but it bothered me to do so, as they were the only things that brought me happiness.

At times, Mother would relax and sing with such abandon, the birds themselves would stop to listen. She had a voice from heaven, the kind that made a body resonate with joy to hear such sound. It was no wonder I loved to dance to her songs and give them form.

"Everything on this earth has a song to it," she said, happy in the moment. "Listen closely, Magdalena, and you can hear it."

I leaned my head into the void and squinted my eyes in earnest, determined to hear something that was not immediately obvious to me. I strained at first, perplexed, but then I relaxed, and when I did, I finally heard it. The gentle sound of leaves twisting in the breeze joined the choir of songbirds and crickets and floated over the steady rhythm of the stream. This was the music that played inside my mother. She was highly attuned to nature and taught me to hear the music she found in the world around her.

"Nature lives in harmony with itself," she often said. "It is only man who silences the music of creation." And with that, I gained a window into her happiness as well as her despair.

At that moment, I recognized for the first time the differences in our ways of looking at the world. Her mind and spirit lived in the beauty she found that always existed, while mine dwelled on what was missing. I fought against injustice with anger and rebellion and wanted to know why things were not right. She knew the pain of the world, so she created an inner life that withstood it. She could not change her circumstances, so she changed her thoughts. While she focused and expanded on the beauty that nature and creativity provided, I was busy worrying about myself. We found joy in our precious secrets, but when we headed home, she warned me to keep our activities between us and to act chaste and subservient when around others. Not that there was a risk of me speaking to anyone besides Father, and I would certainly not tell him of any fun I had. But she constantly stressed that it was better for women not to stand out, to find our freedoms away from the eyes of others. It was a dangerous world for women who did not observe the rules. We could do what we wanted when we were alone, but only then, and that is how we would maintain our joy. And this made me angry.

Another thing that made me angry was being forced to go to the temple. Father insisted, so there was no way out. He needed to have the merchants see him, to remind them that he was devout and active in the community. It was the only time I saw him freely spending money, buying sacrifices when the men he favored were watching. Father loved having the other men look at his beautiful wife with envy, knowing he possessed the woman most would have chosen. He did not realize that no one thought he deserved such a bride, save for his hectares of land and the stain on her from her mother's suicide. I heard this more than once playing at the well.

When we traveled to the temple, Mother and I were immediately separated from the men. We were deemed unworthy, by virtue of our gender, to enter the sacred chamber. I did not care, for the smell nauseated me, and I could not wait to leave its walls. I wondered why I was forced to be there, when my presence pleased no one. Slaughtered animals, entrails, and blood permeated this "holiest" of places. It horrified and angered me. My memories are of the malodorous scent of death. Money changed hands, the more gold, the more sacrosanct the sacrifice, and I quickly learned money was welcomed where women were not, and was certainly more highly regarded.

I experienced the fetid smell, the money changers, and the arrogance of men when I thought of this God they said they worshipped and adored. I preferred God as my mother considered Him. This was a God who was wise and good, who cared for all creatures, and who put stars in the heavens to guide and protect us. A God of creativity and expression, one who gave her the voice of an angel and gifted me with a body that could bend to its sound and make her music seen. A

God of joy, a God who loved the sacrificed lamb as much as He loved me, and would not ask for its blood.

But Father craved prestige and influence, and so we were to travel with him, be quiet and obey; the three things I most detested. I don't know if Father gave a thought to God when he was there, but he was adamant we go. If only it had unlocked his heart in any way, his life, as well as ours, could have been so different. His greatest sin in my mind, if such a thing exists, is that he failed to recognize and appreciate the beauty of my mother's soul. Like so many, he held no true respect for women, believing us inferior.

Theirs was, of course, an arranged marriage, and one she tried hard to honor. Because he was not as cruel as some, and because she knew it could have been so much worse, she accepted her fate and made the best of her circumstance.

Our mornings of trade were among my happiest times, filled with play and other children. But the days before were torturous. Father was so stern and demanding regarding our preparations that even-tempered Mother was at wit's end by the time we set out. We had to impress. That was his driving message. He would go over and over the selling points of the products my ingenious mother had created. Her wares were unique, things he would never imagine could exist until she produced them. He would dictate what to say and how to say it, relentless in his commands and instruction. I should have laughed, for no one had ever seen such lovely oils, soaps, and woven design as she created. She distilled and pressed plants, extracting their essence and mixing them with Father's finest olive oil, creating perfumes and healing salves, anointing oils and cleansing products that softened and nourished skin dried out by our harsh climate. The merchants wanted as much as they could get their hands on, and still she had to bear Father's commands. He had no idea what he was dealing with;

he could not recognize the exceptional art she brought to everything she touched. Somehow, he believed he held ownership and dominion over it all. The worst part was that Father courted the most successful merchant in our city. This was the prize; to gain that man's favor. And he was the one we detested the most.

We would head out, having endured stressful, exhausting days of commands, weary but not defeated. We had our orders, and with an appearance of surrender and acquiescence, we did as we always did; let the beautiful products sell themselves. Once we were on the road, our hearts lightened, and we became ourselves again. Out of Father's sight, we sang songs and enjoyed the day; Mother, our dear little donkey, and me. The town's colors and sounds differed from those of the orchards. It had life and movement unique to the bustle of trade. And I was with my lovely mother without that critical glare of Father's. We could spend half a day shopping for supplies, bartering our wares and bringing home coins as profit. Often, Mother bought a special fruit or date, or even a small honey cake for me to eat. But I was not to tell. Not that I would.

And then we would start it all again, our renewed production of lovely wares, distilling petals and plants that filled our noses and spirits with great pleasure, weaving tapestries of vivid colored wool that we spun and dyed ourselves, singing songs and dancing; a shared creative ideation, all in the guise of subservience. At home, I worked alongside Mother until Father returned from the groves. Life was worth living until he came home.

"Pull off my boots, Girl," he ordered, one evening, with not a look in my direction. He sat at the table and extended his long legs in front of him, expecting me to drop what I was doing and jump at his command. I struggled with the task, and he seemed delighted at kicking me across the room as the boot freed his foot. I wondered at the time why he treated me with such cruelty, and now I understand it was because he could. Feeling powerless in a world he could not control, he at least had sovereignty over me.

After I served his dinner, he waved me off with his hand so he could be alone with Mother, sending me to my alcove to eat by myself. In my cramped nook, set off from the main chamber, I had my straw bed and a small loom, the one on which I wove swaddling clothes for newborns. It was windowless and somewhat dark, but I was out of Father's sight, which made us both happy.

He and Mother shared a larger alcove on the opposite side of our stone house, where he could also be away from me. Sent to my corner, I wove colored threads and sang to myself until I fell asleep. I played with my wooden animals, giving them names and having them dance about my bed with abandon. They were pagan horses and free to do whatever they desired. I wished on my stars they would become real and take me to distant lands, somewhere far from the life I was living.

I was never to go to their bed. This was strictly forbidden, even when I was terrified by frightening dreams. I had a recurring dream of whippings and beatings and abandonment, and when it overcame me, I shivered under my blanket, forcing myself to think of the stream, my mother's songs, and dancing. Praying for the light to appear and banish these wicked scenes from my mind, I clenched my special rock and my wooden animals to my chest, and waited for the precious morning to break. Knowing no one would show up to soothe me, I called out to my stars.

One morning, I made the mistake of trying to tell my dream to Mother while preparing Father's tea.

"Silence!" Father shouted. "I do not want to hear stupid stories from a frightened girl."

And I hated him for the entire day.

Even now, it is difficult to understand why he was so disagreeable. He had a beautiful wife who was pleasant and talented beyond measure, land that provided income, and men to help him work it. I sensed it was because they were not blessed with other children. I had robbed him of his prestigious son, an unforgivable offense, and Mother had not produced an heir. He held this against her, despite her many talents. She was a gifted cook, her stews uncommonly savory with nuanced flavors, and she filled the house with small cakes and delicious bread, even in times of low harvest. She increased his wealth by great measure with her weaving and oils, and still, nothing seemed good enough or bountiful enough for him. He was a man who only saw the empty side of his plate.

Mother and I worked throughout the day. We were lucky, or perhaps wealthy in some eyes, for we had a stone floor, not dirt and straw. It was easy to sweep and keep clean, something I had to do much more often than I felt was necessary. I did it quietly while mother made the fire and boiled water for tea. I would already have prepared the dough for baking when the coals were ready. The day's work would not end until well after the sun had set.

But then we would have more wares to sell and would, after enduring endless hours of adamant tutelage from Father that tested the boundaries of our patience, set off again for a half day's reprieve. I cherished all the information I gleaned at the well, but I felt separate from everyone I met. This was my own doing, aided by my commitment to my mute deception. But something happened when I was five years old that began to alter my way of thinking.

We bought our grain from a kind and gentle man who owned a small tent at the edge of our city. I felt at ease around him, but I was too uncertain and stubborn to look at him directly. I only knew his hair was dark and seemed to abandon the top of his head while carrying bits of white at his temples and in his beard. He seemed in balance with my mother's easy nature. I could tell by the timbre of his voice that he had a tender heart.

Things seemed different on that day. Something about his voice caught my attention, and I looked up at him and into his eyes for the first time. He stared back at me, and we made a connection. But then, his face became featureless, as if breaking apart and dissipating. A bright aura covered his body. I was transfixed. He seemed to be made more of this overpowering light than flesh as he transformed before my eyes into a less solid form. I had no idea what was happening.

"Magdalena," you must not stare at people," Mother admonished, and I was surprised she did not see what I saw. I was frozen in my spot, filled with a knowing I did not understand, but also intuiting that this person shared my experience. Mother pulled me away, saying a gracious goodbye to the lovely, and now mysterious, man.

"Goodbye, Magdalena," he said, something he had not done before. "Have a happy life." I was surprised he knew my name.

I was too confused to tell Mother what I observed, afraid that, even to her, it would seem only a child's fantasy. And I had no words to describe what I witnessed. But I never saw that man again, and I needed to validate what happened. I looked for him whenever we went to the market. I waited, almost patiently, to enter his tent. When we began buying our grain from other vendors, merchants who lacked the beauty of this man's heart, I demanded to know why.

"Mother, I asked, "why do we buy our grain from these men? I like our other man better."

"Yes, Magdalena, so did I," she answered, and I detected sadness in her voice.

"Then why do we go to these other people?"

"Our dear man went to sleep the night we last saw him and never woke up. He told his wife he felt tired and wanted to rest. Bless him, his rest is long indeed."

I did not understand. Although I had seen animals die, often brutally, I did not comprehend the concept of death. How does a person fall asleep and not wake up? Fear gripped me at that moment because it occurred to me that Mother and I went to sleep every night. Should I be afraid? But then what? What is this thing that happens? But the image of the man when I last saw him was peaceful, and in some way, wonderful.

"I do not understand," was all I could say.

"God took the man in his sleep," Mother continued. "Of course, his wife is grieving and hopes their young son can carry on his father's trade, but they are in for hard times. Still, to be taken in our sleep is a blessing. He was a good man given a good death."

These thoughts haunted me. Do we dissolve into light? What does that feel like? We go to sleep, but never wake up? Do we dream? And then what happens to us? I had too many questions and no answers, which left me unsettled. Could I escape this fate? And why would I want to? I hated the life I was living, and felt distant from everyone I met. Why that bothered me, confused me further. I did not even like most people. For some incomprehensible reason, this man's soul reached through the veil between worlds to let me know there was more at play than I had imagined. Leaving this life was not as great a tragedy as I feared. If only I had always kept that in mind.

* * *

After that experience, I seemed to walk with my feet in two different worlds, understanding neither. Many days passed and the weather grew warmer. We went to the stream often to do our wash, collect water, and escape the heat of the day. Mother's songs were abundant and beautiful. I danced with abandon, feeling free with my mother in nature.

Then one day, surrounded by her voice and staring into the stream, my personal, self-absorbed thoughts lifted from me. I looked past my image into a world beyond it, while the strangest sensations stirred me. My body no longer felt real, as if I were a force behind my flesh. I was not this thing with fingers and toes and arms and parts that moved. I was the entity watching those parts. Behind my own eyes, I perceived a shared familiarity. I saw myself in others and recognized them in myself, knowing, without understanding, that this essence existed in every living creature, even animals and the people I thought I despised. I was plunging into the vision, becoming absorbed into something that lives without the body. An unfamiliar sense of belonging enveloped me, a feeling that I was one with everything around me. I, who worked so hard at separating myself from others, was joined with them. I was falling, no longer up or down, but apart, into segments of light that danced on the ripples in the stream. Longing to evaporate, to become nothing, I realized I was a part of everything. I was like the man who sold us grain as he dissolved into light.

And then it was over. I stared again into the still water, trying to understand what I had just experienced, and surprised that I was in my body and still alive.

Mother had been singing this whole while, enjoying a respite from my constant chatting and never-ending questions. She was a woman who loved to sit with her musings. And from the depths of those thoughts, from the solace of her soul and heart, came her songs. Little did I understand then how deep her mind ran.

"What have you been staring at all this while?" she asked, aware I had not moved or spoken for long moments. "A pretty little girl?"

The question hit me as shallow and frivolous.

"That disappeared," I answered, almost annoyed, without taking my eyes from the water, hoping it would begin again. I felt abandoned once it stopped.

"Disappeared?" Mother looked at me, curious about my reaction. "How is that? Is that not your reflection?"

I had no words for what I had experienced. Now that I am seeing my life in review, as it passes away, I can understand and describe things more clearly. Then I had no reference for what I saw.

"Yes," I answered, and I refrained from telling her the truth. I am uncertain why. Perhaps it was the shame of foolishness, or the foolishness of shame; an affliction that kept its hold on me much of my life.

"I watched a girl who wishes she could be as beautiful as you."

But that was not my truth. My words rang hollow to me as I lied to my mother, for I instantly regretted not telling her. She would have understood what I saw better than anyone. But I was so young and unsure of everything, especially myself. I knew nothing of the world, let alone the heavens.

When I stared into the reflection, it lifted me from my ordinary perceptions and beliefs. I viewed life beyond the confines of a physical body. I could have kissed the water a thousand times for giving me a glimpse of something bigger than the treacherous world I beheld. You might say I recognized my soul, but I would disagree. I felt the continuous connection of all things, and the essence that exists beyond form.

This vision also raised many questions. If this essence were true and part of everything, why does disparity exist in the world? Why are women treated so poorly, and men fight against their brothers? Why is cruelty so prevalent? How do we forget we belong together? How do we fail to celebrate our connection?

As I leave this life, I understand that looking into the still water, I no longer remained in the world created by narrow thoughts. I saw with fresh eyes, eyes that existed beyond my body. Perhaps some would call it God's vision. I do not know, nor do I care what anyone calls it, for I see it does not matter, nor does it change its meaning. There is a common essence, something we are all born with, and a thing we forget we share. And perhaps this is the root of all man's problems; the forgetting.

Humans clouded this vision, muddying the waters within their souls, but I saw that animals did not. They are honest and hold to their essence. People, for myriad, meaningless reasons, see themselves as separate and apart. And yet, did I not spend most of my own time doing the same?

Despite my usual errant behavior, this experience created a shift in my thoughts. While I remained inwardly agonistic, another part of me understood that the person or animal standing before me was nothing more than a veil of flesh hiding this essence. Of course, like others, I forgot this lesson while making my way through the world. I let my likes and prejudices rule me much of the time. Life had to shake me hard to reawaken it, but on that day, I became conscious of the realm into which my mother made her escape.

I sat next to Mother and rested against a tree. She glanced at me and smiled, not sure what I was up to, but likely still enjoying my silence. She sang a new melody, and I sank into the caress of her voice, soothed by the great opening of my heart. I stared at nothing, quiet and under the spell of all that had happened, when a young rabbit crept up to my side and gazed at me. I looked into the deep, dark pools of his eyes and settled again into the mystery of the stream, becoming one with the small creature. He peered back as if sharing his essence with me, and then he crawled into my lap, laid his head against me, and fell asleep.

From that moment, an even stronger bond was born between me and the animals, for I could more easily recognize the unifying essence in them than I could in people. It became natural for a small rabbit or marmot to crawl into my lap and rest in its safety. I could stroke them while we rested; they, with no fear. Every so often, a bird would land on my shoulder and join in Mother's song. All of it felt right. They trusted me as I did them. They were my only friends besides Mother and my one ally at the well. Humans silenced the music in their souls and tried to quiet mine, but animals were true to themselves. Even with all of this in mind, despite this gift of vision, I still found it difficult to live with the senselessness I encountered in other people and the rules they inflicted on me.

* * *

When my father glared at me, I thought of the parents in town who held their children's hands. True, most favored were the boys, but some had fathers who actually picked them up and swung them around and even played games with them. How wonderful those men seemed who could enjoy their children. I saw girls laughing with their parents rather than standing silently behind them. It seemed the people who enjoyed their lives and families were the ones with little to show in the world. With meager property to hold, they found their wealth in the smiles and love they shared, rather than in the praise of the priests and esteem of the community at large. They were free from the confines of "devout" behavior. I longed for these riches.

In the colder months, Mother and I spent hours at our looms making the clothes we sold or traded. Sometimes I would stare for long moments at Mother for inspiration. While she was weaving, she entered a different realm, and she brought that world to life with her designs. She emanated such peace and tranquility, it was contagious. I wondered at her ability to pull such beauty out of her imagination and into her work. While her hands moved in repetition, her mind flew into expansive realms I could only imagine.

Watching the threads weave one upon the other, seeing the colors merge, I too fell under their spell. They moved my hands with a rhythm that lifted and expanded me. It filled me with such joy, I would not stop. My mind left this world and swam in the profound consciousness I found in the stream. The feeling between us was unspoken, but it was deep and rich and filled with gratitude. I learned to sit with a quiet mind through a world of suffering. But I get ahead of myself, for I did not know genuine pain at that time. I only thought I did. Those were lovely years compared to what lay before me.

I have neglected to say much, thus far, and for many good reasons, about the Roman soldiers. Our lives changed dramatically when they became an integral part of it. As my life passes before me, I can see why things happened as they did, but until now, I would not have fully understood.

Before they became a part of my life, I only observed them from afar. They would turn up out of nowhere, causing all speech and laughter to cease, as if sucking the air from the sky while the citizens held a collective breath. Being so young and self-absorbed, it did not impress me until I came to know them. I was much more interested in the soldiers' horses and their bright-colored blankets and decorated saddles. The more distinguished soldiers had the most silver medals on themselves and their steeds.

Some soldiers seemed arrogant and proud as they rode through the crowds. The older women told stories of their unreasoned cruelty after they passed, so I recognized which ones were the most dangerous. But some of them looked young and lonely. They watched the families with amusement and even longing, missing their own. What a strange life they must have led, and it caused me to wonder about things. It did not seem that all were bad or cruel, but they were an enemy; an occupier, a force of great concern. They held power over us and stifled our lives. I could not imagine my life being any more restricted than it was, but I still worried when I heard stories of rape and torture and people disappearing, even if I did not understand their meaning.

Although I felt afraid of them, they also fascinated me. It was their steeds that intrigued me the most. I was used to donkeys and thick beasts of burden, but I could tell these animals knew about dance. I could see it in the way they moved. They were lovely beyond description. I spent hours imagining the magical feeling of riding on their backs, like dancing in the wind. Then I heard it whispered that the soldiers were not only ruthless, they were pagans who worshiped many strange, false gods. Ah, the pagans again. Pagans with dancing horses…

* * *

Most people considered Mother's extraordinary appearance when they thought of her, but she gave it little thought. After all, what value was it to her in the way of life she was given? Instead, she undertook to create beautiful things, to spend her time in an esthetic that was not apparent in her life of toil and submission. She sought and encouraged beauty in others, even when they could not find it within themselves. She made everything around her lovelier. She knew herbs and flowers and had great skill in distilling plants and infusing their fragrance into Father's oil. These exceptional goods sold well in the market. It took many plants and much time to produce a small quantity of essential oil, so they were precious and rare. She also mixed oils of lesser quality, and fragrances, into soaps that left the skin moist and soft. The wives valued her creations, and viewed them as a desirable luxury in our dry climate. The wealthiest women wore her oils as perfumes and luxurious lotions, and the devout bought them for holy rituals and anointing loved ones for burial. Many considered Mother a substantial healer, her herbal blends and salves known to cure coughs and fevers, wounds, and skin ailments.

The Romans coveted her wares, buying them as gifts for their wives, or perhaps for the girls I heard they kept in their tents while they were away from their spouses. Mother, of course, was not to interact with the officers and had to give her oils to the merchantmen of our village to peddle to the soldiers.

"They give you one and sell for ten," Father often said, but he knew there was no other way.

It was the way of business in our world. Mother always saved small amounts of oil in the cracked jars she couldn't sell and gave them to the poor women she knew. She wished they, too, could enjoy it for their broken skin or wounds. If she learned a friend lost a husband or child, she gave them what they needed for a proper burial. It was our secret, Mother's and my own, for charity was not a word my father understood.

At season's end, with an ample supply of products to sell, Mother and I loaded our donkey with weavings and many jars of oil, and strapped the extra across our backs with large scarves. We were happy, for we knew we would see a good profit, and we sang our songs along the dry, dusty path to town. Everything seemed promising on that day. The morning was lovely; the sky so blue and deep I thought I could touch it, and the early sun felt pleasant on our skin. But as the walk continued, I lost enthusiasm and complained about the weight of the jars and the length of the road.

"Are we almost there?" I repeated, frequently, and Mother smiled and sang another song to comfort me. Even now, I fear my childish whining was a good part of our distraction on that day.

As we entered the city, we stopped at the first well to let our donkey drink.

"There is a new captain in town," the tall, lanky woman told us.

"Has anyone seen him?" Mother inquired.

"At least that ruthless drunkard has been sent off," the shortest woman, the one with no front teeth, said of the last captain in charge. She grinned with shining gums as she explained, "They caught him bedding down with the wrong girl one time too many." And she laughed.

I did not understand what going to bed had to do with any of it, so I brushed it off, and looked around at the wonders of the market.

"He finally got his due," she continued.

"God knows what this new one will bring," the tall one continued. "But no, no one has yet seen him."

"I suppose none of it matters," Mother said, in her easy manner. "They are all the same. We will be fine if we stay out of his way. Have a good day."

We circled the bustling center to soak up the surrounding excitement. It was uncommonly busy and cheerful. We became absorbed in the lively activities around us as we made a turn to walk toward the most lucrative merchant's tent. As we turned, a fast-moving object came darting toward us, large and looming and out of nowhere. With both of us distracted and looking off in different directions, we did not react with enough precision. Our poor little donkey, frightened and overburdened, pushed against Mother, shoving her and all of her oils to the rocky ground. Trying to regain her balance, she grabbed onto the shaken donkey. As he stumbled for footing, most of the jars he was carrying landed on top of the others. Not knowing what to do, I rushed to her side, slipped on the spilled oil, and I and all my jars dropped onto the heap beside her. Months of labor, a season's worth of income, all ruined. There we were, drenched in lost treasure. A penetrating dread of what Father would do and say overcame us.

Mother was shaken and shouted, "Can you not look where you are going?" and looked up to see the new Roman captain on the largest stallion I had ever witnessed.

The horse mesmerized me. His coat was lustrous and had the color of a deep winter storm. He was large and muscular, yet elegant and proud. Never had I seen a creature such as this. Sensing my affinity with animals, he swept his nose against me. I was thrilled and reached out and pulled him toward me, an act that would bring terror into the heart of any other citizen. I should have thought better of such an action, of reaching for a Roman's prized property, but I felt a connection and instinctively returned his affection.

Mother panicked when she realized she had raised her voice to the new captain in charge. And her child was fondling the soldier's horse. These acts could be punishable if this soldier proved unreasonable. Hardly a good start. As I looked up at the man, he seemed handsome and majestic in a way none of our men were. I could not take my eyes off him, and I suddenly realized he could not keep his off her.

If there is such a thing as time, and if there is a place where it does not exist, the two of them entered that world the moment their eyes met. Drenched in oil, dusty from the fall, and angry in a way I had not known in her, she still appeared a goddess to this man who seemed struck by lightning. He had never felt such an immediate pull toward a woman. She had never had the experience of being seen as the person she was.

He jumped down from his decorated saddle and rushed to her side. Everyone in the immediate area drew to attention at this move, and they fixed their eyes on the scene of broken pottery and streams of precious oil. It was not uncommon for a soldier to run down a citizen and ruin her wares, but it was unimaginable that one would take responsibility for such an act.

"Forgive me," he said, almost reverently, "how clumsy of me to enter a town on my first day only to run down a woman and her child. My horse is too eager to race."

He extended his firm hand to help her up, holding his other out to me as though I, too, mattered. I liked him despite his ruining us. I blushed at the strength of his grip.

I wish our life had been different. From where my soul now sits, I see there are possibilities we never imagined existed, never believed we could own. But it was not so on that day. I wanted the three of us to jump up on that brilliant horse and ride off forever. We would go to a place where Mother could sing, and I could dance without shame. We would live with this handsome soldier, a man I already loved because of the manner in which he regarded my mother and the way he saw me. But we were nowhere near that world, and Mother had to reclaim her mask of subservience and composure as the merchantmen edged toward the scene.

"Fine woman," the soldier said, his voice a song of its own. "I fear I have ruined most of your goods with my carelessness. Let me repay you at the purchase price."

The merchants seemed to understand what he said and moved toward them, afraid of losing their share. The soldier, being a man of the world, read their intention and reached into his pouch. Drawing out a substantial sum of gold coins, he placed them into Mother's palms. I could not help but notice the look between them as their hands touched.

"I hope this is adequate," he said, just as the merchants drew near.

"Dear Captain," the most corpulent of them spoke, "men transact business here. It is our way. Women should not barter with soldiers. It is not proper." He glared at Mother. "We will accept your coins and give this woman her due." And he reached his thick hand in Mother's direction as if to take possession of the gold.

The soldier blocked his arm, to the merchant's surprise. "She is the one I injured, and she and her lovely daughter are the ones robbed by my carelessness. I see no reason you should have a share. This was not a purchase; I am repaying her for what I ruined. This is my way, so if you take her money, I will tax it for their full value. You are not selling these wares and have no hand in their marketing."

The merchants flushed with contempt and anger, but they knew they could not cross this Roman of high rank. They glared at Mother as the soldier pushed the fractured vessels to the side of the road and gathered what little was left. He tied the few unbroken jars and three undamaged weavings onto our donkey's back.

"But who has woven these blankets?" he asked.

"Mother did," I said, more surprised than anyone that I had a voice among adults and used it. After all, he called me her lovely daughter. I was on his side.

The personable soldier, a man I was in love with already, smiled and directed his speech toward me.

"These are the finest blankets I have ever seen. Do you think your mother would make one for my horse?" he asked, conspiratorially, and I felt like dancing.

"Yes," I promised, and Mother looked down at me as the merchants clucked their tongues and stared at us with daggers in their eyes.

"Well, I do not know," Mother started, looking up at the men.

"Oh, I think your partner has made the deal already. You cannot go back on her word. There is no hurry, as I will station here for a long while. I admire the hues of this one," and he pointed to my favorite of the three that remained. He and I were of a like mind. "These colors are extraordinary. You are an artist of unique quality, so please take your time and create your best. I will make it worth your while."

I could tell Mother was flattered and as happy as I to be seen and appreciated, but she grabbed my hand and pulled me to her side.

More daggers from the merchants. If looks could kill, these would have inflicted fatal wounds.

Not wishing to compromise Mother further, yet not wanting to leave without knowing who she was, the soldier jumped back on his horse with a graceful and commanding leap and prepared to ride off, but not without looking directly into Mother's eyes.

"Gentlemen," he said, to the steaming merchants to distract them from Mother. "Thank you for the concern you show this woman, making sure I treat her fairly. I see you are pillars of the community, and I am honored to have met you on my first day." He understood their nature and seemed to delight in this false praise. It brought a smile to my heart to hear him play them. "Please let me know if I can be of service to you in the future."

The merchants could only nod in agreement. The handsome Roman looked at me and asked my name, actually interested in knowing what it was.

"Magdalena." I whispered, shy and uncertain again.

"Magdalena, I apologize for ruining your wares, and thank you for promising a blanket for Zeus. I named him after a god in Greece, where he was born. I bought him there when he was just as small as you are now. He is a beauty, is he not?" I grinned and nodded. He and I had much in common. "I pray you and your mother have a better day than I have provided."

He and Mother avoided looking at each other, each fearing what their heart might reveal. As he rode off, Mother glanced down at me.

"Magdalena, we must go and clean up for Father. Good day, Gentlemen," she said to the traders who were furious about the coins in her hand but unable to do a thing about them. The largest of the men looked at Mother with more than anger in his eyes. It was a look that made me feel undressed and dirty. People were watching, so the merchants were afraid to make a move against us, lest word of it get to the Roman.

Little did I realize just how much strength it took for Mother to proceed as if nothing had happened. Her spirit was awakened in a new way for the first time. Like me, she might have also wished to run away from the life we led and join with this man who was so different from any we knew. But she had lived her years denying this part of her heart, and she hoped with all her might that she could continue.

As we headed for home, women rushed in with small jars to fill with any oil they could scavenge and fought over the soiled, useless blankets. Mother smiled at one, in particular, a friend from the well. She told her she hoped she would benefit from her misfortune. In my mind, there was nothing unfortunate about it. The merchants clenched their teeth, counting even greater profit lost. It was a dark day for them, cheated of an income they did not earn, but felt we owed them.

Once out of town, Mother stopped and looked at the coins. They were gold and worth much more than the merchants would have given us had they sold the oils and blankets for us. Mother handed the largest one to me.

"Magdalena, hide this coin, and we will keep it our secret. Tell no one you have it. A day may come when you may need it. I pray not, but if anything were ever to happen to me, I must know you have something of your own."

Was she looking into our future? Did she perceive from that one encounter with the Roman that her life had forever changed? I cannot know, but I shook at the thought because it hinted there might be a day without her in it. Yet a part of me was happy we had such a special secret. Because the coin symbolized the soldier to me, I also valued it.

"I promise not to tell," I said.

We went home, each lost in our thoughts, but the bond between us was as strong as ever. When we reached the spring near our house,

Mother and I filled large water vessels and washed our clothes and bodies. It took us hours to free ourselves of the oil covering us. We walked home in our undergarments and rushed to get dressed before anyone could see us. We barely had supper ready when Father came in from the groves. I served him and left the table to hide in my bed. From there, I could eavesdrop as my mother recanted a very affable and minimized version of the day's events. The new Roman Captain pushed us to the ground and ruined our wares. He knew the merchants and their greed, so to play with them, he paid us the value of the oil and circumvented them. I heard the clink of coins as she placed them on the table, all but one, and I imagined the delight in Father's eyes at seeing them.

"I wish I had seen their faces," he said, as merrily as I had ever heard him. "But be careful, Rachel, they will not take this lightly. Stay clear of them until their anger has passed." I sensed Father's concern and love for her lurking beneath his absolute need to avoid trouble with the merchants.

"I will," she promised. "Even so, this is a good income from the oil of your fine olives."

I was sure he smiled then and loved her all the more for making him feel valued in the way he craved.

I continued to listen to their voices until my eyes could no longer stay open. It had been a momentous day in so many ways, ways I could not yet fathom. I fell into a deep sleep and had the most vivid dream of my young life. In my last moments in this life, I would realize it was more than a dream.

All I remembered on waking was the sense of floating high above the birds and clouds, filled with happiness unknown to me in this life. Looking down, I noticed angry people, small as ants, beating on a limp and lifeless form. The person wore my cloak, but it could not have been me, for I was flying through the ethers of heaven. I saw, with an insight beyond my years, that the crumpled body was no more than a cloak itself. The angry crowd thought it had beaten the life from it, but rather than feel pain or remorse, I felt free.

Is this, I wondered in the dream, what it is to die? I looked across the water and saw a small boat sailing away. Was it Mother sitting in the boat, looking up at me, and knowing where I was? No, it was not Mother, but someone who held the same expansive love and majesty about her, a woman as beautiful inside and out as she. Above me lay my stars twinkling like jewels in the sky. They broke apart into shards of light, absorbing me and filling me with an unfathomable love.

⋆ TWO ⋆

WE AVOIDED THE market for a turn of the moon. With enough time, the merchants missed the income they generated from Mother's goods and overlooked our dealing with the soldier. No one else produced the quality weave Mother created, and she alone made the coveted oils traded beyond our city. They relied on us, and we needed them. But they would not say it. They wanted us grateful for their patronage, bowing to their benevolence and resting in their mercy. Because they held a united front against us, they managed to keep our prices low and their profits high. We hoped things might return to the way they were before the captain and his coins, but that was not possible. The merchants were now suspicious. In their eyes, we crossed them and sided with the Romans. They felt cheated and betrayed. I missed my friend and the market. I was lonely staying at home, not hesitating to complain about all of it. In truth, I longed to see Zeus and his rider again.

Mother and I spent the month curing the last of the olives and distilling herbs and flowers for their essence and colors. The weather was turning colder, and it was time to begin our winter weaving. I avoided any mention of the blanket, though it strained my patience to do so. Even with my self-absorbed childish attitude, I knew it was a delicate subject. In my heart, I wondered if she had any solid plan. Perhaps a better word would be obsessed. I had patience for mundane toil because of my years without choice, but in this new emotional arena, I had none. I was eager to get this done and see our soldier and his horse again, for, in my mind, they now belonged to us.

I held my tongue, not an effortless task in this matter, as I watched Mother create new dyes and colors for her threads. These differed from the usual hues, and I was curious about how and why she made them and what she had in mind. I helped, and I smiled, and I thought perhaps she was dreaming of her beautiful blanket laying across Zeus' back, or perhaps beneath the muscled thighs of our Roman soldier. Were these pagan thoughts I was harboring? I wondered, but I did not care. Something had stirred within me.

Despite the hard work and constant chores, we enjoyed our time at the looms, just as we did at the stream. But I was not the same. My concentration lacked the purity it once held. I thought of the soldier and Zeus, of town and Mother, and as little as possible of Father.

I worked on a series of smaller blankets and cloaks for children. I used the lower quality thread, as I was not as proficient a weaver as Mother, but I was prolific and could turn out small, useable items people bought for daily use. The merchants picked over Mother's work the moment we entered the central market. They chose the best for their foreign trade or to sell for higher prices to the Romans. We sold the lesser items to women we knew for a fair price. Father preferred she sell to the wealthiest merchant in the city, the one he courted, and I detested most. Mother had no choice in this matter, so I wondered how our blanket would ever get to our soldier. Though I had never heard his name spoken, he was now my second favorite person to walk the earth.

We made a couple of short trips to town. We stayed on the outskirts and avoided the busy trade center, moving about discreetly as we bought grain and traded our cooking oil. When we saw our soldier from across the market, I could feel Mother's heart beating faster. Even from a distance, I could tell his interest was focused entirely on us. Glances passed between them as if a secret conversation had taken place, and then Mother would pull me away and drag me home. I tried every possible way to linger, but even I understood it was too soon for any encounter.

We had no idea what price Mother's wares were bringing in foreign markets, but we knew it was a good deal more than we received. The merchants contrived to get their cut of everything she produced, feeling entitled, because of her gender and their position of power, to give her as little as they could while taking whatever they wanted. When she sold to the other women or traded, they made no profit, so they took most of her goods as soon as we entered the marketplace. They decided the price, and in all their grand benevolence, allowed us to sell or trade my work to the commoners. We had no choice, for to cross them would endanger our livelihood. I fretted over how we would get to see our soldier again with the merchants controlling our every move.

"Mother," I inquired, "how will we get your blanket to the soldier?"

"That is not our problem, Magdalena. We will make some blankets and bring them to the market. He can choose what he likes from the merchants."

"What?" I shouted. I felt robbed. "He asked me if he could buy the blanket. He did not ask them!"

"Magdalena, this is the way of our business. Do not create problems where none should lie."

I felt stricken. How could she do this to me? To ME? Oh, how I thought my concerns were of such great relevance to the world around me. I went on with my work, but now it was just that; work. The joy was gone. A long shadow cast itself across my heart. Each day seemed darker than the one before it. I moved about as if I no longer had blood flowing through my body. I groaned and sighed to Mother's consternation, acting out my displeasure at her giving up. I dared not accuse her of cowardice, but I felt it in my heart and expressed it with every exaggerated breath I took. Mother merely smiled.

The moon turned its full cycle and we were alone for long hours at our looms. Mother sang again, and her songs were lively and poetic. Little by little, light entered my heart because I saw the patterns she was creating. They were extraordinary. It looked as if the poetry of her songs had danced its way into her threads. There were dark blue stars almost as deep a color as Zeus's shiny coat, woven around saffron-colored shapes that looked like fires in the sky. It was a red that would match a soldier's cloak, and Mother created a new color of thread that had the hue of the silver buckles on Zeus's saddle. These designs were the most imaginative I had ever seen her create, but the weavings were too small. She was making a series of small blankets, like separate tiles, of useless dimensions. They looked as if they belonged together, but in reality, they were merely separate pieces not big enough for any use.

In addition to the stars and saffron designs, she created swirls of color to match the golden hills behind our groves. These were the hues of a sun laid down to rest in a darkened sky. They mesmerized me, as did her ability to create, and the way she could give her threads movement and expression.

We headed to town with our wares. We had no anointing oils to sell, but we had cooking oil and the small blankets and children's robes I had woven. There were also several lengths of plain cloth, work

I did during my dreary, insolent days. And then there were the smaller pieces with Mother's new designs. The merchants approached us from their tented stalls and the richest man from his tent at the center of the trading district. They acted happy to see Mother, though I knew differently. Our absence had meant a loss of revenue for them. They were content to welcome her wares, but they cared little to nothing about us.

"We missed seeing you, Rachel," said the corpulent one; the one who traveled the farthest and made the highest profits. There was an arrogant irony in his voice.

"How kind of you to say," Mother answered. She and I understood that these men held not a scrap of concern for our well-being. Still, I knew they were as happy to leer at Mother as they were to fill their pockets.

"What have you to trade today?" he asked, and the other four gathered to inspect her weavings.

"I have cooking oils and children's robes and several lengths of sewing cloth," said Mother.

"Nothing else?" A powerful voice resonated from behind us. The soldier rode up the moment he saw Mother entering the market with goods to sell. He had been looking for her all this time. He also knew the merchants would try to get their hands on his blanket any way they could.

"Yes, that is all." Mother managed to keep her voice calm, but I knew her heart was in her throat.

"Have you not yet had a chance to make my blanket?" he queried.

"No, Captain, I have not." She looked up at the merchant towering over her while profusely sweating under the burden of his weight.

"That disappoints me," the soldier answered. "I look forward to it."

The merchants were not only glaring at the captain, but also fussing over our pile of weavings. Pulling up the samples, they became excited by the unusual colors and designs. Grabbing at them, they fought each other for the small pieces of material.

"I will take these," the corpulent one stated. He held up my favorite with the stars and red swirls. With this pronouncement, he signaled he was in charge. The others needed to defer to his dominant position. He pulled the small woven cloth from the pile and then saw it had no functional use.

"What is this?" he demanded, dismissively. "This cloth is laughable. It is not large enough to swaddle an infant."

"These are new threads I was trying," Mother answered. "I did not intend for them to be sold. A merchant of your status would take nothing so useless. I only wondered if you approved of the designs."

The merchant, Tobias was his name, looked at the captain and then at Mother, puffing himself up to look important. While taking her words as a compliment, he still suspected she might play him. He was good at bluffing and getting the better part of a deal, but was bereft of any artistic sense. He threw the fabric at Mother.

At that moment, I had a hint of Mother's plan. Knowing the vanity of the enemy is one's best weapon against him. She knew they would never realize the value of what looked like small, useless scraps. She also knew they only had eyes for immediate profit. They did not see art. But our captain did.

"You are right about that, woman," Tobias said. "No one would have use for such a thing. I will take these lengths of cloth, but they are very plain. Here is all I think they are worth," and he dropped a few small copper coins into Mother's hands.

"Thank you, dear sir," Mother replied, with a hint of sarcasm and a strong emphasis on "dear."

"I like them very much," Captain said. "They are quite unusual. Zeus and I would be pleased to own such a blanket."

Mother looked down, but I knew she was pleased.

Tobias spoke. "Come into my tent, and we can make the arrangements."

"But this young lady has already made our deal," Captain replied, looking down at me. My face blushed a deeper color than the red on the blanket.

"But, but, but," I stammered, in a barely audible tone, still reluctant to speak in front of adults.

"BUT, BUT, BUT," Tobias stammered louder.

"Merchant, you would not want a Roman coming into your town and breaking his word on a business venture, would you? This girl and I have settled the matter."

"There has been no legitimate agreement," Tobias said, with his false sense of authority. "Girls do not execute bargains in our society. Women do not implement deals. You are to buy from us. This woman sells her wares through us. We make her life possible. We take them to markets she could not imagine." And he puffed himself up larger as he debased my mother.

"I mean no insult to your way of business," the captain continued. "But where I come from, we do not give our word and go back on it. I made the arrangement after ruining this girl's goods, and I honor my word when given. I should think you would be relieved."

He arched one eyebrow, and a stern look crossed his face, one that would have shaken me had I not felt he was on our side.

"And as far as I know, the Roman Government sets the rules here." With this last statement, the other merchants withered, but Tobias seemed to grow angrier. He clenched his jaw tightly.

"I will go to your tent and make a deal for the rest of the cloth to send back home," Captain continued. "They will be very welcome, for although not elaborate, they are of high quality. But this young lady will sell Zeus' blanket."

He looked at me, and again, my sense of being invisible and inconsequential disappeared as it had on first meeting him. My life had changed.

After taking our leave, Mother and I walked home in silence, our faithful donkey relieved of the load he had carried into town, all but the small, mysterious weavings. I suspected matters had gone the way Mother expected, and there was an easy understanding between us. I was entering my seventh year by then, but I was seeing events differently than I had just a few brief seasons before. Several days passed before I saw the full scope of her plan, and it was impressive.

She laid the various pieces of fabric on the stone floor and, with her skilled hand, joined them as seamlessly as if she had woven them as one. Each piece was a section of a much larger picture, made to fit together to create a cohesive image, much like a child's puzzle I once saw by the well. Her threads told the story of my stars leaping in the sky as the sun set on the desert cliffs. It was a magnificent blanket, worthy of our captain and Zeus.

⋆ THREE ⋆

A GAIN, A REQUISITE amount of time needed to pass for Tobias to lose his anger and feel he had regained the upper hand. Understanding her tenuous position and the risk involved, Mother headed straight to Tobias' tent, but not before seeing our captain at a distance and being sure he was aware of our presence.

"Sir," she called to Tobias, "I have finished the captain's blanket and thought I should consult with you on how to proceed."

"Ah, well, let me have it," and with greedy, thick palms, he tried to grab the blanket.

"One moment and I will untie it for you," said Mother, with a false reverence, as she drifted her hands over the fastening ties.

"Is that my blanket?" The soldier strode into the tent. "My trade is with this woman's daughter. This argument has become tedious." The Roman's voice sounded threatening. Tobias' face tightened, as he was not sure how to react to such a strong opponent.

As a girl, I was used to being inconsequential. I had always been meaningless to these merchants. Now, Tobias and his men saw me, but they saw me as a problem. I realized that there were situations in which being invisible held significant advantage.

Mother acted in the manner necessary to maintain our safety, but I soon understood that this, too, was deliberated. "I am accustomed to Master Tobias selling my work." She spoke to the soldier in a voice that carried no commitment.

"Yes, indeed," Tobias added, nervously.

"And in all other matters, so be it," the captain responded. "I have no intention of ruining your business relationship, but I feel I owe this girl and her mother, and I wish to pay them directly for this blanket. I thought we had already settled this matter." His voice grew sharp, and he looked sternly at Tobias who withered under his gaze.

"Of course," Tobias lied. "I was just telling the woman I felt the same." And Mother nodded in agreement, although we all knew differently.

"Come outside then, and let me see the blanket in clear light," the captain said, and he led us out of Tobias' tent.

We were relieved to be out of Tobias' presence, but we could still feel his eyes on us after we left. It was occurring to him, it would be impossible to weave the entire blanket in so short a time. I would be surprised if he had connected the useless squares to the finished product, for Tobias did not see the art and design. He saw an item's commercial value only. Still, there was something about the whole matter that did not feel settled in his mind.

Mother untied the cloth and laid it out on a pile of straw gathered at the side of the road. The blanket was extraordinary in color and design. The captain stared and shook his head, taking it in. I imagine he was thinking more of the mind and hands that created it and less about the actual weaving. It spoke of the artist's sense of color and whimsical nature; the parts of herself that she kept hidden.

"If it does not please you, Captain, I can make another," Mother said.

"Do not play with me," he answered, and I loved the reverent sound of his voice. "I have never, in all my travels, seen a work of art such as this. How did you ever come to this design?"

I spoke up and noticed the shock on Mother's face that I would be so bold, and to a Roman.

"It is a song my mother sings to me, and I move to it. She made the threads dance my dance."

I was reveling in my newfound freedom, but did not miss the look of warning in Mother's eyes. I realized I should not be speaking of dancing and singing. But the Romans were pagans, I thought. He would understand.

"Magnificent," the soldier said. "It certainly has movement. I have never seen such fine work." I knew he would understand, and I was feeling a little defiant even against Mother.

"You have unique talent, it is clear," he continued. " I have never witnessed such skill or vision."

Mother looked at him curiously. He saw into the deepest part of her soul, the part she knew no one bothered to notice. To be perceived as who she was felt liberating rather than dangerous. He was not a man who regarded her as an inferior creature or object, but one who would consider who she was inside. An unfamiliar feeling stirred within her.

The captain reached into a pouch and drew out a handsome sum of gold coins. He bent down on one knee and placed them in both my hands, as they would not fit into just one.

"Well, Magdalena, do you think this is sufficient?" he asked.

I had never seen so many coins, and it was not silver or copper, as Tobias often gave. They were gold. My eyes grew wide, and I looked up at Mother. I suspected she was about to say it was too much, so I spoke up.

"It will do," I answered. Mother looked horrified by my response, but the captain threw back his head in a hearty laugh.

"I knew she was the one to drive your bargain," he said, still laughing. He closed my hands over the coins and stared up at Mother.

"Dear woman, may I know your name? It seems odd to possess such an extraordinary treasure without knowing the artist's name." He stood up and looked into her eyes. He was a good head taller than Mother when standing next to her. I was so excited, I could hardly stand still.

"Rachel," Mother answered, looking up at him. I had never seen such a look on her face. There was respect and gratitude and something I did not recognize.

"What is yours?" I interrupted, and could tell Mother was becoming wary of my newfound sense of self.

The soldier laughed further and looked down at me with kind eyes. "I am Lucius." He bent down again to my height, extended his hand, and said, "It is a pleasure to meet you, Magdalena."

And then he looked up and into Mother's eyes, her green eyes that shone with the brightest light, and said, "I have wondered since meeting you what your name might be. It has occupied most of my thought."

Mother blushed at hearing his words, but they brought delight to her as well. Lucius did not miss this, as he was watching to interpret her response. He had shrewd eyes that were also kind; a rare talent for a soldier. His stare would intimidate most people. I think he recognized that although my mother knew how to act, nothing intimidated her. Although she had known and withstood hardship, within her was a liberated soul, one that understood we were all created by the same force. Women give birth and carry life. How could we not understand the power of creation? How could we believe we were inferior? And yet there was no pretense with my mother. He could sense this and it delighted him.

His commanding features changed when their eyes met. His face softened, and I could almost tell what he looked like when he was a boy at my age. I would have even liked him then.

"Can I get to know you better?" he asked. I could tell he knew the answer before asking, but needed to say what was on his mind.

"I am a married woman," she said, her eyes pointing to me as evidence of this union. "It cannot be."

She noticed the villagers looking our way and whispering. Everything the Romans did was of great interest, but on seeing the handsome new captain speaking with the town's beauty, the tongues could not help but wag. Despite being loved by the women of our city, she was losing favor with the merchants and needed to avoid any trouble and rumor.

"I understand," Lucius said, looking around and also detecting the attention they were attracting. "Still, I have been under a spell since meeting you. Perhaps the gods and fates will find a way."

Even then, I suspected that gods and fates aside, he would find the way.

He tied the blanket behind his saddle with proficient hands. Gaining command of the situation with a mere gesture, he jumped onto his saddle with his easy leap and rode off. His bearing was so regal, it made my knees weak.

Mother gathered her things, and we began our solitary walk back home. When I knew all eyes were no longer on us, I placed the coins into Mother's hands, and she smiled. She had never gone home from the market with such a sum. I wondered if she felt Father would be pleased. I wondered if she thought of Father at all.

A hint of sorrow laced the quiet between us, each wondering why something that felt so right should be denied. Customs, commandments, righteousness; all these words came into my mind, and none of them meant a thing to me. I wished to dance, and craved to ride Zeus across the countryside. I wanted Lucius to be my father.

*   *   *

Every day felt like the deepest part of winter, for joy and fun deserted us. Mother was too smart a woman to speak of the soldier, too wise to consider betraying her marriage and risking her life. I should have learned that lesson from her, but I had a streak in me, one commanded by the stars, or so I told myself. These unreasonable rules should not pertain to me. After all, I could see between this world and the next and knew there was a different way; one not to be dictated by men's commands but by the fairness of the heavens. I was different. I repeated this story to myself, trying hard to believe it was true. Hoping to escape the dreary destiny of being born a girl, I needed to avoid marrying a man I did not love and withering in despair the rest of my days. I wanted to look into a man's eyes the way my mother looked into Lucius', and I hoped upon hope, there would be more encounters with our soldier and Zeus. I was not wise enough to understand the danger.

We wove, but without the new colors or special care. Mother created utility items that lacked her usual artist's touch. We pressed oils and gathered wood dropped by lifeless trees, I, but a shadow to Mother's joyless form. Things were dull and gray and bland. I was losing my childish ways and becoming that odd thing between child and budding woman. When I looked into the stream, I saw an adolescent who cared more about her appearance than the world beyond form. I thought life could get no worse. How foolish a young girl can be.

Mother and Father found a comfortable formality with each other. I wonder now if Father was capable of an intimacy of the heart, or only of the flesh. His speech was uninteresting to me and small in scope. The dull sound of him bored me. When not criticizing me, he spoke of prices and bits of meaningless gossip from the men who labored for him. Mother tried to stay engaged with his verbal meanderings and talk of uninspiring tasks. Her acquiescent politeness made me want to scream and tear out my hair.

As the season plodded along, I noticed Mother's energy waning and her beautiful, rich skin grew hot and flushed. She coughed through a full day, and by its evening, she was suffering from a fierce fever that had taken hold of her.

"Father," I said, daring to speak to him. "What is wrong with Mother? She does not recognize me. She is lying on my bed, shivering, but she is hot to the touch."

Father rushed to my alcove and saw his wife drenched in a fevered sweat.

"Cover her," he commanded, "and watch over her. She has caught the illness going around the city."

I served him a supper of stew with wild onions I had gathered before I knew Mother was so ill. When I finished baking fresh bread, I went to Mother's side and sat through the night. I placed a wet cloth across her forehead when she was burning with fever, and wiped her dry when she became drenched with sweat. I covered her when she was chilled. For five nights and most of their days, I stopped my vigil only to serve Father and clean and cook. When he came into the house and kneeled beside her, I could see the worry on his face. If he was worried, I was distraught.

Neither of us could face the thought of losing her. Father was kinder to me through those days, for he saw I was caring for her as no one else could or would. He seemed ineffective and lost and almost grateful for my presence. I rubbed her special oils over her rib cage, and moistened her lips so they would not crack from the high fever. I placed a cloth soaked in water in her mouth so she would not perish from thirst and heat. Deep into the night, I laid my head on her chest and listened to her labored breath while I sobbed. I prayed to any deity who might spare her, pleading childish bargains for her life over mine. Promising to do anything to save her, I vowed to act like normal people did, and be acceptable. I could be the kind of good they wanted of me. I would give anything.

During the day, I gathered fresh straw to replace that soaked with sweat. I put a dry cloth between her body and her wet robes to prevent a chill from overcoming her. On the sixth evening, her fever broke, and her mind became clear enough to speak.

"Sweet Magdalena," a coarse whisper came from deep in her dry throat. "How long have I been in your bed?"

"Six days," I answered. "I came in from the garden and found you lying here. Father and I have been worried."

"Have you made broth?" she asked, in a faint whisper.

"Yes. I kept some ready for when you woke up." I rushed to the hearth and ladled some into a cup. She was half sitting up when I returned.

"I need to build my strength and get out of your bed," she said, determined.

She sipped the broth, a few swallows at a time, and later wobbled out to the table while I served Father his with pieces of dried meat and boiled root vegetables. He was relieved to see her up again.

I helped her wash and change into dry robes. Exhausted from such little effort, she leaned on me, and I led her into their bed for the night. I cleared the plates and went straight to my alcove, almost nauseous from fatigue. I pulled off the soiled linens, but before I could put a fresh cloth on my bed, I passed out on the uncovered straw.

The following morning, I had considerable work ahead of me. Stiff and tired, I worked to pull the wooden comb through the tangles and broken twigs in my hair. Every muscle in my body ached as I pulled on the last of my clean clothes. I swept the floors and made some order of the house, for I had neglected much during my vigil. I wanted Mother to feel settled and quiet when she rose.

I packed the laundry onto our donkey after serving Mother and Father hot tea and fresh bread, and I headed to the stream for the first time on my own.

At the inlet where we washed our garments, I had to get the work done as quickly as possible, for the winter sun would not be strong for long. I loaded the linens into large clay vessels and covered them with water. I scrubbed them with all my strength to wash the fever from them. If not sufficiently cleaned, the blankets of the sick could spread the illness to anyone who used them next, and I was determined to banish it with my hard strokes and lye. After rinsing them in the vessels several times, I rubbed the cloth against smooth stones until my fingers were red and sore. My arms and legs cramped from squatting over the large casks and from the days and nights sitting at Mother's side.

I finished and hung the laundry on the branches above me, spreading the pieces wide, so they could dry as swiftly as possible. Exhausted, I fell onto the soft ground and waited. I soon became bored with waiting, as it seemed strange being at our spot without Mother. I tried to hear her music, but it was impossible without her guidance. As I missed her, I felt the burden of worry over her illness still weighing on me. There was no joy without Mother.

I peered out at nothing, my mind wandering without form or shape. Water lapped over the smooth stones, but I remained unmoved. Over and over, without change, the water descended over the rocks, until, at last, I heard its rhythms. My heart stirred. I wondered what song Mother would have made of it. Squinting hard, I stretched my ears in all directions and strained with intent. I stared into the water, my mind open and body ready. For the first time in the longest while, I recognized the world beyond form, the wisdom I knew as a younger child before I was so distracted by life.

I no longer felt separate and alone. I heard Mother's music in the great hum of the earth. Birds, loud and rich, joined in. Soon I was on my feet, following the sound, moving the tightness out of my back and limbs. My torso swayed, my ribs arched and rolled, and my arms reached toward my stars as they slept behind the sun. Once again, while staring into the stream, I felt united with the world around me. I had returned to something important without understanding, or even caring, what it was—a force beyond my own. My legs, thin yet strong, grounded me as my arms flowed. My body spun in circles, as if to take flight at any moment. I embraced the music of nature. I loved to dance, knowing the stars made me for it. Great pleasure spread across my face, a smile that had been missing for many long days and nights.

Until I felt someone watching me. Shaken from my trance, I noticed a figure standing beside a tree on the other side of the stream.

I froze in embarrassment, looking about, my heart racing. But it was Lucius. And behind him was Zeus, with Mother's blanket beneath his saddle. I blushed a deep red, and my face pounded with shame.

"Please do not stop," Lucius shouted, holding up his hand. "Do not feel discomfort on my part. You are lovely to watch. I am sorry to have surprised you. I was taking a ride through the countryside." He walked Zeus across the shallowest part of the stream and came closer.

"No one should see me dance," I said, too sternly. "And you should not have watched me." I was surprised by my bold, accusing tone, but I was embarrassed and angry, and like most young minds, I put the blame on the person I believed caused my discomfort.

"We do not feel that way in my country," Lucius answered. "So, you have done no wrong in my eyes." I could tell my attitude perplexed him, and he felt a need to relieve my shame. "I will leave you alone and no longer disturb you, but I am impressed by the beauty of your dancing."

"I see Zeus likes his blanket," I said, wanting to change the conversation as quickly as possible.

"Yes," Lucius said, proudly. "Is your mother here to see how it looks?" And he had a hopeful look on his face. I realized he had been exploring the countryside hoping to find her.

"No, she is home. We come here to wash our laundry, but she has been sick…with fever." As the words stumbled out of my mouth, I realized what I had done. I acted as if he had the full privilege of Mother's whereabouts. I frowned with confusion. Was this wrong?

"Is there something I can do to help? Tell me she is not too ill," he responded, with a serious look. I could feel the depth of his concern, and I lost my anger.

"Her fever broke," I said, still too embarrassed to look at him. I became confused by my emotions and awkwardly aware that this was the first time I had been alone with any man, even my father. Was I wrong to be there? Would I be punished? I felt a hot flushing in my cheeks, uncomfortable with my new feelings, all of them.

"Find me if anything is needed. I will leave you now to your work…and your dancing," he added mirthfully. He walked Zeus across the stream and again jumped onto his back with a strong, masterful leap. With a wave in my direction, he rode off.

I sat quietly the rest of the afternoon, trying to reconcile my concerns and emotions, sitting as still as possible and behaving as I thought I should. This was torture. Why was being proper so difficult for me? And what did proper even mean, and why was it necessary when I was alone with nothing to do? What had I done that was so wrong? I did not understand, but I felt deep, troubling guilt running through me. Whose rules were these they forced me to obey, and why were they so different for girls? I was feeling unsure of my thoughts and feelings and did not know why.

By late afternoon, the robes and linens were dry, and I packed them into baskets tied onto our donkey's back and walked him home. My chaotic thoughts agitated me and shame continued to course through me, but I did not understand why. I was unsettled, wandering as if lost. I had been gone most of the day.

Mother was up, and although she was still weak, she was making supper and moving about slowly. I carried the bundle into the house and made up our beds. I folded the robes and put them into the baskets for clean linens, and then took up my tasks by the fire next to her.

Mother was proud of me, grateful for how I had run the house while she was ill. I did the wash on my own, and had taken over the household duties for days. She looked at me with the melancholy sadness a mother feels when she first faces the reality that her precious child will grow up and leave her.

"How was the stream without me?" she asked.

"Not very interesting," I lied.

⋆ FOUR ⋆

L ITTLE BY LITTLE, Mother regained her strength. Many in our city were not as fortunate. Each time we went to the well, we learned of more women we would never see again. The concept of death eluded me, but it also left a darkness in my weary heart that I could not escape. And then, I was told of my friend, the one with the cloth dolls. She had also passed. I was devastated, and unable to make any sense of it. How could anyone so young die? My only friend? I could not fathom this thing named death. Although we had been lucky, I became even more anxious. I could barely eat and became quiet for a good amount of time, even with Mother. Was it possible it almost happened to her, that there could be a day without her in it? How would I ever be able to go on?

We survived the rest of winter and carried on with our trade, mostly with the greedy and distasteful Tobias. He was the most powerful merchant in our city and the one whose favor Father insisted we seek. Distracted by my misery and grief, I still looked for Lucius and Zeus. When we saw them across the market, Mother would turn and pull me in the opposite direction. I often tried to delay our departure with various schemes, but Mother was too wise and too strong for me to fight and win.

Several times, I saw Lucius turn toward us, and Mother let him know, with just a look, that it was not to be. I wanted to sit defiantly in my spot, but Lucius understood and turned Zeus in the opposite direction. They were working against me, and it infuriated me on top of everything else that burdened me. But they both knew if they were ever to speak again, it had to be in a safe place or it would be the last time they did. I felt an unspoken agreement between them, and this made me happy in a way I could not have explained. Still, it worked beyond the boundaries of my patience.

Tobias regained his control over Mother's goods. She had to appear grateful, as there was no other choice. Tobias had tied up trade with the Romans, selling the most expensive items to those with the most money. He had paid off the soldiers of lower rank, allowing him to carry on as he wished without interference or competition. He was flagrant in his power, and Lucius kept his distance, knowing any trouble with Tobias would mean trouble for us. And so, we carried on much as before. But everything was different.

Then, we did not see Lucius for a long while. I looked everywhere, but there was no sight of him. The weight of this loss exacerbated my grief at losing my only ally, and the allure of going to the market also died. I no longer cared for any of its wonders if Lucius, Zeus, and my friend were not part of it. Life felt abysmally dark, and I had no good thoughts at that time. I was concerned with my loss and sadness, and never considered how difficult and drab it might also be for my mother. He was gone from her life as well.

At last, spring flowers came to light and some heaviness quit my spirit. We went to the stream to do our wash, filled our water jugs, and sang and danced again. I kept hoping I would see Lucius appear, but he did not. He was no longer in town, or anywhere to be seen. Mother was not herself. Father thought it was because she had been so ill, but I knew it was because of her heart. An unknown force had torn it open and then left it to wither. She found it is more unbearable knowing what one is missing than not. It pained me to see her living, day after day, without hope. She could not even entertain such thoughts. I was the joy of her soul and she was mine, but my heart had been changed too. I was in love with Zeus and our soldier, and I dreamed of a different way of life; a world where women mattered, had choices, and we were not the chattel of men. This I blamed on my stars for making me think I could dance to a tune that was not to be played.

It was the heat of summer when we saw Lucius again. He appeared at the stream just as Mother was napping, and I was playing with minnows in the water. I was so startled when I noticed him I almost shouted, but he held his fingers to his mouth in a hushing gesture, so I would not wake her.

"Why disturb her?" he whispered. "She still needs to build strength."

"Where have you been? You have not been in our city," I said, revealing my heart as only a child would.

"I was on assignment to the west of here. It was a difficult and lonely trip. I thought of you and your mother often. I believe Zeus missed you."

"Does he like carrots?" I inquired, thrilled and looking in his direction.

"Indeed, his favorite."

"I have one in my cloth. May I give it to him?" I requested.

"Yes, of course."

We walked quietly the twenty paces to reach Zeus. Brilliant Zeus. I broke the carrot into smaller pieces and handed one to him with a flat, outstretched hand.

"I see you know your way around horses," Lucius added.

"Not at all, but I imagine he acts like my donkey, but much grander," I said, more confident because of Lucius' compliment. He smiled wryly at my pragmatic declaration.

"I can tell he trusts you. Would you care to sit on his saddle?" Lucius offered.

I could not believe my ears. Was this possible?

"May I?" That was all I could say, my eyes as wide as the sky.

Lucius lifted me onto his saddle, and I swung my leg around Zeus and pressed his sides with my inner thighs. No man had ever held me like that, and I had never seen such powerful arms. I thought them beautiful. They were sinewy and strong, and I was nothing in them. This feeling was the best experience of my long seven years of existence, a man I enjoyed carrying me in his arms, and the euphoria of sitting on top of a horse I adored.

I held Zeus' mane and brought my head down next to his. He seemed to understand I loved and respected him and posed no threat. As had been true of animals most of my life, he accepted my nature and knew I recognized his. His body relaxed beneath me as I stroked his muscular neck.

"May I ride him?" I pleaded, reveling in my affinity with this great beast.

Lucius held a curious but concerned look. He glanced over at Mother, not sure what to do.

"Do you know how to ride?" he asked.

"I ride on our donkey all the time, and I should think this would be much better," I said, without hesitation.

"But Zeus is much larger and faster," he answered.

"Please, let me try," I begged.

"All right, but go slowly. He is a smart horse that will follow the commands of your body," Lucius replied.

My legs could not fit around him, so I squeezed them into his flesh to hold on. He turned to the right after I pressed my right thigh into his side. I repeated with the left, and he responded in kind. I beamed with delight. This impressed Lucius.

"You take to it naturally," he said. "See how Zeus follows your body's commands. He is the most intuitive horse I have ever ridden."

I rode Zeus around at a slow walk, and Lucius seemed pleased. He looked over at Mother as she awakened from her sleep.

Mother thought she was dreaming for an instant, but when she realized I was sitting on top of an enormous animal, she rushed to get up.

"Magdalena," she shouted. "What are you doing on that horse?" Her fast movements and startling voice stirred Zeus, and he moved faster.

I could have stopped him, recognizing he would obey my command if I gave it, but I did not. I got my first and only shot at freedom, and I took it. Crouching low against him and squeezing my thighs into his flesh, I allowed him to go as he wished. I shortened my grasp on his neck hairs, and we raced off, Zeus knowing I was on for the ride. He ran across the field, and I felt like he and I were as one. What joy! What magnificence!

Knowing Mother would panic, I turned him around in a wide arc when I reached the far border of the field, avoiding the thick trees of the grove. I did this by pressing my left thigh hard into his side. It is unclear to me why I did it; I sensed the movement I wanted him to do and created it in my body. No longer insignificant, I assumed the bravery of a soldier or maybe even the goddesses the Romans worshiped; a goddess who could fly on horses to the stars.

As I headed back, I recognized a look of fear in Mother's eyes. Without thinking, she held onto Lucius and shouted, "Can you not do something?"

He put his arm around her in an assuring manner and said, "Rachel, do not worry. She has control. She is an amazing young girl."

His words stunned her. He saw me for the person I was, and this, along with his strength and kindness, comforted her in a way she had not known before. Even from my distance, I could see her body relax into his. She turned to him and the look between them was one I will never forget. Oh, how I wanted it to be the four of us, Mother, Lucius, Zeus, and me.

I stopped Zeus a few paces to the left of them by pulling up on his neck hairs. He lifted his magnificent head in an impressive arc and let out a very satisfied snort.

"Have you lost your senses, Magdalena?" Mother shouted, and moved toward me, determined to curtail my rebellious nature. She grabbed onto my waist and pulled me down. Nevertheless, I felt I was a pure smile, barely confined by the borders of a face. I had never been so happy.

"I am truly sorry. It is all my doing. It was my idea to put her up there. I seem to do all the wrong things when I am around you," Lucius said, regretfully.

"No," I shouted. "Zeus ran, and I chose to go with him." I was emphatic.

Mother did not know whether to be furious or impressed. I think she was the latter, but there were so many things about the situation that were upsetting. I had put myself in potential danger, and how could any of it be explained if I fell? And then there was the unspoken fear of what she was feeling inside.

"Please do not be angry. She did an impressive job. You should be proud," Lucius pleaded.

"You may not understand the repercussions of associating in private with a Roman soldier. For a married woman, this is especially dangerous."

Months of thinking and dreaming of each other brought them a sense of familiarity that seemed odd when one considered it was only the fourth time they had ever spoken. Coupled with exchanged glances and looks that communicated intimate consideration and understanding, they felt a deep and empathic bond. Because they were dealing with the deepest parts of themselves, in some ways, I think they felt they understood each other better than they knew any other person.

"I would never put you in danger," he responded. "The truth is, I would like to protect you for the rest of your life."

Mother's face softened, and they gazed at each other for a long while, looking into the parts that were kept hidden. Their eyes held hope and desire and the deep sadness of knowing there were mountains of impossibilities to keep any of it from happening. Or could it? I kept silent, stroking Zeus and kissing him on the nose while analyzing every gesture.

Mother broke away and said, with forced formality, "Come, Child, we must get things ready for the night's meal. Lucius, I should thank you for allowing my daughter such a grand experience; the first, and only she will have in her lifetime."

"That need not be," he protested, trying to regain the sense of intimacy that had just passed between them. "She should be riding. She comes to it naturally, and could be one of the best," Lucius boasted on my behalf.

I had no regard for their concerns at that moment. I had ridden a horse. The most glorious stallion that ever lived.

"And what good would that do her? She is a girl. She will not be allowed. She will have to marry and be subservient and hide her dreams and hopes," Mother said, with sad resignation. She was speaking of herself as well as her daughter. It was the first time I had ever heard her put these thoughts to words. "Today was her only chance at such freedom. There is no sense in getting her hopes high."

Mother and Lucius stared at each other. He knew what she was saying, but there was an unbearably deep pain in their hearts. I saw a tear fall from Mother's eye as she turned away. I wondered how close to tears our Lucius was as well.

I, however, was a child, solipsistic and self-oriented, holding little disposition for the feelings of others, and I had experienced the thrill of my short lifetime. At that moment, I was concerned only for myself. I had ridden the most beautiful horse that ever lived. We danced as if we were one spirit, united in our love and need for movement, flying like wind above ground with no worry and no fear. I wanted to feel that way again. I needed to. It had to happen.

✳ FIVE ✳

SOMEHOW, I MADE it happen, if only by sheer will. Lucius was clever and showed up randomly, assuring that a thoughtful amount of time passed between visits. He was careful not to offend or push Mother. He tried to be respectful of her situation, but now I see he could not stay away. As the season progressed, we saw him more frequently. Mother and I found countless excuses for going to the stream and doing the laundry. Mother's heart lifted on the days we saw him, but it wore on her spirit when we did not. I know she fought harder than Lucius to avoid their encounters, but neither could. Something bigger than either of them was at play. As for self-absorbed, young me, I was delighted every time I saw them ride up. I knew I would be running Zeus to the far end of the field and back, sometimes two or three times in an afternoon.

The situation worried Mother for many reasons. Besides her inner emotional crisis, she was anxious about my fearless escapades on Zeus. Close to the bluff my grandmother used to end her life, there was a long stretch of land that rimmed the precipice. It was almost impossible to see the sharp edge until directly at its brink. There were many risky points where animals lost their footing, never noticing the drop before falling to their deaths. In her haunted visions, she pictured me riding off the cliff, and on a soldier's horse. There would be no acceptable explanation for that. Below the cliff's edge were the bones of unfortunate creatures that died before they knew what happened. Somewhere along that abandoned stretch of rotting animals lay the grisly remains of my grandmother. My grandfather never allowed the retrieval of her body, feeling she deserved the burial she created for herself.

Mother walked me to the cliff's edge and forced me to look at the skeletal remains. She was uncharacteristically stern and spoke in a voice she had never used with me, and which made me rebelliously angry. I was too young and selfish to understand how the very thought of me going over the cliff was a devastating and brutal reminder of her mother's death, and the worst day of her life. I was too stubborn and concerned with my wishes to imagine how I would feel should my mother's bones lie at the bottom of the pit. She warned me to stay as far away as possible, and her voice left no room for argument or discussion. She felt I was becoming too fearless on Zeus and took too many risks. If Lucius had not stood up for me, she might have forbidden me from riding altogether. He told her I was a better rider than most of the young soldiers he trained. I know she doubted the veracity of his words, but she relaxed with his opinion. He had that effect on her. I believed his gentle lies and filled with a physical confidence no girl of my time would have known. Despite her worries and warnings, these were the best days of my life.

When we were in town and crossed paths, we acted as if we hardly knew each other. I thought it was fun, as though it were all a game only the three of us could play. Lucius would give me a child's salute and turn to ride in another direction while I practiced my attitude of disinterest.

It was a confusing year as well. Life was entirely different when we were with Lucius. Those times were permeated with music and laughter. There were endless possibilities. The old world left to us between visits was pure drudgery. That was a life of labor, boredom, and sorrow. The hours were long and lifeless. The contrast was stark.

During our visits, Mother and Lucius talked for hours as our laundry dried in the sun. He told her of the far-off lands, recounted his life as a soldier, and described the horrors he had seen and lived. Sharing these stories with Mother seemed to do him service. She was likely the first person he had ever spoken with about matters of his heart. Her keen and open mind and her compassionate responses comforted him. I felt his tenderness for her and his genuine regard for who she was.

Mother was a woman of greater intelligence than most men cared to recognize. Lucius saw this and was stimulated by her mind and respectful of her opinions and views. This exchange was as empowering for her as riding Zeus was for me. His stories of places and things outside our world mesmerized her. Like me, at that time, she had never been more than a day's walk from where we lived. How mundane and unexciting her daily existence must have seemed in contrast to the vast and colorful life Lucius led.

Mother expressed her intelligence in the only ways open to her— art, her creative healing, and her dreams. Knowing Lucius opened her mind to a larger world, and suddenly, things looked possible. She learned of cultures with ways of living that seemed strange and foreign to anything we knew. And yet, those people embraced and believed in their way of life just as fully as we did our own. Was anyone more right in their thinking? Or was it just that we all live according to our hearts and faith?

I wonder, still, if Mother imagined a different life could be open to her. She and Lucius found an easy and good friendship between them, besides the unanswered longing they experienced. She had not had a man as a companion before. Although friendly with all the women at the well, Mother had not had a genuine friend before Lucius. And she never shared the intimacy of the mind with Father that she had with Lucius.

Lucius had never confided his deepest feelings before meeting Mother, but found it easy and liberating to share them with her. She had a manner about her that opened his heart in a new way. He feared it would close again without her in it. In his soldier's life, he had to be a powerful commander, one who imposed justice and order on his surroundings. He had to silence his mind when he encountered situations and horrors that upset his spirit. In Mother, he met a woman with whom he could entrust those inner thoughts and worries, someone who would bear witness to his pain and soothe his soul. It was possible to be his softer, more loving self, and I suspect that was his true nature.

Most surprising to me, Mother opened up her heart with all its truth to Lucius. She would not be disloyal or dismissive of Father, but she often spoke in secret, thinking I could not hear. She admitted her disappointment at being forced to marry young to an unknown man for whom she had no true feelings. Her art was all she had that was hers; her art, her singing, and me, and she felt surprised and delighted to know these were the traits that attracted Lucius the most. How liberating it must have felt to be completely honest about her inner life that no man I knew, apart from Lucius, imagined a woman would have. I saw they shared similar views despite the vast differences in their cultures.

At times, I saw them brush against each other. Time held its breath for a moment, the touch suggesting a promise of something to come. Words unspoken, an understanding never brought to light, a rare sensation filling the surrounding air, they moved on, acting as if nothing had happened. It was a dangerous thing we were doing, and she knew it, but she felt compelled to continue. She must have believed she could maintain an innocent friendship and not need to give up knowing this remarkable man. She figured that, as long as she did not cross the line into actual adultery, and if no one knew of these encounters, she could continue her contact with him. He brought more to her life than she ever dared to imagine.

She hoped it could continue without incident, without end, but I saw during our times alone that she struggled to find her balance. Some part of her must have known it could not turn out well. I, on the other hand, felt but a minor concern. All I could think of was straddling my scrawny legs around magnificent Zeus. I wanted to ride and dance and sing and live with Lucius.

One evening toward the start of harvest, Father sat at supper talking to Mother, while I was in my alcove playing with one of my wooden horses, the one I had renamed Zeus. I tied a cloth doll on his back, one made from the scraps of a robe I had outgrown, and pretended my missing friend was with me. I strained to hear their conversation.

"Rachel, I sense you do not care much for Tobias," Father said. "But he has bought a herd of sheep and is offering a good sum to graze them on my land. I think he also wishes to expand his trade with your weavings."

Father was blind in so many ways. Not caring for Tobias was an understatement. None of us liked him, but Mother, least of all. Tobias wanted to expand his exposure to her. Even I, with my child's ignorance, felt deep discomfort when he looked at her. His dismissive, greedy eyes watched her intently, as if imagining her with no covering on her body. He was sloppy and greasy and had a rancid animal smell. When reaching for Mother's wares, he often touched her in ways that caused her to become tense. I would pull her away or shout to get her attention and make her leave. My blanket bargain with Lucius and my coming between them made his distaste for me grow as strong as his lust for my mother. My body clenched at the mention of his name.

"Is there enough to feed our animals and his?" Mother asked. I knew she wanted no more interaction with Tobias than was necessary. The closer he was to us, the more discomfort we would know.

"It is a good amount, and I think it will work well on my behalf," Father said, his mind set. Father was not as clever in business as Tobias, nor as conniving. Although he expanded his father's holdings, it was more Mother's ability to refine the oil and create quality items from them that made his harvests stand above others. She was too humble and kind to point this out, but even though I was young and without experience, I knew this from our exchanges at the market. There were myriad reasons Mother wanted to stay as far from Tobias as possible. Besides his foul behavior toward her, she knew he would get the better part of the bargain.

"Your earnings will be the same as now, even though he will provide some wool and have it spun into threads you can dye and weave. That will make the profit larger for us," Father continued. He thought this was a good deal for Mother, as it would afford more yarn, and she could spend more of her time making sellable items. Mother knew Tobias would charge prices unimagined by Father, and his profits would soar much steeper than ours.

"He will make a tidy profit, as if he needs it, but he intends to carry your weaving to more markets. They are in demand, and they may soon bring a much higher price," Father continued.

"For him, I am convinced, while I do the work. What land does he want?" Mother inquired, and the sharpness of her tongue surprised me.

"That has yet to be decided," Father answered, oblivious to her feelings.

"How about the pasture on the side of the western grove by the upper spring?" Mother said, and I froze in horror. She was telling him to put Tobias right by our stream, right where we met Lucius and Zeus. I could not believe my ears. Traitor! I thought with seething anger.

"Oh, Rachel, that is absurd," Father said. "You especially, know the danger of that cliff. No one can use that for pastureland. He would lose most of his sheep in the first season," and he smiled, thinking how foolish women were, how little they knew of business. And I grinned with an even stronger appreciation of my mother's brilliance. She steered him from our spot, using his arrogance while feigning our innocence. Our meeting place was safe.

"I was considering the area opposite the groves on the eastern slope. He can approach it from town. It will save him time getting there, and it is a suitable distance from my sheep and our home here." Father was pleased with himself for thinking this through, and for being so much wiser than his inferior wife. By then, I was peering around the corner of my alcove so I could hear better. I saw Mother's body relax, relieved that Tobias would remain far from our secret life.

Several days passed before we saw Tobias leading his men with a modest herd to the eastern slope of our field. His great arrogance was on full display. He pushed his sheep through Father's new growth seedlings and tore across the small flow of water directed toward them.

Mother had always taught me to respect the land. Any injury to it was an ingratitude for the gift of its use. We must treat it as we would any living creature, she repeated. But Tobias had the entitlement of a rich and careless man. All that existed was there to serve him—his needs, his desires, his fancy. The young seedlings were trampled, the water troughs feeding them were destroyed, and he stopped to let his sheep graze on the remains. We wondered if Father had figured this into his bargain. The entire grove would need replanting.

At least, I thought, he was far from our life, although I hated the idea of him being anywhere on Father's land. Father rode his mule to meet him, feeling clever and triumphant. If he was upset about the seedlings, he did not let it show. He could not admit this grand business deal was anything but brilliant, even to himself.

"Bring wine and bread and some of your sheep's cheese," Father ordered, before leaving. "This is a time for celebration. Let us welcome Tobias properly."

He rode off and left us to prepare the food.

"Mother," I shouted, "he ruined the new seedlings."

"Say nothing, Magdalena, and keep the peace," Mother answered.

"Keep the peace? He showed no respect for the land, for Father's work, or us," I shouted, and I saw regret on Mother's face for allowing me the freedom she did. My tongue, although rarely used in the world, had become too bold.

We followed Father, me riding our donkey and carrying the basket of food, while Mother walked beside us. Tobias looked quite pleased when we arrived with our offering.

"Put the basket down. I will take wine," Tobias shouted, as if he were the anointed master to whom we now owed fealty. Mother's face burned red. He liked seeing her in a role he deemed subservient to him. He was getting more out of this bargain than a place to graze his herd and the promise of Mother's weaving. I believe he thought he was gaining sovereignty over her.

But Father was delighted with their new relationship. He ignored his decimated seedlings and the disrespect to his wife. Tobias stared at Mother making her discomfort grow. I hated him more than ever.

Father, flushed with drink, laughed in a way I had not heard before. There was an affected grandeur to his voice as he spoke. He thought he was gaining stature by being in business with Tobias, but Mother knew he was being used and would end up with the lesser outcome of any bargain they struck.

Father forced us to stand and serve the men while we swallowed our anger and tried to appear gracious. Mother was much better at this pretense than I. I wanted to spit in their wine and waited for the perfect opportunity. Knowing me all too well, Mother sensed my plan.

"Magdalena," she scolded, with a sideways glance. "Do not dare." How did she know my thoughts, and why would she stop me?

As we packed our basket and jars to head home, Tobias handed Mother the cup from which he drank, brushing his hand against her breast. I saw it, but Father did not. I looked at Tobias with disgust.

"Why is that wretched child with you whenever I am near you?" he asked, leeringly. Mother pretended she had not felt his touch and dismissed him politely.

"I am her mother. She belongs at my side," she replied. She turned, but I did not. I glared at him, letting him know I saw him violate her. He sneered at me and turned away. In the pit of my stomach, I knew this would end badly.

* * *

Each week, Tobias rode out to see his herd and bring Father a random market item, something to lure him deeper into his debt. Every day, I felt Father filling with arrogance and pride, thinking he had climbed higher in status and trade. Meanwhile, Mother and I slaved at the looms and turned out as much cloth as possible, so we could take time at the stream with Lucius and Zeus. We were living two lives.

In the beginning, Father demanded we bring Tobias food and wine. He knew his wife was an asset, and he liked to show her off, but he was blindly ignorant of Tobias' intentions. Each time we were alone with Tobias, his gestures toward Mother became crasser and more obvious. She was in a difficult position and tried to handle it with grace, somehow extricating herself without an actual insult to Father's most lucrative trading partner. A man to whom Father was foolishly giving more and more of his trade and power.

At dawn one morning, as I went outside to collect eggs and water, I saw Tobias sitting on his stocky horse, several feet from our house. He was slightly hidden behind a tree, and trying to peer inside.

"What are you doing here so early?" I demanded.

"You have a very bold mouth for a girl," Tobias answered, angry to be seen. Even at that age, I understood he was spying on Mother and hoping to catch a glimpse of her without her knowing. Stupid man, I thought, my father is still in the house. It then occurred to me that Tobias had no respect for my father, whatsoever, and considered himself superior in every way. If Father had something he wanted, Tobias thought he could take it. It was his right as the wealthiest man in our city. With that wealth, he knew he also held power. Only the Romans and the clergy had more than him, and he got his way with most of them for the right price. He felt he could do the same with my father.

"I will inform Father you are here," I said, with false sincerity. "I will ask him to come outside and greet you."

"I was just checking on my herd. I have no business with your father at this time. Begone, girl," he added, and he turned his horse to leave.

"But your herd is not in our house," I said, and he turned with a look so threatening it made my legs shake.

"Little girl, do not cross me, or you will be sorry. One day, you will get your due," he snarled, and he rode off.

*   *   *

Several weeks later, as Mother and I carried our goods to town, we approached the center of the market, hoping to circumvent Tobias long enough to ensure that other merchants would be close by. We hoped Father's new bargain did not pertain to what we had already created, but to future weaving only; those generated from the wool of Tobias' sheep and not from ours. But Tobias spotted us and hurried in our direction.

"Rachel, why are you hesitating? Bring these goods to my tent now," he said, ordering her about as if she were already his property.

Mother moved slowly, trying to delay any interaction with him until the other merchants could crowd around. I knew she was angry. I could feel it raging inside her, but she appeared graceful and calm on the outside. He seemed in a hurry and pulled at her to rush things along. Tobias loved to show his wealth by wearing gold and jewels on his neck and hands, looking, to me, like a decorated ox. One of his more opulent rings caught Mother's headscarf and ripped it off. Her luxurious hair fell out and tumbled onto her shoulders. Tobias flushed with excitement. She hurriedly tried to cover her head, but he was intent on getting Mother inside his tent. He gripped her arm tightly, and dragged her, her headscarf falling to the ground.

Pushing me aside, he untied the cloth and robes and instructed me to wait outside with our donkey. He commanded that I not let anyone in while they settled their important business. I did not understand such things then, but a large bulge grew in his tunic below his waist. Something about it sickened me, but I walked outside as ordered. I searched for people I knew, trying to see what was going on by the well where the women gathered. And of course, I looked for Zeus.

Several minutes passed, and I heard a commotion inside the tent. I sensed Mother was in some kind of trouble. I peeked in and saw her fighting against Tobias. His robe was open, and he was pushing himself against her body while gripping one hand against her mouth.

"Stop this, I am a married woman." Mother tried to speak against the rough pressure of his palm, stifling her screams, hoping to escape without incident. She was dealing with the most influential man in the trade business, and he could ruin us for good. Neither she nor Father needed trouble from Tobias. Her voice was firm and frantic, but muffled by his grip.

"I have much greater wealth than your husband. Perhaps he will not mind. Perhaps we can factor this business into our deal as well," he said. He put his filthy hand across her backside and pulled her toward him, trying to press his greasy lips against hers. "I can make you a very rich woman. You deserve better than you have, a fine beauty like you."

"You could have me stoned for adultery." Mother was still trying to free herself without making a mortal enemy of this man of influence. He held power over our livelihood and existence. If she could conjure a viable excuse without insult, if she could blame her resistance on a fear of retribution, she might escape unscathed. Pushing his enormous stomach against her body, he pulled her robe aside to grab her breast with his other hand. Mother could not bear it. She slapped him hard across the face and pushed him with all her might. He shook his head, somehow delighted by her reaction, and opened his robe wider as he came at her. She thrust her knee into his groin, hard enough to block him but not cause serious injury. He doubled over in considerable pain. His face grew contorted and even uglier than usual. Dazed for a bit, a look crossed his face that was so distorted with anger and excitement, I thought for a moment he would kill her.

He grabbed her roughly and threw her onto a pile of woven rugs, knocking her off her feet, her garment flying up past her knees. He moved toward her with fierce determination. Although still in pain and his robe no longer bulging, he seemed determined to have at her. He wanted access into her, domination over her. As he was about to push himself onto her, I screamed, a blood-curdling scream loud enough that anyone near the tent would hear.

People gathered around me in muted conversations. Many recognized our donkey, and knew Mother was inside selling her wares. Two Roman soldiers of low rank went into the tent, demanding to know why I screamed. I followed behind them and stared at Mother, who was busy adjusting her robe and her composure. She gave me a stern but worried look that warned me not to say a word.

"My daughter was frightened. She thought she saw a snake," Mother lied. "We are fine."

"That child is prone to fits. One might think her possessed," Tobias spoke in his arrogant and confident tone. "I have been worried about that girl for quite some time. She often imagines she sees dangerous things and makes up preposterous stories. Once mute, she now screams for no reason? She froths at the mouth. You should keep a close eye on her."

This accusation caused the soldiers to look at me with guarded suspicion. Tobias was covering himself in case I told Father or anyone what I had just seen. But Lucius was right behind the foot soldiers. On finding Mother's headscarf on the ground and hearing my scream, he rushed to the tent and threw the curtain open.

"What has happened that is of such concern?" he demanded in a tone I had never heard from him.

I began to cry, my body shaking with fear. My reaction played into Tobias' lie, and the other soldiers told Lucius the story of my evil possession and suspected insanity. Lucius watched Mother closely, reading her face, which confirmed his suspicion. He stared at Tobias, who could not hold up against the strength of his glare. With his expression, Lucius let Tobias know he was well aware of what had transpired, and that Tobias was now walking on dangerous ground. But with that look, I fear Lucius also revealed his heart for just one moment. Tobias' eyes narrowed, and he looked from Mother to Lucius with fierce loathing.

The fleshy man's sweaty face held a forced smile, but inside I could see he was raging with hatred and humiliation.

"Just look at that girl. There is something very wrong with that child." He waved his hand in my direction and spoke to the gathering crowd more than to Lucius.

"There is nothing wrong with that child. Something she saw obviously frightened her," Lucius said, his eyes focused on Tobias.

Lucius was making a mortal enemy of the town's most powerful merchant. But as a Roman, Lucius held the stronger hand. Tobias could not touch him, and he knew it. Looking back, I see Lucius did not comprehend the deep wickedness that made its home in Tobias. Lucius believed he was in the position of power. He did not imagine the strength of Tobias' will to exact revenge against anyone who crossed him. Tobias felt humiliated on many fronts. Not the least being Mother's rejection of his advances. The blow to his groin was the ultimate insult and injury. It now occurred to Tobias that the woman he claimed as his rightful conquest was of interest to the captain. And the Roman knew what he had just done. This repudiation was more humiliation than Tobias could tolerate, and he vowed to himself that Lucius would not win.

"Good woman, we meet again," Lucius stated, as if he hardly knew her. "Is everything to your liking here?"

"Yes, of course, Captain," Mother replied. "Something surprised my daughter. You know how children are." She looked at Tobias with courteous eyes, hoping to remove herself unscathed. She was shaken and did not understand what Tobias was now thinking. "Thank you, Master Tobias, for your handling of my goods."

Lucius stood firmly in his place until Mother took my hand and led me outside the tent. Both Mother and Lucius noticed everyone was watching, and they remained cordial and detached. No one would suspect they saw each other beyond these brief meetings in town. No one but Tobias.

As he left the tent, Lucius turned and gave Tobias one last warning look and then bent down toward me and spoke, "How is your lovely daughter?"

I wanted to run into his powerful arms, the arms I wished beyond all hope were ours. I craved to live under his protection and kindness all my days. Confused and frightened, my intuition told me something had been set in motion that would destroy us all. Looking at Mother, I knew not to act in the way my heart was leading me. I stopped crying and hung my head. I nodded in assent, not daring to speak around the gathered strangers and thus blow what remained of my mute disguise, my quiet tears falling.

Lucius dismissed the foot soldiers, telling them I was a perfectly normal child. He had business dealings with my mother and me and knew us to be good people.

"It is that merchant you should watch," he said to them. "He is not to be trusted." As we were about to leave, he looked into my eyes and promised, "Do not worry, Magdalena. I will keep you safe."

Lucius had such generous eyes. It both tears my heart and brings me joy to picture them. He would have given his life for us, though his knowing of us was so limited. In his mind, he would allow no harm to come our way.

Something in me doubted that was possible. I was too young to grasp all that had just happened, but in my soul, I could feel the dark clouds gathering.

⋆ SIX ⋆

AFTER THAT DREADFUL day, we stayed away from town for a long while. Lucius made his presence known throughout the city, doing his soldier's work and intimidating Tobias as he did. He needed to be seen, and we desired to be forgotten. When we went to the stream, it was stark and depressing without Lucius. Mother seemed desperately sad, but also relieved, when he failed to show. We felt an undefined danger hanging over us, and I worried Mother would put an end to our meetings. It filled me with great anxiety, dreading but not understanding what was unfolding. My greatest fear, the concern that unsettled me the most, was going back to our old way of life, a life without Lucius.

But neither of them could resist the other for long. As the season passed, we saw him more regularly. When we were with Lucius, we lived in a better world. But Mother seemed plagued by anxiety before and after each visit. It lasted longer each time we met with him, as if there were only a finite number of meetings possible, and each one, although wonderful in every conceivable way, was one closer to the end. She fought to delay our going to the stream with a determined strength. I held my tongue, for I knew it would not last, and we would soon be together again.

I suppose I could have felt threatened by my mother's feelings for Lucius. I had been the only one she ever loved before meeting him. But I loved him too. I had always craved to know what having a loving father would feel like, one to whom I held a special place. I thought I had a family when we were together, and I resented how we lived when we were not with him.

We tried to push Tobias out of our thoughts, making excuses at every opportunity to have Father carry our products to him when he went into town to discuss their business. We told Father we could no longer afford to bring food and wine to Tobias, protesting that any time away from our looms would mean a loss of profit. This argument appealed to his unending desire for money and success.

We delayed our market visits until later in the day, when the crowds were fuller. It was not the ideal time to trade, as most had already finished their business, but we needed to be surrounded by other people. When we saw Tobias, we waited until his tent was full, so we could make our exchanges, taking whatever meager coins he thought he could get away with paying us. He knew Mother was uncomfortable in his presence, and he used it against her. His eyes held a thinly veiled threat to our safety, daring us not to speak of the incident. He still stared at Mother distastefully, but there was something else as well. He was angry and humiliated by Mother's rejection, and it fueled his need for vengeance. And now, he hated her for preferring a man he knew, but could not admit, was superior in too many ways. She reminded him of it every time he looked at her. How dare a woman of such low standing not bow before his wealth and power, not give in to his desires, not consider herself fortunate to have his attention? With his insatiable need for dominance, he paid her as poorly as he could and glared at her with such arrogance it made me want to spit in his face. Tobias was a most unscrupulous and conniving man, and I felt dirty and threatened every time we were near him.

Lucius kept a sharp eye on Mother every time we entered Tobias' tent. I wondered if people were watching him watch her. I could also see Lucius' love for Mother becoming more evident. Going into the city felt threatening, and we tried to avoid it.

What Mother was thinking during these days, I cannot know. She never spoke to me about the incident in Tobias' tent. I am sure she thought I would not understand at my young age, and that was true. I only knew he wanted revenge, but even my daringly creative and mischievous mind never fully imagined the evil in his heart.

And then things shifted beyond our control.

*   *   *

The morning began well enough. The sunrise was fading, leaving layers of wispy white clouds dancing through the deep azure sky. I skipped along, my mind occupied with thoughts of Zeus. I had become fearless on his back, and I liked to believe he loved having me there, as I was so light compared to Lucius. He must have felt unburdened and filled with as much freedom as I experienced. We carried our laundry in baskets loaded on our donkey, and had prepared a lovely feast of figs and dates, sheep's cheese, and freshly baked bread. We were hoping to share our meal with Lucius, but we never spoke those words out loud. I knew, by the happy baking of fresh bread the evening before, that I would soon have my legs wrapped around my beloved Zeus.

Lucius was already resting by the stream when we walked up. He seemed eager for us to arrive. As we did our washing, Lucius relaxed and told us the town's news and gossip. We soothed his soul as much as he did ours. We laid our meal before him, and he smiled his honest, generous smile, finally at ease. He complimented our food enthusiastically, but I knew his pleasure came in sharing it with us.

The crisp chill of the morning faded, and the sun warmed our skin as we finished eating. Too energetic to sit, I danced about while Mother sang, feeling free and unencumbered. It no longer seemed strange being so at ease with Lucius. It was a strong contrast to how I felt around other men, including my father. But I trusted Lucius as I trusted no other, and he had a disarming way about him when he was with us. He was a much different Lucius from the man I saw in town and the soldier who so intimidated Tobias. He was what I imagined a father and husband should be. Lucius made me feel safe and seen. Although we were happy in that magical moment, it still seemed a cloud was hanging over the day.

I studied Lucius' face as he spoke. It fascinated me how different he was from the other men I saw in town. His eyes were a dusty blue, and his bronze skin was more golden than the others. He and Mother looked as if they belonged together by decree. I loved the lines around his features. Although they could underscore a ferocity when he was angry, they danced when he smiled.

After our meal, I rode Zeus for the better part of an hour. I could now jump on and off by my own effort, even though he was so tall next to me. He allowed me to wrap my fingers in his mane and use it to pull myself high enough to reach the saddle. Then, with a swing from the center of me, I could throw one leg around him and land on top. I felt very accomplished in all aspects of riding and would have become quite the braggart had Mother not quelled my tendency. She was still apprehensive about my running such a powerful horse across the field, and worried over the risk I was taking. But Lucius had great confidence in me, and that settled her nerves. Because her own soul loved to see me feeling so free, she let me go.

We ran faster than ever before, Zeus delighted to have such a light and willing rider on his back. My natural ease and physical grace matched his, so he could run freely and still follow my directions. In harmony, we shared our great love and need for movement. When I returned to Mother and Lucius, I was a sorry sight with tangled hair and sweaty robes, but neither of them noticed. Something was wrong.

"There is no telling how long I will be gone," I heard Lucius saying to Mother as I slipped off Zeus' back. "There is an uprising three days' ride from here. They are killing our soldiers."

I crept toward them, feeling the weight of the moment.

"Is it dangerous?" Mother asked.

"I feel confident we can overpower them and settle this in a short time," Lucius answered.

"I pray you are not injured," Mother added, "and yet I am sad you fight my people."

"Are you supportive of this rebellion? I respect your beliefs, but you must know this is politics. It is not about faith or community," Lucius replied, in a voice that was oddly both soft and strong.

"To them, I think it is. I understand the hatred of not being free, of being dominated. And these fighters are still my people."

Lucius seemed to be at a loss for words, not wanting to upset Mother to express his thoughts. How could he tell her he considered them cowards who murdered his men in the dark of night rather than bravely on a battlefield? Still, Lucius admired their commitment. He understood how difficult it was to have the Roman army occupying their land. Lucius was not a man who held prejudices. I can see that even more clearly from this distance. He was an unusual captain, one who had no cruelty in him, who had and used his power to do what he thought was right; here to protect his soldiers and bring peace to the region. In our city's eyes, he and his legions had a stranglehold on our throats.

" Will you be careful?" Mother pleaded, now thinking only of her love for him, her dearest friend, and more.

"Rachel, I have to say what is in my heart. If anything were to happen to me, I would die unhappy if I never told you how much I care for you. I have never felt this love for a woman before you. I dream of you at night and regret all time not spent with you. The risk you take by meeting with me is untenable, and I have thought long and hard about how to change our fates and protect you. When I get back, I can arrange a stationing far from here. Will you go with me, you and Magdalena? I know this goes against your faith and tradition, but this life holds nothing good for you. We can find a way. We can spend our lives together."

I could not believe what I was hearing. Lucius was putting words to all my hopes and dreams. I searched Mother's face for a sign she might agree. She sighed, and her face filled with sorrow as she rested her head against his willing shoulder.

"How is this possible?" she asked. "How can we so change our lives?"

Lucius put his firm hand under her delicate chin and raised it toward him. "We can find a way," he said, and he leaned in to place a kiss on her lips.

Just then, at the far edge of the field, there rose a great rustling commotion. A moment later, from out of the olive grove Zeus and I used as our turning point, came a thick, brown horse with a thicker and triumphant Tobias bouncing on top. It took him several minutes to cross the field to reach us, long enough for Mother to regain her composure.

"Good day, Rachel," Tobias said, huffing from his effort, and making his voice lower and louder than usual. "And Captain, how strange to find you so far from your station. I could not help but notice you from where I rested in the shade of the trees," and he tossed his stubby fingers toward our grove. "Engaged in sordid behavior, I fear. Adultery comes to mind." Tobias continued, "I have often rested in that grove and have seen you together on several occasions."

The three of us then realized, Tobias had been following us and watching Mother for some time, since the incident in his tent.

"I can not imagine what it is you think you saw," Mother protested, in a determined voice. "For nothing inappropriate has occurred."

Lucius quickly rose to his feet with a stature Tobias could not dream of possessing. Even Tobias' horse seemed to cower in his presence.

"This entire area is my charge, Merchant," Lucius said, putting Tobias in his place. "What is it you are accusing this woman of doing? I was comforting her for a moment when her daughter fell. Is this what you call sordid? It could not be easy to know what you saw from such a distance. Even a younger, more vital man could not have such good vision." I could not stop my smile at this well-landed affront. "Perhaps your mind is purposefully tricking you, for your eyes cannot be as keen as most predators." More insult to the gloating Tobias, his sweaty face now showing a hint of confusion. This could be feasible, for I was disheveled and messy. My admiration for Lucius swelled with his fast and confident thinking.

"I came across them in distress while riding these hills," he continued. "It seems you are taking such a ride yourself. I would hate to think you were spying on these good people if you have been there several times. Should I be concerned?" With this, his eyes narrowed into a fearsome expression.

If Lucius was worried, we did not detect it. Mother froze with fear, but I thought she hid it well.

"Dear Sir," she responded, addressing Tobias. "You know me and my family better than this." She used a voice I did not recognize, one that floated above suspicion as if accusing her accuser. "It is as the captain has said."

Tobias calculated his odds, and a scheme came into his mind, one none of us would have imagined.

"Of course, of course," he said, with a constipated grin. "And fine Captain, how good of you to come to the aid of this dear woman. How fortunate you invariably seem to be in her company when misfortune strikes." He stressed the word always and leered at Mother with a knowing glare. He let his suspicion hang in the air for a long moment.

"It seems strange that you are ever present in her times of strife as well," Lucius countered, his suspicion shot back at Tobias with a knowing look.

"As long as everything is in order, I will leave you," Tobias answered, struggling to regain his upper hand. "What a tragedy that child is so clumsy and regularly in need of rescuing," and he looked me up and down, working to intimidate me after having no success with Lucius. I stared back at him with pure hatred.

He made a pretentious bow to Mother and Lucius and rode off. His poor horse, I thought, how does he survive the weight and clumsiness of that wretched man? When he was gone from the area, Lucius turned toward Mother.

"That man is dangerous, Rachel. Please take my offer seriously, and consider leaving with me before he can do you harm. I want nothing more than to care for you and Magdalena and get you away from here. I think it will give her a better life as well."

He pulled her to him, and concerned only with his love for her, he kissed her. I saw my mother melt into his arms, my mother who never lost her mask of imperturbability and always hid her true heart. She let all inhibition go and lived that moment of truth in its totality. I felt her power ignite. Would she finally free us? The kiss lasted so long, I thought I would get my wish—the gift that we might all be together as a family and live the life of our dreams. Mother had never known this feeling and had never felt such emotion. I marveled at the mystery between men and women, what happiness seemed possible, and yet for reasons I could not, and refused to understand, was so often denied. Perhaps Mother would get nothing more than this one kiss, no other authentic occasion of freedom and desire won, but it was worth living or dying for. Their physical longing at last realized, the true importance of the moment was the awakening in my mother's soul.

Just days after Lucius and his famed legion left our city, and we were under the control of the older and less capable foot soldiers, Tobias felt free to move forward with his plan. He started spinning rumors, first among the merchants who came for trade, and after getting a good deal of satisfaction from their reaction and practice telling his tale, he spread his salacious gossip to the village men. The men shared their stories with the women, and soon all tongues were wagging with the news that Rachel was an adulteress, a harlot who had taken up with the handsome and powerful Roman soldier.

At first, the women could not believe this of the lovely Rachel, whom they cherished. Tobias, being skilled in deception, tied the episode in his tent to Lucius. He said he confronted Mother, but she was too emotional and too determined to continue her liaison to listen to reason. When Tobias defied her, she became hysterical, and I screamed at seeing her so upset.

His lies were well-considered and plausible. The villagers remembered the incident, remembered that both Mother and Lucius were there, and began to believe the thread of lies that Tobias wove. Anyone who knew my mother and father could see it was no love match, and I suspect any woman with eyes would recognize the allure of the captivating captain. He seemed a temptation few would refuse if provided the opportunity. And so, they believed.

Tobias was relentless. He wove exaggerated tales among those eager to believe anything scandalous about a Roman, even if it meant sacrificing Mother to reap revenge. Eventually, Father heard the rumors. Possessing such a beautiful wife had always afforded him a taste of prestige. Losing that standing and being ridiculed was as death to him. He confronted Mother angrily. She promised that nothing improper had taken place. We had run into the captain frequently. He was always kind to me, and she appreciated his wish to pay for the goods he ruined. Father knew Tobias was angry with us about the blanket and that he was a spiteful man; all the more reason he would rather not be on his wrong side. Father wanted to avoid trouble, but he felt diminished by the circulating gossip. His feelings of shame led to an increase in hostility toward Mother.

In absolute fact, Mother told the truth, but in her heart, she was an adulteress, and she wondered if it showed. She loved Lucius as she had loved no one before him, and wanted to be with him. I knew Father wanted to believe her, but he felt damaged and lessened in the eyes of the men whose approval he sought. He hated to be the object of the city's demeaning and salacious gossip. These rumors were a humiliation he could not bear. A cold and suspicious distance grew between them.

Mother and I hid from sight, avoiding town and anyone we knew. We wove daily, but at a slow pace. We both hoped, without sharing our thoughts, that Lucius would return and save us from whatever trouble was brewing. But Tobias had perfected his scheme and summoned fabrics, clothing and oils from Mother for his upcoming journey. It was an important trip, a very lucrative one, and he warned Father not to miss this opportunity. Tobias was stern and emphasized that if Father did not produce exceptional products, Tobias would seek goods from others. Once he started a new trade, his business with Father would be over. There was no telling how damaging this would be to Father's future. Tobias increased the pressure daily, and finally sent word that all items were due in his tent within two days or their business was over for good. Father fell into his trap, feeling he had no choice but to bring our wares to Tobias immediately. He promised to accompany Mother and me to the market, thinking his presence would help to avoid trouble.

Mother resisted going. "You take these things to Tobias, Gal," she pleaded. "There is no need for us all to make the trip." But Father would not hear of it, fearing it would cause him to appear inadequate, and her guilty.

"We go together," he commanded. Weak though Father was, he was also stubborn, a dangerous combination. He was determined to regain prestige and dismiss the rumors, and craved to be the one behind the wares that made Tobias so successful. He wanted his due. With this idea stuck in his mind, he could not consider another one. His standing and wealth rested on it.

When we arrived in town, we noticed a crowd gathered outside Tobias' tent. They were calling out with heated, discordant voices, creating a cacophony of impassioned banter we could not decipher but could feel in our flesh. Rage stirred the air around us as the men pushed about angrily, and without direction. They just heard that Lucius and his soldiers killed the leaders of the resistance, and would track the rest until each one was dead. This news increased their agitation, and they shouted and waved sticks and stones as they moved about. They wanted revenge, some way to cut the head from this growing monster.

"We should kill these Roman dogs," one burly man shouted. His words fomented a fury against Lucius and his men, and increased their appetite for violence. Tobias had been agitating them for days, anticipating our arrival. He fed them gossip and stirred their anger. There was little truth in anything he said, but his telling was passionate, and these recent killings created greater outrage and a strong desire for revenge.

We were fools to continue walking toward the tent with our goods. We should have turned and fled. I took Mother's trembling hand as Father pulled her by the other. He naively believed he held sway with Tobias because of their business dealings, but I knew better. Tobias had loyalty to no one but himself.

It felt like we entered a hornets' nest with nothing to shield us. Tobias stepped forward with the sense of authority he assumed with his lies and position of wealth.

"There she is, the Roman's whore," he shouted, and pointed his thick, greasy finger at Mother.

"Liar!" I cried, and Mother pulled me behind her, shielding me from sight.

"Here. Here," Father spoke, looking surprised by the attack. "What is all of this talk?"

Tobias stared at Father with contempt, and Father wilted under his gaze. He was confused about his standing with the man, and at how quickly he turned on him. Tobias repeated, "There she is, the Roman's whore."

The meaner and angrier men held large rocks in their hands and waved them at Mother. A sense of defeat numbed my body as I struggled to find my voice, but my tongue defied me, and I sat frozen, unable to move.

"Stone the adulteress!" A cry rose from the crowd. The words rang in my ears, but my mind would not let them in. "Stone the Roman's whore!" several men called out.

For the briefest moment, I thought Father might fight for her. I saw him shield her with his body as he spoke.

"You have no proof. Where are the two witnesses to this accusation? What lies are these? My wife is not an adulteress. I know her too well to believe this." His voice sounded pleading, making a case for himself more than her.

Tobias stepped forward and pulled at Mother, grabbing her roughly by the arm and away from me. "I observed her with my own eyes. I saw her with that captain out by the stream on your property and in my tent. The crime of adultery calls for stoning. With a Roman occupier, the punishment is too kind."

He looked at the enraged men. Many of them shunned Mother just for her unapproachable beauty and the thought that she would give it away to the enemy and not to any of them. They hated all things Roman and craved an opportunity to fight back. They felt helpless against them, and furious at the death of the rebels. Tobias stirred their anger. He argued that their hopes for freedom were over. The resistance was destroyed. He shouted to the crowd, his voice rising, stirring them into an uncontrollable mob.

"That is not what happened," I shouted.

Mother looked at me with such strength, I lost my voice again. I knew she wanted to silence me. She did not want me to speak up for fear they would drag me into the fury with her, but I felt compelled to do so.

"That girl is possessed," Tobias shouted back. "When I confronted her mother regarding this affair, the child screamed hysterically. She is nothing but trouble herself. You know her as a mute, and now she speaks? When the devil gives her tongue? She, who rides and possesses the soldier's horse, while her mother lies with the man."

I was about to tell the truth about Tobias forcing himself on Mother, but she looked at me and said, in a stern voice, "Magdalena, no."

I was at a loss, having no clear sense of what to do. I had to save my mother, yet how could I disobey her when she demanded my silence?

"That child should be stoned as well. She is the source of this trouble. A demon dwells in her," Tobias went on, waving his hand at me. Mother knew the angry men would kill me alongside her if I continued to tell what happened. No one was going to believe me, for no one wanted to. They craved revenge and blood. It would be my word, a useless girl with a history of strange behavior, against the mighty Tobias.

"Rachel is the Roman's whore, and her daughter is demon-possessed. Who knows what evil will come from the two of them? We should cut them down before that demon grows in strength."

I understood then that Mother knew the plan better than anyone. Tobias wanted me, with my knowledge of what had happened in the tent, to be done with as well. I would remain a threat for the rest of my life, and he had always resented my very existence. Mother realized this, for she saw the nature of the man all too well. Saving me was her only concern.

At that moment, I recognized Father was helpless against Tobias. A part of him thought it might be true, and this possibility weakened him even further. He knew we had spent a good deal of time at the stream, and there had been a strange distance between them for months. Filled with doubt and rage, his need for acceptance from these men tipped the balance. He looked at Mother with disgust.

"Is this true, Rachel?" he demanded.

"I have not committed adultery," she answered.

"Liar." Tobias shouted. "I have seen you with my own eyes, and more than once."

Mother recognized there was no rescue, no way out. She would have told the truth of the incident in the tent, but her only thought was to save a life for me. If she exposed Tobias, very few would accept her word, for they wanted to believe the lies. They needed a win against the Roman occupiers. They required a scapegoat of any kind, and Tobias would offer me as a sacrifice. He would convince the angry crowd to have me stoned for demon possession and cavorting with Romans and their animals. If a few believed us, if we escaped execution, she knew Tobias would destroy Father's business and leave us all in ruin. Of this, she was certain.

The most she could say was, "You and I both know the truth of what happened in the tent, Tobias." And she looked at Father.

For a moment, I thought he understood what she meant, but his vanity blurred his thinking. He could never see Tobias' lust for Mother as dangerous, could not tolerate the idea that their business was a ruse to get access to her. He needed to believe he was a good businessman worthy of trade with the illustrious Tobias.

"Yes, we do," Tobias shouted, "and you must pay the price for adultery. It is our law."

I approached, intending to tell the truth about Tobias' actions, as I could not risk Mother's death, even if it made her angry with me for the rest of our lives. I would rather lose her love than have her taken from me in this way, hoping to die in her place. Sensing what I was about to do, Tobias struck me hard to the ground. Father did not flinch. At that moment, I meant nothing to him. Mother, with grave fear in her eyes, not for herself but for what would happen to me, gave me a look I dared not cross. She wanted me to remain silent and to step back. I was afraid to cross her. I could not match her strength, and for this, I still cannot forgive myself. But she knew I would go down with her if I spoke up. Her only thought was to save me.

Looking back with the wisdom of one crossing to the other side, I also see Mother realized her life could not continue as it had. She needed the struggle to be over. It had waged within her for too long, and she understood she had no viable resolution. She knew there was no way to choose Lucius, to sever herself from her culture and its laws. Despite her liberated soul, the law stated that once married, always married. Her marriage would feel more intolerable after knowing Lucius. To love Lucius and be with him would be a joy she could only imagine, but there would constantly be the risk of being found, of looking over her shoulder, of living in fear. To run from a husband was punishable by death. And yet, she feared she would choose her love for Lucius anyway, and what kind of life would that provide for us?

Where would we go? Even if we could hide, was a soldier's existence a decent one to give her daughter? Were we to live in Rome in a fashion we could not even imagine? What would it mean for me to have no father, no lineage, no status other than as a concubine's daughter? No, death seemed the only suitable ending. She found peace in realizing the choice was made for her. Her battle would soon be over. But her child, her love, she must survive. I must somehow rise above the situation in which I was born.

Tobias walked over to Father and placed a large, jagged rock in his hand, and pushed Mother to the center of the crowd. The other men shoved her about, and the frenzy mounted.

"You must throw the first stone. Rachel is your wife," Tobias shouted, as if he were the grand authority on all justice.

"I have seen no proof of what you say," Father almost mumbled, speaking with little force or conviction. I knew he loved Mother, and the last thing he wanted was for her to be dead. As Tobias stared at him, Father understood that his trade would be over if he crossed the most powerful merchant in the area. All of his olives, his oils, and wool would have no market if Tobias forbade it. If he could not sell his products, he would lose his land. Father was a ruined man one way or another. He would give up his wife or all that he owned.

"Throw the stone," Tobias shouted, and he waved his hand at the crowd.

"Throw the stone," the angriest man in the crowd shouted, and he stared down at Mother. He raised his arm with a large jagged rock clenched in his fist. He was eager for the bloodshed to begin.

Mother looked up at him, her eyes calm and clear. She knew she was now on the threshold of seeing her God. She was already looking beyond this world, and the physical beauty she possessed was nothing compared to the full force of her soul. Perhaps she entered the place beyond form that I found in the stream. More than likely, she always lived with that vision, but now she held it in its full power. She looked into the man's eyes, past the hate and fear and right into his humanity, the sacred part we all share even when we forget. He stopped and stared back at her, a part of him meeting her there, moved by a feeling he did not understand. He let the rock drop from his hand as he wrestled with the guilt that filled him.

This unsettled Tobias, and he sensed the crowd's anger might dissipate at seeing the man leave, and he would lose the momentum he had taken so long to build. He puffed himself up and spoke even louder to distract anyone whose eyes were now on Mother.

"Her lover just killed many of our own. We will never be free of the Roman yoke unless these occupiers are stopped. Stone this adulteress and send our message. Leave the captain's whore under stones." Tobias spoke with such enthusiasm, he incited the men again, and they shouted and waved their rocks over their heads. "Show that we have our own laws. Laws they cannot touch."

"No!" I shouted, and ran toward Mother, blood running down my face from the cut left by Tobias' blow.

One woman, one who did care for Mother, and who was crying out for her rescue, pulled me away from what she knew was coming. She understood there was no escape. A woman of my time had little chance against forces driven by men. Mother glanced up at her in gratitude, knowing I was safe in her care. She then looked at me and said, with the calm of a person who can already touch the other side, "I love you, Magdalena. Remember all I have taught you. I will always be with you. We will be together again."

Tobias grabbed Father's arm and forced the first throw from his hand with a pronounced thrust. I sensed Father recoil after the stone hit Mother in the back, causing her to fall to her knees. The crowd was untethered once they watched her stumble. I saw her blood spill, soaking the ground where she lay. She tucked her beautiful head under her arm as the stones buried her. The crowd had an ample supply, gathered by Tobias and his men and at the ready. They were in the grip of hatred and anger and acting out the deep resentment they held for the Romans. It had nothing to do with Mother or any crime she may or may not have committed. They needed to kill, to release the rage and fury consuming them. I watched in horror, held back by my mother's friend, a shrill animal wail coming from the depth of me. I pulled away and ran to Mother. The image of her bloodied and broken form melded within the savage emotions of our townspeople. It created a tenebrous impression within my soul that would now and forever haunt my mind. I flung myself over her, trying to absorb her essence into me, to feed her my life force or to leave with hers.

"Mother…" I cried, in a shrill voice. As I threw my body onto hers, the last stone struck the side of my head. I fell back and looked into Father's confused and panicked eyes. He saw only hatred in mine. And then my world turned black.

⋆ SEVEN ⋆

THE ROCK SKIMMED Mother's body before it struck me, thus sparing my life. I believe this was her last protective act for the child she loved. It was fortunate I was unconscious of what came next. Tobias kicked Mother's body to roll it over and expose her still beautiful but bloodied face. She had tucked her head when the first stone caught her back. I know she did this for my sake, to avoid the horror I would feel should I see her face disfigured. Tobias ordered his men to drag her body to an unmarked grave before night fell, as was the law. Father, struck dumb with grief, reached out to take hold of her, but Tobias grabbed his arm and pulled him away.

"She is unclean, a sinner. Be done with her," he said.

Father glared at him, but it was a whimpering expression without effect. To have chosen his trade and future over his wife would no doubt plague his conscience for the rest of his time, but he had to choke back those thoughts. Father could not face how weakly he had given her up. He needed to shield himself from his own faults and accept Tobias' lie. To own the truth would have broken him further.

"I am sorry to be the one to bear witness to what I saw, but I saved you from ruin, my friend," Tobias said, and he placed his arm solicitously around Father's shoulder. "Your trade would be over once people knew Rachel was bedding that Roman."

Father winced, hating the thought of those words and still wondering if any of it was true. Somehow the woman he knew, and the one Tobias described were not the same person.

"I realize this must be difficult for you, but it is for the best," Tobias continued. "She was a beauty, but we all know what trouble that brings. You will marry again, this time to someone more worthy, and I will help you extend your trade to new markets. I can grow your business in ways you never dreamed possible," Tobias promised. "And you still have that troublesome child to weave and work."

Father looked with dead eyes at the torn and bloodied shell of his beautiful and talented wife as two clumsy and thoughtless men dragged her in the dirt. I doubt he had a single thought of me.

Someone in the angry crowd carried me to the home of the woman to whom Mother entrusted me. She washed my wound and held me through the night, offering water with wine to soothe my nerves. I clung to my despair as I craved to hold on to my mother. My mind drew further and further away until it looked as though I might follow her to the grave. Oh, how my soul wanted to leave this treacherous world and be with her.

The dear woman cared for me as if I were her own child. I recognized her as one who gathered spilled oil on the day Lucius knocked our goods to the ground, the memory of it bringing a delirium of dreams through my traumatized mind. Beautiful images turned into hellish nightmares that terrorized me. Lucius and Zeus appeared as they did when we first met; stunning and magnificent, but they soon turned wicked and frightening. Mother sang while I danced to her songs, but we were out of sync, discordant and at odds. Her voice was sad and heavy. She was sinking into the earth, deeper and deeper, while I floated on clouds trying to touch my stars. I struggled to grasp them, stretching desperately to feel them, but they were unreachable. One last attempt failing. And then falling…falling…faster and faster over a precipice, my Grandmother's cliff, unable to stop…onto the stones, surrounded by decaying bones; falling into the stark void of nothingness. Lost and alone.

I remained in the care of my mother's ally without recognizing where I was, nor would I have cared. Mother befriended her at the well after her husband died, and slipped goods to her from time to time. Now she would repay Mother's kindness by looking after me. She dabbed some of the familiar oil on my wound, knowing it would help me heal and prevent infection. The scent stirred recollections within me, some good and some treacherous. The older woman would not leave my side, caring for me as she would have for my mother. I moved between light and loving images to the last, tragic moments of my mother's life.

I hovered between this world and the next for several days and nights. I wanted to follow Mother, to forget everything that I was and had been. But some unknown force kept returning me to my body. It would not allow me to surrender to the allure of death.

On the last night of this dark struggle, Mother returned my spirit to my body for good. She was so close, I could have reached out to touch her. Circled in golden light, looking more radiant and loving than when she walked the earth, she spoke to me without words, reaching between our worlds, and touching me one last time. It was no mere dream.

"Magdalena, it is more beautiful here than you can imagine. Get up and stay true to your courageous heart. Follow your stars and let them protect you. Do not worry about me. I have found peace at last."

Her indelible serenity filled my soul. I rose from the bed and stumbled to the table of the woman who saved me, still dizzy from my blurred vision. My brain's command to my legs faltered, so I almost fell, but I kept my pride and gathered my strength.

"I must go home," I said.

"Rest one more day and get stronger," she pleaded, a worried look on her face, and I did. My sudden turn of mind surprised her. She was concerned about sending me home without Mother. If my father allowed such a fate for her, what would become of her daughter? But I was determined, and she felt more comfortable with the resolve I held despite my faltering steps. I would let no one see me cry again, I swore. They would not beat me. My mother taught me to value freedom, and I would honor her by living it. I would not forget a single word she ever told me, and prayed Lucius would come to save me and exact revenge on everyone who hurt us.

The following morning, the older woman fed me broth and bread and provided water with which to wash. She had cleaned my robe, supported my weight while I dressed, and then escorted me back to the only home I had ever known.

I cannot say Father was happy to see me, but there was relief in his eyes when I walked through the door. The emptiness of our house must have haunted him the days and nights I was gone. What could he have thought? What did he think had become of me? Or did he consider me collateral damage he could easily afford? He looked thin and absent. I believe a part of him was grateful to see I was still alive. At least some piece of Mother remained.

I did not say a word to him, but looked down and performed my chores. I acted as if things were normal, as if the only good part of our life was not now missing. My face flushed red with anger, and my lips quivered with emotion, but I would not admit my distress. The cut over my eye and my swollen face must have caused his guilt to stir. My head pounded with pain. I moved slowly and clumsily because of my impaired vision. I was a living reminder of the tragedy that had befallen us, and so he also said nothing.

We spent days like this—I, serving him and doing things as Mother had taught me, and Father pretending things were as they had always been, with not a word shared between us. Days turned into weeks. Weeks moved into seasons. I did not care. I went to the stream and sobbed when I could be alone, finding some vestige of relief in my hot, stinging tears. At least, they were genuine and of my own making. There was no longer a chance of joy in my life. I might never see Lucius or Zeus again, but that paled in the face of never seeing my beloved mother. The donkey and I and the stream. No song. No music. No dance.

I now had twice the chores, as I had mine, as well as Mother's. Father commanded me to weave robes and blankets and cloth for Tobias to sell. I made them carelessly, at first, for I resented his profit and Father's. Father found his voice only to criticize my work, and I became angrier still. If ever I would look at him, it was with a glare of contempt.

Things became even more strained between us. My childish revenge drove me to make his stews bland and tasteless. I knew how to use Mother's herbs to create the savory flavors Father liked, but I refused to gather them or the wild onions and ramps he loved. I wanted him to taste what he was missing, as I tasted my misery with every day that passed. The bread I made was hard and dry, and he had to soak it until he could chew it more easily. For this, he did not dare complain, afraid he would unleash my evil tongue, and I would shout my accusations at him. I was determined to make him suffer for what he had done. Perhaps I was wrong in my ways, but I could not do better for the man who allowed the murder of my mother.

The winter cold fell hard, and I could not stand to be alone with Father, so I sat at my loom and worked. He seemed satisfied when I produced something that would sell. I settled into a fantasy that when I wove, I was still with Mother. Her hands guided mine, and I let her lead me toward the work in new ways. I let my mind, once again, fall into the magic of the threads, into the patterns of a world I could not see. Art became my only solace because it was a way to hold my mother near. Soon, my work became exceptional because I thought it came from her hands and not my own. My art would keep her present. I would breathe her life into the fabric, and she would travel to places she had never been, and live lives she only dreamed of. I brought all of this into the cloth. Believing this kept me alive, though I daily begged death to claim me.

Father was wise enough to keep me away from Tobias, wise or too afraid of what I would do should I see him. My weavings were apparently doing very well in foreign markets, and Father's income grew. I rarely went into town, so I had no news of Lucius, no word if he was alive or dead. I believed, with all my heart, that he would take vengeance on Tobias if he returned. Tobias was regrettably still alive, so I had to assume Lucius was also lost to me. I had no friend left in the world, only my weavings and my little donkey. These were the darkest of days.

I cannot even tell how much time passed like this; I suspect it was over a year. I was still a child of only nine years when Father brought home a rather plain and stout woman and announced that she was his wife. I looked at him with disgust, and it did not go unnoticed by him or Abigail, my new "mother."

I will not pretend I tried to get along with her. I barely tolerated her, and she wanted nothing to do with me. There was nothing in her face that showed kindness or even good thought, not that I looked to find it. I will not say she was not clever, for she was, at getting what she needed. She took possession of the house immediately, as if she were queen of the domain. Father seemed reluctant to cross her. His weakness was no match for her uncompromising nature. I also knew he needed to have a new life that might help him forget the one he had traded for material success. She loaded me with chores, as she was lazy and unimaginative, but they kept me outside and away from her. I was less miserable when I was alone, so she did me a favor without suspecting it.

Abigail had a sharp tongue and could easily manipulate Father to get what she desired. She doted on him, but it was always on the back of my hard work. Besides the wash, gathering water, and tending the garden, I ground the wheat, baked the bread, gathered wood, cleaned the house, tended the newborn lambs, and anything else she could think for me to do, plus my weaving. She was not a good or practiced cook, so I found satisfaction in again gathering Mother's herbs to use in my stews, thus making hers taste even more common and bland in contrast to mine. I knew the flavors reminded Father of Mother, and I harbored secret pleasure in that as well.

I had become a child of ill intent and wanton revenge.

* * *

I found Abigail lazy, loud, and without manners, but she complimented Father and built his confidence. I wondered if Father organized his thoughts to believe he had done the right thing in allowing Mother's murder. It was my love for my mother that prevented me from becoming more fully poisoned with hatred. Often, I wanted to pick up a stick from the fire and strike one of them, strike them hard and without mercy, but Mother's image appeared again in my mind to stop me.

I would pick up a knife and wonder how it would feel to push it deep into Abigail's or Father's flesh. Could I? Would I do it? And then Mother would again warn me to abandon my need for revenge. When Father looked at me, he hated me for reminding him of how he had given up my mother to protect his trade and livelihood. I believe Father knew she had not yet acted against him. But he likely understood he was not the man she loved.

Abigail, however, adored Father. I suspect she would have fancied any man of even meager means who would marry her, for she was well past the age of marriage, and prospects were slim until Mother's death. I only vaguely remembered her from the market when Mother and I traded. She was younger than Mother, but so much plainer, and I think she felt it her great fortune to replace his dead wife and gain her land and status. I say status because Tobias did see to it that Father's income grew. Of course, Tobias' fortune grew at a far greater pace, as Father's harvest and my weavings and essential oils brought him untold new income. Abigail believed it was her influence that created the increased wealth. She refused to recognize my contributions to the prosperity, and more and more, she commanded Father's workers and dictated how he did his business. She saw his weakness and used it to her advantage.

Abigail was shrewd, I must give her that, and her greed was a match for Tobias'. She loved the game of trade and barter, using flattery and my talent to make her way into higher circles. She came to believe she was the driving force behind Father's success.

Occasionally, Abigail made me accompany her, so I could carry any extra weight the donkey could not bear. Abigail felt it beneath her station to do so, and considered me her servant, leaving me more resentful with each day. My pride would not allow me to show the rage I felt in front of Tobias. I held firm and kept my tongue, as hard as that was. I struggled to find ways of crossing both of them without drawing enough attention to my actions to bring retribution. Mimicking Lucius' stance when I stood in front of Tobias, I both confused and irritated him. I was silent, but I would not back down.

I watched Abigail flatter Tobias and stroke him as if they had been lifelong friends.

"What an outstanding man you are," she told him, over and over. "Your success is an inspiration! You are a pride to this city, so pious and holy. You, Tobias, personify all that is good in our people."

My stomach churned, and I choked on swallowed contempt. Of course, Tobias would not acknowledge my presence, which made me bolder in my underhanded attempts at rebellion. He wanted me to feel insignificant and of no consequence. Even though he thought me a powerless girl, I always recognized the threat in his eyes. I sensed his fear that I would somehow tell the truth to Father about what I had seen in his tent that fateful day. I would be lying to say it did not shake me, but it also gave me an insight into his insecurity, as covered with bravado and bullying as it was.

Abigail forced me to weave into the late hours, and I suspected she had struck a bargain for any extra weaving I produced. One by one, treasures from distant lands replaced our simple household items. She had new furniture made by the finest carpenters in the city. Silver trays covered the stone ledge above the hearth. Rich, luxurious tapestries hung on the walls, most notably to block the entrance to the alcove where I slept. That cut most of my light, which put even more strain on my eyes and nerves, but it accomplished the important goal of keeping me from their sight.

Nothing was too good for Abigail, and her lust for luxury and material riches grew each day. She loved to mention how Father's luck had changed for the better the day he married her. Abigail claimed he was fortunate to have a woman who could help him manage his holdings and see them grow; a wife who could curate his talent. It was true that Father had become more wealthy due to Tobias' patronage. This was the bargain he made in exchange for my mother's life. I wondered how Father truly saw it.

Wealth filled Abigail with an unending desire for more. More of everything. She had become wider of girth and less appealing each day, despite the colorful, textured robes she demanded I make for her with the finest threads available. I dressed her like a queen, and she treated me as her personal slave.

But I was beginning to look like my mother, and Abigail's commonness was more evident in contrast. She wanted me gone from her sight. I was a constant reminder of the beautiful wife Father once had, and I was coming too close to my young womanhood and my full beauty for her comfort. Yet, it conflicted her, for she was growing richer by the day, and although unable to admit it, she knew it was on my back. She became more determined to work around me. She hired additional villagers to help around the property, girls who struggled to do the jobs Mother had done. Lacking any sense of art or quality, Abigail felt it would be easy to supplant me with any other girl—one in need and nonthreatening. Once my presence was no longer essential to her success, she could get rid of me. Father had no say in how Abigail ran things. This was apparent, but Abigail had a talent for making him think he was in charge. She flattered him and praised him as a person of affluence and prestige. He did not need to do the work himself, she repeated, for he was a landowner, a man of influence. Flattery was the only music my father ever heard.

The hired help did not result in less responsibility for me, but it allowed Abigail to keep me at the loom longer. She enlisted unfortunate girls desperate enough to work for her meager offering, but she had no skill in teaching them how to do the things she demanded of them. They were all young, with little experience. They found it impossible to follow her orders.

She brought one girl up to the stream to do the wash, but could not be bothered to use the vessels we kept for separating the lye from the flowing water. To save time and effort, she tainted the water downstream that others used. Mother would have shuddered at such behavior.

"Always consider what your actions do to the land." I heard Mother's voice echo in my mind as I watched with grave disapproval. "We are stewards of the soil and water."

Defending my mother, I corrected the young woman and showed her how we had always done it. Humiliated and angry, Abigail slapped me across the face. "You are a stupid, stupid girl," Abigail shouted, and she threw the water back into the stream, breaking the clay vessel. " We do it this way now!"

I hardly flinched. At that moment, I understood that every aspect of my old life was behind me. Everything my mother and I had cared about was dead. I wanted to be as well.

I lived my life honoring the truth of stewardship and acted accordingly, as did so many of our women. If we failed the land, what did we have? But to Abigail, people and things were there to be exploited. In this, she was a perfect match for Tobias, as if cut from the same cloth. It mattered not the cost of their actions, as long as their wealth provided an endless supply of all they desired.

Abigail hired a poor, inexperienced girl, Hana, to operate the olive press. Hana was desperate for work, as her father had died when his youngest child was two years old. Being the eldest of four children, it fell on her to earn any money she could, so the family might survive. Father, oblivious to the rarity of Mother's talents, gave the task to Abigail after their marriage, thinking she could take over the job. He meant it as an honor, but she found it tedious, as she did most chores. She did not understand what it took to press rich and pure oil, and she hated and avoided any comparison to Mother. She wanted to be done with the task as quickly as possible and showed no interest in learning. Father tried for months to raise her to Mother's skill level, but it proved futile. Her oil was as crude and unrefined as Abigail herself. She cared little about excellence, only profit, and it showed. But she knew Father was losing his reputation as a producer of the highest quality oil, and she wanted to avoid being seen as the cause. So, she gave the task to Hana, a girl who had never been near a press in her life. Why she thought Hana, who was unfamiliar with olives or pressing, could do the job was beyond comprehension. The girl would work for almost nothing with the most rudimentary instruction. That was enough for Abigail.

I taught Hana to net the olive trees and catch the fruit before it could touch the ground. Olives begin turning rancid the moment they hit the dirt, and that lowers the quality of the oil. Mother taught me this at a very young age. Taking this care made Father's products stand out above others, but Abigail refused to follow my lead. Mother used the fruit that escaped the nets for lamp oil only. This oil brought little profit, and Abigail derided me as wasteful and foolish, but I knew her true motivation was to make me wrong and have Mother's ways forgotten.

Once netted, the olives needed to be run immediately to the press, for the longer the time between harvest and pressing, the cruder the oil.

Abigail could not afford to have me away from my loom and soon ordered me back to the house, leaving Hana alone to do the work. I knew she listened to me, not Abigail, and she tried hard, day after day, to crush the olives and press quality oil. In return, Hana received Abigail's criticisms, which were much more forthcoming than any constructive advice on how to improve. Abigail did not understand how to make high-quality oil herself. She was too lazy to take the care needed and had no way of teaching Hana. Her sharp tongue only disoriented and agitated the poor girl. She would have the olives scraped off the ground and brought to the mill to be dumped into the press with the ones Hana netted, confusing her further.

"The oil is too cloudy and too sharp, stupid girl," Abigail would shout. Hanna tried to mention the tainted olives and how they ruined the batch only once. The hard slap across her face discouraged any future attempts.

"What is all this pulp? We cannot sell this as oil," Abigail would screech.

"Can you not get more oil from each pressing?" she shouted, when Hana used only her netted olives, even though the oil was of good quality. Never a word for support or encouragement. Never a compliment to assure more confidence in the girl.

Hana became so nervous around Abigail that she could barely exercise her power of thought. Abigail knew how desperately the girl needed work and felt entitled to take advantage of her in every way she could, including bolstering her pride at the cost of Hana's. Hana struggled for months, her anxiety growing by the day. She grew so afraid of making a mistake that she could no longer think straight. Forced by Abigail to stay at my loom, there was little I could do to help Hana, who was even younger than myself. When I saw her, I gave her little tips and words of kindness and tried to build her confidence. But nothing helped. Hana was a girl with jittery nerves, and Abigail's constant criticisms only heightened her condition.

Late one afternoon, I could hear the loud barking of Abigail's criticisms aimed at poor Hana as I wove some new cloth. I tried to ignore the screaming, struggling to surrender to the creative escape I often found in my work. But over Abigail's screeching tone, I heard a wail of utter fear coming from Hana. I jumped up, knocking over my loom to see what was happening. I tripped on a tangle of threads and fell over the loom, cutting the bottom of my hand as I stumbled to Hana's side, a trail of blood and broken yarn behind me. Hana had become so distracted and nervous in reaction to Abigail's harsh criticisms that she did not notice her sleeve as it caught between the turning stones. Hana was struggling to pull it loose, but could not manage by herself. Abigail never thought to tear Hana's clothes from her body or place one of the thick, wooden paddles between the grinding wheels to stop them.

I arrived just in time to see Hana's arm dragged between the weight of the pressing stones. She and I watched in horror as the press crushed her bones and severed much of her hand. I pushed the paddle between the two discs to free her arm, her blood spraying across our faces. I pulled off my headscarf and wrapped it tightly around her lower arm, trying to slow the bleeding and screaming for help. No one came.

"Oh dear," Abigail said, brusquely, as if trying to deny the scene before her. "Take her to her family. They can help her. There is nothing to be done here."

I looked at her in disbelief. She cared nothing for the welfare of the girl. Abigail just wanted to be free of the gruesome sight.

"Hurry, you wretched child. Take her home and then come back to clean up this mess," she sputtered. "This oil is ruined, tainted with your blood. The whole thing is a waste."

Abigail left, coward that she was, hoping to extricate herself from the reality of what had just happened.

I grabbed anything I thought might bring comfort to Hana. If I had slowed the bloodletting, I knew it was not by much. I tied her onto my donkey with a shawl and loaded my stolen goods behind her. She was faint and struggled to remain upright. She was almost unconscious by the time I reached her family.

Her mother screamed at the sight of her daughter. Her cry sprang from the same bottomless well of anguish I fell into when I saw the stones crush my mother's skull. It binds its victims, this endless dark chasm from which there is no escape. We were now compatriot souls who would never again walk the earth free of sorrow. We recognize each other when we lock eyes, but we do not speak of it, nor do we acknowledge it. But we know.

She and I and her son carried Hana from the donkey to a straw bed in the hut's corner. They rushed about, muttering in despair and fear. None of us understood what to do, but I felt I needed to take command and at least act as if I knew enough to help. I bandaged her arm as Mother taught me when a lamb caught its leg between stones and tore it. It never turned out well for the lamb, and I had little hope Hana would fare any better. I was false in my words, lies spilling from my tongue as I told her mother I was stopping the bleeding and that it would lessen her pain. I worked to wipe the gushing blood away, but it kept coming, mixing with mine until I could no longer recognize its source. Changing the bandages as they became saturated, I continued to wash her, but it was futile.

I had medicinal oil with me and a crock of wine. I poured the oil onto the bandage, believing it could help the wound. At a loss, I tried to copy my mother's air of calm and confidence. Giving the rest of the oil to Hana's mother, I told her it would prevent infection when the bleeding stopped. If ever it could stop, I thought to myself in horror. I brought the drink to Hana's mouth, hoping for any relief she might find. She swallowed it in large gulps. I also had a small flask of valerian root oil I hoped might help ease the blinding pain, and I mixed it with the wine. If lucky, she might lose consciousness. I told her mother to let her have as much as she could tolerate.

As I worked on Hana with her mother, one of Abigail's bond-women arrived with an offering for the family. She sent a basket with a small bottle of our lowest grade lamp oil and one of the used robes she had outgrown. This useless present was her compensation, a worn robe many sizes too large for any member of Hana's undernourished household. The girl's mother stared at me in disbelief. Was this the price for her daughter? I could only shake my head in understanding, but there was nothing I could say. Besides the tragedy of losing her beloved daughter, Hana was the only child old enough to bring bread to the table. This woman's husband was dead, and her only son had barely seen his seventh year. This accident brought ruin to the family I could only try to understand.

I tended to Hana as best I could, but soon sensed my presence was both futile and irritating to her mother. She realized everything I was doing was a lie. I was unsettled and on the verge of tears. As I took my leave, Hana looked at me with vacuous eyes, not a glimmer of light left in them. She and I both knew that no better outcome lay ahead.

Her pain was intolerable. She hoped only for the end of suffering, as did I for her. She died of blood loss that night.

Hana's eyes haunted me for days, as did my elevated disgust for Abigail. Was it possible she cared so little for others? Was her need for power and wealth so strong that it blinded her to the feelings of anyone who did not serve her purpose? How was this conceivable in a human heart? How could she entirely ignore the consequences of her actions and be so uncaring? And yet, was I not also without compassion, but differently? Did I not hold enmity toward Abigail from the first moment I met her? My rancor only intensified with this incident. I saw only Hana's side and condemned Abigail, never questioning whether I was fair in my absolute judgement. Loathing her with increased fervor, I blamed her for Hana's death, and she knew it. If she held any guilt, it transformed into an increased hatred and resentment of me.

Abigail decided I should take Hana's place at the press the following day, most likely hoping the same fate would befall me. Her ignorance and inability to see or know me increased my disdain for her. I had a lifetime of experience, as young as I was. I understood the care of olives and how to produce the highest yield with the best quality. My oil quickly rose to Mother's quality. I brought her pride and artistry to my work to honor her and her memory. And my devious heart wanted nothing more than to cause Abigail to look incompetent in comparison. It was the only way I could go on.

When Father inspected the oil, he sighed with relief. He recognized the quality had gone down since Mother's death, but he could not admit it and would not dare confront Abigail. He now saw things in a clearer light. Perhaps he could regain his reputation with me at the press. Despite Tobias' backing, people preferred oil from other growers who produced superior products. Father's profits were dwindling, as everyone understood Mother was the excellence behind most of what came from Father's land. Word spread that things were different under Abigail, that perhaps Father had let greed and wealth go to his head. Rumors circulated that his best days were behind him. On seeing the quality advance to the level it had been with Mother at the press, Father's sales rose again. He seemed pleased with me for the first time in my life, finally recognizing Mother in me. But Abigail saw only rage and jealousy. And her profits would dwindle with me weaving less cloth, so she ordered me back to the loom despite Father's whimpering protests.

I was still worth more alive than dead.

But Abigail was a clever and greedy woman and knew she could not allow the quality to revert to what it had been without me. She had Mother's old loom brought to the olive press, so I could oversee and train the next girl hired to run it. This dual-task divided my concentration and was distracting at best, but I was back in a better light. My eyes felt less strained, and the headache that seemed my constant companion finally abated. I had the young woman to keep me company, and we were friendly, although she knew what had happened to Hana, and I felt that distance between us.

I slipped bread and oil and even some lamb to Hana's family through the new girl. The more successful I was at this, the bolder I became, and she told me the mother was grateful I understood the hardships they faced. I sent cloth and minor items of clothing as often as I could. Helping her family assuaged some guilt and anguish I felt over Hana.

I became too bold in my exploits, however, for soon Abigail discovered what I was doing. She stormed up to the olive press one afternoon after the new helper had gone home.

"I know you have taken a shoulder of lamb from the shed. Bread is also missing. I had that girl followed and found she was delivering our property to that other girl's family. She admitted you had given them to her and told her to do so. Cloth and robes have been missing as well. What right have you to give my goods away?" she shouted.

I looked at her with contempt, but held my tongue. My silence enraged her further.

"I ask you what right have you?" and she slapped me hard across the face. I became so angry, I almost struck her back, but I refused to react.

"You have no right to give our goods away!" she screamed, incensed by my steady nerve.

"You had no right to cause Hana's death," I answered, with as much control as I could manage. "Do you even know her name?"

"Who do you think you are, you wicked thing? It is not my fault that the girl was stupid," Abigail screeched.

"I am my father's only child. The one given him by his rightful wife." I spoke louder but kept a flat tone.

"You steal from me and my husband," she cried, with a loud emphasis on the word "my." Abigails' face was as red as a setting sun but with none of its beauty. It was ugly and contorted with hate.

"I am the one who bakes the bread and weaves the cloth. This is my rightful home. I have every right to help the family you robbed of a child," I shouted.

This worked Abigail into an unreasoned rage, no doubt fueled by the guilt she felt about Hana. But she could not own that truth, and had to direct her anger at me. She seized a large wooden paddle and came after me with such ferocity I was almost amused. She thrust it against me several times with all her strength, hitting my arms and hands, and then my legs and chest. I stood my ground despite the pain, making her angrier still. She swung the flattened blade with all her might, aiming it directly at my head. I laughed in her face and grabbed the stirring stick from her.

"Do you think you can beat me?" I laughed, too hysterically.

"You evil child, you are possessed," she screamed, and stepped back in fear. "Tobias has been right about you all along."

"You and Tobias are a match, that is certain. It is him you should have married. If he would have an old ox such as you," I said, and I lifted the heavy paddle over my head as if to strike her down. I delighted in watching her cower. It made me giddy to see her afraid. I laughed again, an evil laugh, and threw the paddle down. "You both use people and care nothing about destroying them, good as they are. May God strike you both." And I left.

I ran to the stream and spent the night there, alone and cold. I was afraid, but I could not bear to be in the same house as Father and Abigail. They were relieved I did not come home and probably did not care whether I was safe or not, alive or dead. I was becoming too great a problem.

I was being held hostage in a life I detested, hiding in my thoughts and fantasies when I wove or escaped to the stream. When our donkey died that winter, I was inconsolable. He had been the last link to my old life. How could I live without my trusted friend, the only creature who ever helped ease my burden? I dug his grave myself, for no one else would. They would have dragged his body in the dirt, heaved him over the cliff, and been done with him after he spent his life serving us. Each day was the darkest day of winter in my soul.

* * *

At last, Abigail became pregnant, and my father grew joyous at the hope of having a son, maybe many. I was an asset only in the goods I produced. I was a liability in too many ways.

As the seasons passed and Abigail's stomach grew, she began preparing for the upcoming birth of her baby. I returned from the stream late one afternoon to find a cradle where my straw bed once was. The thick tapestry had been removed and placed on the stone floor for warmth. My bed lay in ruins outside.

"You can make a place in the sheep's birthing shed," Abigail said, without a look in my direction.

"Fine," I said, without betraying emotion. I left and picked up my meager belongings and moved them into the small stone shelter. It was fine with me, though the wind blew through the cracks and rain and sand leaked through the roof. I was happy to be out of that house that had changed in so many ways and yet was so eerily the same. I never spent another night in that house.

My workload increased as Abigail sat about and gloated over her upcoming delivery. She demanded that I rub my perfumed oils on her belly and her thick, swollen legs. I washed her hair and smoothed the tangles with the comb my father had once made for my mother. I distilled more plants and rubbed my finest oils into her hair and scalp. Father seemed pleased with the prospect of having an heir. I knew he could not possibly love Abigail, but he benefited from her aggressive manner in business and her relentless pursuit of a new position in life. And he needed desperately to forget Mother. He believed a son would bring him higher standing and more respect with those he courted, and hopefully fill the hole left in his heart.

I was suspicious when Abigail hired a woman to help with my work. It was inconceivable she would care to make my life any easier. I told myself she must want to have someone around who knew about birth and babies, but a nagging doubt stayed with me. There was an air about Abigail that suggested something more devious was afoot. I did allow that my unfailing distaste for her had poisoned my mind, and perhaps I was wrong in my thoughts. Impending motherhood may have softened her, at least for a short time. I tried to convince myself, but a part of me knew something was not right.

The night before Abigail was to leave for the birthing shelter, I finished serving the two of them and broke off a small piece of bread to take to the shed for my supper.

"Magdalena," Abigail said, coolly. "Your father has some matter to discuss with you." Father looked uncomfortable as I looked him directly in the eye, something I rarely did. "Go on, dear," she pushed.

Your mother and I have decided it is time for you to wed and leave this house. There is no room for you here with the new child coming."

"Wed?" I shouted incredulously, "I am not yet eleven years. How can I wed? I have not yet become a woman."

"You are certainly old enough to be a wife," Abigail protested, angrily. "Many are married off younger than you."

"You did not wed until much after your twentieth year, almost thirty," I shouted, with more than a hint of sarcasm. "I am not ready to marry anyone." Marriage would be the nightmare following a bad dream. It meant a life of servitude and the loss of all freedom. Being married was the last thing I wanted, being even worse than the life I was living. It would be the end of any hope that a better day might come.

Father flushed, and I imagine he thought of Mother, but he was easily overpowered by Abigail. Her mind was made up. "Your mother..."

"She is NOT my mother," I shouted, and stared daggers at Abigail.

"Do you see how she looks at me, Gal? She has no respect. She has evil in her, like her mother. Destined for the same end, I am certain. She will bring nothing but shame on us and your new son."

Even Father flinched at her words, but I became enraged. I was so close to striking her that I could already feel it on my fingers.

"You will NOT speak of my mother like that and get away with it," I shouted, and my ferocity frightened even Father. If he felt any guilt, fear of what I might do overrode it. The only thing that kept me from sticking the table knife into Abigail's back was the greater fear that Father would then sell me to someone so detestable, it would be her final act of revenge against me.

"She will poison our new son," Abigail added, to strengthen Father's resolve.

"It has been decided, Magdalena. Abigail is right." He spoke with a broken voice. "I will seek a suitable husband for you quickly. It is time. Your mother and I have said our piece.

"She is not my mother. And on the day you allowed the murder of my real mother, your wife, you ceased to be my father," I screamed, and I ran outside to my shed. I threw myself on the straw and wept through the night. My life, difficult as it was to believe, was getting worse.

Three days later, Father arrived in the late afternoon after a day's trade in the city. Abigail was with the women waiting for the birth of her promised son. I was sweeping the stone floor and boiling bones for broth when he came in, looking triumphant.

"I have made a promise for your marriage, Magdalena. Things will be easier for you now, for you will be a woman of substance. It has cost me greatly. Your dowry was high due to the stain on you from your mother's disgrace. I had to make a promise of future trade as well. It was not an easy bargain to make, but he has agreed, graciously, out of respect for Abigail and me. This marriage will redeem your good name and mine. You should be pleased." He seemed proud of himself.

"You will marry Tobias."

✴ EIGHT ✴

ONCE I HEARD Father say the name Tobias, I knew any hope or dream of a better life was dead. I needed to be as well. I desperately wished I had thrown myself over Mother's body to catch the flying stone an instant sooner, and perished with her. I would be buried with her in the same unmarked grave for all time, and I would be happier by untold measure. Now I had to kill myself to escape a fate worse than any death. My grandmother's cliff was the first thing that came to mind. Throwing myself over its edge would be risky, but it worked well enough for her. But what if I did not die and became crippled and unable to use my body? It would be unbearable and would save me from nothing. Dancing was the only joy I had ever known in my life. To survive and never be able to move again might be more horrible than even Tobias. And that act would be the ultimate betrayal of my mother.

What if I became food for wild beasts, and they tore me apart while I was still alive? What level of horror would that be? It was a terror I could not face. I then remembered the poisonous plants Mother had so carefully warned me to avoid, and thought I could make a potion of them and drink it. I was not confident how to do this, for Mother shunned these plants with heated warning and would not even discuss the subject except to forbid me from going anywhere near them. Still, I knew which they were, and I would have to trust them to the deed. I had no idea what kind of death it would be, how it would feel, or how quickly it would come. Nor did I know how to dose it properly. Still, it would not be as wretched as being wed to Tobias, and it seemed infinitely better than the cliff.

I gathered and carefully purified the plants while Abigail was off with the women waiting for her exalted son to be born. Wanting to assure its efficacy, I took special care in preparing the distillate, condensing it into a thick, potent liquid. I fought the temptation to put some of the brew into Father's stew. I would leave him dead and render Abigail a widow with a fatherless child. That thought pleased me in so many ways I should have felt great shame, but I did not. Still, I could not hate him with sufficient force to go through with it. It must have been Mother who guided my heart, for I know I was capable of much evil on that night.

It was a wicked evening in every way. I fed Father without a word, and then poured my thick brew into a cup and carried it into the storm. The wind howled ferociously, throwing limbs against my legs and whipping dirt and sand in my face as I stumbled forward in the dark. I clung tightly to the cup as I made my way, sheltering it in my cloak, for the force of the wind made it difficult to move. My hair slapped my face so hard it stung my skin and eyes. I struggled to close the heavy door once I pushed through it. I felt exhausted in every conceivable way.

It was a perfect night to die.

I put on one of Mother's robes, one I had hidden after her death. I wanted Father to see his dead child in his murdered wife's clothing. He needed to know he drove me to this, that it was his doing. I wanted to haunt every remaining moment of his life, so he would never again rest without a thought of Mother and me. I wanted him burdened forever with guilt. And I wanted him to believe that wherever she was, she knew what he had done. He sold her beloved daughter to the very man who destroyed her. I never imagined so much cruelty existed in my father's heart. Was it possible he believed this was for my good, or was he so obsessed with his desires that he never considered mine? I could not imagine he understood, in any way, what this marriage would do to me. I hated him at that moment. My heart brimmed with it for both Father and Abigail. It was more potent than the poison I was about to set to my lips. Was it wrong to go to eternity with such loathing in my soul? I did not know, but I gave myself to it fully.

I cried to Mother and begged for her forgiveness and guidance, wondering if what I was doing was wrong. Would it separate me from her for eternity? Was there any place in the afterlife for one who ends one's own life? I regretted that, like my grandmother, I was giving in to despair, the very thing my mother fought so hard to prevent. I was denying everything she taught me, rejecting every gift of spirit she created so I could survive. I was, in essence, making a lie of her life. No, I thought, she would do the same in my place. What stood before me was no life worth living.

The thoughts, the fear, and the disgust filling me were too great to absorb, so I became numb. I felt foreign in my body, as if already separating from it, as if the poison were already running in my blood. My hand shook as I held the cup. I trembled from the cold of the shed, the cruelty of the night, and the barrenness of my soul. I brought the cup to my lips, and as I did, the wind pushed suddenly and violently against the shed door, throwing it open. The clay cup fell from my hand and shattered on the ground. Frightened, I screamed into the void, into the space where no one cared. But then I sensed it was Mother who took the cup from my hand. I had prayed to her for guidance or at least forgiveness. If not her, who or what would want me to live? What reason was there for me to face the horror of my impending future? Was this marriage my punishment for all the hatred I held in my heart these past two years?

Where the cup spilled, the straw withered and melted into a thick, dark sludge, and it burned a hole straight through the cloth of Mother's robe. How painful would this have been having ingested it? I realized Mother did not want me to die in this way. But did she want me to live? Was I meant to marry the detestable Tobias?

"Please, Mother and God," I prayed, "if you exist, take this from me. Show me how I can end my life if you have it in your power."

At the very least, I had to turn my heart to stone and free myself of any hope. A hope that would be killed day after day and make it all the more unbearable. I had to shut my feelings down and pray my end would come quickly. Was it my destiny to relive my grandmother's fate? Oh, Mother, you tried so hard to save me. Never again would we have a song, never again a dance of joy. I would not live but merely exist, with as little feeling as possible, until I could escape this life. I prayed for it to come, sooner rather than later.

In a rushed ceremony in the outer chamber of the temple the following day, I was handed over to Tobias by Father.

"I wish you great happiness in your new life," Father said, as if he meant it. Had he any genuine knowledge of me, or of Mother for that matter, he would have seen this was impossible. But he only saw things from his perspective; he never once thought of mine. He felt the union would benefit his trade with Tobias, and I was, after all, but an asset to use to his advantage.

"If not for my mother, I would curse you through all time," I said, and looked at him with the full coldness of my heart. "I would rather you kill me than send me to this fate."

Tobias, now my husband, pulled me roughly by the arm and pushed me out of the temple to wait for him. He was angry at my insult, but my misery at the situation satisfied him on another, more sordid and satisfying level. Tobias now owned me.

"I expect the rest of your payment soon for taking that unruly girl off your hands," he said, pausing to lick his lips salaciously. "But I will be paid in other ways tonight."

Father suddenly realized what he had done in executing Abigail's grand plan. He had a glimpse of what would become of the child he and Mother created together. I think he truly regretted his actions, for he seemed smaller and weaker when he came out of the temple with Tobias. Determined not to cry, I looked away and did not take his leave. Tobias then dragged me to my new home.

I am sure anyone else would have described his house as grand. To me, a prison holds no beauty. Rich tapestries hung on the walls, layers of thick carpets covered the stone floors, and an entire area for the preparation and storage of food opened to the large hearth. There were silver pots, gold utensils, and painted plates and cloths everywhere I looked. It smelled stale and rancid, like Tobias himself. There was no hint of love or harmony within those cold walls, only expressions of avarice, vanity, and greed.

Tobias pushed me into a separate room, one holding a large, carved bed. No small bed would hold his weight. Covering the bed was one of Mother's loveliest weavings. I could not help but think that he hoped to own a part of her through this acquisition. And then I thought of the beauty she wove into it from the grace of her soul, and this made me want to cry. On top of her exquisite art was a showy array of gaudy fabrics tossed over it in a pretentious show of wealth. The floor was a hard white stone so highly polished I could almost see my reflection in it. Tobias loomed over me, and with one look at his face, I knew I was in trouble.

I hate to tell what happened that night. It was too wretched to relate in full and with honest emotion, but I will give an understanding of the torture I endured. Tobias threw me immediately onto his bed, scratching at my thighs as he ripped at my robes. He pushed his heavy body on top of mine and began to pull the cloth from my breasts.

"What is this? You are a disgusting, undeveloped child." He sneered in disgust at seeing me without clothing.

"I am a child, you ugly fool!" I shouted back, and he quickly slapped me across the mouth, splitting my bottom lip in two with one of his opulent rings. Tobias was not only large of girth, but also tall and stocky. He could have killed me with one hard blow, but he seemed to know how to use just enough force to hurt me and still keep me alert. He wanted me aware of what he was doing. I tasted the blood in my mouth and tried to spit it at him. His mouth spread into an evil grin of satisfaction.

"Child or not, you are mine now, and I will do what I want with you," he said, as he pulled his leggings down to bare himself and then pressed hard against me. Disgusted at the sight of his mostly naked form, his rolls of hairy flesh and the small bare appendage now revealed, I pushed against him and struggled to get away, but that only excited him. I had never seen a naked man, and I felt nauseous with the disgust and fear of him touching me. He scratched long cuts across my chest as he tore my robe from my body. He then threw me onto the floor, pressing his enormous leg on my chest to pin me down as he tore off my undergarment. My head ached from hitting the stone and the blow across my face, yet I fought as hard as I could manage, flailing my arms and legs at him wildly. My fear made him grow larger. He used my undergarment to tie my hands behind my back, so I could no longer push and scratch at him, and then he roughly pulled my legs apart. He tried to enter me, but I was small, a virgin, and had not yet begun my menses, so he could not. He slapped me again, and I realized that violence escalated his desire, and he grew larger and pushed harder until I screamed.

I felt warm blood run between my legs. He pushed relentlessly into me, and his smelly sweat poured into the open wounds on my face and chest. I screamed, and it seemed to make him even more intent and aroused. He was tearing my insides with his roughness, and the pain was almost as horrible as the humiliation and hatred I felt.

"You are not beautiful like your mother and I would have preferred to do this to her, you daughter of a whore, but I will take you as often and as much as I like. You will know I own you. After all, look what I did to her."

His words enraged me. The depth of grief mixed with overpowering pain and disgust made me suddenly fearless. "You swine!" I shouted, and I spit in his face. "You can't take anything more than you already have. You can do what you want with my body, but you will never own me," I shouted, and spit again.

I knew this was a mistake before the words left my lips, but I did not care. He hit me across the face, this time with his fist, and he pushed harder and harder into me, ripping me from within, mercilessly tearing me until I knew that bearing a child was now impossible. And for this, I was glad because to carry this man's child would seem a sin to mankind. But my defiance made him even more determined to hurt me, so he threw me back onto the bed, turned me over, and pushed himself hard into my backside, pulling my hair so I felt it would tear from my scalp. He was destroying my body, and the horror of it frightened me to my core. The more I begged him to stop, the more determined he became. He beat me in every possible way. Knowing no one would come to save me, I offered my body and soul to whatever God would listen. Darkness enveloped me, my last thought a hope that death would finally claim me.

I fell into sickening darkness until the morning light came. With my first conscious thought, my plan came into being. I have no idea how it came to mind, but I clung to it immediately. With it, came a glimmer of hope and a resolve I could hang onto. I would pretend he beat me into submission. He could think I was weak and without a will of my own. I was too swollen, bloodied, and spoiled for him to have at me again, so he pulled the covering from my body as I put on my robe. He ordered me to make his morning meal naked to add to my humiliation.

I did as Mother taught me and pretended I was fully clothed. I refused to cower in his presence, and I glared at him malignantly as if he were the one with no covering. At times, I almost sneered at the thought of his grotesque body. Still, I cooked an impressive meal and began to clean the house as it had great need. I could tell he was not only impressed, but also confused and suspicious of my sudden surrender. He ate everything I prepared without a thought of leaving a morsel for me. Not that I could have eaten, for I was too sick of body and soul, but I would not show it.

I summoned strength from where I did not know, but I would not let him win. I would be acquiescent and mysterious, and keep him guessing. It would seem satisfying to have a servant and object of sexual pleasure wrapped up in one person, but he found it confusing to trust that the recalcitrant girl he had beaten the night before could have such a sudden change of disposition. But I looked like the woman he had always desired, and Tobias was always stronger in lust than wisdom.

He ordered me to get ready and go with him to his tent. He wanted me under his watch, weaving at my loom, with no opportunity to run. I washed cautiously, for thick blood caked on my thighs, mouth, and chest, and it hurt to put water to the open wounds. I put on my lightest clothing as gently as I could. Everything that touched my body caused great pain. Every movement brought waves of nausea and humiliation with it. I had carried Mother's oils with me to have something of her close by, and I tenderly dabbed some on my wounds. What would she do if she knew this was their use? I suspect that even she, as good a woman as she was, would thrust a knife into the man's heart.

At midday, Tobias ordered me to the house to prepare a meal. He could see how difficult it was for me to walk after what he had done to me, so he let me go unattended. I would not get far if I tried. Tobias' men smirked, and Tobias gloated that they thought he had such sexual power. No matter that I was a mere child. How did they justify the bruises and cuts on my face, the split lower lip that showed despite the cloth he forced me to wear over my head? But of course, the beating of a wife was of no concern to them.

I passed Father on the way. I was surprised to see him and wondered if he had business in town or needed to see how I fared through the night. One look at me told the sordid tale. I was beaten and ravaged, and he knew it. I could barely walk, and as a man, he knew what that meant. As he looked into my vacant eyes and across the massive cuts and bruises on my face, he saw he now had two sins against the only woman he ever loved.

"Magdalena, you have a brother. I have a son," he said, with the last real pride left to him.

"I have no one," I answered, and I turned to walk away. Father looked concerned and put his hand on my shoulder to stop me. I flinched at the mere touch on my battered body.

"Magdalena, I fear for you with this mouth of yours," he whispered. "You are too bold and lack respect. You are on danger-ous ground."

"I am on the ground you put me. I curse this life you have forced on me," I answered, and then I walked away with what little grace remained in my body.

The days passed, and I worked diligently and without complaint. My docility surprised Tobias, for he expected a fight. Only his vanity allowed him to believe he could conquer me in one night. He let go of the women he had used to do his cooking and cleaning because he now owned a servant of his own. I looked like the model wife to the patrons while enduring the horrors of the night in quiet submission. My lack of reaction made me much less appealing to Tobias. He would beat me to excite himself, and I infuriated him when I would not react. Seeing this made me even bolder in my plan. He became more violent, trying to incite my hatred and fire. I remained still and compliant, despite the pain, gaining an inner resolve and power that surprised even me. My acquiescence deflated his excitement, and he frequently lost interest in the fight. It was not worth his effort on many nights, and I could begin to breathe. But I no longer cared. If his blows ended my life, I would be the better for it.

When he thought he had rendered me completely submissive, he lost interest in me except to relieve his need. He enjoyed thinking he owned me, that he was my master and overlord. Lying with me became merely a way to keep me in his control and to satisfy his desire as it came. Sex became routine and fast and, for me, easier to endure. And I say "endure" most generously. Each encounter ravaged my spirit and damaged my psyche in ways I dared not fully recognize. The beatings were less satisfying for him and not worth the effort if I would not wither under his strength, so they became less frequent.

I think it unsettled him that I could withstand his blows without a whimper. He was a brute who understood power and submission, not the kind of control I displayed. My restraint, I suspect, caused him to wonder if I might truly be possessed, as he had always claimed. There had to be some unseen power that helped me withstand his torture. I hoped and believed there were times when Tobias began to fear me.

In many ways, Tobias was pleased with his bargain despite my lack of sexual appeal. I was a good cook, a prolific weaver and a good worker. I was attractive, when not swollen and bruised, so he beat me less. It was good for his image to have a beautiful wife on display. Mother's stoning seemed forgotten, or at least never mentioned. I inherited her unusual looks, so I seemed a prize. I kept my head down, stayed quiet, and kept hope with my plan.

I must confess, there were times when I thought of slitting the man's throat in the middle of the night. I could not imagine it was wrong after what he did to me. What kept me from doing so, I am not certain. Perhaps it was the plain and justified fear he could stop me before I completed the deed, if I dared to go through with it. His retaliation would be unimaginable. It would also mean the end of any plan of escape. Perhaps it was Mother who stopped me. Maybe I still had some belief in a God. But right and wrong made no sense to me at that time. Was it honorable to torture women and own them? Was it wrong for that woman to fight for her life? I had my plan, and that is what kept us both alive.

When Tobias went out to Father's land to oversee his sheep and discuss business, I was left in the tent to sell to the women of our town. Most of them preferred doing business with me instead of my overbearing and greedy husband, so they waited until he was gone before they came to shop. It was clear that they also detested the cheating and calculating Tobias. As soon as word circulated that I was selling the goods, more and more women came to the tent. Sales were best when I was alone, so Tobias left more often. He probably felt I had settled into what he considered my privileged life. It also left him free to go about the city and make his presence known. He soon felt he was too important to sit in a trader's tent. He was the one to make the deals and collect the coin at day's end. By owning me, he had a capable wife, a claim to my weavings, and a woman to do the selling. He drank wine with the other merchants while their wives also toiled away. They told stories of their trips to foreign lands and bragged about the profits they made. I imagined each tale grew in scale and import with each telling and each cup of wine.

Tobias frequently spent his afternoons with prostitutes, and then stopped by the temple to give coins to the priests, so they would praise him as a pious man. I heard these stories when the ladies came and repeated the tales their husbands told. Once Abigail came into my life, I lost all access to the women at the well. With Tobias forbidding me to go anywhere alone, I was still kept apart from gossip and news. Once he trusted me to make the sales, I could finally interact with the other wives, and it lessened my loneliness and pain. I felt less isolated. Of course, his men were around to watch over me, but they paid no attention when the women came in. We shared tea in the tent to make the days more tolerable when the men were drunk and useless. The other wives knew I had no good feelings for Tobias and never held their words against them. At last, I felt a part of the women's community.

* * *

On nights when Tobias stayed out late, I could breathe more naturally. My fierce state of anxiety would abate long enough for me to realize how afraid I was most of the time. I could feed him, and he would quickly fall asleep, and I felt temporarily safe. He had undoubtedly spent his desire on women paid to satisfy him in ways I did not. But there were times when he came back belligerent and violent, and on those nights, it took all my will to keep from using a knife against him. If I had not had my plan, I would have eventually succumbed to his murder. Such was the state of my mind and the poverty of my soul at the time.

My plan was simple. I had the one gold coin from Mother and I managed to keep it hidden in the threads I used for my weavings. Eventually, I sewed it into my outer robe, where I knew Tobias would never find it. But this was not enough to keep me alive for very long. So, with every sale I made, I kept a bit for myself. It was not enough to be mentioned or noticed, but I kept the coins in a hidden pouch. As the amount grew, I traded those of lesser value for gold so they would take less room to store. I thus began to amass a tidy sum.

As Tobias trusted I had resigned myself to being a good wife, and he saw how capable I was, he did not question me. He recognized my intelligence and that, like my mother, I was good with numbers and counting. Tobias also believed my position as his wife was an honor any woman would be happy to hold. How ignorant and filled with himself he was, but I used it to my advantage. Soon, I was left to all the selling, so Tobias had even less to do. He did not suspect I was clever enough to have a plan. His profits were higher than they had ever been.

Sometimes I wove small children's clothing without his knowing, and I kept those profits entirely for myself while giving the women with little wealth a good bargain. I often sent cloth and weavings to Hana's family. Sometimes I sent money to them as well. Tobias never suspected. I knew I was taking my life in my hands if he ever found out, and only rarely did I even care. I would die at his hand, as long as it was quick and efficient, or I would carry out my plan. Which end no longer mattered to me as I held no love for life. I also knew charity and kindness were not words my husband knew, so he would hardly suspect I had such thoughts.

My scheme was working as planned but for one thing. In the two years of my marriage, I had developed more fully into a woman. My breasts had grown, and I was taller and more voluptuous. I no longer had a body that could bear children, but I knew this was a good thing under my circumstances. I could have mourned the child I would never have but for the conviction that I would not condemn my own to such a fate as I was living. My relationship with my mother was the only good thing in my life, and it did not last. I was robbed of that precious bond, and look what fate met the child she so loved. I could not bear to witness the same outcome for my own.

Tobias threatened to trade me for a woman who could give him heirs. He would have had the law on his side, even though it was his own doing, but his profits would have suffered and he was in no hurry. I was not yet fourteen, and Tobias could take his time before it became an issue among the other men. He must have known somewhere in his vacant heart that it would bring me great relief if he cast me aside, and that made him less inclined as well. My blossoming body, however, heightened his desire for me, and I suffered again, frequently, under his detestable body. I cannot put into words the tortured hell each of those moments brought me, the screams I held down, the vomit I held in my throat, my fevered desire to murder him with each violation of my body. He often forced me to stay naked, both to humiliate me and to satisfy his lust. If I refused, I was given a fist across my face, and he tore the clothes from me anyway. I knew I would have to make my move and soon.

*   *   *

The season passed slowly, each day seeming to be an endless lifetime of misery. Each day I wondered how I would make it to its end, and I feared the night even more for what it would bring. Finally, it was time for Tobias to plan his trade expedition. I could not wait for him to leave. He was excited to pack the bulk of my weavings for the voyage, for I had done work worthy of Mother's best. He seemed to believe I was interested in his business, and he felt secure enough to leave me under his men's watch. I tried to do my best, not just because it was a part of my plan, but because when I wove, it was the only time I returned to memories of my childhood. My weaving was my meditation, my way out of a world I despised. I wove constantly, and Tobias was almost kind to me when he saw the results of my labor. These weavings would make him renowned and sought after on the trade routes and richer still. My value as a wife had risen.

At last, he left, and I enjoyed the many weeks without him. I went to the well, for there was no one to stop me. His men were ordered to stay alert to my actions, but what harm was there in going to the well as all their wives did? They followed me the first few times as ordered, but satisfied that I was gathering water, doing the washing, and gossiping with the other women, they relaxed their watch and drank the afternoons away.

The women were kind and took me into their confidence, aware of the hardships I endured despite Tobias' wealth. They saw the evidence of his beatings. Not one of them would have traded their place for mine. Not just because he was wretched and cruel, but because they understood the piercing pain of being abused by the very man who murdered my mother. They seemed to know and hear everything that happened in and around the city, so I caught up on all the news I missed in the tent. Few of them, if any, held regard for Abigail. They resented her superior air and her disdain for women of lesser positions. She demanded higher prices for her oil, although hers were no match for Mother's. I wondered what Father thought. His reputation for quality oil had gone down since Mother's death and his selling me to Tobias. He no longer had income from my weavings, as they and I now belonged to Tobias in full. Their little son ran Abigail around as if he were a prince, and Abigail seemed old before her time. The boy would be nothing but trouble, the women said. She had not produced another heir in the two years since, and many thought she would not. Perhaps, they said, my father found the life he deserved. I was surprised by the sadness this caused me. I knew the women remained loyal to Mother in their hearts, but this brought only unsatisfactory relief.

Finally, after waiting as patiently as I could, I heard the news of Lucius' whereabouts. I had been afraid to ask, afraid it would conjure memories of Mother's stoning and supposed adultery. I never stopped hoping for his return, but after these long two years, I had little trust I would find him. He was injured, quite seriously, and sent home to Rome to recover. A new captain, one of little grandeur or good humor, had taken his place. There was concern over the actions of this new Roman, although I had not yet seen him, for I was rarely allowed out of Tobias' tent. Now that Lucius was gone and another was in his place, everyone realized what a good and fair man Lucius had been, a rare thing for the occupiers of our cities. Things had gotten worse without him. No one knew if he would ever return, and I understood, with profound sadness, that he was gone from my life.

This loss would have been paralyzing but for the fact that my days were so much happier without Tobias in them. I felt some semblance of belonging to the city again, some remembrance of my life with Mother. I liked the other women, and to my great surprise, I even smiled a few times at the clever things they said. The burden of Tobias' domination was made ever more evident by how much better life was without him. But just as I felt the heavy layers of tension leaving my ravaged body, word came that Tobias was on the last leg of his trade journey. I was to prepare for his homecoming.

And this I did. I had been saving large bones from discarded carcasses, and I wrapped them in my cloak after soaking it in blood. Most of these I stole from behind the temple; sacrificial waste too holy to be handled by a woman, and no doubt, one more sin ensuring my eternal damnation. I laughed as I soaked the robe in sacrificial blood. What could be more damning than the life I had been living?

I gathered food, a bladder filled with water and my coins. I placed them in a small woven bag next to an old cloth that held the bones and soiled robe. All of this I tied inside my thickest blanket. I put on several layers of clothing, wearing only my best robes, hoping to present a noble face to whatever future might be before me. I waited until Tobias' men were sleepy with their mid-day wine and then headed out inconspicuously as if carrying wash to the well. I walked quickly for several hours past Father's land, past my old stream, and toward my grandmother's fateful cliff.

I tried not to think of the past as I crossed the land, but my mind was weak against the old memories. I had not been near our stream for the two years of my godforsaken marriage. Images of my past flooded my mind; my beautiful mother and her songs, my dances that made them visible, transcendent visions, and my beloved donkey. My body shook with uncompromising grief. I fell to the ground, sobbing and clutching the earth that had once held my mother. I gripped the tears-soaked dirt and watched it slip through my fingers; nothing to hold onto, not now, perhaps never. I remembered Lucius and his eyes as he looked at Mother, my magnificent Zeus, with his deep, radiant color and high spirit. Haunted by the memories and impact of two years of torture, I felt more alone than I could have imagined possible.

How many lifetimes had I already lived and failed? Who was I now, and who was I then? I wanted to give up, give up everything, and disappear. Perhaps I should just jump over the cliff, join my grandmother, and be done with it. And then I heard my mother admonishing me, telling me to get up, to keep going, and to find a destiny that would honor us both. I must not allow grief to stop me. I had to force these memories from my mind and concentrate only on what was before me.

I had to accept that I would never see our stream again. Everything of my past was dead to me, and I needed to be as well, at least in the eyes of all who knew me. I forced myself to concentrate on the task ahead, fight the bitter tears that stung my cheeks, and refuse to think of what had once been.

Approaching the cliff, I recognized how easy it would be to fall over the edge. One careless overstep and any animal could easily slip on the loose rocks and meet its end.

I threw the bones wrapped in my bloodied robe over the cliff, and they fell directly onto a pile of bones that had been there for years. And beneath them, I realized, from a generation before, lay the unclaimed bones of my grandmother. I tried not to hold that thought, it could be too crippling, and instead, I said a prayer to her and asked her to guide me out of the despair she could not escape. I then scattered rocks to look as if they shook loose when I approached the edge. I tossed a few of my lesser coins about to look like they spilled as I fell. It would seem

I had run away but met my deserved death below. I would be considered a thief and sinful woman, but I would be dead, and no one would continue to look for me. I was sure the women would not blame me. Abigail would lose any profits she still made from goods I produced, and this brought a genuine smile to my face. I carried a long olive branch with me for the last part of my climb and used it to sweep over my footsteps as I walked away from this land that had cursed me two times over. I was free at long last. Freedom was all I ever wanted. Now that it was finally before me, I understood, viscerally, that freedom was a foreign and dangerous reality for a woman.

⋆ NINE ⋆

I T WAS SUNSET when I crossed the last of Father's land. I had no idea where I would go or what I would do once I got there, yet I felt an odd sense of euphoria. Being off Father's property and away from Tobias, I felt a weight lifting from what remained of my crushed spirit. I was finally free of that life and all of its misery. All I had ever wanted was to own my own life. But what choices were before me? What would the world allow for a single girl on her own?

Had Mother been free to choose, she would be alive and living happily with the man she loved, the man we both loved. I would be riding Zeus, or maybe even a horse of my own. I reveled in these fantasies while I walked. But as my legs grew tired and the dark began to envelop me, reality seeped into my thoughts. What dangers were ahead? How would I protect myself? If wild beasts tore me apart, I consoled myself, it would still be better than another night under the weight of Tobias. I felt this with all my heart.

I walked long into the night, under the light of the moon, until my legs refused to move. As I looked down on my bloodied feet, I realized I had nothing with me to care for my wounds. My legs burned with exhaustion, and my back ached from carrying my load. And in my great weariness, I starkly faced what this grand freedom meant. Nothing if I was dead. What was I going to do? What childish plan had I concocted? And yet, the idea of never again having to see the man who tortured me and killed my mother gave me strength enough to face whatever fate might be before me.

I thought back to the night I tried to poison myself. I pleaded then to be shown a good way to die, and I was now closer to the answer. I found peace in knowing that death might finally take me, though it made no sense to have lived the past two years of torture before it came. Why such agony before the gift of death? To what end? I wrapped myself in my blanket under the shelter of a rocky ledge, and I cried myself to sleep.

That night, I dreamed of Mother, and my spirit danced through the night to her songs. Not even in my dreams had I danced since her death. Was I free to move again? Would there be some joy in these last days before I left to join her? But then, I tossed and turned, moving from freedom to fear in my dreams. I clutched the stone in my pocket, the only physical object, other than the coin from Lucius, that connected me to my mother. Hers was buried with her in that damned unmarked grave, and I had worn mine smooth with constant stroking. It was my only way of touching her.

"Mother, I will find you soon." I spoke into the desolation of the desert around me, and eventually I fell into the gift of sleep.

When I woke, it was to the image of Mother in my mind's eye, as if she were sending a message. As was true throughout my life, I had only her. God most likely wanted nothing to do with me, as I was now considered a faithless sinner who deserted my legal husband. Was there a covenant in which I had no say, and no rights? I did not know.

I was not sure I even cared. I was now a woman without a husband, family, or entry to a temple. I must be a pagan, I decided, and I had better learn to embrace it.

The next several days were increasingly difficult. I continued to walk, not knowing where I was going or even why, but I felt the need to keep moving. If I stopped, I might collapse and not get back up. My water went quickly, but I rationed the bread to make it last. I knew I would not survive long this way, hoping to find a city or caravan soon; unwilling to face the desperation and futility I felt through the nights. I missed my people, the women at the well, those who came with their children to the tent, and even the Roman soldiers. The great value of community and people never struck me before these barren nights. I had always felt separate from everyone. But being so very alone, I finally saw their great value. I finally understood the inherent need humans have to share life, to know others are around. Confused and frightened, I realized I still had time to turn around and return before Tobias landed. I might be able to save my life if he had not yet discovered my disappearance. Perhaps his men would neglect to tell him for fear of retribution, which I was sure would be harsh. I might get away with it. But the thought of him touching and ravaging me again, of ever allowing him to beat my body and take command of me, I could no longer endure. I only survived the past two years because of my plan. How would it be with no hope? No, I had to continue. My death would at least be of my own making.

On the sixth day, I came upon a small city. I had no idea where I was, but I was almost breathless with the joy of seeing people again. I needed them, though I never understood that until I was so alone. I craved to see others, to hear them speak, to know they were around. My loneliness was stark and visceral, and I ached with a fierce hunger that gnawed at both my body and my spirit.

I hid my blanket and belongings behind a large rock before entering the city center, and I found the communal well where I drank and refreshed myself. I tried to look as respectable and clean as I could in my fine robe, presenting myself as a woman supported by a man with his coin to spend. I had nothing to trade, so I had to appear above such action. I covered my head and walked into the market as if I belonged there; a woman of means out to enjoy the day.

It seemed odd being in a town I did not know. I thought back to the freedom I enjoyed with Mother on those mornings we could escape to the market, and I felt uplifted until I again witnessed the truth of humanity. Walking past homeless beggars, some blind, others bent and stooped from crippled bones, my heart ached to look at them. Why do some have so much, men like Tobias, who do nothing to help others, while many are left to die in the dirt? What justice is there in man's world? I could not walk by them without placing a few of my coins in their cups. My desperation was no match for theirs.

As I walked toward the market's center, I saw a woman slapped repeatedly by a man I assumed was her husband and then thrown onto the ground and kicked several times. I burned with rage, for her and for all the beatings I had endured. I dared not interfere and bring attention to myself, and I knew it would do no good anyway. But I wondered what she had done to deserve such brutality. Anything? Nothing? Our eyes locked, and with one look, she knew I understood. And that I, too, had endured such treatment. Nothing unusual had occurred, and nothing would change. I knew this same woman would go back to her home and give love and comfort to her children, prepare a meal for her family, and carry on as she always did. She believed this was her lot in life; this is what happened to women. I missed people through my lonely nights, but what about them did I want? The injustices of life seemed even more unbearable when separated from them and seeing them anew.

I drew suspicious stares, for no one recognized me as anyone they would know. I walked as arrogantly as I could toward the tent of the kindest looking man I could find. While he did not seem to notice me as anything but a prospective customer, his rather sharp-looking wife eyed me as if she knew all my secrets and disapproved of them all. I refused to let it shake me. I had two years of experience in a trader's tent, and I knew the actions of the wealthy who came in to intimidate with their money. It went against my temperament to act superior, but I well understood the nature of this business.

"Bread and wine," I said, with such command the woman sat back down on her cushion and seemed to shrink a bit.

Her kind husband quickly gathered a rich, hearty loaf and a goat's bladder filled with dark wine and brought it to me.

"Will this do?" I said, more than asked, and threw a coin on the tray, one worth much more than the bread and wine. The wife suddenly smiled warmly and busily scurried about should I care to purchase more.

"Perhaps you would like some sheep's cheese," she offered, now my dear and devoted servant. "And some dates." I dared not bargain like a commoner. I had to present a noble face. No one asked questions if the price was right.

"Why not?" I replied, and tossed another coin onto the tray. She wrapped my goods in a scrap of cloth. I smiled at her as if I were doing her a favor, and she grinned back at me with stained teeth.

Fine, I thought, so this is how I must play the game. I walked to the central well and smiled at the women, acting as if I were doing them all a favor. I found this worked quite well. Soon they overlooked me and gossiped openly, thinking I would have no interest in their mundane lives. But I cherished their talk. The women's gossip was music to my ears, a melody I had not heard in too long a time.

They talked of other women in the city: who had given birth, who lost a family member, and the daily happenings of life in their world. I wrapped myself in their conversations, feeling warmed and comforted by their words. When they began to speak of the Romans, my ears tuned intently to their speech. For no logical reason, I hoped they could shed some light on what had happened to Lucius. But it was not to be. It appeared their Romans were unusually unpleasant, especially the captain in charge. He punished citizens freely for the lightest offense and had an eye for women, married or not. It was rumored he pulled those he wanted off the street and into his living quarters, where he would force himself on them. These stories may have merely been salacious gossip the wives liked to tell for the sake of excitement, but it made me nervous to hear of such men. With a building panic tightening my chest, I hurried out of town.

I quietly made my way, walking as fast as my tired legs would take me. I did not need one more man to violate me. I would put as much distance as possible between myself and these Romans.

I made this food and wine last for several days even though I was so hungry I could have eaten it all without hesitation. I rationed carefully and became thinner and weaker as I went. I saved the bladder and filled it again with water when I came across a spring. It lasted through several fillings before it split and became useless.

When the heat became too oppressive, I hid beneath any protection I could find. The hot, sun-baked ground burned my worn feet, and I dressed in only my under garments to keep from overheating. I wrapped my good robes in my blanket so they might appear clean and proper when I came across people. The road was so dusty and dry, my nose often bled, and the skin of my throat became so parched I could barely swallow until I again found water. If I came across sticks or dried brush along the road, and they were rare, I saved them for a fire at night. When I found a long wooden pole dropped from a trade or soldier's cart, I was giddy with joy at such a treasure. I used it and several other sticks to prop up my blanket to make a small makeshift tent so I could rest through the hot afternoons, thus avoiding the worst heat of the day. I continued my walk through the early mornings and evenings, walking until I could no longer see the road in front of me; my belongings rolled up in my blanket and tied to the ends of the pole, carrying them across my back as I made my way nowhere.

If I found a small ledge or rock away from the main road for my night's rest, I stopped there. These were few and far between, and what hurry did I have? The road was now my life. My woven blanket was my home. The wine relaxed my aching legs and helped to quiet my mind. I saved the scraps of cloth that held the food I bought and used them as bandages for my torn feet. If the desert nights became too cold, I wrapped myself in everything I had to stop my body from shivering and my teeth from chattering. For distraction, I stared up at the stars.

"Are you protecting or cursing me now?" I asked. They did not answer, but still, they brought me comfort, helping me to feel closer to Mother. I told them my thoughts throughout the day, my feelings, hopes and fears at night. I spoke to myself constantly because I was the only one who would listen.

I had no idea where I was going, and I began not to care. I was not being beaten or raped by a man I detested. I would rather die of starvation than humiliation, so savage was my pride after all I had endured. Even though my throat was dry and cracked, my skin burnt and rough, I felt I was better off without Tobias no matter how bad the situation became. All these things I told myself to make some sense of what I was doing and to try to maintain my sanity.

I say this because there were moments in the stark isolation when I questioned whether my mind had turned. I had only my own company to keep, and I pretended to be someone I was not when I did run into people. Two years of torture can easily bend a mind. And I had no idea what was done to mine after witnessing the murder of my mother. Who was I? What would I become? Was I my past or some possible future? Did I have a truth or purpose of any kind? I wondered about all of this, but I had no answers. I had no sense of what I was doing, as I had never known anyone in my circumstance before.

I kept count of the days and nights on my fingers and toes. On what seemed like the twelfth night, I relived Mother's death in my dream and woke up to the sound of my own scream. Why, when she was such a good woman, did she suffer this fate? She followed the rules, and she was dead anyway, tragically murdered by the man who took me as payment. Why are women treated this way? God created us as well as men. When I was a child looking into the water, I saw all creatures as equal, not a truth for one gender and a different one for the other. Lucius was the only man I ever knew who had respect for women, or at least one. What allowed these injustices?

Were there other Romans who felt and acted as Lucius did? Did pagans see women and men equally and have different laws than ours? It hardly seemed so based on many of the occupiers in our area. But Lucius was a fair man. More must exist. I stayed awake, shivering and anxious, well into the early morning wondering about these things. I was free now, whatever that meant, and for however long. Under the dictates of no law, neither did I have its protection.

I cried uncontrollably for hours, confusion and despair rocking me. I was lost to everything I knew. As the sun rose above the rocks, as I sobbed with exhausted breaths, I felt a reassuring hand touch my shoulder. Startled, I turned quickly to see whose hand was on me, but no one was there. Was it my imagination, my need to think there was a force in existence that would hold me in its arms? Or was I imagining an embrace because I needed it so desperately? Was I indeed going mad?

I learned to read the road after a time. When it showed heavy use, I knew I was near a town or city, and I followed the path most travelled, able to gauge how many travelers had passed and how long since. I knew if a trader's cart had used the road or if the prints were from Roman soldiers and the wagons that carried their supplies. If a detail of soldiers had recently passed, I was as inconspicuous and quick about my business as possible. I was adept at fitting into crowds to purchase what I needed and slipping away to avoid questions or notice. After a time on the road, I was afraid my bloodied feet would give me away, for no woman of wealth and substance would have feet as worn and weary as mine. I wore the robes of a rich woman but had the feet of a peasant. I needed to wash them whenever water was available to avoid infection, but I had to be careful not to be seen doing so. I also needed to soak my hands and rinse the dust and dirt from my hair and skin. Because I understood the habits of women at the well, I went when I knew I could be alone.

I sat by the well and waited late one morning after most of the early trade had finished, covering my feet with a shawl and waiting for the moment I would have the well to myself. I kept my hair covered and tried not to betray my youth or looks. To a practiced eye, I would seem suspicious, and I knew soldiers were well-trained and vigilant. I dared not risk being taken by one of them.

I was about to dip my bloodied foot into the shallow lower pool of the well when an old, wrinkled crone suddenly appeared behind me. I gasped at her unusual appearance. Her clothes were tattered but wildly colorful. Her unkempt gray hair was loose and uncovered, and many of her teeth were missing. She eyed me with a predator's gaze.

"My dear girl, what are you running from?" she asked, with a crackling voice.

She took me by surprise, and I must have betrayed my own vulnerability for she grabbed my foot with her thin and bony hand and looked at the open sores and then at my fine woven robes.

"Oh, you have quite the story to tell," she said, sitting uncomfortably close to me.

"Do you think you know me?" I asked, as arrogantly as I could, but even to myself, I was unconvincing.

"Better than you know yourself, I suspect," she continued, sensing my unease and using it to her advantage. She then pressed her thin, knobby finger into the wound on my foot. I quickly recoiled and withdrew my leg.

"Your secrets are safe with me. I am the truth-teller in this town. I keep the secrets of everyone I read…for a price."

"What business do you have with me?" I asked, defensively. I was becoming increasingly uncomfortable because I sensed this woman did see through me, and the truth was trouble for many reasons. But something in her seemed to metamorphose as she placed her hand on my shoulder.

"Do not worry, girl. I sense you have a destiny before you. You have had a difficult time in your short years, I can tell. Let me help you."

Her words softened me, and I began to relax under her gaze. As we stared at each other, she transformed, looking suddenly younger and more beautiful. I found myself drawn to her as if she were suddenly the closest person in the world to me, this strange world in which I was sure my mind had left me. I wanted to follow her, not knowing or caring where it would lead me. I needed to feel close to someone.

"Give me a few coins and let me read your hand," she said, directly and with authority. I had two silver coins beside me I had not yet returned to my hidden pouch, and I handed them to her, suddenly mute and under her command. She took my hand in hers and turned it palm up, tracing the lines of my hand with her sharp, bony finger.

"Yes," she said, "as I suspected. Your life has not been easy. You are a good worker…oh you are most unusual. You see many things that most cannot. I see…" Her eyes brightened from whatever she was seeing, images not from her dim eyes but from a different source. "A talented woman…a dancer of great beauty and intuition, and the art of dance will bring you many gifts. You create treasures with this hand."

I was no longer afraid of her. I felt she knew me as only my mother had. I fell into the comfort of being seen for who I was.

"You have a destiny you will choose not to avoid. Most will not see the truth for ages, but you must fulfill it despite their lies. I am confused, for the timeline is beyond what I can see, and I cannot read your fate fully. I do see love in your life, yes, some love…hmm, different kinds of love." Her voice drifted off. I was baffled, for surely the only people I ever loved were Mother and Lucius, but they were both gone. I wanted to hear more. I wanted her to tell me my life could be better. I suddenly wanted to live. I wanted to be seen and free to live this destiny. "But…" she traced a short line on the side of my thumb, and her hand suddenly tightened. "You have had nightmares of whippings and beatings as a child, have you not? Glimpses of future events. You see beyond this world."

I thought back to the recurring dream that frightened me so often as a child. But I had not had that dream for years. Why would she bring it up? The nightmare of Mother's stoning had replaced it in the dark caverns of my mind. But how could she know? What did she see?

"Those dreams are a part of your destiny somehow," she continued, a worried look starting to tighten her face. She then narrowed her eyes and looked up at me with great apprehension. Her aura of beauty and comfort disappeared faster than it manifested, and she became even more ugly and shriveled than at first sight. She threw my hand down quickly and dropped the coins as if they were poison to touch. She stared at me for a moment with wild eyes.

"Too much surrounds you even beyond what I can see," she cried. She looked around apprehensively. With frantic movements and a curious snort, she wrapped herself tightly in her worn shawl and stood to leave. She made a quick, sharp turn in my direction and stared straight into my eyes one more time. "Who are you?" she asked.

"I thought you would tell me," I answered, surprisingly not shaken by her sudden turn. I smiled in a way that upset her even more. She made brusque movements with her hands, brushing the air as if trying to remove any trace of me.

"I do not know who you are, but you travel a strange path in this life, and with unusual companions," she said. "Good luck to you. You will need it." And for an old, bent woman, she almost ran from my sight.

Bewildered, I sat still and considered what had just occurred. Who or what was this woman? And should I take anything she said seriously? And yet, she seemed to intuit so much about me. Did she say these things to every woman she met with coins to spend? But she had thrown the coins down in fear. Her discomfort amused me for some odd reason. And then fear shook me as I seriously considered if any of it did happen, or was I just so weak with hunger and exhaustion that I conjured her up in my mind? I no longer knew what was real and what was not.

I wandered over the dry, dusty earth for weeks. I started to lose track of time. How long had I been separated from everything I once knew? It seemed forever. I tried to adjust my thoughts to fit my new life, as sparse and fragile as it was. At least I had lived some days making my own decisions, as limited as they were. I would wander until I ran out of money, died of hunger, or found work as a weaver, which proved incredibly difficult, for I knew no one and usually had to make my way through a city too quickly to establish any relationships with other women. I was hesitant to enter the tents of merchants, men like Tobias. What if I came across one who knew my husband? If anyone recognized me, I would be in the worst kind of trouble.

If I saw a woman handling cloth, I tried to get close enough to begin a conversation, but I found it difficult to explain who I was or how I came to be there. If her husband came near, I affected a haughty attitude and walked off as if I were too good for their wares. I could almost read the questions in the women's minds as they recognized the quality of the cloth I wore. I dressed too well to be considered one of them. How could I explain I had woven them myself, that they sold far and wide and for high profit? The truth would expose me. What would happen if anyone recognized my work from Tobias' trade? Any success I provided for another trader would only bring attention directly to me. If recognized, Tobias would come to claim me, or worse. Settling down in a small village and busying my hands and mind creatively again would surely restore my mental and physical health, but how could I relax fearing I would be found? After several clumsy attempts, I recognized the futility of this idea. I belonged to no one and needed to leave my fate to my stars. I had no other ally in this world. To keep my thoughts trained on these things would only curse my survival.

A brilliant, full moon rose, shining its light on a large overhanging ledge with soft sand beneath it. I noticed a small spring just a few steps away. It was a paradise compared to what I had endured the past nights. I had been traveling for more than two moons, and all that had any meaning anymore was food and water and a safe place to lie down at the end of the day.

It had been a relatively good day. After traveling through arid and desolate terrain for several days, I came across a fairly busy city that seemed moderately populated. After many days of staring into barren nothingness, the market felt rich and diverse, and I bought as much food and wine as I could carry, afraid I might not find another town for some time. I moved about slowly, absorbing the sounds of people talking and children playing. Longing for contact with other people, I lingered leisurely by the well and listened to the women's gossip. I meant nothing to them, but I did not care. They were alive, and I cherished their company, as shallow as it was.

Had it not been a full moon, I might have missed this rest spot completely, and for this, I felt blessed. Blessed by what, I no longer cared to know. I bent down and drank my fill and washed the dust from my face and hair. My legs felt heavy, and I could see many of the cuts on my feet were hot and bloody. If only I had Mother's oils to heal my wounds. If only I had her embrace, her kiss, her smile. I missed so many things about home and family, as estranged as my family life had felt at the time. Still, at that moment, having water was a great luxury, and I was grateful. Keeping the cuts clean would give me a chance. I rested my feet in the spring for long moments, feeling the cool water wash over them. After wrapping my feet in the scraps of cloth I saved from the markets, I drank large gulps of the wine and fell into my exhaustion.

My body was too tired to allow restful sleep. Strange dreams haunted me; images of people I recognized, but did not know, appeared and turned into frightful creatures. Scenes of whippings, beatings, and betrayal rose again from those childhood nightmares I thought were long forgotten. In that strange twilight between sleep and conscious thought, through the haze of images coming from the deep turmoil of my mind, an eerie noise aroused me. I struggled to distinguish the sound. Did I hear something real, or was it part of my confusion? I sat up with a start. What if a wild animal objected to my presence at the spring? How foolish to think no other creature would fight for its use. I grabbed my sticks, my hands shaking, and pointed them straight out in front of me, hoping to defend myself against the beast. The cry continued, and I trained my ear in its direction, listening until it was all I could hear. Was it a moan? Could it possibly be a person, another poor traveler like myself?

I pulled on my sandals and walked in the direction of the sound. Not knowing if it was human or beast, I made my voice as loud and frightening as possible. If it was not human, I needed to appear strong to discourage an attack. The moan grew louder but no more distinguishable. If this was a person, and I hoped it was, I thought he, or she, had heard me. I walked about, listening intently, trying to decipher the source.

Finally, I saw an outline in the faint light of the moon. I walked cautiously toward it, pointing my sticks, fully ready to fight if need be. A thin line of blood streaked the earth where he, or she, had been dragged. I put down my sticks and approached cautiously, wondering if the poor soul was still alive. As I got closer, I saw it was a young man, his clothes badly torn and bloody. Was he the victim of an animal attack, or was it something more sinister? The sight of him made me shudder with visceral memories of Tobias' beatings, and a strong impulse to help him came over me. I knelt close to him, placed my ear next to his chest, and listened for a sign of life.

Although badly beaten, I heard his labored breathing and knew he still had some strength. I cleared the branches and leaves covering his torn body and quickly walked back to the spring to gather my things. There was no way I could move him. He was taller than me and maybe just a few years older. He appeared muscular and much too heavy to carry or drag even if I had not been in such a weakened state. And I had no idea how badly hurt he was. Moving him might only make things worse. I set my things down next to him and squeezed some of my wine into his mouth. His lips were torn and open, and even in his delirium, he winced as it crossed them. I pulled some cloth from his torn robe and walked again to the spring to soak the pieces in cool water. Once back to him, I squeezed the water from the cloth and let it run over his wounds. I was afraid to touch them, afraid to bring him more pain, so back-and-forth I went from the spring to the poor beaten man until I felt I had done a decent job of cleansing his open cuts. I used some of the cloth I had collected to bandage his deepest wounds and used my blanket to cover him. I was wet and cold by then and soon began to shiver uncontrollably. With some hesitation, I moved closer, sharing my only blanket for warmth. I had no idea who this was or what this man had done to end up in such a state, but surprisingly, I found an unfamiliar, deep comfort in lying next to him, a man I did not even know. I had never slept next to a man who did not beat or rape me. I had only lain in fear through each night of my marriage. I had no experience with any male my age. I had known my father and Lucius as a child. I was given in marriage to a violent man three times my age. I had no idea what men my age were like. Was I wrong to lie next to him? But I quickly realized I had no choice. My hair and clothes were wet, and I could catch a chill from which I might not recover. I took off my wet outer robe and pulled my body next to his for warmth. And I had been so alone. Feeling his flesh against mine, hearing his breath, as labored as it was, knowing a living person was close at my side, it all shook me. How alone I had been. It was an unspeakable comfort to be with another human being. To rest next to a man without fear or loathing seemed peaceful in a way I had never known. But something told me this man would not try to hurt me under any circumstance. I felt it from him immediately. I drank more of the wine until my thoughts, folly or not, finally fell away and guided me into sleep.

In the morning, I suddenly remembered where I was and I sat up quickly. What was I doing lying next to a strange man? But I had been cold, and there was only one blanket. The poor soul was still moaning and in terrible pain. I carefully lifted his head and brought the rest of my wine to his lips. He swallowed hard, and I felt it relax him.

He was a very handsome man beneath the swelling and blood. His features promised to be more delicate than most and chiseled when not battered, unusual for a man in this land. His limbs were long and muscled. He had an artisan's fingers, long and nimble. Who was he, I wondered. If he had any coins on him before the attack, they were now gone. I starkly realized the risk I took on the road alone. If this young, strong man could not survive, what chance had I?

I brought water to him and urged him to drink. After making a shelter with my blanket and poles to protect him from the harsh sun, I walked back to town and bought more supplies, carefully marking the path with small sticks and rocks to find my way back. I collected herbs I found along the way, remembering potions Mother made for sleep and easing pain. At the market, I bought a small piece of lamb and a clay pot, more bread, and as much wine as I could carry. I collected twigs and dried weeds along the way, enough to make a small fire when I returned. I struggled to carry all that I had gathered and was already exhausted when the sun was low in the sky. I first made a brew with the herbs and wine and set them aside, as they would become more potent as they sat. I boiled the lamb in water, but not having enough fire left, I could hardly call what I made a decent stew. Still, it was warm and I carried it to the beaten man. He struggled to sit up, and I was glad to see some life in him.

"I have something to help you gain strength," I said to him.

"So you are real," he said, in a hoarse and weak voice. "I thought you were a goddess preparing me for the Afterlife."

I smiled and told him to save his strength. He managed to swallow a bit of the stew and broth, and I followed it with more wine and my potion. Waiting a while for it to take effect, I cleaned his wounds again. He winced and took a deep breath to steady his nerves, and then closed his eyes and fell into a deep sleep, the herbs finally relaxing him. I watched him closely. So many things about him were attractive, his tall build, his young skin and his facial features. When not battered, he must be one of the most handsome men I had ever seen. I smiled at these musings, fancies of a young girl who had never had the privilege of such thoughts.

I ate the rest of the broth and lamb and felt revived. It was a relief to have the pot for carrying water back and forth. It would be one more thing I had to carry on my walks, but it made things easier. My coins were going quickly but for a good cause.

He slept through the night and most of the next day. When he woke, I gave him more of my brew and continued putting water in his mouth and cleaning his wounds. The third night, he sat up again.

"You are still here?" he asked.

"How could I leave you like this?" I answered.

"But why would you help someone like me?" he asked, and he looked broken.

"You are a fellow traveler on the same road as I. I would hope you would do the same for me. What thieves did this to you?"

"I am a fool. I brought this on myself," he answered, his voice low.

I was somewhat shocked at this forthright confession. But here we were, two souls with apparently nothing but the clothes on our backs on the verge of ruin one way or another. This unusual situation seemed to bring a closeness we would not have ordinarily found. Feeling he could trust me or maybe just needing to trust someone, I felt him opening to me.

"What is your name?" I asked. "Where are you from, and where are you going?"

"Seth," he replied. "And yours?"

"Magdalena."

"I work in a traveling tent down the road. A music tent with dancers and entertainment," he continued.

Dancing? Music? Oh, how this aroused my soul. But I had a confused look on my face. I could not imagine such a thing existed, and I realized with embarrassment how little I knew of the world. Torture, abandonment, and despair, yes, I knew these all too well, but of the actual lives of people outside my small world, I knew nothing.

"I am an orphan," he said, without emotion. "I never knew a mother or father. I was given to an old woman when my mother died giving birth to me. I can hardly remember her, but she was kind enough. She died when I was seven. I was on my own from then on."

"I am an orphan as well," I said, as my father was more than dead to me.

"Sorry," Seth said, and I knew he meant it.

"But I had my mother for close to nine years." I looked off into the distance and fought back the tears that always came when thinking of Mother. "What did you do on the streets?" I asked.

"I survived one way or another. It was not easy, but I managed. A little begging, some small jobs when I could find them, and even a bit of larceny from time to time, I hate to say. When I was almost of age, a Roman soldier took me in. I lived with him for several years, and I was happy for the first time. I truly loved him as I had never loved anyone before him." He looked at me curiously, and he then looked down as if embarrassed.

"That sounds quite nice," I said. So naive. So unknowing of the ways of the world. "What happened to him?"

"He was sent back to Rome and left me behind with a few coins in my pouch and not a hint of regret. My heart was broken."

"Well, of course, it was," I continued. "He was your friend, perhaps even your brother."

Seth looked at me directly, taking measure of me. Would I understand what he was about to tell me?

"Have you ever been with a man?" he asked.

My face dropped, and sadness and disgust spread over my features.

"I was given to a man in marriage, a most detestable man, the very man who murdered my mother. They were the most wretched two years of my life. That is why I am now alone on this road. I ran from him. Being with a man that way seems worse than any fate I have yet met."

"I am very sorry you had that experience," Seth continued. "It is not always wretched and unkind. Being with someone you love is the best feeling in the world. I hope you can know it some day. I had this with my soldier until he discarded me without a hint of remorse."

I looked both perplexed and hopeful. I was attracted to this lovely man in a way I did not understand. Was it because he was kind and open? Because he was my age? Seth realized I did not understand what he was telling me.

"Magdalena," Seth said. "I am different from the men you know. I have not been with a woman as you were with your husband."

"That is good. It was torture," I responded.

Seth looked at me curiously. He half-smiled at my innocence but was contrite.

"Oh, how I wish I could love someone like you, such a beautiful and graceful young woman. A lady of kindness. How easy and how wonderful life would be." He looked off wistfully.

I blushed at the thought and looked at him, searching for his meaning. What was he saying?

"Magdalena, some call me an abomination. I am not attracted to women. My soldier was my lover. He was my heart's love."

I laugh now at how blank my expression must have been. It even brought a small smile to Seth's face. I mulled these thoughts over for a while and finally began to understand.

"Oh," I said. There was no judgement in my tone or my thoughts. I was proud of myself for vaguely figuring it out. "How does that work?"

"Not very well it seems," Seth said, with a smile.

I was not sure what to make of this information. I knew I should be shocked and think it was sinful, but I did not. And who decided who was good or bad in this world? It seemed reasonable to me, for what was a person who was alone in the world with no family and without means to do? If he was born one way, how could he force himself to be another? Because society so dictated? I could not force myself to conform to the tortures of life with Tobias. Was I sinful? Who made these rules? People who knew nothing about me or my captor, this man and his life? Although I had seen much hardship and had suffered much abuse, I had still lived a very sheltered life and knew little about these things. But I knew wrong was wrong, and seeking love and shelter did not seem as such to me. Perhaps ignorance and naiveté were to my advantage, for I had no set prejudice against many things. Seth seemed a good and kind person, so it made no sense for me to question his life.

He continued. Tired and hurt as he was, he wanted to tell his story. He talked of Roman merchants who traveled through his city and brought many of the exotic customs, treasures, and spices of his colorful and rich land back home. I was fascinated by what he told me, imagining the richness of a life I never knew existed. The Romans particularly loved the dancing girls who were uninhibited, talented, and as beautiful as the land itself. One man, in particular, being clever and having a good head for earning money, started a business featuring music and dance. Over time, he gathered a large tent and several musicians of quality and traveled the roads between Egypt and Rome, stopping outside cities and around the soldiers' camps to set up his show. He provided entertainment for anyone with the coin to enter his tent, and he began to be known for his exotic performances and erotic dancers. His nomadic show was a success, especially in Rome, and he made a decent living for himself and the misfits he gathered along the way. Seth heard of the tent and the dancing girls and was intrigued.

Listening to Seth tell his story, I felt like Mother must have when Lucius spoke of distant lands and people with different thoughts and customs than our own. The world was growing in my young mind, and I begged to hear more.

"When I was living with my soldier, I thought my life settled, that I had a home at last. But when he left without a thought of my happiness or survival, I was devastated. I had no will to live any longer and nowhere to go." Seth's voice trailed off and softened as he recalled the memory.

I urged him to tell me more, and he continued softly. He recounted the night he stumbled into the tent after walking the streets, lonely and broken. Being Egyptian, nothing about it was foreign to him, and the soft, rhythmic sounds were medicine to his ailing heart. He used the little coin he had left to buy a cup of wine, and he sat through the night nursing that one cup, his eyes dreamy and sad.

The man who owned the tent, Makas, recognizing loneliness and despair when he saw it, struck up a conversation with the boy and found him disarming and kind. He was friendly and welcoming even in his sorrow, something Makas lacked but knew his entertainment business sorely needed. The old man had become tired and lonely, and he did need help running his business. Seth seemed the right fit, and Makas welcomed the gentle young man into his life by hiring him that night.

Seth quickly proved his cleverness and showed promising musical talent. The two became good friends and then, in time, more like father and son, as Makas was not in judgment of Seth or his tendencies. Makas was a worldly man. The Greeks had once inhabited the land in which they traveled, and Seth's ways were not uncommon among them. The Romans, too, were familiar with these differences. To Makas, a customer was a customer; a person was a person who might become a customer. The rest made little difference to him.

Seth felt comfort and acceptance in his new life. Sadly, he was prone to melancholy and heartache, but he was comforted by knowing he had someone and some place to count on.

"The second winter we were together," Seth continued, his energy coming back to him as he told his story, "Makas was struck with fever while we were in Egypt. He was close to death for weeks, and it took him months to get back on his feet. How could I forsake such a good man who would have no income and no home without his tent? And where would I have been without him? Makas is the only family I have ever known."

"What did you do while he was sick?" I asked. "How did you know what to do?"

"I had been working with him for two years by then and had a good idea of what was needed. And I always had ideas I kept to myself, afraid to insult Makas by thinking I knew a better way."

I smiled. I had never met a man with this kind of humility and kindness before. Oddly, I was not so shocked by his stories of a male lover, most likely because he was so honest and sincere about it and because I knew nothing of willing love or lovers. I had only known rape and torture. His story did not make any clear sense to me, for I was naive to the world, and the thought of sexual union as enjoyable was more perplexing than who the partners were. My only hint of what love might look like was what I had seen between Mother and Lucius, so it was an inexplicable mystery to me. Seth's apparent goodness struck me as innocent and blameless. I intuitively felt he would not intentionally do anything of ill intent, and without doubt, his experiences had to have been better than those inflicted on me.

"I found that I have a good eye for beauty and movement. I was, after all, born and raised in Egypt. I gathered silk scarves and tunics from merchants I knew and dressed the dancers in rich, colorful new costumes. I showcased each dancer in her best light. The tent took on a more exotic and intoxicating air, more Egyptian and less Makas if I dare say without insult to my dear friend. The girls were excited by the changes, and it showed."

These improvements drew in more and more customers, and the business grew in reputation and treasure. Seth sounded almost apologetic as he told his story, as if he had criticized Makas and his abilities, but he was also proud of his work. He had never before taken on such a challenge, and he felt proud he had met it with success. He kept the changes from Makas while he cared for him, which he did as any loving son would. As far as Seth was concerned, Makas needed only to heal and get well. When Makas recovered and discovered his business was not only still standing but also thriving like it never had, he was thrilled, both for the increased income and for Seth's dedication and loyalty. A lasting bond had grown between them. And so, Seth had work and a family for life.

"Makas was grateful when he saw what I had done. What I feared might be seen as arrogance, Makas took as devotion and care," Seth continued. "I was happy again for the first time since my heartbreak, for Makas was well, and I had done right by him."

"My success with the tent did not cure my poor judgment," Seth continued, after a long, stilted pause. "We have been slowly making our way back from a winter in Rome. We set up our tent not far from here to rest and make a little coin. I saw a soldier who reminded me so much of the man who left me behind that I immediately attached all of those feelings to him. He came in every night and watched me closely, following my every move, so I let myself believe he might have feelings for me."

"I might have thought the same thing," I told him, understanding his desire to be loved.

"I can see now that he set me up, but at the time, I only thought how lucky I would be if he returned my affection. What a young fool I am. I was so happy to see him enter the tent, I overlooked two other men who were with him that last night. As I think back, I remember they whispered among themselves throughout the show. At the end of the evening, my handsome soldier came over to me in a flirtatious way. He invited me to join him for a cup of wine. One thing led to another, as they seem to do, and the soldier asked me to meet him after I closed the tent. We agreed on this spot. I should have been suspicious when it was so far from town and our tent, but I could not see any of this at the time. I reasoned that this kind of liaison was new to him, and he wanted to be far from the other soldiers."

Seth looked away and I felt him flush with shame. What a tortured road he must travel with so many in judgement of his nature, I thought. I put my hand on his in a reassuring gesture.

"Those who reach for love are never wrong, Seth," I said. "Perhaps you were not wise, but you were not wrong."

Seth melted with my words, and on feeling his pain, I wanted to cry. Judgement killed my mother and ruined my life. How or why would I condemn this gentle man for his actions?

"When I met up with him, the two other men were also waiting. They were hiding behind that rock formation by the spring.

"I ran up and embraced him. He slapped me hard, and I fell to the ground. I was confused and hurt, more by the rejection than the blow. The other two moved behind me, and one hit me over the head with a large stick. I fell to my knees, and they beat and kicked me until I lost consciousness. I only remember their drunken breath as they shouted obscenities and called me an abomination. I had been too distracted by my passion. I am a stupid man."

"Please, do not say such things," I admonished. "The desire for love is not stupid. Unfortunately, he was not worthy."

Seth could not remember what came next. They took any money he had on him, as that was their intention all along. I like to think it was the soldier who made them stop before they killed him, feeling some remorse for his actions. They dragged him into the brush, covered him with dirt and broken branches and left him lying in his blood. Leaving him alone was a sure death, but they could reason it was not directly on their hands. He would surely have met his end had I not found him. Unable to move under the heat of the desert sun, he would have died of thirst and his wounds. I put my arm around this stranger who had opened his heart to me.

"Seth," I said. "I will care for you until you are strong enough to return to Makas. I am sorry there is such evil in this world. I have known it in my time as well."

Seth looked at me strangely, this young girl in fine robes, alone on the road with no protection, who came to his rescue seemingly out of nowhere.

"What manner of woman are you?" he asked. "Have I passed to the other side? I would believe you are an apparition sent from the gods, if only I were worthy."

"I already know you are the worthiest man I have yet to meet, perhaps save one," I answered, and Lucius came to mind. "And I am not sure my God even knows me now, for I am in many ways a lost woman. But if my last act in this world is to save you, I will die happy."

I wrapped Seth in my blanket and helped him lie down. A gentle tear fell from his eye. I knew then I would spend all the coins I had to save this man, my first true friend since my mother's death.

✶ TEN ✶

I LOOKED AFTER Seth as if he were my brother. I knew Mother would have cared for him, as he had an artist's soul. And like her, he deserved a better world than the one in which he was born. As the swelling left his face and his wounds began to heal, I saw he was even more handsome than I first imagined. As Lucius looked so different from the men in my city, so did Seth, but more distinctively. He had a delicate look and a refinement I had not before seen in a man. Seth moved about slowly, in great pain, but ate as much food as I provided. He was young and lean and needed to regain his strength.

I hesitated to bargain with the merchants, afraid to draw attention to myself. If I paid whatever price was asked and acted like a wealthy woman who did not care, the merchants were happy to see me. My coins were going quickly, and I knew I would soon have only the one given to me by Mother. At that point, what did I care? I saw how foolish my plan had been. How far did I think these coins would take me? What did I think I would do when they ran out? It did not matter. I wanted to save Seth. Perhaps I was stopped from drinking the poison to do one thing of value with the life given to me. Is this the fate the old crone predicted? Once he got stronger, we could travel to Makas together. Having a man at my side would offer protection.

Seth did not want Makas to see him so badly beaten, but he also knew the old man would worry when he failed to return to the tent. In another three days, he felt strong enough to attempt the walk back. What a tragic sight we must have been; Seth with battered legs, cut and bruised, his every step slow and painful and me with raw and blood-ied feet, on the verge of debilitating wounds. Seth's clothes were torn and stained with blood, and mine were elegant but caked in red clay dirt. We were both so broken, each in different ways, but I felt heart-ened to be with another person. I was in no better circumstance, and my coins would last no more than another moon cycle at best, but I had done a kindness to another, enriching me in a comforting way. We had to stop and rest many times, for Seth leaned on my shoulder to keep going, and I often stumbled while trying to support his weight. My feet pounded with pain.

When we arrived, Makas dropped what he was doing and ran on hobbled legs to greet us. There was tremendous relief in the elder's eyes as he looked upon the closest thing to a son he would ever know. He was so grateful to see Seth that he barely noticed his condition. The reunion shook me, and all I could think of was my mother, her love for me, and the tremendous grief of losing her. The exhaustion of caring for Seth those many nights and days, the loneliness that haunted me, and the terrible void that never filled, all of this hit me at once. This, and knowing how close I had come to losing my mind. I shook with emotion and choked on my tears as I fell against Seth. He seemed to summon strength from being home and seeing Makas again. He stood upright and held me tightly.

He put his other arm around Makas and said, "Father, I was a fool and nearly met my end. This woman has saved me and I owe her my life."

"Then I owe her as well," the wrinkled, gray-bearded man replied. "Come, please, come in and rest. Let me bring you nourishment."

Seth led me into a spacious tent. Almost numb with grief and fatigue when I entered, once inside, I quickly became speechless. I stared at my surroundings. Silk veils undulated above us creating a floating canopy of color within the main tent, the hues more brilliant than I had ever seen. The fabric danced gracefully, yet wildly, in the moving air. Patterned carpets lay on the ground, and tapestries covered several long cushions arranged in a circle around a central platform.

I was so stunned by this visual feast, that I momentarily forgot my pain and exhaustion. I stood in wonder, my eyes wide as a small child's and almost as innocent. Where was I? What world had I entered? Did I die in the desert and not know it until this moment? Was I now in Paradise? But my body ached and refused to be ignored, so I knew I was very much alive and every part of me was burning with pain. I collapsed onto one of the cushions, needing to get off my tortured feet. It was the first time in months my body had rested on anything but rock or hard ground. In its comfort, I surrendered to the physical toll of the past many days.

Makas left and returned a while later, carrying a large metal tray. On it was a steaming pot of hot tea and hammered copper cups. They were more beautiful than anything I had seen in Tobias' tent, having thought his were so unique. How small my vision had been until that moment. I was in a world I never imagined existed while I savored the warm tea and its sweet taste. It had been too long since I had known this kind of comfort. On the intricately etched tray was a small silver plate with date cakes covered in honey. I ate like a queen with Seth beside me. We ate every morsel.

"When you have finished, I have prepared a place for you to rest," Makas told me. "You must be tired. Seth is the only family I have, and I am grateful to you. You are welcome here as long as you wish to stay."

I followed Makas to a small, recessed alcove behind the main tent. Inside was a lovely blanketed bed with pillows to rest my head and layers of fine Egyptian cotton should I become cold. Before I could thank Makas for his hospitality, my eyes closed, and I fell onto the blankets. The tea had relaxed me, and my body, with its own wisdom, knew I was safe in a way I had not been since Mother's death.

* * *

The sun was painting its magic over the distant hills when my eyes opened. In the great calm of my badly needed rest, I found myself floating in dreams of color and music. The tender sound of flutes kissed the air above me while my heart beat with a rhythmic and steady pulse. Everything seemed luscious and inviting, and something familiar woke within me—a physical desire to move again, to dance to the music playing within me. I jumped up, thinking I had, once again, fallen into the vision of my childhood stream. But it was real.

I straightened my robe and pulled my fingers through my long, thick hair to untangle the knots that had formed. I found a large vessel of water and a washing bowl set next to my bed, and I tried to make myself as presentable as possible before venturing out. Out to where I had no idea. Quietly I crept around the outside of the tent until I found a moveable flap on its side. I pulled it back just enough to peek through without being seen.

Two men with drums on their laps sat on one side of the large central carpet. One drum was made of hammered metal with etched drawings on the sides and thick, tight goatskin pulled by laces over the top. The other was formed from baked clay with the same tight skin covering. The drummers beat their fingers and thumbs methodically against the skins to produce the deep, resonant sound that created the heartbeat of the tent. Two men with wooden flutes sat cross-legged on raised cushions and wove their notes through the drumbeats like feathers floating on a summer's breeze. I was mesmerized. I had seen men at the marketplace pound on drums to attract customers to their wares. I had heard flutes played by children and merchants, but never had I witnessed such sound. Yet another musician played a stringed instrument that balanced across his lap. He had what looked like rings of thinly carved bone on his fingers, and he used them to pluck sounds from the strings. His rhythms were complex and hypnotizing and brought all the other sounds together in a haunting melody. His fingers danced across the instrument, light and quick, holding the complexity of the rhythms together as if by magic. The beauty of this music had to come from the majesty of their souls, I mused, for how could it be otherwise?

At that moment, I believed that music was life's only truth. Nothing but music could hold the essence of heaven and earth in their purest form. While this does contain a most divine truth, I laugh now with my final breaths at how naively I translated the scene before me.

And then came the dancers. First, two stepped onto the carpet, and then three, all covered in light layers of softly colored silk. Gold coins sewn on the edges of their fitted belts made rhythmic sounds as they shimmied their hips. Their legs and stomachs were almost bare, covered only with the lightest layers of moving fabric. They were almost naked but for the mysterious moving outfits—veils, coins, and streams of silk carrying on a dance of their own. Light layers of colored fabrics were placed in front of lanterns on the side of the large tent, creating different colored hues that washed over them and changed in the moving air. It was as if they wore the changing tones and not clothing. This tent held a world I could not understand, and yet, color and sound and movement spoke to my essence.

I was more intrigued than shocked. The only naked body I had ever seen, other than Tobias', was my mother's when we bathed in the stream when I was so young. Seeing this was so foreign to me that I could not reconcile it. But their bodies were magnificent. The dancers seemed to feel no shame and seemed proud. They were fearless, and that confusingly inspired me. I stared, wide-eyed, watching their long muscles move to the beat of the drums as their hips swayed and shimmied. They undulated their bellies in ways I could not fathom. No wonder their bodies were left uncovered, so the movements themselves could be seen and appreciated. And yet, they were covered in color and light. Was that enough? It started to make some odd kind of bewildering sense. Their graceful arms moved like slithering snakes and played metal discs tied to their fingers, two on each hand. The sounds of the discs answered the patterned sounds of the drums as if the dancers were speaking to the musicians. They responded to the music but were a part of it as well.

Are these people free to live this way, to enjoy this kind of freedom? I wondered almost out loud. Will they not be condemned to some dismal and painful end? Stoned at best? They seemed to exist in a world of their own making, one in which this was not only possible but also allowed and celebrated. In the back of my mind, I feared we would all be seized and punished severely, yet the light and sound, the color and movement, all made an indelible imprint on my soul so deep I almost cried.

I stood in that spot for what seemed like hours. I could not take my eyes from the scene before me. Soldiers, filled with wine and laughter, gathered on the cushions piled around the large carpet. Some shouted out to the dancing girls, and a few seemed to look on with a hint of awe and respect. This respect fell quickly with each cup of wine.

One of the soldiers threw gold coins at a dancer he fancied, and she answered by moving close to him. He then tucked more coins into her belt, his hand slipping deep into the front of it and she kissed him on the lips and lay beside him on the cushion. I felt a pulse go through my body that left me teetering on the edge of shame.

Everything taught to me as a child was assailed by what was before me, yet some part of my mind could not find fault in any of it. I cannot say if I was upset at that moment or merely trying to absorb the impressions of what I was seeing. I stood there, hiding behind the open flap, frozen in my spot, observing and trying to reconcile everything around me, when I suddenly felt a hand on my shoulder. I jumped, frightened for my life, instinctively fearing punishment for the mere act of witnessing such a scene. And the fact that I was enjoying it as much as I was would surely guarantee my eternal damnation. But it was Seth, and he looked like an entirely different person. Clean and freshly dressed, he leaned on a carved wooden stick, a lovely, well-used one that Makas had made for occasional use. He seemed well. Being home, as uncommon and unusual as it was, proved to be his best medicine.

"What do you think of our dancers?" he asked.

"Magnificent," I answered, "and the music must be from heaven itself."

Seth laughed, the first I had heard from him. It was a good laugh, an honest laugh that came from the very center of him. "Are you shocked?" he teased.

"I think I am, but I know the joy of dancing. I just have never seen it so free and to such sound. Their bodies are so bare. All of this is allowed? This freedom is unknown and unforgiven by my people."

"Where I come from it is allowed and, in many ways, respected," he answered.

I could only look at him, wide-eyed with disbelief. Was there such a world and life outside the confines of the one to which I was born, one that existed without condemnation and punishment? Were these people the pagans Mother had described?

"I play music. Maybe you will dance with me. I am not a soldier, and some would question whether I am even a man. That should keep you safe. I would love to bring you any joy I could, for you have given me my life."

"Perhaps," I said. Mother's warnings flooded my mind, and I could not rid myself of the guilt I was feeling. Seth had carried a cup of wine with him to help me sleep, and we walked back to my bed. We sat together while I drank it slowly.

"I thank you, Magdalena, for being the unusual woman you are. I am fortunate fate brought you into my life. You seem to judge no one. That brings me great comfort, for I am used to being treated poorly, except by Makas. I think of you as my family already. Rest well, dear sister," and he kissed me on the forehead and closed my eyes with his hand.

His words moved my heart. Here I was, in a tent of sin by my father's values, yet treated better than my family ever thought I deserved once Mother was gone. "You have saved me as well," I whispered.

My body obeyed his touch, and I fell immediately into a deep sleep. He covered me with the softest cotton blanket, and I felt a comfort

I feared I would never know again. I have no recollection of what I dreamed that night, but I know it was full of color, light and sound.

* * *

Makas made me feel at home immediately, and once I told him and Seth my story, they insisted I travel with them. I would be safer, and I had nowhere else to go. They needed help with cooking and serving the patrons of the tent. Although I had no loom and no experience with fabric as fine as the silk from Egypt, I did know how to sew and could create clothing for the dancers. Seth had clever ideas for their outfits. He had an artist's eye Mother would have appreciated. Makas collected myriad treasures as his caravan traveled the land—colored cloth and sacks of dazzling beads that he wanted to use in new ways. The girls needed belts and veils and even leggings. Though it seemed they wore next to nothing, I did know dance and could imagine improvements to make their clothing more attractive. I felt there would be more mystery with more coverage if that covering took advantage of their movements. Art and creativity stirred me, and with it, a spark of life began to return to my heart.

For a long while, I felt shame at what my mother might have thought of the life I was living. It was everything she wanted to protect me from knowing. But Mother was dead, taken from me for no just reason. What did obeying the rules do for her? What was given to me in place of my life with her was worse than any violent death. Was there any other choice left to me? I could join with these people who seemed only to wish me well, or I could perish in the desert, be taken by a Roman, or return to Tobias for an even worse fate. And so I joined a traveling band of musicians and dancers and embraced my new life.

Seth became the closest thing to a sibling I would ever know. Makas was kinder to me than my own father had ever been. Their embrace led to eventual contentment and a sense of well-being. Little by little, I became accustomed to seeing the girls moving about with so little clothing on their bodies, and the music brought me untold joy. And so, I slowly settled into my pagan life in a traveling tent.

The guilt and shame lessened. After all, without this life, I would have met my end in little time. Or I would have been taken by a Roman who was not kind and respectful and be made to suffer again under the dictates and abuses of a man I detested. I saw my new clan did not harm anyone. They brought happiness and amusement to those around them, often people who also had hard lives. Could this be immoral? Yet it starkly contradicted the beliefs held in my former community. In living that life, I believed that oppression and condemnation were wrong and unjust, but in finding myself in such a world as this, the old ways and judgments plagued me. Once again, I found no peace within my heart.

At night, while the tent filled with merriment and music and I wondered what else, I stayed in my little side tent and sewed costumes for the girls. I grew to know and like them. Not one had chosen this life, but each felt grateful to have found a way to survive with decent men to shelter them.

Some, but not all, went off with the soldiers into private tents. I dared not even imagine these trysts after the horror of my nights with Tobias, but they seemed happy enough about it. At least they felt they had some choice in the matter. And some reward. The days of men forcing sex on them and treating them as worthless chattel were behind them, at least in their minds. Makas put no pressure on them and allowed them any income they procured. They felt a sense of control, as odd as that seemed to my still naive mind. Lying with strange men seemed a detestable fate to me, one to avoid at all costs. But these were the girls with the most coins on their belts and the ones who were courted by the soldiers most often. I saw the coins were a way of signaling they were readily available. They were the girls with experience, and they knew how to use it.

The younger girls tried to lie with the soldiers as infrequently as possible. They knew a day would come when money would be the only thing to help them survive, but they could not suspend their guilt and disgust as well as the others. If an offer was not too distasteful, they made the coin when they could. They liked to see themselves as dancers, a step away from prostitution in their minds. In some lands, it was considered an art. I wanted desperately to believe this. These girls held on to their pride as long as they could and made their own choices regarding the men. The pay for dancing was next to nothing. They received food and shelter from Makas, and on occasion, the kinder, sympathetic soldiers left coins for them just for dancing. But they would have little to show for their efforts when they were no longer young and beautiful. When looks faded, and they had nothing to their names, what would they do?

As they grew older, they understood they needed to make as much money as they could in the time they had left. There was no chance of survival in their later years without it. They came to understand it did not even matter. On one side of the desert, the side I was from, they were considered prostitutes whether they were paid to lie with the men or not, just by being there. By that measure, so was I.

To protect me from such decisions, Seth suggested that he and I should marry. Marriage would shelter me from the drunken men and guard what little virtue I might still have. Sadly, I could not, for even though I had falsified my death, I was still married to Tobias under the law. I had no idea if that law mattered and who was to decide what merit it had, but I was haunted by the old rules of my former life and had no idea what was possible. I would have found much comfort in being

Seth's wife. He was kind and understood my pain better than anyone else could, and we purely loved each other. Is that not the grounds for a good marriage? I had no idea what love between a man and woman could be except as I saw it between Mother and Lucius. Knowing how that ended only confused me. My only experience of marriage was being ravaged, owned, and mistreated, or the lonely distance between my mother and father. Still, at times, I often wondered and dreamed of things I did not understand and felt I was missing. Seth offered safety and respect, and this is what I assumed was the basis of a good marriage. Knowing I could not rightfully take Seth as my husband, we pretended. As we moved from town to town, we presented ourselves as man and wife, and this gave me the protection I needed.

Art was the only refuge my mother and I had ever known, and when I created the dancers' costumes, I lived in the grace of those innocent days with her. I remembered watching her bring exquisite images from her imagination into her threads, making daily items magical and delightful. They brought smiles to those who saw them and a little more pleasure into the lives of those who owned them. I marveled at her ability then, and felt my own way to it now. Perhaps art is born when we have a desperate need to find joy.

Makas had baskets of colored glass and clay beads he collected in his travels. I sewed them onto fabric and created designs as I once did in my best weavings. For the girls who had few coins, I created beaded belts that fit snugly on their hips and beaded breast plates that made their bodies even more alluring. They no longer felt diminished by their lack of experience and coin, and their renewed excitement showed in their dancing. The new designs were so attractive that the old belts soon lost their appeal. The girls with all the coins wanted my new designs as well.

Creativity and art brought forth the better parts of myself, parts I had forgotten. While working with the beads, something indecipherable stirred me, causing a curious restlessness. The beads called to me in the same way the threads once had, but there was something more, something to which I could not put clear thought. I would stare at them for what seemed like hours, hypnotically watching the light move through each prism while illuminating the landscape or tent walls. And then, mysteriously, I felt the light shine directly into me, into the very center of my mind and heart, and I was able to enter, once again, the inexplicable vision of the stream. I was standing outside of time in the moment of my childhood, or perhaps both the child I was then and the broken girl I was now joined together in this realm of unconditional love. Was there a life outside of time where I existed now and then? Could I reach across this vision to look into the eyes of my mother and remember the love and the spirit that exists in all living things? Maybe it was so in those moments of creativity. Perhaps this was the great secret my mother handed down to me. The beads that guided my hands offered some mysterious meaning I needed to uncover. The more I worked with the beads, the deeper into their spell I fell. They communicated a promise of some kind, but I could not tell what it was. Perhaps to work with beauty, to be consumed in innocence and art, or to bring me closer to my mother's soul. I did not know.

Soon all the girls wanted my new outfits, and I was kept busy. The demand for my work proved a good turn for me as it kept my mind on what I could create and not on what my life had become as I approached my fourteenth year.

*   *   *

Toward the end of winter, we came across a bustling city and decided to rest in its comfort and restore our supplies. As Seth wandered about, he came across a girl even younger than me. She was filthy, bloody, and exhausted, sitting at the outer well of the city weeping in despair. With his enormous heart, he folded his lanky body to the ground and sat beside her.

"What is your name?" he asked.

"Anna," she whispered, almost afraid to speak.

Seth had a most disarming charm about him. He was a man who knew pain and never wanted it for another. With his relaxed gestures and wide, ingenuous smile, Seth coaxed her story from her and she quickly unloaded her troubles. He had the gift of never seeming a stranger to anyone and was able to hold a person's heart with his first glance.

She immediately told her story as if bringing it to the ears of an understanding person might somehow ease the pain she carried with her to that well. She had been raped repeatedly by her father's brother for two years. In fear, she held her tongue, not understanding what any of it meant for her. It was her father's oldest brother, a foul and unpleasant man who was known to beat his wife and drink heavily. Yet her father idolized him.

The first time it happened, he dragged her into the stable and told her to lie down as he held a knife to her throat. He warned that if she made a sound or told anyone, he would use it to cut out her tongue. There he took her, roughly and without concern for her young age. She cried for weeks, yet no one cared to notice.

Every time the uncle visited, he pulled her aside and did the same. She began to hope he would use the knife and end her misery. But Anna was promised in marriage to a boy she deeply loved. She hoped to endure the abuse long enough to be married and gone from her uncle and family. But the uncle became rougher with her and came to her more often. She feared she was ruined for her wedding night and sought the help and counsel of her father. Her father became enraged and put the entirety of the blame on Anna, cursing her as a liar and harlot. She must have enticed his brother to have it go on so long, he shouted. She had enjoyed it and tempted him. She would have been ten years when it started, but still, her father refused to find fault with his oldest brother. Despite her mother's pleading, she was driven from their home and left without a coin, without a blanket.

She walked and struggled for days without food or water until she found this city. She had no idea what she would do from there. The water from the well revived her enough to restore her panic and worry. She had no money for food. At best, she would have to beg. She would die, be forced into prostitution, or be taken by a Roman, for there were no other choices for a ruined girl in her position.

Seth suggested that perhaps she could dance and work in the tent. He knew Makas would not take on another mouth to feed that could not bring in income, so the only solution would be for Seth to teach her to perform for the men. Even if she had no talent, there would be wine and food served, and to some, it would not matter. She was young, and with enough care and kohl, she could be made to appear attractive.

Seth brought Anna to Makas, who resisted furiously. Seth would not give up and continued to argue, albeit with kindness, until Makas could no longer refuse him. He could not see it as anything but a very bad idea. But even his heart was moved by the sight of Anna. He hesitantly agreed. She came with us that late afternoon, and we made a bed for her and fed her until she could eat no more.

Seth desperately wanted to believe she had talent, though no one else saw it. Some of the girls laughed at her and were unkind. Most of them felt it was a waste of time and food to have her around, yet each knew what would happen to her without our protection. Seth worked with her every moment he could. When he felt frustrated, he did not let it show. Anna was a young and shy girl burdened by scars of shame, but she possessed an inner beauty and sense of rhythm only Seth could recognize. Makas remained skeptical and worried Seth had added a burden to our lives by taking on this broken girl, a girl he thought had no allure whatsoever.

Seth begged me to dance with her, to help her lose her shyness and sense of shame. He thought I would be the one to show her it was a decent enough life or at least a way to survive. We met for hours each afternoon, and I was immediately filled with that old, almost forgotten pleasure and mystery of dance. My joy was contagious, for she also began to love and understand the music and how to interpret it with her body. It became fun for us, something with which she had no previous experience. I told her all my stories of dancing with Mother, being at the stream and even of Zeus, and we made it a game to pretend we were there. In that world, our life was good. We believed that if we held these thoughts, they were true, at least at the moment. It would be our private secret, and Anna began to remind me of my one friend who had been my ally and co-conspirator as a child. Having someone with whom we share our secrets is empowering, and I saw Anna shed some of her angst and sorrow as we worked together. We laughed and acted as young children together, for neither of us had had many opportunities for fun in our lives, and we formed a bond. I told her that dance had always been my escape. There were no rules other than sound, rhythm, and space. There was no judgment, no dishonor, only joy, and art. If she could lose herself in the music and find her place within it, as I always had, no one and nothing else would matter. She would survive.

"It is the one thing that is yours and yours alone," I told her, and her eyes lit up with the thought.

I styled Anna's hair and taught her how to put kohl on her eyes to help her feel attractive. Seeing her confidence grow, I decided to make a belt and veil for her as a gift, an act of friendship that might inspire her, though most thought she deserved it least. The girls who sold the most drinks and earned the most coins for the tent demanded my best work, so I hid her gift and worked on it secretly. I selected beads that reminded me of Lucius' blanket, and I tried to recreate some of the designs. Whenever I did work on it, I fell into memories of sitting beside Mother in those long past days when we wove together making Zeus' blanket. Some of these recollections wrenched my heart, and some shook me with tears of joy until I felt her hands in my own. In moments of melancholy, I wondered where her blanket was. Was Lucius using it daily and dreaming of her as I was? Or was he dead and buried in it? And where was my Zeus? I feared I would never know.

I worked on Anna's gift in my spare time, what little there was, through the summer season. I began my project hoping it would bring Anna confidence and a sense of belonging, but my attachment to it became too strong. I conflated the veil with memories of my child-hood—my mother, my lost dreams. Even after finishing it, I kept it hidden. I began to avoid Anna, the guilt of my deception creeping into our relationship as deception always does. A distance grew between us, and she became shy and uncertain around me. I had created the exact opposite of my original intention.

There were times in my life when I felt directed by a force I could not name, nor did I know from where it came, but it seemed deter-mined to guide me to better action. I believed it had to do with my visions and my stars. I found it comforting, as if something real or imagined cared enough to watch over me after Mother died. When my life held so much resentment, hate, and despair during my life with Abigail, it fell silent, or perhaps I was too angry to listen. When I did listen, I was guided to better decisions even if I did not recognize it at the time. The night of my attempted suicide, it took the cup from my hand. Into the great despair of my marriage to Tobias, it brought my plan of escape. That plan was all that kept me alive at the time. This force seemed to lead me along the right roads and ultimately to Seth, to the path of rescue. When I was younger and more recalcitrant, I fought this force when it went against my shallow interests and desires. I refused to listen. I only welcomed it when it brought things of wonder and delight, but I came to understand that my resistance always delayed my best interests.

I was now in one of those moments. My selfishness was blocking this wiser voice. I knew, in my heart, I needed to give the veil and belt to Anna as I had planned, but I continued to resist. I adamantly insisted I could not. They meant too much, had too much significance, and should be mine. I was mistaken to believe they should go to Anna, I argued. I was the one with talent. I was the one chosen by the stars. Oh, the pride that had set up its household within me. But still, it nagged at my heart and caused me continued unease. Finally, I had to surrender. There would be no rest until I did.

"Anna," I said, one afternoon as she was sitting alone beneath the shade of an old, gnarled tree, "I made this veil in memory of my mother and a blanket she once made for someone very dear to her. In truth, I made it for you, for you have become very dear to me. You have become a talented dancer, and I want you to wear these to bring our time together into your art. You possess a special gift."

Did I lie to her or only wish it to be true? I cannot say even now. But words sometimes take form and I hoped.

Tears ran down her face as she knelt at my feet sobbing. Through her tears, she thanked me. "My own sisters have not shown me kindness such as this. I think of you as my sister now," she said.

"Then it is so," I said, and I meant it.

Her story poured out of her as if the vessel containing all her pain had suddenly shattered. There was no stopping it.

"I deeply loved Abid," she cried to me. "I long for him still. I have known him since we were small children. I always felt he would be my husband one day. We loved being together, first as children playing, and as we grew, we talked about our happy future ahead. He is all I ever wanted."

Anna hung her head for a moment, unable to speak. I sat beside her and placed the veil across her shoulders. She fingered the colored beads and fine stitching softly as if pulling comfort from them.

"Abid was my protector in all things," she told me. "I know he loved me. We had a special bond. I told him about my uncle, and my father's response, hoping he would step in to save me. I believed he would come to my defense." Again, she paused and looked away. She held onto my arm for strength as she told the rest of her story.

"I thought he would understand and be angry with my uncle, would cut his throat and avenge my honor. I begged him to take me away to safety and a life together. He was angry, yes, but not for the reason I hoped. Like my father, he blamed me."

"'How could you lie down and take this time after time?' he shouted at me, his face so red it hurt to look at him. 'You are ruined! Spoiled for me. If you had honor, you would have let him slit your throat.'"

"'But I wanted to live, to be with you,' I cried to him."

"He slapped me across the face. 'Do not speak to me. I cannot look at you any longer, you disgust me. How could you allow yourself to be ruined like this?' He shouted with so much anger I began to cry."

"I could only stare at him. Was this the same boy I had loved since I was born, who was promised to me for as long as I could remember? I could not believe my ears. How could he change his feelings for me in but an instant?"

"'But I am the same girl,' I cried to him," 'I am the same girl who has waited all my life to marry you. This was not my doing.'"

"He left me and gathered his parents," she continued. "His father spit on me and his mother did the same. They wanted nothing more to do with me or my disgraced family. The only way my family felt they could restore their honor was to send me into the desert with nothing, and declare me a harlot to save their name. They felt it a kindness over stoning. I would have preferred the stones."

My heart broke for her. She was an innocent girl ruined by a man and sent to her death. I was tired of these stories, sick of the sentences men so easily handed down to women. Not only had she had to endure the torture of her uncle's continued raping, something I knew only too well, she was also no longer seen as herself by the boy she loved. His feelings for her changed in just an instant, and he would see her die before he would defend her, underscoring the fact that women were commodities and she no longer held value. What had she done to deserve any of this? Her uncle would be free to continue his ways, more than likely with one of her sisters, while she was left to die. At least her sisters would learn the lesson and never tell of the abuse. At the age of twelve, Anna could not begin to understand.

"I know some of this pain," I told her in a quiet, resigned voice. "We are together now and will protect each other. Our lives are not what we had hoped they could be, but we can be a family."

We sat together for a while, staring into the barrenness of our pasts and the nothingness of our futures, and then I stood up and took her hands. I pulled her up, wrapped the veil around her, and showed her how to dance with it, how to allow its beauty to become her own. I showed Anna how to move the sorrow out of her body. The gift of giving brought healing to my own heart, as well as hers.

Seth's kindness showed her a different life, a strange one but a life nonetheless. He became her brother and made her feel loved and accepted. With our help, she grew into a decent dancer. Dancing now had meaning for her. She began to enjoy its gifts. Even when it was simply an escape from thought and judgment, it had passion. She moved like I felt when I rode Zeus—free and unbridled. And like my riding Zeus, she would only get better the more she did it. She began to feel physical confidence as I had in learning to ride.

I think she needed to dance, needed to escape her past and her feelings. Breaking free of her shame, as well as she could, restored some measure of her heart and sense of worth. She could not bear to think of a soldier touching her, but some threw coins at her sympathetically because she was so young and lacked experience. Dancing came to matter to her. She lacked refinement and possessed a clumsy grace, but she had a wild and unusual spirit once she set it free. When one has lost everything, often a gift is found buried in the rubble. What a lot we were; a collection of broken souls finding solace in music and dance. We would stay together in a world of our own making, a world of art and liberation, hoping to be free of the judgment, shame, and condemnation the other world held for us. We would be family to each other and survive.

I began to feel close to all the dancers, each in a different way. Most were not as kind or innocent as Anna. Some were raised by prostitutes and knew no other way. Most learned to use men better than men could use them. Several had suffered abuse as Anna and I had and found their way to the tent. Two others were orphans with no other life offered to them. Even though I was younger than all of them, save Anna, I felt motherly toward them. I needed to belong to something, to have a family, to have some reason to live. And I was no longer alone.

When finished with our morning duties, Seth and I rested together and prepared for the night's activities. We took walks or sat by a stream or in the shade of a tree if one was near. We talked about all manner of things much as Mother had with Lucius. I often did the wash if water was near, and it brought me back to forgotten times. I had never felt this closeness with anyone other than Mother, and he became the sibling I had always wished I had. I would tease him about a soldier he thought charming, and he would tell me he would find a suitor for me and then describe the most intolerable drunkard we had seen stumble into the tent the night before. We would make up wild stories of our imagined liaisons and laugh until we cried.

Often, he brought a drum or a flute and played music while we rested. I came to understand the rhythms and songs and asked him endless questions about the melodies and the instruments. I worked with my beads and fabrics, enchanted by the music and wishing those carefree moments would never end. When I became stiff and cramped, I stood and stretched to the rhythms, feeling the need to move. The memory of dancing to Mother's sweet, lyrical voice and the magic of the stream lived in my flesh. When I moved, these forgotten moments came alive again and transported me back to my safest and happiest times.

I often pretended the flute was Mother's voice. Sometimes I pictured Lucius sitting with us, looking lovingly at her while she sang. I became lost in dreams of the past. Seth said very little, knowing it was a potentially tender subject for me. We carried on this way for a season, and I came to anticipate and interpret his music with ease.

As a musician, Seth enjoyed watching me give form to his music just as Mother had when she sang. I eventually just closed my eyes and let myself go. As I became more comfortable, so did he, and his playing became more inspired and complex. We shared a deep, creative pairing; a gift to us both.

One day, Seth looked at me directly and said, "Magdalena, you are the most intuitive and graceful dancer I have ever seen. It seems you were made for it, as though the gods themselves blessed you with this gift."

An ancient memory came to me, and I thought back to a time before recollection.

"Mother always said I was born under stars that summoned me to dance, that this was the choice of the heavens and not my own. How strange this is where my life has led me, as if this were the destiny she predicted." I had a perplexed and troubled look on my face. "But she warned me to keep it hidden, for my community would surely take it wrong, and I could bring misguided attention to myself. They would think me a godless pagan."

Seth laughed his pure and throaty laugh. "It is too late, Sister, for there is little doubt about that now. Just look where your life has brought you."

I scowled at him angrily. Not having been raised under the strict religiosity into which I had been born, he found my discomfort amusing. Did he not see how troubled I was by the memory of this? I became furious.

He mocked my angry scowl, making his face stern and distorted, and laughed harder. I became more indignant. He looked ridiculous, but I could not shake my anger. I contorted my face in pure displeasure and he twisted his right back, fighting a crooked grin. I stubbornly held my rancor, glowering and squinting my eyes. He imitated me again, looking so ridiculous, so ludicrous between his stifled laughter and attempted outrage, I finally had to laugh, for I saw the absurdity in all of it. There was nothing left but to laugh. I finally recognized how hysterical I must have looked. And why should I be angry with him? He held no judgement against me.

Mother, I thought, wherever you are, is this the fate you predicted—the one our stars laid before me? How is it you always thought I had a destined purpose? Or did you tell me that to give me hope when you knew only too well a woman's fate? Did you ever, in all your imagination, think I would be living in a musicians' tent? And would you have secretly preferred this for me over the other life forced on me? It was this or the bondage of a hateful, abusive marriage, one that could easily have ended my life in a sick and sordid manner. What choice did I have? I believed that from where she existed, and I did believe with all my heart she did exist, she saw this new life brought more to me than anything she or I had gained from the other. Is one's destiny only to find peace?

As winter descended, the soldiers made camp close by, and Makas decided to settle in for the season. The business was hearty, and I cooked large quantities of food to feed them. Seth and Makas made wine by the barrel, and we earned good money each night. The girls were happy to be adding to their coffers. The day when they were too old to dance would arrive much too quickly. They needed a way to survive beyond this life in the tent. What they would do was never discussed and perhaps never planned. But without money, there were no options.

*   *   *

The winter turned uncommonly cold, and a deadly fever swept through the soldiers' encampment. In little time, it spread through our tents as well. Those not sick had to dance without rest, and it soon wore them down. They, too, began to fall. The soldiers who were well came nightly, if only to drink and escape the depressing illness infiltrating their camp. They found the music soothing, and our tent became a respite from the cold weather and stench of fever. I often made pots of tea and honey cakes to serve with their wine. It nursed their bodies and their lonely hearts.

We were more a shelter than a traveling show at that time; a needed distraction from the stress and loneliness of their camp, maybe even a kind of home away from their native land. I wondered if I was wrong to bring comfort to the Romans. After all, my people despised them. But I was no longer with my people, and they were the ones who stoned my mother for no wrongdoing. And Lucius, one of the few people I truly loved, was a Roman. These were my people now, and I chose to believe, in my still childish fantasies, that Lucius was my father. I wondered if he found refuge in tents such as ours. I longed to know if Lucius was alive and if he knew of Mother's fate. I feared my heart would never rest, for too many ghosts had set up camp within its fragile walls.

The soldiers regarded me as Seth's wife and, as such, I was shown a modicum of respect. I never enjoyed the benefits of marriage until this false one we concocted. How could I have been married to Tobias when Seth seemed more like God's intention for me? Here I was speaking of God again when I had so little faith left to me. Dance and music existed. That was all I knew with certainty. And there were good people in the world, and sometimes I believed I was one of them. But the world, at large, did not regard me as such.

It was at this time that a true break from my childhood teachings became clearer to me. I saw the hierarchy of the clergy as merely political, based on a financial position, something to be bought or handed down. These men of power wielded their influence as they saw fit and used God as justification. Tobias could buy his sanctity and beat and rape me. We were considered lowly prostitutes and fallen sinners when we only tried to survive and bring happiness to those around us. We were less than because we did not serve as they dictated and did not give them their due.

Or was it possible that we were inherently evil and only justified our lives? Who or what issued these decrees, and who decided? Are raping and stoning more pleasing to God than dancing? We were only trying to survive. The best person I ever knew, my mother, was murdered for only her heart's desire while living a righteous life. What kind of law creates these injustices? No God I would cherish would condone such actions.

This life was all I had, and I saw my new people as good and worthy. I would do whatever I could to help them survive, and I trusted they would for me. Eventually, and I know now that fate and my stars had their hands in this, I had to leave the comfort of my safe position. It fell on me to abandon my past and protect the livelihood of those I had come to love.

We heard some of the soldiers did not survive, and sadly two of our dancers did not as well. I cared for our girls as I had for Mother so long ago, praying they would pull through, but a few came close to the edge of demise. Our musicians, Makas, Seth, and I escaped the fever, but soon, all but one dancer fell ill. I seemed immune somehow, perhaps from caring for Mother so many years before, and it became evident that the girls who brought the soldiers into their tents were the most vulnerable. From there it spread. The last dancer standing, little Anna, was left to perform many nights without rest. The soldiers appreciated my nurturing food and tea and the copious amounts of wine, but they were bored and agitated and expected us to be a better distraction. They saw that Anna was too tired to dance with spirit, and they were impatient for variety. Seth and I feared for Anna's health if she did not get rest and considered closing the tent until we could move on.

The soldier of the highest rank sensed the growing unrest among his men. They were drinking more than usual in their boredom and had become rude and boisterous. Trying to find some distraction to bolster their morale, which was low due to the loss of comrades and fear of fever, he shouted out, "Can we not have Magdalena dance? We need a change and this one has become tired."

The other soldiers jumped on the notion and took up the chant, "Yes, have Magdalena dance!" they shouted. "Magdalena! Magdalena!"

Makas became concerned and protested that his daughter-in-law could not perform. It would not be proper. The soldiers laughed, believing us to be outside the rules and protection of ordinary customs. They paid their coin and felt they owned at least a part of us.

The captain said, "We will do her no harm but surely she is the only one well enough to dance. The men need variety."

Makas continued to argue gently, pleading against the idea. Seth could feel the tension and excitement building and put himself between the men and Makas.

"Magdalena is my wife," he said. "I cannot have her exposed."

Again, the soldiers laughed, stomped on the ground, and shouted for me to begin. The voices grew louder and the chatter more confusing. Seth knew it could turn violent if we did not appease them. Even if the tent survived, some of us might not. It would be difficult to pick up and move the tent from the area with the girls so ill. There was no telling what might happen with a group of angry soldiers set against us.

Seth spread his disarming smile across his face and tried to offer other ideas; perhaps they would like something new to eat. Maybe they would prefer a different type of music. But they would not stop, and their shouting took on a more threatening tone. They pounded the ground ferociously.

Seth then said, "She is a talented dancer, and I give my wife permission, but fully clothed and with me playing for her." He strongly emphasized the word "wife" to make his point. They did not own us or our time, and he wanted to make it clear he considered them guests in our tent, and this was his decision. They were paying surely, but we still ran our own lives. More than ever, I admired Seth's ability to bring calm and order to those around him.

The soldiers were satisfied, at least at the moment. I knew they wondered about me. Not all had been polite in their dealings, but they did maintain a sense of suitability regarding the old man and his son. And they did not want to risk the winter's entertainment pulling out of camp and moving on.

"We have respect for you and your father," the high-ranking officer said, "and for your wife, but entertainment is your business. We appreciate that you will have Magdalena dance for us."

It was clear the captain did not want trouble from his men. They were standing, stomping on the ground, and shouting loudly for me to dance. He needed to avoid a fight while protecting his relationship with us, not wanting to lose our hospitality. We were a welcomed diversion for his men through the winter season. With an air of grave command, he sat back calmly, folded his arms, and looked on respectfully. With this one act, he regained a modicum of order, and the men began to settle down. Despite my unease, I was impressed.

Fear and all of Mother's warnings flashed through me. I would hardly be thought shy, but I had spent most of my life hiding my true self from others. Now I would be revealed in ways I could not yet fathom. Seth handed me the veil I had fashioned for Anna. I clung to it as a child does its favorite blanket, hoping to hide behind its protection. I had no choice. There was no telling what might happen if I refused. I had to forget about the soldiers and let go of the shame that still clung so clumsily to my spirit. I needed to remember the beauty of movement and nothing else. I half-closed my eyes and let the rich colors of the tent wash over me. It was between me, Mother, the music, and nothing else.

Seth picked up his flute and joined the other musicians, taking a close seat to where I stood in a very protective manner. He led the others with a familiar and haunting melody. The beauty of his sound settled the soldiers, and they took their places on the cushions surrounding us, following the captain's lead. I stood on the carpet close to Seth and wrapped the veil around me. Lanterns of etched metal spread designs and more colors on the floating cloths above us. It created a magical atmosphere, one that made it easy for me to lose myself in imaginings.

I moved slowly, trying to hear only Seth and his flute. And then, the oddest thought came into my mind. They all thought they were watching me, but I was seeing them. I could read into their hearts and minds and could understand their intentions. I had the advantage as a performer. They would see what I showed them and nothing more, but I could look straight into them. These thoughts set me free. I lost inhibition, for ultimately, I cared not what any of them thought. After all, who were they to me? I saw they were all lost in themselves anyway. I cared about the music and the dance. I cared about Seth and my new tribe, not about them.

I felt a freedom I did not understand before that moment. Freedom comes from having nothing to hide, from living bravely in truth and giving up fear and pretense. This dance was a gift to me most of all. Dancing was my one enduring talent, and nothing they could do or say could change that. With these thoughts, I felt only joy. I moved freely from my heart. I moved as if I were with Mother and our lives had taken a different path, and we were together again in the loveliness of that moment.

My mind lifted higher, and I felt I was no longer a body. I was in the space between music and form, moving within the reflection in the stream. I was myself as only I knew myself to be. I would be considered a sinner and lost woman to anyone I knew in my past, but at that moment, I felt far beyond such judgement. For the first time since Mother's death, I was part of all that was good. At that moment, I was a soul without fear or contempt, ill will, or pride.

When the music stopped, I finished my dance and opened my eyes. The soldiers' faces shone with an odd kind of awe and gratitude. They lacked the lascivious looks I had seen so many times before. They felt the honesty of my love of movement for its own sake; the sincerity of owning one's truth, whatever that is. They recognized art even if they did not know it. Men who stand on a battlefield, an arena separating this life from the other, with the power to quell another's existence or end one's own, these men have a unique knowledge of life. I had struck that chord within them. They stood respectfully and threw gold coins on the carpet at my feet.

"Well done, Magdalena," they shouted. "You have hidden the best from us. Thank you."

"I cannot keep your coin," I said, fearing they might think they owned my time.

"You cannot refuse us. We appreciate your entertainment," the high-ranking officer said, and he seemed to hold an appreciation I rarely saw. "You are an honorable married woman. These coins are for the gift of your dance, for you are highly talented. It was a pleasure to watch you."

As we cleaned up, we gathered the many gold coins. I gave a third to Anna, who deserved it for all the nights she worked so tirelessly by herself. A third I gave to Seth and Makas, and I kept a third for myself at their insistence. Although I had no plans to leave that life and nowhere I could go, I remembered Mother's wish that I have money of my own in case I should ever be in need. The next day I sewed a sturdy purse of soft lamb's skin and tucked the coins away.

I truly loved the dancing, but when I went to bed that evening, I felt tortured and conflicted. Dancing was the best part of my life. Once I started, I no longer thought of the soldiers, and I became lost in the creativity that always nurtured me. I left the values of this world and made my own. But guilt has a strong hold on a mind, and I was confused. Even though I had always fought against these rules, they were the bedrock of my early life. I did exactly what Mother wanted to avoid. How could I defend my actions? Would there be a need? Surely she, of all people, would understand. My rebellious mind argued the point back and forth.

Music held much more weight for me than the thoughts of men. Was I not born to dance? Did not the stars claim me? Was standing naked and humiliated before a husband I detested, a man who caused my mother's death and nearly my own, better than dancing before strangers? A man who ruined any chance of motherhood for me? Why? Because of a marriage thrust on me without my consent by a corrupt priest and father who cared more for Tobias' money than his daughter's safety?

I could not stop my thoughts. I felt safe under Seth's protection, but what would the priests say of him? And with that thought, my mind set firmly. Any person who would condemn Seth would no longer carry weight in my heart. I would leave these old opinions behind for good and decide my truth. For, do we not all make a faith of what we believe and so craft it?

I thought again of Mother and Lucius and Zeus and what might have been but for rules and doctrines. A deep melancholy sat on my soul, and for the first time in a long while, I wept uncontrollably.

*   *   *

From that night on, the soldiers demanded I dance at the end of each evening. I still served their food and wine but closed the evening with the final song. Although I was still unsure of what I was doing, I found myself secretly happy with the opportunity to dance with all the musicians playing, to revel in the luxury and beauty of their sound. The soldiers were forbidden to approach me as they did the others due to my "married" status, and I did not wear a belt or transparent clothing. This status set me apart and this made me feel safer, but it created a distance from the other girls.

Finding my thick robe restricted me, I sewed a thinner one that was modest but flowed with my movements. Colored beads and layers of silk reflected the tent's lights and gave me a decent amount of cover. I felt I maintained my honor this way. But truth be told, no matter how one viewed it, I had become a dancer in a traveling tent; in most eyes, a soulless pagan, a harlot, and a lost sinner. I fooled only myself, and for but a little while.

It became a habit that the highest-ranking officer, Gaius was his name, would call for the evening to end, and I was the one to perform. He was the man in charge, and the others knew to leave once he had decided the night was over. Many needed the support of their comrades to walk back to their camp, some laughing, others cursing beneath their breaths, close to crossing the line between civility and disorder. Somehow, Gaius recognized the tipping point and the request for my dance was the signal that the evening had reached its end. As time went on, I learned a lot about men and their habits. Many of them chose only to drink and lie with the women. I considered them our best customers, as they spent the most and came every night. They were rough and arrogant and made me afraid. These soldiers reminded me of Tobias in their disregard for the girls or anyone they deemed less than themselves, but they were much stronger than my soft husband, and he would tremble in fear if ever they crossed him, as evil as I thought him to be. And then there were the lost and lonely men who tugged at my heart because I carried so much of the same pain within myself. Toward the end of the evening, after much drinking, some of the men would try to be inappropriate with me, but Gaius would put a stop to it immediately and call for the last dance. I became grateful for his protection, knowing that now that I was dancing, I had become more of a commodity. I was no longer regarded as just a married servant woman.

I found a rare few, the high-ranking captain most of all, possessed a higher mind and just desired time away from their camp and rounds. Gaius commanded respect by his very presence. He was there for the entertainment, the respite our environment offered, and to keep an eye on his soldiers. In time, Gaius began to remind me of a younger Lucius. He had the same dark sand-colored hair and eyes the color of a winter sky. He stood out from the others.

The kinder soldiers found solace in the music and the beauty of the dance. I like to believe they had art in their souls. They stayed until after I danced and then stood and cheered, respectfully laying coins on the carpet as they left. My joy and my treasure grew with each dance. Sadly, the kinder these men were to me, the harsher the girls became, except Anna. They came to resent the protection I received from Gaius and Seth and envied how easily my purse filled without having to lie with the soldiers.

* ELEVEN *

I T WAS A night like any other. The girls danced while I stayed in the background serving food and drink to the soldiers. As the evening drew to its end, I took my place for the final dance, as had become the custom. I was comfortable dancing, no longer worried about what anyone thought. I was more myself in those moments than at any other time. I was my mother's daughter, connected to art and spirit. I felt separate from my environment and all judgement of it, and yet in union with something much bigger.

I closed my eyes and followed the hypnotic rhythm of the music, but it sounded as if it were echoing from a far distant shore. My body felt fluid, no longer bound by the weight of flesh. I flowed within the vision in the stream, under the reflection, into the wisdom that had so often called to me and I had always tried so hard to understand. I was dancing to the songs of my mother's soul, merging with the darkness, past the light and without fear.

This infinite void then lit up with the radiant essence of my stars, and the light surrounded me, absorbed me, and led me into the timeless and abstract heavens. I became witness to the collective knowledge of every soul and event, as unimaginable as that may sound not having experienced it. I felt I had lived through all ages, in one form or another, merging with everything that had or ever will exist, as if all time happened in the same instant. Dancing in the totality of all my destinies, what had once been my body, was now a multifaceted crystal jewel consisting only of light. Each facet held a different aspect or story of me, a moment in my life. Without fear, I let each prism go, knowing none mattered. Nothing solid existed, only the pulsing, colored crystals that created a grand pattern of light. Was this the message these beads had always called out to me?

I remembered the merchant who turned into this light on the day he died when I was so young. Was I no longer alive? Or had I entered a place between time and death? I did not know, nor did I care. It filled me with tremendous joy and possibility beyond my limited imagination. What a small opinion we have of living. How could we conceive of a God who judges, who desires sacrifices, and who punishes? Love and creation surrounded me as I had never imagined it to be. I did not exist as a dense body. I was not mortal flesh. Each thought I had of myself was as useless as the facet of jewel dissipating and just as insignificant. Each image I held onto, right or wrong, good or bad, was just that; a story I could let go. None of it could haunt or hurt me again. I was free, made of the same substance as my stars, a part of the heavens themselves.

When I opened my eyes, I was on my knees with light tears rolling down my cheeks. I did not know what anyone had seen or noticed, nor did I have a clue what my dance looked like to others. As I gathered my wits about me, my gaze rested on Gaius. He leaned forward and stared into me and I felt I looked at him for the first time. I thought he also saw me.

Seth was concerned for me, but also very moved himself. Of course, no one knew my inner experience, but my dance had conveyed an unusual emotion. If nothing else, they recognized art over entertainment. The tent cleared, and the soldiers retired to their camp. Gaius and I locked eyes when he left. He wanted to linger and speak with me, but did not want to upset my "husband." I cleaned up and gathered the coins on the carpet, stunned by the amount before me.

What did gold have to do with the revelation I was just given? I was confused in a strange way. Two of the girls walked into the tent, and I felt their hostility as they eyed the pile of coins before me.

"Why is Magdalena stealing our job?" one demanded. "She is not even one of us."

Seth answered in a firm tone, "Magdalena is the one who saved our business when you were so ill. And she cared for all of you until you were well. You owe her thanks, not resentment."

"Look at all the gold she has taken. You always take her side over ours. We have been here longer and have worked harder. There will not be enough for us. She took advantage of our illness," the other complained.

After the glorious unity I had just experienced, this talk felt wrong. Is there not enough of everything for everyone? The heavens are without limit, as I was just shown. Why are my sisters speaking this way? I had a difficult time feeling my place back in the world.

"Are you concerned about gold?" I asked, and the girls just sneered, thinking I was mocking them. I filled my hands with coins and handed them to the women. "Here," I said, "If it is about money, please take it. This should not come between us."

How will women ever rise, I thought to myself, if we fight to deny each other?

The girls looked at me as though I had grown two heads, but they grabbed the gold and hurried out, afraid I would change my mind. I am uncertain whether they resented me any less, but the money assuaged their immediate anger.

Seth and I talked about all of this the next day, and I described what I had experienced. He understood as best he could. He was sure I received a message from the gods. Being Egyptian, he had many gods, and I knew nothing of them, but I believed something had happened that was not of this world. I felt a shift in my perception of many things that night, but could not describe it at that moment.

Seth also noticed the looks between Gaius and me, and he cautioned about getting involved with a Roman soldier. Nothing good would come of it, he warned, and I remembered both his experience and Mother's. Still, I dreamed of Gaius that night and many after.

Gaius continued to come to the tent every evening, but it was obvious something had changed in him as well. He was quiet and thoughtful, but always stayed until after I danced. At first, I could not look him in the eye, afraid I would betray my heart to anybody who saw me, but soon I found I could not avoid looking at him. I had no experience wanting a man in this way. Indeed, I had never wished for any physical intimacy before, and it was disconcerting. I did not understand how I wanted him or what any of it meant, but seemed drawn to him. I felt not only self-conscious and timid but also excited and anxious.

When our eyes met, I imagined I was looking into my own soul. He returned my gaze with as much wonder and directness as I did his. Now I understood what Mother felt with Lucius. The more I looked at Gaius and the more I got to know him, the more he reminded me of the only man my mother ever loved.

Then an awkwardness grew between us, and I did not understand my feelings. I had never been around someone I wanted to touch. I had been abused before I came into my womanhood. The closest I had ever come to fancying a man was Lucius, and that was with a child's innocence and admiration. Gaius was experienced and powerful, and it frightened, intimidated, and thrilled me all at the same time. I did not know how to even imagine being intimate with a man I liked and respected.

We shared an obvious physical longing for each other, but I was, in his eyes, a married woman. How could I explain this, and should I even try? For I was married, but not in the way he thought.

When serving him, if my arm accidentally touched his, I felt a sharp longing to have it linger. He would look into my eyes with the same hunger. I did not understand the physical sensations I was experiencing. I associated touch with terror and humiliation. This all moved something deep and artistic within me. A brush against Gaius' arm could take me to Lucius and the way he looked at Mother. It was a kindness and feeling I now longed for. I needed to experience everything about it. I wished to learn what touch without torture could be. Obsessed with these emotions, I had to confess my thoughts and feelings to my truest friend. Seth, of course, understood. He was no fool and had seen what was between us. He wanted me to know this kind of love and felt my life would be incomplete without it. But Seth worried what might happen to me, how I would be hurt, for, he knew I would be later if not before.

Still, it pained Seth to see me so tortured by this unmet desire. If Seth understood anything, it was this. His affection for me was so pure and kind that his only wish was for my happiness. I think he also felt, in watching our exchanges, that maybe Gaius was sincere in his feelings for me. For Seth would always have a heart that wanted to trust in love. He took matters into his hands and sat Gaius down and explained to him what existed between us. He avoided any mention of Tobias. He spoke of my saving his life and how we pretended to be married for my protection. Hoping Gaius was worldly enough not to hold prejudices against him, he explained his story as well.

Relieved by this revelation, Gaius confessed it upset him to think I belonged to another man. With this news and the heightened state of energy it produced, he never thought to question what I was doing on the road alone at night. Gaius then, with direction from Seth, found my alcove and walked through the closed curtain. I was lying down, still in my dancing robe but lost in thoughts and dreams, for I found it difficult to rest my mind after being near him. I gasped at the sight of him and sat up, folding my legs beneath me. My heart pounded so hard, I feared it would break my chest. I must have looked to him like a frightened girl with no experience in this realm. And I was. He walked toward me, his strength almost frightening, looking like the decorated soldier he was.

When he reached my side, his posture softened, and he was no longer the confident and indestructible Gaius. He was a man willing to make his heart known. When he was with his men, his eyes held a distant, detached gaze, one he had perfected for their sake and his ability to command. I only truly saw him after the dance that so affected me, when he looked at me as if to know me. As he came closer, he seemed almost vulnerable, and I could bear it no longer. At that moment, my heart was his.

I rushed into his arms and held him at last, without reservation, without fear. I would trust my body to lead me as it always had. They murdered my mother for a kiss, yet I no longer cared about the conse-quence. My life meant so little. Should I deny any pleasure offered to me before it ended? I would die for a night with Gaius, and some would say, I have.

I was naive to physical love, and it showed. I hesitated, the residue of trauma clinging to my flesh and spirit as I tried to respond to his touch. Gaius seemed to understand and treated me with the respect and caring of a girl on her first night. So much of what I was, of what I thought I was and what I expected to be, faded into the past. Never had I suspected, after the horror of being tortured by Tobias, that I could experience pleasure. Before that night, I did not even imagine the pleasure a person could know. I became a true dancer again, following his lead, blending into the rhythms of his beautiful body. But my mind struggled. Is this love? Why are there are so many rules against it? What could be wrong with this and right with the way Tobias handled me? Why was my mother murdered for less than this? I was confused, not knowing if I was wrong in my act, or accepting refuge in the arms of someone who actually cared for me. Yet, where I was at that moment, sin or no sin, damnation or not, it was where I wanted to be. I had no respect for the rules of the men who killed my mother. I damned those who considered us corrupt and worthless.

Gaius reached into my soul and touched my essence. All those nights of fantasizing and wondering could not have prepared me for the experience of being with him. None of my fantasies had the strength and mystery of what I felt. I had not realized, until he caressed me, how closed my body had become to touch, how traumatized my flesh had been. Dancing allowed me to remain viable, but only in his arms that night did I find true healing, did I reopen after shutting down from Tobias' humiliation and violence.

"My Magdalena," he said to me. "Although I have desired you for so long, I had no notion I could experience a gift such as this."

"Gaius," I whispered, "I had no sense this kind of pleasure existed. There is so much you must know."

"Not now, my love, that must wait, for I must get back to camp or they will think me a deserter. You are so innocent. I hope I have not done wrong to bring myself to you as I have. I could not bear to be without you any longer."

I shuddered at his statement. I had behaved as a girl with no experience making love, for until that night I had none. How would he take it, knowing I was still married under the law? Somehow, the strength of dancing had restored my youthful body, and he perceived me as untouched. In so many ways, I was, for never had a man held me with care or respect. I had been abused and used and beaten close to death, but I had never given myself to anyone before Gaius. I would have to find the time to tell him my truth.

But that moment did not come. He left me with such joy and love in his eyes, I could not bear the thought of that look ever leaving his handsome face. Each glorious night we spent together, I meant to tell him my past, and each time he took my leave with so much care and passion, my resolve faded, and I remained silent.

We spent the remaining nights of winter in each other's arms. I danced, and I loved, and I stopped looking back. Circumstances had changed for the better the day I left Tobias. The depth of change that took place within me the night of my transcendent dance, coupled with my joining with Gaius, made me think my life was now my own. So true, and yet so beyond what I then thought.

Although Seth was content to see me so happy, his life had taught him only disappointment. He was sad I spent my evenings with Gaius and no longer with him. He worried about the fall he was sure would come my way. Still, we found time to be together, as he was my dearest friend. Because of my relationship with Gaius, Seth felt free to be himself and not have to pretend he was a married man for my protection. It allowed him a few flirtations that winter, but they never manifested into anything of substance. After his initial heartbreak as a young man, Seth determined to never let another destroy his heart, but he did this with kindness and not bitterness. I sought to cultivate this trait in myself; a lesson that would serve me well in times to come. I watched as he picked himself up and tried repeatedly, each time bringing his best to everyone he met. If I could have had a son, I would have wished him to be like Seth.

But I could not bear a son, and I needed to find the courage to tell Gaius. As time passed and our feelings grew more serious, I thought I could keep it from him. I could live this new life and forget my past. It nagged at my spirit. I knew, in my soul, that it was a lie, and I was playing with the truth, but I tried to believe. As I was busy convincing myself, he told me he was being sent to Egypt and had to leave within a few short days. On hearing his words, my heart dropped like stone.

"Magdalena, my dearest love, do not look so worried. I will find a way for us to be together. I could never leave you now that I have found you."

Somewhat comforted by his words, a chill still crept up my spine. I could not go forward without telling him I was, in the eyes of most men, only half a woman, and a future with me would be a childless one for certain. I struggled many times to say what was in my heart, but I failed. Every time I tried, Gaius swept me into his powerful arms and laid me across my bed, making me forget I had ever been the girl I once was. How I wanted to believe it. I almost did.

Makas and Seth began preparing for the return to Rome. The weather was warming, and the conditions for travel were good. The girls were eager to greet different soldiers and additional sources of revenue. They needed costumes and veils and expected me to create them. Their resentment of me was clear, but they tried to hide it to secure my finest designs. But I was the protected mistress of the highest ranking and best-looking soldier in the camp, and a distance had grown between us.

How could I go to Rome with Gaius traveling to Egypt? After hearing this news, I could not sleep, not understanding what would become of me, of my heart. I clung to him at night and he to me as we struggled to make some sense of our future. Was this the end of our time together? Had we found such love only to lose it?

I prepared my things, packing them as I had all the other times we moved the tent, but my heart was no longer willing. My hands turned without thinking. I knew I was losing something important one way or another.

Two sleepless nights after he first told me of his plans, Gaius came to my bed and handed me a present wrapped in silk material. I smiled at him, for no one had given me an actual gift before that moment. But I feared this was his way of buying me off, of saying goodbye forever. As I slipped the cord from the cloth, I was stunned. It was a necklace made of gold and magnificent green stones that matched the color of my eyes. I held it up and marveled at its beauty as light danced through the clear gems. He picked it up and put it around my neck, kissing my shoulder.

"It does you justice," he said, "for it compliments your incredible eyes. Eyes I wish to look into for eternity. Magdalena, come with me as my wife. When we can go to Rome, we can be married at my family's home."

My mouth dropped open. Marry him? But what of Tobias? Did he still matter? Wasn't this a new life, a life where he did not exist? And what if I was wrong? Perhaps I could bear a child. Maybe our love was strong enough to overcome this improbability. Could I possibly avoid telling him? I struggled with my sin of omission, bargaining with my better self and struggling to find adequate words. Could I get away with pretending my past had never happened? Was I lying, or just owning my new life? Gaius took my unease and confusion as rejection of his idea, and a dark look crossed his face. Seeing his reaction, I lost all strength.

"I see I was mistaken, and this is not your desire," he said. "Perhaps you have been playing at love this whole time."

"No…no!" I shouted. "Not for a moment. There is nothing in this world I want more than to be with you forever. I cherish you, Gaius, more than I ever thought possible." Relief washed over him, and he pulled me close. I whispered, "I have never received a gift before, and I have not met such kindness before you." I started this way and thought I would then explain what I experienced in my former life, but Gaius was a man who now felt he had the world at his feet.

"Say no more," and he put his fingers across my lips. "Forgive me for not understanding. You have shown me nothing but the most beautiful devotion since we met. And soon you will be my wife. You have a depth I have never seen in a woman, and the ability to love that would be the envy of any man." His hand remained against my mouth in a hushing gesture, while his other slid down my torso. I lost all words. Perhaps speech and explanation had no use. Maybe none of it mattered. This was the only communication we needed, our bodies dancing together, our only truth.

Oh, silly girl that I was.

I told Makas and Seth about my plans the next day. They both said they were happy for me, but I could tell by their eyes they were lying.

While I was with them, they felt I was safe and cared for. I was family to them now, and they were with me, but I had to follow my heart. Neither of them felt this would turn out as I hoped or even as Gaius promised, but they both recognized I would not change my mind.

I met with Anna and gave her a small pouch with some of my coins.

"Anna, my mother always wanted me to have my own money should something ever separate us. Please take these coins and keep them hidden. I know you have your own, but I wish you to have enough. I want you to feel you have choices in life. I pray you never have need of them as I once did. I love you as my only sister. May your path be safe and happy," I said, and Anna wept.

I set out with Gaius and his special detail of men the following morning. Seth and Makas and my tribe in the tent headed toward Rome. We would travel apart, not to see each other again, and I could not bear the sorrow of leaving them. A second family lost to me. I fought my tears as I held on to Seth, not wanting to let him go.

"My brother, we will meet again. I know it," I promised.

I could see the doubt and resignation in Seth's eyes, but he said, "Then this will be, my sister, my dearest friend."

"Oh, Seth, the day I found you was the beginning of my new life. I love you with all my heart," I cried.

"Not all your heart," he said, smiling generously but not genuinely, and he turned me toward Gaius. "Now, be off with you and follow your handsome soldier to a new and brighter life." Seth was a miserable liar, and I knew he feared none of this would come to pass. He had a harder time than me in saying goodbye. I kissed him on the cheek and mounted the horse Gaius had given me to ride.

Despite the deep sorrow that sat on my heart, my spirits lifted once I stood before the lean, muscled stallion. I peered into his lipid eyes, and he looked back into mine. My affinity with animals had never left me, and he pushed his nose into my arm and I stroked him, the love I had for him moving through my fingers and into his flesh. He showed no resistance as I pulled myself up into the saddle. I sensed a familiar oneness with this horse of incredible strength and intuition. How many years had passed, how much misery and sorrow since I last sat on top of my magnificent Zeus? The physical excitement filled me as it had in my childhood. The horse, sensing my light weight, tested me, trying to discern my ability. He arched his back, and I allowed him his freedom and yet guidance as he flung his proud neck to see if he could take control. I met his challenges with my practiced movements, kind but firm, using the skills I learned when riding Zeus. Knowing I was capable as well as safe, he gave me the lead and seemed content with me at the reins. Gaius looked at me with utter surprise.

"I was afraid the horse would be too spirited for you." He laughed, "but now I fear it is the other way around."

I grinned. "I learned to ride as a child. It is one of my great joys," and I left it at that.

*   *   *

From the deep and haunted recesses of my mind, I saw the rocks flying again, spilling my mother's blood. These images would torture my dreams for the rest of my life. They would never leave me. Separating from Seth and Makas must have registered a much deeper loss than I expected, and as I watched the blood draining from my mother's lifeless body one more time in my sleep, I screamed. Gaius sat up and took me in his arms.

"What is it, Magdalena?" he asked. "Have you had an unpleasant dream?"

Unpleasant? Each time I had that dream, the horror of her death seeped deeper into the marrow of my bones. I would never be free of it. I sobbed uncontrollably for several minutes, my head buried in the crook of Gaius' hard, muscled shoulder, the shoulder I adored. At last, between sobs, I told him of Mother and of a Roman soldier and his magnificent horse; the story ending with the death of the most beautiful person I had ever known. I was short on details and was so upset, Gaius hesitated to ask questions. As he looked at me, I could not discern what thoughts crossed his mind. I hoped he would not, as my people had, think I bore a stain because of my mother's stoning. This fear, as undeserved as it was, had prevented me from ever speaking of her, so she had no life in his mind, the mind of my beloved. How strange that seemed. I wanted him to know her in whatever way he could, but I made the story short and said little of the soldier she loved. Did I feel a sense of shame at the manner in which they took her from me? I had so many emotions I needed to sort out in my heart. I was, on that evening, not yet sixteen years, and they killed her before my ninth. Almost half a lifetime without her.

"She sounds impressive," he said at last, to my great relief. "That Tobias deserves an early and gruesome death."

With those words, my heart seized. How could I tell him that Tobias had not only taken my mother, but any future children as well? I had no strength at that moment to confess all of my secrets, so I remained silent. The last of my tears dried on his tight, bronzed skin, and I fell back to sleep in the safety of his arms.

I was in no hurry to reach Egypt. I was living in a space separate from time, independent of the past, and with no thought of a future reckoning. It was a dream I wanted to last forever, a life renewed, without ghosts or the burden of sin. This was the closest I had come to any real happiness. Through the days, Gaius told me of the places we passed, and I marveled that such a world existed. I was awed by my worldly and knowing lover. In the evenings, we took rides in the open areas surrounding our camp, alone together. I felt safe in his love, wishing those days would never end. I was so removed from my past, it seemed to no longer matter. Like it had never been. Gaius looked surprised that I met each of my horse's challenges, perplexed that a woman could ride so well. We made it a game to race along the countryside, laughing, flirting with each other, enjoying the land, the stallions, and the passion we shared.

One extraordinary evening, as the sun threw brilliant color across the vast, open sky, we stopped to enjoy the moment and each other.

"You are a woman of great mystery, Magdalena. Never have I seen such depth and such skill in any person…and yet a girl. How have you come to be such an expert?" he asked.

"It was a magnificent horse that taught me." I smiled, thinking of Zeus. "He and I both loved to move, and we found our way together."

Gaius smiled. I became uneasy, as I felt he was about to ask more. I turned my horse to avoid what I perceived was coming and saw one of his men approaching us. "Gaius, look," I said, interrupting his thoughts. His man reached us in short time.

"Captain," the soldier reported, "Your uncle has arrived with his detail. They are headed toward Samaria to settle another uprising. He asked to see you, as he will set out at first light. We are caring for their horses and feeding his men."

"Good," Gaius said, in his voice of command. "I will come directly." He turned toward me as the soldier rode off. "Well, my darling, duty calls. You will soon meet my legendary uncle."

How odd, I thought. I knew nothing of his life before we met, just as he did not know of mine. In keeping the details of my story hidden, I saw it prevented me from learning about his. I never asked a single question about his way of life beyond what I saw before me, fearing any inquiry would invite questions about my own. We were strangers in so many respects, and yet I felt we were, in conditions of the heart, one and the same.

As we rode back, I made a game of keeping pace with him. He loved challenging me, and he delighted in how I met each nuanced change of speed. Although I could easily jump on and off as I pleased, I relished his powerful hands on my waist, and loved feeling small and feminine in his arms. What a game I played then, unaware that life would reveal I was the one with the greatest strength. But I giggled then, a silly girl, as he lifted me and placed me on the ground and into his embrace. Taking me by the hand, he pulled me into his tent, where his uncle was waiting.

I was laughing as I entered, but all humor left me the instant I saw who was before me. I froze, only my eyes moving, trying hard to clear them to be certain what I was seeing was real. Were they playing a trick on me? Was I only seeing what I wanted to see?

It was Lucius, our beloved Lucius, sitting on a cushion drinking a cup of wine. He looked much older and a scar traveled across his left cheek from the outside of his eye to his chin. A second dropped across his shoulder and down his chest. I shuddered to think what had happened to him in the years since I last saw him. I rushed to his side, tears running down my cheeks.

"Oh, Lucius, is it you?" I asked, and I threw myself on my knees before him. He looked at me with disbelief, but seeing Mother in my face, his shoulders shook and tears welled in his eyes.

"Is this possible?" he asked. "Is it you? Magdalena? I heard you were dead." He used his soldier's strength to maintain control, but I could see the great pain and yet relief in his eyes. I looked over at Gaius. He had a stern, confused look on his face.

"What is this? You two know each other?" he demanded, and I suspected he thought something apart from what was between us.

"Nephew, I knew Magdalena as a child," he answered, and I saw Gaius' face relax. "I was in love with her mother and wanted to marry her."

"Wait," Gaius shouted, his mind trying to make sense of what he was hearing. "My uncle is the Roman soldier your mother loved?" I nodded, as my voice was impossible to find at that moment.

"Rome dispatched us on a mission that kept me away longer than any of us thought it would," Lucius continued, looking only at me. "While saving one of my men, I was injured and sent home to Rome to mend. I tried sending messages to your mother through soldiers who were stationed close by, but none could find her. It took almost three years to get back, and when I returned, everything was gone. That bastard Tobias had murdered Rachel, and the fault was mine alone. I caused her death, and all that passed to you, and for this, I will never forgive myself." His face held such grief, I wanted to die in Mother's place. "I am sorry, Magdalena, although saying so cannot make up for what has happened to you."

"No," I cried, "Tobias caused her death, not you. You are the only person besides me she ever loved. You brought her more happiness in that short time than she knew in all her years before."

"That cursed man will harm no one again," Lucius answered. "When I heard what happened to your mother, and to you, I lost control. He begged for his life like the coward he was. 'Did Rachel beg for hers?' I asked him, as I drew my sword from his flesh. He is dead, Magdalena. He can never hurt you again. I thought you were as well. They told me you threw yourself over a cliff to escape him."

"Why escape him?" Gaius interrupted. "What did Tobias have to do with you besides cause your mother's death?"

He looked confused but sensed there was more to the story. Weeping, I crumpled at Lucius' feet, and he held me. My life had been tragic beyond imagination, and he blamed himself for all of it. The sight of his uncle in such distress made Gaius uncomfortable. He stormed out of the tent and left us alone for a good while, needing time to settle his thoughts. When he returned, I was sitting next to Lucius, not only relieved to see him alive but also afraid that now my secrets would be exposed.

"So, I am off to Samaria, Gaius, an unworthy assignment at the end of my career. It was not wise to kill the richest merchant in the city of my last post, but I could not let him live after what he did. There has been too much tension between Rome and these people under our command. If I survive, this will be my last mission, and I will return to Rome to lead a life I no longer want. The woman I will always love and the life I wanted are gone. Knowing you are alive, Magdalena, seeing your mother in you and all of her beauty has brought me a bit of peace at last."

Gaius was moved by Lucius' pain and passion, but did not know how to deal with this new information.

"I must leave you and Lucius alone to talk," I said.

I kissed both of Lucius' hands, washing them with my tears, and he stroked my hair with a reverence that left me unspeakably sad. Stumbling out of the tent, I wandered out to care for the horses. I patted them down and secured their blankets, making sure they were comfortable for the night. I led them toward the other stallions, and there I saw my dear and glorious Zeus. He looked a little less magnificent than when I had known him, but he remembered me. He nuzzled his nose against my shoulder, and I held him close to my heart.

"Oh, Zeus," I cried, on his still sturdy cheek, "save me as you always have." I cradled his head in my arms and held him for a long while.

Later, after Lucius left for his camp, I joined Gaius in our tent. My heart barely dared to beat. His first instinct was to hold me, and I softened in his arms. There was evidence of love between us, and his talk with Lucius seemed to help him understand my past better. Through the night, we spoke of Mother's death and of my near demise by the rock meant for her. I then told of Father and Abigail, and I explained about Tobias. When I described, in all truth, the horror of my life with Tobias and the nights of torture, Gaius shook with such rage it frightened me.

"Thank the gods my uncle killed that man," he shouted. "I should have liked to myself. But your father and his wife, they should be next."

These words stung my heart and my thoughts turned to Father. I had blocked him from my mind all this while, not having laid eyes on him since that morning after my first Godforsaken night with Tobias. In my child's mind, my father died the day of my mother's stoning. It was the end of any family life for me. Looking through Gaius' eyes, I could blame him for my fate, but somehow, I did not.

"But," I said, " fate has a way of winding its path, does it not? Had they not forced me to marry Tobias, I would not have run away. I would not have found Seth, and had that not happened, I would never have met you. Even if you believe I am no longer worthy of your love, these times with you have made my life worth living. It is the only happiness I have known without Mother."

My words moved Gaius, and he held me in a strong embrace. "That man is dead. You are no longer married and are free to take a husband. Lucius has done a good deed for the daughter of his beloved."

Was this possible? Could Gaius still want me? Still cherish me? Whatever the consequences, my conscience was finally clear. Lucius was alive and I felt some part of my mother still lived within him. And Gaius, my lover and my soul, he was different that night. His passion was unbridled, though not as tender, as if he had to purge demons from my body. He swept me away with a carnal, sexual power that surprised and thrilled me. He kept at me with such stamina I felt I would faint, but with a joy this tainted flesh had never imagined. We finished, exhausted in each other's arms, two bodies made to fit together. But in the depth of my soul, I knew everything had changed.

⋆ TWELVE ⋆

AT FIRST LIGHT, I walked to the sheltered grove where the horses were tethered and found Lucius standing next to Zeus, preparing to leave.

"Sweet Magdalena," he said. "At least you are alive and under the care of my nephew. Gaius is a good man, a magnificent soldier, and someone who will keep you safe. How curious that fate would find you with him. May you share the life I should have had with Rachel." He was subdued in a way I had never seen in him. So much of Lucius must have also died with Mother.

"Oh, Lucius," I cried, thinking more of myself than his pain. "Do you think Gaius finds me spoiled, knowing now the truth?"

A look crossed his face, one he tried to hide, and he gave me a half-hearted smile. I had seen too much in my short life not to recognize his expression. But denial is a powerful potion.

"Magdalena, you have done no wrong. Even if you had killed that man in his sleep, you could not be blamed. Perhaps Gaius will take time to understand what it all means, but you are blameless. If anyone is at fault, it is I."

Lucius then reached into a sewn leather sack tied on Zeus' saddle and pulled out a narrow pouch. I noticed, with melancholy delight, the worn but still beautiful blanket Mother had woven resting on Zeus' back. That it still existed, and she did not, was incomprehensible. He closed my hands around the small bag and said, "Please, I owe you and Rachel so much more than this. To even think it has a monetary value is an insult to the truth, but I know she would want you to have something to count on if ever you should need it." I was so absorbed in his love for my mother and his incredible grief that I gave no thought to the concern that lived behind his words. "I told her I wanted to care for you both," he continued. "Take this and keep it to yourself. Do me this favor, so I can try to find peace in what remains of my life. I beg the gods to allow me to see you again and care for you better than this."

I could not find sufficient words, but I knew refusing would only sadden him, so I took the pouch and threw my arms around his neck, kissing him on the cheek. His pain was so palpable, I could feel it in his flesh.

I cannot fully describe the feeling I held as I stood before Lucius again, wrapped in his arms. I had only known him as a child, and a remarkable amount of time had passed. We were both so much older. It pained me to see how he had changed, and yet I knew the grief of Mother's death and life without her had aged me as well. I wondered how we both would look if she had lived, and we had shared a life together. Looking at him with the eyes of a woman, I recognized more than ever what an extraordinary man he was. As he held me, I felt his incomparable strength and inner power, and I knew I was safer in is arms than I had ever been. He was a man I could and did love. Perhaps the greatest love of my life.

"Lucius, she loved no one in the way she did you. You meant more to her than you can know. And to me as well," I said, almost shy again.

"If it is half what I felt, it is beyond the luck of most men," he replied. "I can never forgive myself for what I caused you and your mother."

I protested, but he placed his fingers on my lips.

"I was so taken with her, I could not help but pursue her. It was only out of love and admiration. I should have understood the risk, and I overestimated my power in the situation. I see now how selfish I was." He looked away, and we both feared a tear might again fall from his eye. "Hide the coins even from Gaius."

I tucked them deep into the folds of my robe to his satisfaction. Gaius then approached us, and he wished Lucius luck and success on his mission. The high esteem he held for his uncle was obvious. We watched as Lucius leapt on Zeus, still with the commanding grace I had always admired, and he rode off without looking back. Gaius kept his gaze on him, sad to see him go. I averted my eyes for a moment, unwilling to watch Lucius ride out of my life one more time. When I looked up, an eerie dread took hold of me. Life would no longer yield to a future. Grief would have felled me at that moment if I had given it its due. But, once again, needing to survive, I danced with denial, blocking my gift of intuition. I looked away, refusing to admit what I perceived in the deepest sanctuary of my heart. The image of Lucius froze in time, and my spirit realized he would not make it back to Rome.

We were just a few days' ride from Alexandria. The nights held a conflicting combination of passion and fear. Gaius' desire for me increased, as if he needed to erase any trace of another man from my body. But his lovemaking was different—rougher and more demanding. At first, his fervor excited me. But it seemed much less personal, as if I could be any woman beneath him. And the sweet innocence with which he once held me was gone. Deep into the nights, loneliness seized me. I was so far from Seth and Makas, a lifetime away from Lucius or anyone who cared about me, and I felt Gaius' love for me changing by the day.

When we arrived in Alexandria, it was like entering a magical new world. It felt exotic and foreign, and the possibility of beginning a fresh life and a different story seemed possible. My worries gradually faded. The Egyptians set us up in a home overlooking the sea. It looked a palace to me, a girl raised in a one-room house in the orchards, but Gaius assured me it was a shelter suitable for a Roman of his stature. His detail made camp outside the gates, and a few of his high-ranking men built posts around the city. They would remain after we moved on.

We had an enormous bed with silk netting hanging on all sides and covered with fine light blankets and sheets of soft cotton. Even Tobias' extravagant prison held none of the elegance and comfort of this exotic dwelling. From our bed, we could look out through massive stone pillars to the open sea beyond. A gentle breeze kept our chamber cool and airy. Servants brought bowls of fresh fruits and dates each morning with pitchers of clean water and wine. We ate and drank while watching the colored sails of ships coming to and from port.

I felt I was living in a dream I never imagined could be mine. I wondered if Mother knew such things existed outside her imagination, and I described them to her in my thoughts. Believing we had returned to our former closeness in this little paradise, I became blissfully cheerful. We laughed and teased each other and had long hours alone in each other's arms. Gaius also seemed pleased in our foreign oasis. Once again, the child in me picked up the lead, and I believed all was well.

Paradise did not last. It was interrupted by Gaius' fits of rage.

"How could you keep this from me, that you were married, that you could not bear children?" he would shout at me.

I tried to explain my sense of shame, my confusion, and my overwhelming love for him. I had been so very young when this was thrust on me, inexperienced and unprepared. The blame was not mine. Maybe I could bear a child. Perhaps it was only my hatred and revulsion of Tobias that prevented it. I argued to Gauis' scorn.

"I was but a child, a girl with no choice or decision," I cried. I explained I had never felt the touch of passion before, and in every good way, I had never been with a lover before him. All these things had tied my tongue, and for this, I was sorry, but, he had to know the only man I ever loved, could forever love, was he.

This would melt his anger, and we would lie together as in our past. I would think the matter settled, and we had an understanding. Peace would reign for several days and then, after a night of drinking with the other soldiers, it would begin anew. I would beg for his forgiveness, ask for his sympathy, and remind him that Lucius himself knew it was not my fault. This is what life did to young girls. The actual crime belonged to the men who believed they owned me. My only sin was in being born a woman. This would bring forth his compassion and I would feel safe again…for a while.

While Gaius was busy with his soldier's duties, I walked for hours around the city. Alexandria was an intriguing, civilized, but complex world. Everything about it awakened my senses. I found it strange they worshipped so many gods; some were even part animal and part human. This confused me, but my mother's thoughts and opinions had prepared me to be open to things I could not understand. I supposed the Egyptians were what my people thought of as pagans, but they seemed uniquely intelligent, and that made me wonder about the judgements that people make of others. I sensed a knowledge and wisdom behind their beliefs. My uncertainty over my relationship with Gaius clouded most of my thoughts, so I tried to settle my mind with these long walks. My unending anxiety caused me to miss Seth more than I thought possible. Thinking the Egyptians would all remind me of him, I was surprised that the men did not look very different from those in my city. They did not have Seth's lanky build or his fine, chiseled features. I wondered what made him so distinctive.

As I thought about it, I realized he considered himself Egyptian because it was where he was born. As an orphan, he never knew his parents. His was a country of vast trade and merging cultures. I wondered if his mother had been a prostitute and his father unknown to her. He could be anything or anyone. His tall forehead and lighter eyes hinted of something foreign, but his sharp intelligence had to come from this unique Egyptian environment. I decided I needed to know everything about his homeland.

I walked to the grand library many times. People said it was the biggest and most comprehensive in existence. Since I had no experience with such things, I believed it. Of course, I could not read or speak their tongue, but I picked up information from travelers from my side of the desert. They considered Alexandria the great learning center of the world, famous for its scientists, astronomers, and physicians. This was a different world from anything I had ever experienced. The city itself seemed to be a work of art. The lighthouse especially fascinated me, and I walked to it daily. I had heard tales of the Great Sea, but to feel its expansive power and vitality awakened my spirit in new ways. I spent hours sitting at its edge, staring into its endless expanse.

As I wandered through the markets, I noticed women were freer in Egypt than in my homeland. They could wear their hair as they wished, sometimes long and free, but most often tied in wonderful ornaments on top of their heads. The climate called for lighter clothing and freer movement. They wore light, gauzy gowns that flowed as they walked to allow the air to cool their bodies. Some of their gods were female and were worshipped as highly as their male counterparts. This both shocked and delighted me. I came to believe Seth's opinion that dancing was an accepted art form, as women seemed less judged and more liberated here.

I was interested in knowing about Isis after hearing she was the goddess of mothers and children. I could honor her for the memory of my mother, but I feared even Isis could not help me bear my own child. Still, I begged for her mercy. Though I was not a follower of hers, and she had no allegiance to me, I pleaded with her to change my fate. I visited her temple daily, hoping my devotion might persuade her. Then I learned she was also the god of sinners and the poor, and I feared this was how she regarded me. But it comforted me to know there was a god somewhere who would befriend a lost and fallen girl.

I forgot myself in the temples and buildings and felt expansive when I was out and about. But I became small again when I entered our chamber. I lost my sense of self and waited with frayed nerves to see how Gaius would feel about me when he returned, and therefore, how I would feel about myself.

*   *   *

After a welcomed month's reprieve, we had to leave Alexandria. Gaius received orders to travel up the great river to Memphis. I was never told what their business was in Egypt, whether they were to collect fees or merely maintain a Roman presence. Although I should have felt ashamed, I cared nothing about the reason or the benefit to Rome. I was sad to give up what I thought of as our haven in Alexandria and the tranquility of the sea. But being so inexperienced in the world, the adventure of it soon took hold of me. We boarded a barge, the likes of which I could never have dreamed existed. I was a child in wonder as I climbed onto it. They decorated it with gold paint and carvings of birds with great orbs above their heads and jackals with human bodies. These Egyptians did everything with precision and detail and grandeur. Everything seemed bigger, even the sky above us, where the sunsets blazed richer and deeper than any I had seen. I felt an ever-expanding fascination with the world around me.

We traveled by water for several days. Our nights were quiet and tender again, but the rest of the time, Gaius greeted me with cold, unmasked anger. The more he thought of my past, the more I became a stranger to him. Our physical fascination with each other did not leave when we were alone together, but with his men, in his role as an important captain in the Roman army, I no longer seemed to fit. I became too anxious to eat and could only sleep when I was in his embrace.

Though I was filled with fear and anguish, the days also brought wonder and delight. This unusual land held a magical feeling, one that went beyond what my eyes could see. My body, always a measure of my surroundings, felt open, as if, despite my personal life falling apart, some force was stretching my heart in new directions.

Sailing up the river, we sometimes passed the ruins of ancient shrines. There they stood, homages to some grandeur of the past, almost miraculous in their architecture and scale. To the men, they were impressive and grand, and I would agree, but in my heart, I found them shallow and vain. Their ruler erected them to serve his vanity, his riches, and power over others. These temples celebrated their kings with the forced labor of poor, downtrodden workers. Where was the temple of spirit? I wondered. And then I questioned why such a thought would come to me.

When we arrived at our destination, Gaius and I were set up in another house, this one even more opulent than the one before. It contained many rooms, and we were treated with respectful contempt by the servants who were made to wait on us. I was told we were in one of the oldest cities of Egypt, a place of great importance. We pretended to go on as we had before, acting pleased with the luxurious surroundings, but I felt more estranged from Gaius with each day that passed.

Soon, messages came from Gaius' family in Rome. After each scroll, Gaius began bringing back treasures he found for me in the city. He presented them in bed at night; bracelets of gold and precious stones and jeweled rings for my fingers. He was loving in those moments, and I sensed a great sorrow in him. It seemed he felt regret over how he often acted, about the unreasonable anger he unleashed on me. I saw these gifts as apologies for his roughness and his unkind words. I believed things might become right again between us.

Gaius became absorbed with his duties and left me alone a great deal, so I spent most of my time walking and exploring this new city, as I had in Alexandria. It took my mind off the immediate worry of my life, and I could pretend I was happy. I thought if his soldier's business could satisfy Gaius, and I was no burden to him, we would become as we had once been. This went on for a season, although the climate was so temperate it was difficult to tell by any change in weather. The Egyptians marked the seasons by the rains and rise of the river, different from what I was used to. I missed the open sea of Alexandria, and I missed Gaius. I tried to avoid any thoughts of the future or the past, for both haunted me.

Gaius entered the room one evening, more energized and happy than I had seen him in a long while. In those turbulent times, his moods always affected mine, and it lifted my heart to see him so enthusiastic. He and a few of his higher-ranking men would soon make a journey to inspect the strange and ancient structures rising from the desert floor; a two-day ride from the city.

"You have spoken so much of these structures. Perhaps you would like to join me?" he said.

"Oh, Gaius, I long to visit them. Yes, yes, thank you," I cried, as excited as a child. I put my arms around him in delight. My youth and exuberance were often the reasons he found such refuge in my love, and he grinned.

I was thrilled. I had been curious about these structures since we first arrived in the area. It seemed everyone had some grand tale about them. Most said they existed long before anyone could remember, some saying longer than time itself. I laughed at such a notion, but everything I heard intrigued me, and I had the greatest desire to see them. But if I remain honest, the overriding emotion for me was my hope that this trip would make all things right again with Gaius. My relationship took precedence over any knowledge or insight I might gain. I was such a young and mistaken girl.

He was warm and tender to me as we prepared for our journey, and I was feeling happy and secure, Gaius delighting in my enthusiastic telling of the tales and legends I gathered on my walks. In a few short days, we headed out on horseback and had a small contingent of guides to lead us and carry our supplies. Gaius rode ahead with his top man, and I stayed back with the others. I rode a good part of the time but often got off to rest my horse and walk along beside him, especially during the heat of the day when I hated to add burden to the poor creature. He was kind, but old and tame for my liking, having been used to the likes of Zeus. But I cared for him and felt his needs, and he was responsive in kind. And I liked to feel the earth beneath my feet, for it had a unique hum and vibration to it. I could feel its rhythm and often got lost in my thoughts and musings. In my mind, I created dances celebrating the land I crossed. I heard songs my mother might have sung. I found movement everywhere except in my heart. And this should have concerned me.

I became friendly with the oldest and slowest of our guides, for it seemed whenever I sank into my deepest reveries, I would find him next to me. I often lost myself in daydreams similar to those I experienced looking into the stream as a child, higher thoughts not of this world, but of a better place. When my thoughts became so transcendent, I could not know them as my own, I would look up and see him smiling at me. Often, he hummed or chanted some sound I did not recognize. He walked separately from the other guides, and I assumed it was because he, as well as the camel he led, were much older and slower than the horses.

He was a wizened man with failing eyesight, his skin drier and more lined than the hide of the camel he led to carry our water. Yet, a kindness came from him that set me at ease. He told me stories along the way—strange, entertaining, preposterous tales—the kind that made time go by quickly.

"You are interested in the pyramids?" he asked, early the first morning, as we walked.

"Why yes, the pyramids," I answered. "You have seen them before?"

He smiled and his cloudy eyes almost twinkled. "Many times," he said.

"What are they like?"

"People perceive what they want to see," he continued. "Most do not recognize the true power. They find them intriguing and wondrous, even hard to comprehend and perplexing, but nothing more."

"What is the truth then?" I asked, feeling he was teasing me. Yet, for some nebulous reason, I trusted the man.

"They came from a venerable culture, one that stood at the dawn of time itself; the Sons of God. Most have forgotten them, or perhaps never knew they existed. This was very long ago."

"What was their purpose?"

"Ah, now that is the part most do not understand. The Ancient Ones possessed great power; God given. They used the pyramids to control the workings of the earth, the weather, and the laws of nature, but only for the common good." His words stretched my imagination, but it seemed everything about me was being disassembled. I found solace in the old man's company.

Truth tellers had told him tales of the pyramids since he was a small boy. To look at him, I thought that must have been a long while past. He looked a hundred years if a day, and I marveled he had the stamina to travel the desert as he did.

He was eager to share his stories with me, believing I was the one who would understand them. More than likely, I thought, he knew I was the only one who would listen. He spoke in a low, hushed voice, and I sensed he did not want anyone else hearing what he said. It made me sad to think the others would consider him a fool. I realized they would as readily laugh at me for sharing his foolishness. But I found him charming, entertaining, and of good heart. What harm was there in allowing an old man his fantasies? It was obvious he relished these tales of an ancient race who upheld what he called the Divine Mysteries, and had the tools and knowledge to manage the balance of the earth and sky. When he continually included women in his ramblings, it easily seduced me into paying greater attention. Just the thought of it, imaginary or not, made me happy.

"The Ancient Ones built these pyramids as temples for initiation. The power they wielded, and their expert knowledge, are no longer known to this world," he went on. "Women and men studied and served, yet few rose to the highest level. All the people benefited from the wisdom of these initiates. They were the guardians of the land and assured the abundance and health of the citizenry."

Even if only a tale, his stories guided my mind beyond my self-centered worries and into better thought. I wanted to believe women were also eligible for these sacred rites; to think there was a time and place that existed where we had the respect I felt we deserved. I was not allowed into the inner sanctum of my temple as a child, let alone share in any blessings that might be had.

"Egypt was a different place in the long distant past, countless generations before it fell under lesser men's control," he continued. "Kings have come and kings have gone. Some claimed them as their tombs, wanting the grandeur and mystery of the pyramids to reflect their names and grant them immortality. These were not the men who understood their purpose and function, knowing nothing of the Divine Mysteries. Arrogance and pride filled these lesser men. Over the years the power of the structures lowered, for without the ancient rites and knowledge, without the Initiates, their energy waned. They were no longer used for higher purpose. Although memories of the ancient rites have been lost, it cannot completely change the true nature and meaning of the pyramids. They cannot be claimed by proud and ignorant men forever," my guide declared. He said it with such conviction, I almost believed him.

"These were the very kings who tried to erase from history the known power of the feminine. They wanted nothing to dilute their hold on the people. They allowed stories of female gods for a short time to appease those who remembered, but little by little, they blocked these memories by decree. I am sure you have seen evidence of the female gods. Some cannot be dispelled altogether, but they were overshadowed by the men who ruled the land. The pharaohs declared themselves gods. They misused their rule, denying any power higher than their own." His eyes became almost clear, and he looked different as he told these stories he held so dear.

"The Sons of God disbursed when man's quest for domination corrupted society. Knowing the rulers would usurp their knowledge for personal power and not the common good, the Initiates left and took their abilities with them. They scattered to the far edges of the earth. They settled among men and went about their work unrecognized for what they were."

His stories made more sense to me than anything else I heard in my life. I wondered what Mother would have thought of this. I could not help but think she would find it fascinating.

"Some mated with common people, thus mixing the races. Some left earthly bodies behind and worked from another level of existence altogether."

With this, I stood still and stared at him, wide-eyed and suspicious. My look of utter confusion seemed to amuse him. "How is that?" I questioned, with an edge to my voice. He had lost me with this preposterous notion.

"You will understand in time," was all he said.

His words made no logical sense, and yet somehow, I resonated with them in a profound way. I watched his eyes light up as he told these stories he trusted with all his heart, his vision seeming to come from faith in what he believed, not from anything he saw before him. What a lovely thought, to believe women were the equal of men; that they were learned and respected. I found it comforting to be around this old man, for he inspired a stronger part of me. Even if his tales were pure fantasy, they were better thoughts than my mind held.

A half-day's travel from our destination, we stopped at a tomb in what seemed like the middle of nowhere. The men had no interest in it other than to rest their horses and take some nourishment, so they ate and drank and carried on with their soldiers' talk. I was so filled with anxiety, I could not relax or eat. I was anxious about Gaius, who all but ignored me through the days and was now distant through the nights. He and I both wondered why he had asked me to join his expedition, for I seemed a bother to him. The weariness of my thoughts exhausted me.

I wandered around the simple building to get a better look. Why, I wondered, would anyone place a monument so far from people who might pay respect? It stood isolated within a stark and barren landscape. I entered the tomb, not knowing what I would find. It was a two-room structure, not especially opulent. There were no impressive statues, just carved writings on the walls in the odd pictures and script of the Egyptians. It was not large but there was something majestic and important about it. I sat on a ledge in the first chamber and closed my eyes.

My blood ran cold, and then my lips, arms, and legs grew numb. A tingling sensation crept over my face and I trembled. My chest pounded as if a small bird were trapped within my ribcage and fighting to escape. Crystal jewels of light spun around me, moving in sequential patterns, each one reflecting an image or story I could not decipher. Images came in dizzying patterns, each significant and with meaning, but I understood none of them. I could not comprehend their meaning. I was disoriented, as if lifting from my physical body, moving upwards again as opposed to falling down, without reference to anything around me. Confused and yet stimulated, I felt of two minds, one the observer and one the person observed. Whose images were these, and why were they being shown to me? My heart pulsed stronger and faster than seemed possible for my small body. Yet, despite this physical upheaval, I filled with joy, feeling almost giddy. I was ready and willing to leave this world for good, to forsake my body and happy for it, longing for death's comforting embrace, when Gaius entered and broke the spell.

In a deep, condescending tone, he asked, "What are you doing alone in this tomb?"

I paused for a moment and could not recover words. I needed to settle back into my body and clear my thoughts, but Gaius lost patience with me. Struggling to regain my composure, I fought to find my voice.

"Seeking relief from the heat," I lied, unable to meet his eyes. I realized I was afraid to share my deepest revelation with this man I so loved. This caused me to wonder about the meaning and nature of love. Can it exist without truth? I was now a stranger even to myself.

"Come along, Magdalena, we need to leave," he said, and he held out his hand to lead me back to our horses as he would to a petulant child who needed his guidance.

Every part of me wanted to stay. I was desperate to understand the images I had just witnessed. I felt I was being ripped away from something important to my life and growth. But my small human mind, the one I wore so clumsily at that time, returned, and I disavowed everything I had just experienced. I must have been dizzy from lack of food and rest. Perhaps it was the heat. Perhaps…

That evening, the guide found me by the horses and tapped my shoulder. "So," he said, "I see Ptahhotep has communicated with you."

I looked at him. "What can you mean?"

"You visited the tomb of the high priest, Ptahhotep. He was the greatest Initiate ever to live and rule over Ancient Egypt in the Great Age. Even now, he reaches out to souls who seek; to those with vision. When needed, he comes back in a distinct form, in a different body."

I looked at the old man with curiosity and annoyed suspicion. Who was he, and why did he tell me these things? His words were preposterous. They only fed my confusion. I became irritated with him, but I was unsure why. How did he know about my experience or that I had ever had any visions? Who was this funny little man? He was a person most would dismiss as insignificant—old and poor—someone who made his life leading a camel about the desert. By and large, he was invisible and of no consequence. And yet, he seemed to know what happened in the deepest parts of me. Was the heat of the desert affecting my mind, or was this strange little guide amusing himself by playing with a girl he thought was simple? Was I that easy to see through? And yet, how did he know?

"I cannot follow what you are saying," I said defensively.

"Do not be afraid." He answered in a calm, reassuring voice. "The images can be confusing. It takes time to learn. That is how they communicated with each other, how they still do."

I became angrier and turned my back on him. These ancients he spoke of had been dead for generations, if they ever existed. How could they be communicating? But what were those images? And how did this little man know I had seen them? And why the crystal jewels again? I turned back to face him, filled with questions, but he was nowhere to be found.

Early the next day, I could see the grand structures rising out of the desert sand, and it began again, the sudden quickening and pounding of my heart as I had felt before. Now it came with greater force, as if I were nearing the source of some power I could not understand.

By mid-morning, we reached the base of the Great Pyramid, the largest of the three structures. I could not speak. I could not eat. My body trembled with a curious excitement. Gaius was busy with his soldier's business and never noticed me or my reaction. I sat with folded legs facing the structure, and it filled my mind again with strange and foreign images for which I had no words.

I became anxious and unsettled, so I walked toward the largest structure, as if pulled in its direction. I ducked into a slight opening in the pyramid's side and stepped onto a slope. Without thinking, I crawled deeper inside to a short, walled landing that led up to a steep, narrow crawlspace. The ramp had thin strips of rock carved systematically where I could place my hands and feet. Using them, I climbed in a deeply crouched position up a long, inclined corridor. I crawled up, using my hands and knees and feet in ungraceful reaches, and the higher and deeper I went, the thinner the air became. I felt hot and lightheaded.

I became afraid, for I was entering deep within a solid structure and did not know what I might find once the passageway ended. I wondered if there would be air to breathe or if I would faint before getting back down, and I saw the absurdity and foolishness of my actions. Should I slip and fall onto the earth below, would it matter to anyone? Why was I compelled to continue? I was becoming more and more confused, but I carried on. My back ached from the crouched position needed to make it through the low, narrow passageway. In despair, I surrendered and tried to back down, but I could not see where to put my hands or feet. There was no room to turn around, and I panicked.

Gasping for breath, more from fear than lack of air, I came at last to a chamber at the top of the passageway. It was small, but the walls were very high, and I could stand straight at last. There was a raised bed of stone, large enough to lie upon, an altar of sorts, and nothing else. But there were no bloodstains in evidence, and I doubted any creature had been sacrificed in that room. I wondered what its purpose might be. There was no window, for I was deep within the top center of the structure, but somehow, there was light.

I stood there, transfixed. Being in that room was like standing outside of time, as if it did not exist, as if I had never been anywhere but there. And then the trembling began again with uncontrollable force. Something of great significance took place in that room. I knew it, but I could not, in any way, explain it. I shook as the images flew repeatedly through my mind's eye, the faceted beads spinning about, suggesting stories and lives I could not understand. I felt my mother around me as if I were once again within her womb. An increasing energy pulsed through my person, and it soon overwhelmed me. I did not belong there; this became clear. I needed to leave, for I was not wise or strong enough to understand or control what was coming at me. My heart raced so fast, I knew my body could not hold up to the force of it. The images came faster, my mind spinning until I felt I was losing consciousness. In great fear, I tumbled and crawled backward down the ramp and onto the desert floor below. I ran back to our camp and found Gaius with his men. I was so shaken I was sure my face had no color to it at all.

"Where have you been?" Gaius asked, without affection. "I was thinking a jackal had taken you." I wondered if he wished one had.

With a faint smile, I told him I had just been for a walk around the pyramid. Another truth withheld from my beloved.

"Strange, is it not?" he said, and I just shook my head.

He was oblivious to my obvious distress. There was no way I could explain what I had just been through. He would not have understood, and would have laughed at my childish imaginings. To Gaius, these structures were a conquest for Rome, for whatever use I was sure he did not even care.

Gaius stayed out that night, drinking with his men and discussing the land and its benefits to Rome. I sat alone and stared ahead. I could not face away from this thing that pulled at me with such force. It would not let me go. When Gaius came to bed, I saw he was sleepy with wine. I was glad, as I did not want his touch. My body felt too energized to think of being used in that way. I stroked his head until he fell asleep, and I faced the Great Pyramid, my heart stretched wide, my mind a flurry of thoughts and pictures I did not understand.

I fell into the twilight between waking and sleeping, that precipice between thought and knowing. A quickening hit me suddenly, coursing through my body as if a bolt of lightning had struck me. Once again, the images flooded my mind as they had in the tomb, and I recognized the writings on the walls. I saw them, but could not understand. I grasped that someone or something was communicating with me, or maybe the communication was always present, and I had just stumbled onto it. But then, the quickening and images withdrew as quickly as they began, and I felt abandoned. The loneliness left in their place was as sharp as any I had ever known.

A voice that had no sound, whispered. "You could not have survived more.

"Why am I seeing these things? What do they mean?" I asked aloud, to no one.

I received no answer. I made no sense even to myself, if I ever did. I had feared so often on my trek through the desert that my mind had forsaken me. I now believed it had. Without comfort, I fell into an exhausted and dreamless sleep.

We traveled back to the city, each absorbing the wonder of what we had seen at the site of the pyramids. My old guide and I barely spoke, but he smiled at me often with a twinkle in his cloudy eyes. I had no words. What was there to say?

I looked around and watched the others in our party. They seemed unaffected, and yet, I had changed. I did not know how, or why, or to what use, but I was different. Like my message from the man who sold us wheat when I was a child, the merchant who died after I saw him turning into light, these experiences were profound and visceral. I tried to understand the reason these pictures had come to me. They were living replays of events, not limited by the ability of the person interpreting them. Was I receiving someone else's experiences directly rather than a description of them? Was this some elevated form of communication like the guide said? I felt I no longer belonged to anyone or anything; no longer familiar with the world I inhabited. I searched for my old friend but could not find him, and then I felt guilt over the anger I had shown him the day before.

As we rode back to our post, the mystery of the pyramids faded from my mind, and the worry of my circumstances plagued me once again. I had hoped our journey would recreate intimacy between Gaius and me. It seemed to bring him closer to his men and further from the person I was. Where it brought me, I could not yet fathom.

When we arrived, I looked everywhere for my guide, wishing to see him one more time and take his leave after my rude behavior the day before. I felt closer to him than to anyone. When I could not find him, I felt desperate. I wanted to ask questions I knew only he would understand.

I found Gaius and asked if he had seen the old guide with the camel, but he said he did not know of any old man or any camel ever being in our camp. He looked at me as if I had lost all reason.

"What use would a soldier have of such a pair?" he asked, in a mocking tone.

I stood there, bewildered. Perhaps it was more than the heat that tricked me. Perhaps the trauma and betrayal that defined my life had finally taken their toll on my mind.

With great relief, we spent three lovely days together on our return. I believed Gaius was mine again, that the journey had brought us closer. On that third day, I headed out early to find some delicacies for our mid-day meal. After a lovely few hours, I walked into our bed chamber carrying a basket of exotic fruits and cakes, delighted with myself and my treasures. I found Gaius slumped on our bed, his hands cradling his head. A scroll lay at his feet, the obvious cause of distress.

"My darling," I said, holding him by the shoulders, "what news is causing you such worry?"

Gaius looked at me, a deep sorrow gripping his features. I had never seen his face so distorted and anguished. He hesitated to speak, to tell me the cause. At last, he let out a groan from his deepest core, a sound that sent a chill through my heart.

"Lucius has been killed…slaughtered," was all he could say.

"No!" I shouted. My cry sounded like an animal as it falls prey. "No, it cannot be. Not Lucius, no dear God, please not Lucius." My tone shook Gaius as he realized the depth of my horror at the news.

"His body was unrecognizable. They buried him where he lay. He never made it to Rome for a proper burial," he lamented, in a voice I hardly recognized. "They even mutilated his horse."

Zeus? No. No. Lucius? Both gone? Butchered? My mind could not absorb these thoughts, and I became faint. Once again, I saw the stones flying in my mind's eye, while the sound of my mother's cracking skull resonated through my soul. I was back in my nightmare, more real than the life before me. I fought for consciousness. Too much violence. Too much death and horror. The image of a fallen Lucius, a torn and ravaged Zeus, was more than my mind could hold. I fell onto the floor before him, sobbing and shaking at his feet. Gaius lifted me into his arms, shocked by the level of grief that had overtaken me. Lucius was my only link to my mother, the only man alive who knew the better days of my childhood. And I truly loved him, as a father and as a man. Gaius and I held each other and sobbed, our tears mixing as our faces pressed together.

After a time, he spoke. "I saw what the two of you meant to each other, and it brings me comfort to know you cared for him as I did. Lucius was my mother's older brother. My father died in battle before I knew him. Lucius was the only one I have known. We come from a prominent household in Rome, and we have counted on Lucius in all things. Mother was always angry with him for not marrying and having children to carry the family name. Oh, how she tried to make matches for him, but he would never hear of it. It is now up to me."

Had I had my wits about me, I would have known the full meaning of this immediately, but I was too overcome with grief. My mind went to Mother and how much Lucius had wanted her to be his wife. Had he been waiting for her? I thought of how things might have been if Lucius had stolen her away, if she had had children with him, and they had had a chance to be happy, if he had been my father. I would never have wed Tobias. I could have children of my own and would not have known such torture. We could all have been happy but for the unjust rules of man, laws that forced a woman to belong to a man she did not want or love. But what would Gaius' family have made of us? We would be strangers to them and they to us. Would any proper marriage have been possible between them?

We spent the night in each other's arms, crying and consoling. I was so grateful for Gaius in those moments, so thankful for his love. The only hope my heart could hold was that somehow, in some after-life, Lucius was with Mother.

Correspondence continued from Gaius' mother. I assumed she was concerned with family business and exchanges that had to do with Lucius, and so I never questioned him about them. Gaius became agitated and upset after reading each scroll and, in frustration, left to drink with his men. He would return later with an expensive gift or exotic flower he found in the surrounding gardens, a gesture to show he cared. Through these nights, he was tender and held me as if he were afraid to let me go. I took this erratic behavior as a sign of his grieving for Lucius, and I was relieved our shared pain was bringing us closer. We seemed to return to the way we had been before Gaius learned of my marriage to Tobias.

The last scroll came, and with it, an order for Gaius to return to Rome. That gift was the most precious to date. It was a long golden chain with rubies strung within the links, well-crafted with a length that reached my breasts. The stones looked like little hearts, and I thought it symbolized Gaius' love for me. It was the most beautiful man-made object I had ever received. I had no desire to wear such wealth on my body, only cherishing the jewels because Gaius chose them and because it made him happy to see my surprise and delight at his gifts. I wore them to please him and not myself.

On hearing we were to continue to Rome, I, of course, remembered how Gaius had first asked me to be his wife. "We will go to Egypt and then to Rome to be married."

Gaius sat me down and was thoughtful as he told me his intentions. I was both nervous and excited, as he seemed serious. Perhaps the plans to marry would be complicated, and there were things we needed to sort out. I sensed he might think I would not understand the Roman ways, and I became self-conscious at the prospect of being around his family and people I did not know. I held my breath in anticipation as he told me a new captain would arrive soon. Gaius was to bring his detail of men back to Rome. They had been away too long, and as Lucius' only heir, he had much business to attend. I nodded with a slight smile, young girl that I was, anticipating how our wedding might take place.

And then he dropped the earth from under me. His mother was demanding he marry but she had her own plans. It was time for him to present an heir for their affluent, high-ranking family. With Lucius gone, there was no reason to delay. She had found a suitable wife for him, a young and fertile girl from a good Roman household, and their prestigious line would continue. He was not to take any chances but to travel home quickly and safely, and the arrangements would be made by the time he returned.

I stared at him in disbelief. Who was this person sitting across from me? Where was the man who said he loved me?

"Can this be true?" I asked, and I saw his face fall. I felt our love take its final breath.

"Magdalena, how can I explain this so you can understand? I come from an important family in Rome. Somehow, I told myself my mother would fall in love with you as I have and as anyone of worth would. I always felt my uncle would see what an extraordinary woman you are and would support our marriage. But when I found you could not bear children, and had already been married, I realized that was too high an obstacle to overcome.

"And yet, you took my love, knowing you would not keep it?" I shouted, and I felt guilt wash over him.

"I tried to bury these thoughts and hoped it would not matter. Lucius was the head of the family then, and his opinion would weigh more than anyone's. If he could create heirs, the responsibility would not fall on me. But when Lucius died, I lost hope. As these messages came from home, I could see, more and more, my mother would never accept you. How could I present you to the nobility of Rome—a dancing girl, a barren one at that, a once married woman who abandoned her husband to dance in an entertainment tent?"

I could not believe my ears. Is this what he thought of me, or was he looking through his mother's eyes? Was I this thing he described? I only stared at him, unable to speak.

"Magdalena," he begged, "this is not the end of our love. I will marry but for the children and my heart will always be yours. I will make a place for you here and come back to you whenever I can. After I have produced my heirs, I can send for you, and you can stay closer to Rome, so we can be together. I will take care of your needs. I promise."

"You are betraying your wife before even meeting her?" I asked. "You betray us both and your future children as well?"

A flicker of anger crossed his face, but his heart was heavy with guilt and remorse. "Magdalena, my dearest, you will always be the great love of my life, but things are not possible for marriage between us. I cannot fail my family duty."

"But you can fail me and betray your word? What if you care for this family you create? Will you just cast me aside?" I shouted.

"I have made no promise that your lies and secrets have not invalidated," he answered, his voice harsh. He stood, and for a moment, I feared he would strike me.

"Have you not kept secrets from me as well?" I demanded. "This is the first I have heard of your important family, and your need to continue this prominent line. It seems I hardly know you."

"I never saw how any of this would fit together," he answered, frustrated.

"And yet, you accepted my love? You took me away from Seth and Makas and anyone who cared about me just to serve your desires?"

"I have provided for you better than they ever could," he shouted back at me.

As my mind went back to Seth and the tent, I remembered it was Gaius who first made me dance for the men. It was he who put me in the position for which he now judged me. Are women to be moved about and used as fits his important position in life? Yes, he found me different and maybe extraordinary, and he wanted to experience and bask in all my heart's love, but I saw he still regarded me as just a woman. I was not an equal in his eyes. And I did not hold an "important" station or position in life. To him, I held little value. He felt he could judge me and dictate my circumstances as he willed.

"I have gifted you a small fortune in jewels that can keep you housed and safe should anything happen to me. I did not forsake you." And here I saw the planned strategy of his gifts. He did not give them in love so much as guilt.

"And this is how you see me?" My voice became soft and resigned. "A woman to buy, a ruined dancing girl from an entertainment tent?"

"That is how I found you," he replied, and the words stung my heart.

"Then everything between us is a lie," I said. I could tell this struck Gaius hard, and I thought he would take it all back, his faced etched with regret. I could see the thoughts running through his mind as he remembered the initial moment our eyes locked and the magic of our early nights together. Never would we find this kind of love again, and we both knew it. He was throwing it all away for his sense of obligation and propriety. So be it.

"Magdalena, I must do this for the honor of my family," he said, after a lengthy pause.

"In my eyes, you have lost all honor," I answered, and I left our bed chamber.

"Honor? Do you call it honorable to keep your sins a secret?" Gaius shouted.

A firm resolve then overcame me. Sins? Was I to be held responsible for the horrors of my life? Being at the pyramids had transformed me. I felt an invisible force beside me. I was no longer a woman who would allow a man to decide who and what I was, for I had seen a larger thought. My wound was deep, yes, but I was no stranger to pain. I would never turn back. This must have been a great surprise to Gaius, who regarded me as a weak and helpless woman who would settle for any arrangement made on my behalf. I had acted as such throughout our time together, but something in me changed at that moment.

"Magdalena, wait! Come back here," he shouted, in a very commanding voice. I did not turn back.

"Magdalena," he demanded, louder and with more anger.

I gathered my things into a folding basket: all my jewels, several robes and scarves, and the many coins I had collected. I fell in love with Gaius the moment I looked into his heart for the first time. And it disappeared the instant I saw the deficiency of his thought. I had had my fill of men's abuses, these "noble" and "important" men who regard women as objects to fulfill their needs and uses. He would have a woman who would give him children. If he had his way, he would also have my love, my body, and my devotion until I was no longer desirable. Then there would be a new girl, and he would cast me aside with a few more trinkets to assuage his guilt. I was done with all of it. Something or someone had shown me there was a higher thought available to me. I had all the coins I saved from my days in the tent, the gold Lucius gave me, and the precious coin from Mother. I had jewels worth even more. I was now a woman of means.

But I was also a woman with no meaning in the world.

✶ THIRTEEN ✶

I**T WOULD SEEM** I left in a fit of anger, but I had been preparing
to leave Gaius longer than I realized. My mysterious experiences
had stretched my mind open, and my spirit was weary of the constant
worry. I was tired of the torment, sick of believing I was not worthy.
In the depths of my heart, I knew it was over long before the child in
me would concede the fact. When I saw the veracity of his opinion,
that he felt entitled to do with a woman as he willed without regard for
her feelings or thoughts, my heart closed to him. Seeing how he saw
me, I was both devastated and liberated. I would not be this thing he
thought me to be. I would fight again, to the death if need be, to prove
my independence and to own my truth. If my life had taught me any
lesson, it was this; if things went badly, they often got worse. I left while
I had some modicum of dignity, in my mind if nowhere else.

It was late afternoon when I stormed out of the house, with only
a few hours of daylight remaining. I had no notion where I would go.
I was in a foreign land and I knew little about it. Yet, I realized I could
never return to my old existence with Father. That thought was laughable. Abigail would march me straight to the stones. My life with Tobias
was over, and they would blame me for his death. I could not imagine

how to find Seth and Makas. Despite all of this, I could not consider crawling back to Gaius, although I knew he believed I would. My pride would not allow it.

I refused to let fear overtake me, though it tried with all its might. I had to walk. Although I had no idea where, it had to be away from Gaius and my life as a soldier's woman. Maybe it was just a stubborn last march to death, but I would not go down in weak defeat. I would not take my life over a man's opinion of me. I would just move forward. At least, I had this discipline left. Like my mother and Lucius before me, I would face my death with dignity, grateful that the struggle was over at last.

I set my mind to the first task before me; finding a secure place to spend the night. How foolishly intent I was at staying safe while waiting for a righteous way to die. But it was not the time to determine if I had a future. I needed to leave and take the most obscure path available to make sure Gaius could not follow me, yet every part of me knew he would not try.

As I walked on, my arms ached from carrying the heavy basket. I thought it might be easier to wear the jewelry, so I hid behind a building and put all of it on my body, hiding much of it in my undergarments. I then covered myself in my lighter, lesser clothes to both hide the jewels and to look as unremarkable as possible. With a melancholy sadness, I realized the great treasure Gaius had given me, as if love and heartache had a price. In his mind, he had done right by me. These thoughts enraged me as I realized his complete inability to know me, but I had to forget my pride and concentrate on survival. If seen, I would be easy prey for any thief. I wrapped my floppy woven basket across my shoulders and distributed the weight across my back and chest so I looked like any plain, inconsequential woman doing errands.

I walked to the outskirts of the city, looking as busy and occupied as I could, after using a few of my coins to purchase a bladder of wine and some bread and cheese. The more secluded road called to me, for what reason I was not sure. I thought it best to trust my intuition. When I left Tobias, the land was as unfamiliar to me as this, so what did it matter if I was not in the country of my birth? I summoned my courage, or perhaps it was the apathy of a deepening depression, and I moved on. I had nowhere to go and no one to greet me anywhere in the world.

I stopped by a large rock and dug a small trench at its side, nestling against it for protection as the sky darkened. Within moments, a celestial show lit up the sky. The stars appeared close enough to touch. Were they the same I had lain beneath as a child, the very ones Mother said commanded so much in my life? I wondered if they connected us even now. Was she a part of them, and Lucius with her? I had too many questions and no answers, but their light was a balm to my soul. And then one shot through the sky, losing its place in the heavens for all time. Of course, I thought, that was mine, the one that has fallen from grace.

I stayed awake a good portion of the night, cold and without comfort. I ate half of the bread and swallowed some wine to ease my nerves. My thoughts were of Gaius. I became possessed by the memory of him. His rejection stung my heart, but what hurt most was the narrowness of his thought. He was never the man I believed him to be. He was like most others, and that was the biggest blow. Yet, I was used to sleeping next to him. I was used to his touch, accustomed to his smell, his strength. That was gone forever and I was now, once more, alone. I wondered if I would ever know love again, or was that entire part of my story over at only sixteen years of age? One relationship of torture, the other of abandonment? A ruined body and a broken soul in the bargain. I felt truly sorry for myself, miserable and angry at him for taking me away from Seth and any possibility of another, perhaps more fulfilling way of life.

But in the vast expanse of the desert, under the stars of my youth, on the same sands that held the pyramids, these thoughts faded. I thought of Gaius, of our times together, and I felt sympathy and forgiveness for him. My misfortunes were not his fault. He had been one of the best things to come into my life, at least for a while. Without him, I would never have known what physical love was, after knowing only torture and pain. No matter what society dictates, a soul should not be allowed to wither and suffer knowing only abuse and never love. Gaius healed my broken body; he and dance. How could I blame him for needing to fulfill his family's legacy? Would I so disappoint my mother if she were alive? In that context, I saw he would only resent me in years to come for cheating him and his family of his progeny. It was better I left when there was still a hint of respect between us, for Tobias was my fate and not his. These better thoughts settled me, and I fell asleep at last.

I was awake before the sun rose. I gathered my things and set out. There was a slight layer of morning dew on the rocks, and I licked the water off as best I could, trying to get as much of it into my mouth as possible. I could last a few days without finding food and water, but no more. Again, I felt drawn to the path I was on, but I did not know where I was going or even in which direction. Was I headed toward the pyramids or back to the land of my birth? I hardly cared. I just walked, casting my fate to the winds.

Through that day and the next, and the one after, I swallowed only sand. I ate all my provisions the first morning, and my stomach ached from lack of food. Dirt and dust filled my nose and eyes. How I needed water, a place of shelter, and bread. I became dizzy and disoriented, but something about the hum of the land beneath my feet kept me moving.

I struggled on. It was getting harder and harder to breathe as my eyes and mouth filled with clay from the trail, and I tasted only the dried blood that was caked in my parched throat. At night, I dug a trench next to anything I could find to shelter me, alone with only my thoughts of missing my mother, and of Gaius. I clenched the small rock I kept hidden in my pouch and rubbed it. I had worn it smooth with years of worry, and I thought of the other stone still in Mother's hand. Perhaps it was now one of my stars.

Over and over, I dwelled on Gaius' demeaning remarks and his judgments of my life. They ran through my mind, filling me with distress and rage. I had no answer to his accusations. I kept from him the most important details of my existence, and his castigation tortured me. But I had allowed his judgement and opinions to own me. Was that not my failing? What was my responsibility in it? I only tried to survive the world I was handed, but was I as innocent of wrong-doing as I imagined?

I knew I could not survive this way, weary of the endless repetition. Realizing how these thoughts weakened me, I tried to put myself in his position. Was Gaius' interpretation of what happened different from how I saw it? Was he hurt by my deception and omission of truth? What was his version, and did it carry as much weight or value as mine? I realized then that there were more sides to the story than just our two. How did God see it, if indeed there was a God?

I recognized that the sorry version I continued to weave was one part of our relationship. Had I thought of him at other stages of knowing him, my reaction would be different. There were many joyful moments connected to him, many healing experiences, and many filled with laughter. But I chose to repeat the part that brought me pain. My pride was leading me. Gaius was Gaius. In his totality, he was many things, things I did not even know or understand. My current opinion of him held a strong judgement of one moment in time, separated from the whole; one facet of the crystal bead.

In my past visions, I sensed each facet contained a feature or aspect of me, none more real or important than the others, and none mattered, for they all dissipated and became a part of something bigger. To hold on to one piece would not tell the entire story. Gaius' opinion of me differed greatly from the one I held myself, as did my idea of him. We were seeing through our own experiences, neither being able to see the entire other person.

I looked up at the stars shining above me, and they now appeared as jewels in the heavens; complete records, maybe a recounting of all the souls that have ever lived. If written, both the scribe and the reader could translate or dilute the accurate account. It could become altered and less accurate with each telling. The prejudices, agenda, or emotions of each party would influence the story. The images I saw at the pyramid seemed to avoid all of this opinion. Those pictures recreated the experience rather than an attempt to interpret it. These larger thoughts led me out of my self-pity and misery.

The stars became my guiding lights. I grew wiser and more forgiving with each night that passed. When everything is taken away, our arms are then free to hold on to something new. I cherished these long, nightly introspections, my thoughts guided by the wisdom of my past visions. They were all I had. The desert was my muse, my teacher, my only friend.

Three days after I left Gaius, I spotted a small caravan in the distance. Delirious from heat, thirst, and starvation, I could not be sure what I saw was true. I rushed to catch up to it after putting all of my jewelry, save one bangle, into my floppy basket under my blanket and dusty clothes. When I got close enough to know it was real, I approached with apprehension. I suspected my appearance was questionable; a clay-baked waif carrying a blanket with one bracelet on her arm. I was alone, without a companion, and possibly running from someone or something. I would invoke pity or suspicion in anyone who saw me. A weathered woman, old enough to be sympathetic and kind, sat behind an array of lovely fruits and breads for sale or barter. My stomach ached at the sight, and I looked at her with glazed and imploring eyes. She returned an understanding expression.

"Would you be willing to trade this bangle for food and water?" I asked, my voice husky and dry.

The woman looked me up and down. She was much older than my mother would be, and I could tell I had struck a maternal nerve in her.

"Yes, Child, let me see the bracelet."

She had a practiced eye and much experience. I could tell she was quite interested in the quality of the bangle, and also curious that such a lost child would come to own it. No doubt she suspected larceny but I knew that would not stand in her way. It was offered, and that was what mattered.

I took it off and handed it to her. It was worth a great deal more than the supplies a desperate girl would take for it. It was thick with delicate etching, a work of fine art with significant weight. Pleased, she turned the bracelet over in her hand and eyed the details, happy with the bargain. She narrowed her eyes and smiled, sure I had stolen it, but not caring a bit.

"Sit down, Child," the woman said, shoving the bangle into her pouch. "Take some water first," and she passed a cup laden with fresh water from the large vessel at her side. I choked it down, sputtering as mounds of dust and sand washed down my parched throat. "Slow down, there is more," she said, with a thin-lipped smile. She filled it again and handed it to me. I gulped it down, feeling a bit of life returning to my body. She handed me a slight cut of bread, and I gobbled it down without taking a breath, following each bite with a mouthful of water, so I could swallow.

The woman took a large cloth and filled it with fruits, fresh and preserved, strips of dried fish, and two more loaves of bread. She then gathered bladders of wine and water, while I finished all she handed me. My stomach ached, cramping from the sudden onslaught of food and water. I tucked the goods into my basket, under my blanket, and the woman seemed satisfied that I was happy with the trade.

Her face dropped as two brothers, younger than her but older than me, approached. They walked toward the tent while eyeing me, one curiously, and the other maliciously. One had a handsome, though weathered and unkind presence, and the other was grisly and dark. I had seen the look in their eyes too many times as a child when men stared at my mother. The elder woman assumed an aggressive posture.

"Who is this? And where is she from?" the grisly man asked the woman.

"A hungry girl who needs food," she answered. I could tell she neither liked nor trusted these men, but they apparently held some footing within the group.

"What does she have to barter with?" he demanded. Now that I could think more clearly, I realized the risk I had taken, walking into a strange caravan with no protection. They could take my basket, all my belongings and anything else they wanted from me, and who would stop them?

"No matter to you," the old woman said, and I looked at her, betraying my fear, hoping she could stand between us. "This is not your business. It is enough for a small bit of food."

They eyed the bread and water before me, unaware of all I had pushed into my basket. The bracelet was well out of sight in the woman's leather pouch behind her.

They scrutinized me, making me feel deeply vulnerable, the taller one especially. I must have appeared much older than my sixteen years with the layers of dust caked on my skin, and my hair matted and filthy. I could not have seemed attractive, and yet I knew all too well that did not matter to some men.

"This is no issue of yours," the old woman sneered. I took some courage from her tone. They laughed, as if to say everything was their business.

They turned around and walked off, but I sensed they were not done with me. She turned to me.

"Those two are no good. Their family is decent enough, but they look for the easy way. They will never make decent merchants, even in a caravan." She snorted and handed me a fistful of dates. I could only smile at such a treasure, despite the fear that now ran through me.

The sky darkened, and the clouds picked up their hazy blush of color as I rested at the woman's invitation. Her family gathered to share a meal, offering me a cup of their stew. I ate as if I had never seen food before that day. Afterwards, the older woman's young grandchildren rolled themselves up in blankets at the back of her tent, and she suggested I stay the night, hoping I would be safer. I thanked her and laid my blanket at the outer edge, next to the sleeping children. The son and daughter-in-law left for their own beds nearby, but they exchanged knowing glances as they retired. They well understood the cause of my anxiety. A girl on her own had no protection.

I pretended to rest until the others were asleep. Once I looked into the eyes of those two traders, I understood the danger I was in. They would be back, and they would take from me anything and everything they wanted. I was helpless against them. I did not know how well the old woman and her son could or would protect me, or how much power the other men held. They would likely return as soon as they felt we were all sleeping. I had learned to think like a soldier.

I stuffed as much water and food into my basket as I could and slipped away. I believed the bangle was worth much more than what I took, but I felt guilty taking more than the old woman offered. In gratitude for her kindness, I laid a few small coins next to her, hoping she would understand. In the distance, I saw two figures moving closer, and I knew I had little time. I crawled out of the tent and ran with all my might, weaving back and forth, crossing my own steps several times to confuse anyone trying to follow my footprints. I ran as quickly as I could, my frail body weakening with the effort, my stomach aching from the sudden onslaught of food and water after being so empty. But I had a good start ahead of them.

I heard a rustling noise in the distance. My breathing became loud and labored, and I feared they would find me by the sound of it alone. But I kept on, driven by fear.

"I can hear her," a heavy voice spoke from some distance away.

I carried on, running, almost in circles, tripping over my feet, sand filling my nose and mouth and making my breath even louder as I coughed.

"I think she went that way," a raspier voice shouted, but I could tell they were facing in the opposite direction. "I heard her coughing." There was no telling how close they were, but they could hear me.

What force came to my defense at that moment, I do not know. But a fierce wind swept up from the desert floor and whipped at me and the sand at my feet. It overtook all other sound and covered my footsteps.

Collapsing with fatigue, I pulled out my blanket and wrapped it around me as tightly as I could. I rocked my body back and forth, trying to slow my heart and breath. Cold and frightened, I rubbed the small, worn stone in my hand, the only thing left of my mother besides the coin still sewn into the hem of my robe. On any other occasion, the shrill wail of the desert wind would have pierced my soul like the barren call of death itself. It would bring such loneliness into my bones that I would beg for its end. But on that night, I was grateful for its protection. I prayed it would cover my footsteps and drive the brothers away. I shivered and trembled until it stopped some time later. The men would not have stood through such a wind storm for so little reward, so I was confident they had given up.

I hurried through the midnight hours, putting as much distance as possible between myself and the caravan. The next day I hurried on, stopping often to search the landscape for any sign of those frightful men, until I was sure I had traveled off their path.

I forced myself to ration the food and water and drank the wine at night to ease my aching body. Completely alone, facing only the nameless space before me, I had no escape from myself. I had to fight my fear and find some kind of resolution, or I would surely go mad. I stumbled toward my death, all the while debating the meaning of life. Was death a punishment or a sweet reward? An end or a beginning?

Are we victims, or do we have a say in how our lives unfold? Alone in the desert, under my stars, I came to think my death might be the beginning of a new life.

I did not understand what would or should become of me, nor did I know who I was. I had been Mother's daughter, which differed vastly from a girl child of Father's. After Mother's death, I was Abigail's resentful stepchild, and then Tobias' abused wife. Next a traveling dancer under Seth and Makas' care, an infidel by most standards, a harlot, and a pagan. And the girl with Gaius—a sinner, adulteress and outcast—a woman abandoned without worth or standing. By what decree? What ordained these judgements over women? When I tried to fit into the life given me, I made ruin of it.

I had always lived under the control of a man, and he dictated the circumstances of my existence. To Father, I was an insignificant girl, an inconvenience, but also a bargaining tool, hardly a person at all. Had I not possessed such an independent mind, I would have fit, albeit miserably, into the wretched life laid before me as Tobias' wife. Rather than run away, I would have withered in torment until he had beaten any inner or outer beauty out of me. No longer young or attractive, my husband would have pushed me aside for not providing heirs to the rich and powerful Tobias. I would be left with nothing, thrown away as a meaningless, childless, and manless female. And no one would have cared. Had I not stood up to Gaius, I would have been a kept woman at the mercy of his will and desire until thrown away for committing the crime of becoming old, inconvenient, and undesirable.

Seth and Makas were the only men who held me with respect, but they, too, were outcasts. Society considered them as pagan and as worthless as I. The person who did not seem to fit this pattern was Lucius, a soldier of strength and power who could treat a woman as she deserved to be treated. How did he come to this? Were there others like him? Perhaps the good man who ground our grain and died so young. What was it that made most men feel so superior to women? Were they not all born of one? Do they not owe us their very lives?

Mother recognized my nature and feared I would succumb, like my grandmother, to depression and death under the weight of this oppression. So, she planted the seed of creativity, hoping it might sustain me as it had her, at least for a while. Seeing my mother punished for the mere hope of following her heart in no sense diminished my independence. It made it fiercer. I lost myself as a girl in love, but I would not allow Gaius to own me, not in the way he suggested. If I had, I would never have left him. I would have accepted whatever fate he offered. But my prophetic vision the night of my fateful dance had changed me in ways I still did not understand. It lifted a veil to reveal a truth that seemed more real than anything I had seen with my body's eyes, as odd and mad as it sounds. Once I saw the other side, I could no longer pretend it did not exist. It was one of the holy instants of my life, and it now guided at least some part of me and could not be ignored. As a result, I was on this dusty road alone, wandering the desert, and I preferred it over a life of slow death and depression. When I saw the truth of Gaius, I could no longer love him in the same way.

Somehow, I was granted the gift of vision. It began with the merchant's death and then my experiences looking into the water—visions that opened a door in my heart and spirit that would not fully close. After Mother 's death, they were all I had that were mine. My dance of the crystal beads came to me when I struggled to reconcile my life with the one I had been born to. It seemed as if someone or some-thing wanted me to realize the world did not have the final judgement. The inexplicable images at the pyramid came to my tortured soul as I struggled to understand my place with Gaius. But why? What claimed me from such a young age? Or were they all mere fantasies of imagination conjured up for survival?

Mother and my stars dared me to own my mind and protect my truth. But what had that principle ever done for me, other than separate me from the rest of the world? I was alone on the verge of death once again. But, on those lonely nights in the desert, I no longer felt afraid. An end to this story seemed a gift. I had prayed for it countless times, believing it better to own my death than suffer a life I could not bear. If death is inevitable, if it comes to every living creature, if it unites all beings, what is there to fear? If God is kind and merciful, as my mother believed, how could He condemn His creations to a fearful, desolate, and meaningless outcome? And if He is a punishing, harsh God, why should I care about Him or even try to be good? I should hate Him for His vengeance. And He most likely already hated me, for look what life He set before me. Or is death but the conclusion of one reality and the start of another? And if it is simply the end to everything, so be it. I would no longer exist along with all the pain I carried.

I stared into the night sky at my stars and became lost in their glow. They lifted me into the wonder of the other side, and I realized I had not yet fully grasped any truth. I was traveling between two worlds.

In the mornings, I began my wandering again; my meandering, pointless walk through the desert. I stopped if I discovered shelter and rested. I sang Mother's songs if my throat was not too dry and I could utter a sound—faint, hoarse brief whispers barely echoing the strength of her magnificent voice. A vague memory of a dancer, still living within my battered flesh, moved with the quiet hum of the earth beneath my feet. I was an aimless woman; lost, but feeling found in the oddest of ways. I was lonely beyond expression. I had no comfort or future to expect, but I owned my life, and that gave me a rebellious sense of satisfaction. At night, I sat beneath my starry temple and learned how to think with the wisdom of a sage.

In moments of despair, when thoughts of Tobias invaded my soul, I clenched and sickened with the hatred and revulsion I felt for him. My body harbored too many memories of his abuse, and it responded in terror at the mere memory of him. And he had caused my mother's death, which was worse than anything he did to me. I thought of Lucius ending Tobias' life, and I was glad in ways that made me ashamed. But it led to the circumstances of Lucius' death, so I found no lasting satisfaction in revenge. These tortured thoughts owned me while they lasted, haunting me with their wickedness and weakening me until I had to stop and rest. Carrying so much buried grief and hate was exhausting.

"Will you not free me of this pain?" I shouted in anger at my stars. I threw myself onto the ground and hugged my knees to my chest, spent in every way.

And then, as if in answer, in the stark void of desert sky, I heard a voice, not my own. It spoke to me, but it came without a word or sound. A picture appeared in my mind of Tobias, a living image much as I had seen in the tomb, and I saw him with a new perspective. He was an ugly man in every way I valued. Far from attractive, repulsive in fact, he quickly found that using his power and treasure gave him a standing he always doubted he deserved. His father, who was rich and harsh, berated and mistreated him, and despised the very sight of him. How do these things twist a man's mind? His position of wealth, inherited to begin with, afforded him cruelty and abuse over those he deemed to be of lesser value. It offered him a means of revenge against a world he felt was against him. His sense of entitlement allowed his brutality to grow with the power he gained over others. Under such circumstances, would I have done better? This thought shook me. I had considered nothing from Tobias' perspective. I hated him from the first moment I met him. His avaricious desire of my mother and her rejection of him fueled his desire to destroy everything she loved, me most of all. I had done nothing to assuage his anger or contempt. In fact, I had never been the least bit respectful or kind to him, at any time in my life. I felt an actual tinge of guilt over my part in it. I was not free of blame, and this realization forced some compassion into me, as scarce and incomplete as it was. It was only in this forgiveness that I could find a hint of relief from the memories that haunted me.

If Father or Abigail came into my mind, I forced them from my thoughts. I refused to spend a moment on them. It never freed me from the disgust I held in my soul at their cruelty and betrayal. It was as poison in me until I realized that burying anger did not free me of the pain it caused. Hiding it from sight, only made it fester. Their actions and my reaction to them chiseled away at any happiness I tried to hold.

I walked on, exhausted in every way, and then, once again, at what seemed the end of my ability to continue, a power came to fill me from some nameless source. All the sensate experiences gifted to me through my life embraced me at once. Empathy filled the abyss of despair that held my soul. I felt united with knowledge beyond my reasoning, as I had as a young child. Was I insane and weak of mind and flesh from lack of nourishment? Was I so beaten that I needed to imagine there was something better available to me? Or was this a conscious event? I did not even care, finding some peace, at last, in the desolate world I was ready to leave behind. Was this the beginning of death, this separation from life? And if it was, how beautiful it seemed.

But I did not die. I slept through the night. I felt my mother's hand brush against my cheek, and her tender lips touch my forehead. My dreams were joyous, filled with dance and vibrant colors and images. The songs of my mother's heart cradled me as they had when

I was born. I was a dancer again, moving ethereally through light and sound, dancing to the choir of the heavens and to her illustrious voice. Maybe I was going mad once and for all. Maybe in those solitary nights in the desert, alone with only my thoughts, all sanity abandoned me. But I felt at peace there, half buried in dust under my stars. Perhaps minds go mad when there is no better option before them.

I gained insight during those lonely nights, mad or not. I realized how close we are to wisdom as children until our lives and emotions distract us. How quickly the stream becomes clouded by vanity, greed, ambition, pain, and pride. I came to understand how free thought threatens authoritarian rule. Vain men punish and kill to maintain their power and dominance. I was not wrong in my beliefs; I was over-powered. Men, as I knew them, carried little value for women and anyone who refused to follow their rules. They used fear and judgement, even God, to keep others under their control. But from where I sat under the desert sky, these men held no power over me. They would die of thirst the same as I. They would starve or be buried in sand just as any woman would. There is justice in nature. If a beast ate me, it would be for honest hunger, not for any desire of prestige or power. Nature was not cruel. Nature was practical.

I walked on and on, not knowing where I was going or why. I craved to meet people, but I needed to see them differently; to share truth and speak without deception or fear. Longing for a life in which I need not hide who I was or what I had been, I asked my stars to show me the way. But Magdalena, whoever she was, knew of none that existed.

* * *

The sky held its breath and a foreboding stillness covered the earth. And then, everything changed in an instant. A bitter and wild wind rose, whipping my scarves across my face and threatening to tear them from me. I clung to them, fighting the tempest and struggling to remain upright. I looked to my left, to the force pushing against me, and saw a huge, dark wall closing in on me. It raced across the desert floor and cast a shadow that seemed bigger than the land itself. It was a sandstorm, the magnitude of which I had never witnessed, burying everything in its wake.

I scanned the area, searching for shelter. I was near a large rock formation and I ran toward it, running on fear more than thought. Looking back at the great wall rapidly closing in on me, hopelessness seized me. I had wished for death so many times, but when it came this close, I was afraid. A small part of me wanted to surrender and let it bury me. But a deeper, more mysterious part urged me to stay alive and continue.

Half crazed, I dug a trench against the largest of the rocks, hoping it could buttress me against the brutal force of sand already blasting against me. My hands, trembling with fear, struggled as I rolled up my scarves around my nose, eyes, and throat, and shoved my basket and provisions beneath me. I hoped my weight could hold them and me in place. I then folded myself as tight as possible in my blanket and faced into the rock. The wind pushed me against the boulders with such force I did not know if they were protecting or crushing me.

The sand was already pounding at my back, feeling like a thousand tiny knives piercing my skin. Wave upon wave of hard clay pushed against me. My frightened, hot breath became moist and thick within my blanket and scarves. I tucked into a tighter ball as the soil built up against me, closing me in. Sand was everywhere. Air was nonexistent. My breathing quickened. I feared I was suffocating, being buried alive.

"Help me," I shouted, without thinking. And I realized I did not want to die, not there, not in that way.

Did I endure this for hours? I could not tell, for each moment felt a lifetime. A minute became a year; such is the relevance of time. But then it all stopped. Silence embraced me. That now familiar trembling coursed through me, pulling me out of the tight restriction of my body. I lifted from that dark hole into brilliant light, which I experienced more through my spirit than with my body's eyes. Once freed, energized and fluid, I moved as if dancing in quiet essence.

Waves of energy flowed through me, and I gave myself to them, thinking it was the solace of death finally coming to claim me. I saw my life in pictures; scenes of my past moving through my mind with a preternatural understanding and forgiveness of each, all without words. Mother, Father, Abigail, Seth, and on it went until they moved with a speed that was almost dizzying. A continuous flow of images moved past my existence into a time before. These were the visions I witnessed in the tomb and the great pyramid. In the new and rarified silence surrounding me, I understood them at last. My thoughts had been too narrow to decipher them before, too cluttered with petty emotions and personal fears to understand they had nothing and yet everything to do with me. These images held the stories of life lived since the dawn of man.

Resting in a quiet I had never known, I saw into a far distant history when women and their nurturing ways of love were honored. I was witnessing it as if I had experienced it myself. Life was fair and just. Beauty and bounty rested over the landscape. Peace reigned without conflict. People shared what they had, with no desire to fight for more. Children were happy, girls and boys. It was a better world than the one I left behind.

Picture after picture passed through me. This was the life that humankind threw away. People with misguided goals dominated others with brute strength. The wise agents of higher mind dispersed with their knowledge to keep their secrets out of the hands of those who would misuse it. What rested within the feminine guidance, within the mother, was denied more and more. Men created a new order based on physical supremacy and power.

Men fought for dominance. War, greed, and uncertainty became the norm, while the women's voices rose against it. They needed to be silenced and judged inferior. These images reflected endless war and strife, with women and children suffering first and most. And yet, the solution rested in the hands of those who caused the pain.

Would a sane mother wage war or allow her children to starve and be brutalized? Love prevails in the hearts of women and in men who can cherish, protect, and respect them. But those of greed, lust, disrespect, and imperious desires created a world that held the righteous down, creating societies and theocracies that judged women as temptresses and objects of seduction; unworthy because of their gender, of God's true blessings. These rulers used their interpretations of God and religion to control the thoughts of men who were confused or felt they had no other option. This was the world into which I was born, but it was not the natural order of creation.

Who was served by holding women down? Did our very nature pose a threat to their plans of war and authority? Or was it because they could, and to have power over others fed their need for dominance? We were easy victims with a strength of will and heart, but not of body.

A vibrant image lit before me; someone I recognized but had never seen. I knew that something significant tied her to me. Through lies, deception, and ignorance, she would be discredited and disavowed.

The patriarchal order would not allow such power and knowledge in a woman. I had a role in this, but I could not see what it was. The last picture would not come into focus.

Time will erase all who live, and yet, truth will eventually prevail, somehow, perhaps after great misunderstanding for centuries. In creation, death does not exist, but in the world, it provides endless suffering. Mother was right. I was born for a reason, but I could not see it.

An even deeper silence dropped over me. Nothing looked as I had ever known it to be. I moved as if without a body. The colors of the sky and earth were vibrant and drenched in ethereal light. I stepped forward into the silence, and standing before me was my guide from the pyramid. He held out his hand and smiled, and his murky eyes twinkled and became clear.

"But how have you come here?" I asked. "Are we near the pyramid?"

"I am always near," he explained.

"Why are you here?" I continued.

"To show you more," he answered. "I thought your experiences were too overwhelming before. You needed time to absorb them and think things through for yourself. You are a lot like your mother."

"You knew my mother?" I asked, incredulous.

"Yes, a good woman. She did not realize it, but she descended from the sacred lineage. Many generations have passed and few remember. Did you not notice how different she was?"

"Yes, of course, everyone noticed it, but they just thought her beautiful."

"She had great creativity and talent and a rare connection to spirit. She brought exceptional beauty forth in everything she touched, did she not?"

I just stared at him. Nothing was real and yet, maybe it was more authentic than anything before that moment. I did not know where I was or why.

"Follow me," the old man said, and we moved together through misty columns of light. He sat down, on what I could not say, and I sat with him.

He put his hand on my shoulder and the quickening began again, stronger and more vibrant than before. Connected by his touch, I saw with a context far beyond the one that little Magdalena held. Sitting within a non-spatial continuum, between time and events, I found myself suspended in eternity. I was witnessing a viewpoint much bigger than that which the world holds. I understood, that if one truly had the knowing and strength of mind to hold this thought and perception, all things were possible. For is our world not but a sum and consequence of our beliefs and interpretations, and could we not change our reality? Was this the vision and power of the Initiates?

I was a visitor by my guide's invitation. I still held doubts and limitations, and I could not control my abilities or emotions in most ways. But with a mind that dwelt in this state, what we thought of as miracles could happen. Within this vision, I grasped how the impossible was indeed possible. For with this bigger intention, the collective mind no longer had power over a mind that could suspend such beliefs.

I had not the faith nor knowledge with which to instruct this potential or to hold these thoughts. But I understood it was not about sovereignty and commanding the world. It was about working outside its boundaries and limitations; to avoid common perception and command true spiritual strength. I saw there are endless possibilities. Was this the role of the Initiates the guide had spoken of? Was this the energy they held in the pyramids, the force that had hit me in that upper chamber? I saw that, if one owned such a state of mind, one could heal and make the perceived impossible come to pass. There was more at play than most of us could comprehend.

I was still so attached to my human form, my fears, desires, and experiences, that I was incapable of suspending my faith in perceived physical order. But I gained a glimpse of how the laws of nature and man are all organized perceptions fixed in time and thought.

Revising this belief could mean a change of reality. There had been men and women on this earth, and maybe there would be again, who knew these truths. Just understanding this was a possibility changed my thinking. I would never be the same. For in seeing how miracles could happen, I could accept my own.

As I looked at my old guide, he became younger and more vibrant. He was beautiful in every conceivable sense. Who or what was this person before me, if a man at all? Was he an Initiate? The one of whom he spoke?

His eyes burned clear and bright, and I felt he had the strength of ten men but the sensitivity of a mother; the perfect blend of male and female qualities. He cared for nothing in the physical world, and yet I saw he held unconditional love for everything in it. His power grew so great, I knew he could face down a lion if need be. All of it overwhelmed me; everything I had witnessed, my guide's transformation, and the knowing that filled me.

And then it stopped. As quickly as it began, everything disappeared. I was surrounded by darkness, wrapped in a tight, suffocating knot. I remembered the sandstorm and fought again for my breath.

In the far distance, I heard a faint sound, a voice, penetrating my consciousness, becoming more discernible, and waking me to my circumstance. I thought I felt something digging behind me, but I was confused. Was I still alive? I was disoriented, choking and spitting out mouthfuls of dirt. Pain brought me back into my body. It took several moments for the air to break through the sand caked in my nose. Air. Blessed air. I sputtered and gasped until I realized I could take a full breath.

Standing before me was an apparition so lovely I knew I must have entered Paradise. Death was the only explanation for all that had just transpired. At first, I thought it was Mother coming to claim me. I stared in childish wonder for several moments, eyes wide; silent, hoping. As I tried to move, I felt every part of my body pain me. I was, regrettably, still alive.

"Dear child, are you alright?" my apparition asked.

With a hoarse, faint voice I responded. "Where am I? Who are you?"

She seemed familiar. For no rational reason, I felt I knew her.

"The sandstorm buried you. The end of your headscarf was blowing about and caused us to notice you. I had the strangest feeling someone was close by. I thought I heard my name."

"Where are we?" I inquired, still confused by all I had just been through. I no longer knew what was real and what was not.

"The better question is, what are you doing out here?" she asked, concerned. "Are you alone?" And she glanced about, a worried look on her face should there be more sad souls buried in the sand.

"I am very much alone. I left the man I was to marry and set out on this road," I said, in a heavy, coarse voice still affected by the dry sand and air. "He disavowed me when he found I was barren and had kept it from him. His family made plans for his betrothal to another." I surprised myself by this immediate confession and willingness to tell this stranger my story on just meeting her, but there was something wise and loving about her. I trusted her from the start.

"You are alone?" she repeated, needing to confirm I was coherent enough to understand what she was asking.

"Yes, very." I said, choking back tears.

She helped me up, and I saw she had two women and a man with her, all older than myself, and a small donkey to carry their supplies. I dug my basket out of its deep hole and took what water I had left, gulped it down, and choked on the mouthfuls of sand in my throat. I sputtered and coughed until I felt I could swallow without fear.

"Can you walk? Where are you going?" she asked.

I shook myself off and moved my arms and legs to see if they still worked. I was intact.

"I… I am fine," I answered, not sounding convinced. "There is nowhere to go, so I will just follow the road." As I looked out, there was no pathway to be found. The sandstorm had covered everything. I felt like laughing; a desperate laugh at the futility of my untethered plans.

"We are going to Bethany," she replied. "Why not travel with us?"

"But what are you doing out here?" I asked, curious about this magnificent, kind woman.

"Our friend and teacher had a gathering south of here. We started our journey home, but seeing the storm in the distance, we found shelter and waited. Fortunately we did so we could find you."

"I thought I had died, and it made me happy," I said, after several moments, still confused.

She smiled, as though she understood my thought as very few could. She had a deep and wise look that comforted me in ways I had not felt since I was a child. I wanted to remain as close to her as I could.

"Come," she said, helping me with my basket. She then wiped some caked sand from my eyes as a loving mother would, and put her arm around my shoulder. I could no longer fight back tears; a lost girl, always yearning for her mother's embrace.

"What is your name?" she asked, when we reached the others.

"Magdalena," I replied, my voice still coarse and fragmented. "And yours?"

"Mary."

We walked the full day, stopping for rest several times along the way. Although my muscles ached from weathering the fierce storm, they loosened up as the morning wore on. It took me several hours to feel as though I owned my body again.

Mary was traveling with two sisters and their brother. Martha, the eldest, was a serious woman who kept her mind on the task ahead. We stopped for a light meal and water, which she had carried with her on the donkey. She was formidable, organized, and had not a second's hesitation in sharing what she had with me.

"I have some food with me," I offered, and I dug the last piece of bread from my basket, the one I bought with my bangle at the caravan. It was hard as a rock, and I felt embarrassed as I handed it to her.

She smiled and accepted my offering, although I suspected it pained her to think of eating such a paltry morsel. She was too kind and of good manners to reject what I had contributed, and this filled me with a great appreciation for her.

"We can save this for later and eat what I have already set out," she said.

I was starving and ate everything she gave me and then drank every bit of water offered. Martha was a very kind woman, although I could see how many would find her serious and without humor.

Her younger sister's name was also Mary. She was enthusiastic and lighter of spirit, which I could tell often irritated Martha, for Mary was a daydreamer, and left Martha to organize and care for the group. Absorbed in thoughts and ideas, concepts, and wondering, Mary mused while Martha was practical and got things done. Mary had a deep inner life and loved to ponder life's mysteries, much as I did. I liked them both.

The entire time we walked and rested, the younger Mary spoke of the gathering from the day before. She was excited by the teachings and asked my Mary, for by now I regarded the woman who saved me as mine, to explain the things they heard.

My Mary seemed very learned. She explained, with great precision, the meanings of the lessons and stories. How wonderful this was, I thought as I watched her, a woman with knowledge, like my mother, but one who was valued because of it and did not need to hide it. Oh, how I wished Mother could have known women such as these. What would she have made of it? How much richer her life would have been.

Their teacher seemed very different from the priests and elders of my old city, those arrogant men who demanded sacrifice and debased their followers, keeping them down, so they could control them with threat and fear. As Mary spoke, I felt their friend considered people as brethren and family rather than as strangers with a hierarchy of order. Their words touched the deepest parts of me.

The man with them was Martha and the younger Mary's brother. He was quiet and gentle, and the three were good friends of the preacher's. My Mary was close to them all, but I could not tell in what capacity. Still, I felt fortunate to have met these exceptional people who seemed not to judge or worry about whom, or what, I was, but only wanted to help me. I felt familial with them after only a few hours together.

We traveled most of the day, walking and stopping when we came across a home or small farm. The families we reached greeted us and gave us shade, water and well wishes. I seemed to have come across individuals who shared kindness and were met with the same. This all felt foreign to me. I had always believed myself separate from others. This had been true most of my life, but here, within just a few hours, I was accepted and cared for. Were these people so different from those I had known, or was I the one who had changed?

We arrived in Bethany just before sundown at the home of Martha and Mary, whom I called Little Mary to avoid confusion, and their brother. Martha's house was large and welcoming, well run, and I felt safe the moment I set foot in it. Martha was a widow of some means, and it showed.

They invited me to stay a few days at their home. How lucky and grateful I felt, for I had no direction and no one in my life. I sensed I was safe around them. Martha gave me a simple robe to wear while I washed and dried my own. She led me outside to her well and supplied soap and fragrant oils, a comfort I could only have dreamed of during my last trek through the desert. I had become accustomed to luxury as Gaius's woman, but the period of dust and depravity quickly returned me to a more humble state. I was embedded in dust from the storm and had never felt so grateful for water and lye. I poured multiple buckets of water over me, working the oil through my matted hair for what seemed like hours. Sand was in my nose, my ears, and every crevice of my body. The water brought me back to life, and I returned to them a renewed woman.

Feeling grateful, I helped with the chores as much as needed, for which Martha was very pleased. She often sighed at Little Mary for sitting about, talking of stories from the gatherings and asking endless questions, absorbed with her thoughts, while Martha did the tasks at hand.

I loved listening to the vivid exchange of ideas as Mary spoke. All the many revelations I had experienced in the stark quiet of the desert resonated with their beliefs. It was a much bigger thought than most individuals held. Mary said more and more people were traveling the countryside to hear their friend speak, and the crowds were growing larger by the day.

I worked alongside Martha listening as intently as I could, much like I did as a child at the communal well. I asked if I could go to hear a sermon, and, without hesitation, Mary said she would take me with her when she left in a few days' time. Martha and the others planned to stay in Bethany and meet with her in a few weeks. I had mistakenly headed toward the land of my birth when I left Gaius, not knowing in which direction I was walking, and I was close to my old home. But I was a very different person from the girl who had escaped two years before, was I not? I had to hope no one would recognize me. I had to believe I was safe and could live a new life after so much had changed.

I craved to be near Mary. It was hardly a rational thought, but I wished to be like her. The attachment I formed and the great admiration I already held surprised me. Perhaps it was because she reminded me so much of my mother; perhaps it was more. I told Mary I had some money and could pay my own way and help fund their group as well. Mary smiled and thanked me with a kindness I rarely saw in another.

She conducted herself with grace and good manners, and I assumed she had wealth of her own, but none of it seemed to concern her.

We walked a full day and arrived at her cousins' home in the late afternoon. On meeting the family, I surprised myself by feeling at ease among them, I had so many scars on my spirit from the likes of my father, Abigail and Tobias, that I expected most people to be judgmental and unkind. Until that moment, I had not witnessed truly ingratiating, generous people, except for Seth and Makas. I was long years away from the tender times with my mother.

They gave me a small mat on which to sleep, and I shared a meal with the family that evening. They all spoke of this teacher and of his wisdom and goodness. I felt self-conscious, knowing nothing of the man or his teachings, and feeling I had little to add to the conversation. But in my heart, I understood. My strange but varied life had taught me many of these lessons. It excited me to hear my thoughts validated.

The following day, I went with the family and Mary to hear their teacher speak. A sizable crowd had gathered, the largest I had ever encountered. I felt overpowered and frightened, being amid so many bodies. I was basically a girl of the land, and although I had seen more of the world than I could have imagined, it was in small groups at a time and under Gaius' care. In the very beginning, the music tent was overwhelming for me. There were so many men I did not know. It took some time to feel comfortable. This gathering was much larger, and I found it difficult to breathe normally, being very unsure of myself and trying hard to hide my discomfort. But there was a calm that prevailed, and I finally relaxed. I watched their teacher as he stood in the crowd, smiling and disarming everyone around him. I did not know what I expected, knowing only the priests of my childhood, they who embellished themselves in rich robes and headdresses. This man wore a plain robe and adorned himself with kindness. How he attracted so many people with such a humble presentation surprised me.

I remembered how our priests put out their hands and accepted Tobias' bribes for acceptance and praise. They did not care what my husband did to me. They cared for the riches he possessed and his status in the community. This man did not seem to condemn or judge, but smiled and laughed light-heartedly. He did not act superior or self-righteous, and seemed to only offer support and kindness.

I stood in the back of the crowd watching after the children, still adjusting to the number of people assembled. Even though I was too far from the preacher to see his features, I could not help but feel good in his presence. He held a gravitas that commanded respect without a hint of fear, despite his simple presentation. This confused and delighted me. I strained to hear as much as I could. I wanted to know everything about these individuals. Some said this man had cured the sick; others claimed he healed lepers with just a touch. At any other time, this would have seemed preposterous to me, and I would have negated everything as foolish gossip. But my vision in the sandstorm, real or unreal, led me to believe these things could be true. Was it possible this man could navigate that state of mind? Was he what the old guide would call an Initiate? Could any of this be credible? It felt like absolute reality in the sandstorm, but what was that? A crazy thought in the mind of a girl on the verge of suffocation? Did this teacher know of these things? If these miracles were true, I had to believe he was a most unusual man, the likes of which I had never seen, but someone my old guide might know. But who or what was he? Did he even exist? I was more confused than ever, but I felt a deep need to hear more.

I knew the miracles were not the devil's work, as many claimed, for what is the devil but a means of teaching a child's mind what temptation and ill intention are? Or controlling the masses through fear?

Even when very young, most likely because of my mother's influence, I did not believe such a fallen soul existed. Why would God, as I and she understood Him to be, ever create a creature so evil and unloving? No caring parent would tempt his children to test their resolve and destroy them if they failed. He would only guide and protect them. A devil made no sense to me except to explain the danger of evil thought and to frighten people into desired behavior. Yet, perhaps I had known this type of devil in Tobias.

But even he was just a human with defects and failures of spirit because of his lot in life. I was shown under my stars how he had become twisted and cruel. The fear of being without his power was the driving force behind his cruelty. What would he be in his mind and the minds of others without it? He never had a woman who loved or chose him. Was I in a position to judge him? Me, with my own faults and questionable decisions? How could I, while looking at only one side of things and not the whole?

And so, when the preacher said, "Love your enemies," I understood what he meant. An enemy is only a person separated by misunderstanding. Tobias was not a devil. He was a broken man who was taught cruelty and learned his lesson all too well. I found I couldn't hold true forgiveness for him, but I was understanding it might be possible, if only for my own sake.

A small group of fellows surrounded the teacher and looked to be in his inner circle. I asked the cousins about them, and they explained he chose each to follow him. I watched them, interested in what each possessed that would make him worthy of such a role. They appeared to be good men, but very common. Perhaps that was why he called them, for they were like the people he taught and could understand them. Some seemed coarse, one appeared young and of tender heart, but one of them was more refined. I assumed he might be more politically minded than the rest, sensing he hoped their teacher would free our people in a physical sense from the occupiers. I felt none of them understood the man as Mary did.

After a brief reprieve at the cousins' house, I set out on my own again. I stayed close to the gatherings, if for no other reason than to feel I was near people I might trust. If I am honest, it was because of Mary. She pulled at me. I felt I knew her from another time or perhaps even another life.

I sometimes found children lost in the crowds and helped them locate their families. This often led to offers of lodging for watching the younger ones. I loved every moment playing with them and teaching them Mother's songs and my dances under the stars. As I became fond of the young girls and boys, I struggled with the deep pain and loneliness of knowing I would never have one of my own. In better moments, I fantasized Gaius would love me even now if I had been able to bear his children, that this would have tied us together for eternity. But my heart knew the truth of how he saw me, and it tortured me to admit that no other outcome was ever possible. I would become depressed and move on, often to lonely stays in the desert, with my blanket as my home, again with only my stars to protect me.

When I could no longer tolerate my loneliness, I moved to another household, another group of children, and I began again. In every situation, questions arose; questions about my family, my past, my reasons for being out on my own, and I would need to disappear to avoid anyone knowing my truth.

My outstanding talent for deciphering and gathering gossip served me well. I was able to keep track of Mary's comings and goings, and I followed her as if she were my guiding star. When she noticed me among the crowds, she always greeted me with the warm and understanding love I so admired in her. She treated me as family, and her acceptance restored me. When I lost track of her, I became disoriented and depressed until I again found her.

So much confused me then. Having returned to the land of my childhood, I again felt the political pressures of occupation. The crowds in the streets were angry, and I could feel their brewing resentment. But at the gatherings, things were different. It was a salve to my soul to hear about love, kindness, and right action. I did not know if the people gathered took it to heart, but I sensed the man's words also soothed them. But I also noticed men on the fringes of the crowd who appeared calculating and conniving, and I determined they were trouble. I had lived among soldiers long enough to sense when men were dangerous, and everything in me understood them to be.

When I was alone and without children to watch, I would rent a room in the homes of people I met at the gatherings. How strange my life had been, I often thought. I had lived so many lives already and was but sixteen years. As I moved from place to place, I presented myself in whatever way the situation required. No one knew who I was, including me. I had to believe my stars were guiding me. But where was I going?

*   *   *

Caring for children helped to fill the hole in my heart. I had had but one genuine friend as a child. She, the one who died of fever and who owned the cloth dolls, came to mind often when I took the young ones on long walks, sang Mother's songs, and taught them to dance under the open sky. I stayed from home to home, and tent to tent, until again, people wanted to know more about my past. How could I explain my life? A mother wrongly stoned for alleged adultery, an adulteress myself, a whore? A dancer in an entertainment tent? All of

Gaius' prejudices still haunted me, and I could not free myself of the shame I felt. And how could I explain my dead husband? I quickly moved on to a new family, another home, or the desert close by. What thoughts and opinions I left behind, I could not know.

I attended the gatherings as often as possible to hold some sense of direction, albeit a still lonely and uncertain one. The crowds were big enough that I could evade the families I wished to avoid, those wanting to know more about my history. I kept my eyes on Mary. She beguiled me. She had the beauty and grace of my mother but was given, or had taken, a life that allowed her more choice. But I could also feel the prejudice and envy she had to face from men around her, even the ones in the inner circle. Some resented her closeness to the man they all admired, thinking a woman had no place in the hierarchy. Her intelligence and importance were undeniable, but even she still stood in a man's world. I wondered why she felt so familiar to me.

*   *   *

I roamed about for a season, summer yielding to the harvest months. Still so naive despite the myriad strange experiences I had already endured, I secured a room in a woman's house I met at a gathering. She was a widow and rented rooms for income. She was a kind woman, much older than me, warm and friendly, and I stayed for a full turn of the moon. I seemed almost content. Mary was close by and I often saw her at the gatherings, and she was always kind and welcoming to me, so I felt somewhat settled.

I had been staying with the woman for some time when a husky man much older than me came to the house and secured the chamber next to mine. I felt intimidated by the way he watched me come and go. He commented on my being alone and asked questions of and about me, but he did not ask in a friendly manner. There was an edge to his comments and insinuations that made me uncomfortable. Convinced I was under no one's protection, that I was indeed alone and vulnerable, he entered my room one night in the late hours.

"What are you doing in my room? Please go!" I shouted, surprised and afraid. I stood up and wrapped my blanket around myself.

"A woman like you must surely be waiting for a man to enter her chamber," he snarled.

Angry, I shoved him and said, "You are mistaken. Leave here immediately."

Memories of rape and torture shook me, and my mind flew into the rage I could never unleash on Tobias. The man's face broke into a twisted smile, just as Tobias' had so many times; feeling excited by the pain he could cause me and the sense of power he held over me.

He shoved me back, and I slapped him hard on the face. He slipped his fingers under my robe and tried to push them into me, his other hand reaching for my breast. I lost all sense at this violation. I grabbed the closest thing I could lay my hands on and threw it against him, cutting his face, a large gush of blood spraying on us both. He screamed so loud, the old woman ran into my room, and seeing the blood from his cut and the broken chair, she cried, "What are you doing, you crazy child?".

"The whore invited me in and then attacked me," the man shouted. "She must have planned to rob me!"

I was too consumed with fury and fear to speak. The woman looked at me and was surprised, but immediately believed the man's words.

"Pick up your belongings and leave this house now," she shouted. The brute smirked, with a gleam in his eye, knowing the widow would believe him over me.

I gathered my things, still reeling with anger and disbelief. I looked at the woman and shouted, "Nothing this man has said is true." But she held the door open and stared at me coldly until I walked through it.

I spent that night and several others in the desert, fearing any future I might have before me. Was I destined to be tortured by men for the rest of my life? Did I not have any worth or opinion of my own?

Several days later, I ventured into the city and sat by the well, hoping for gossip and news. A large gathering of some importance was to be held around a small mountain rimming the sea. I needed to see Mary, to remember there was good in the world, and to not feel so lost and isolated.

I started walking and joined a small group of followers heading toward the gathering. The crowd grew larger as we continued, as more and more travelers headed toward the site. By the time we arrived, I was stunned by the number of people that had gathered. It was the largest I had yet seen. A light scarf covered my hair, and I wore a plain robe. I traded my beautiful, woven robes for plainer cloth as soon as I realized I was approaching the land of my birth. I could not risk anyone recognizing my weaving, and I hid my jewels on my body or in my folding basket.

Mary found me as soon as I arrived. Frightened, I held on to her and cried, at last releasing the terror I carried with me to the gathering.

"You are safe here, Magdalena," she said. She acted as if she expected me and, somehow, understood my trauma. "I am pleased you are here. Stay close." She kissed me on the forehead and left to join the group close to the teacher. None of this confused me. I did not overthink it. I just wanted to remain as close to her as I could.

Although I was very near the city of my birth, I felt different in every way. I believed I was no longer recognizable as the old Magdalena, yet a shadow of worry darkened my mind. Should I be recognized and Tobias' death held against me, I would face the same fate as my mother. I now feared for my safety in ways I had not for a long while.

I strolled the perimeter of the crowd, still keeping my eye on Mary from a distance. The diversity of characters gathered intrigued me, and I felt soothed by the quiet that had settled over the group. But then I saw the same group of unseemly men who always concerned me at the gatherings. They huddled along the outer reaches of the crowd, but they kept their eyes fixed on the teacher. They were conspicuously different from the people who came to listen to the sermons. I insinuated myself close enough to hear what they were saying, acting like a worthless woman with some meaningless task at hand. They spoke in low voices, but I was always clever at deciphering gossip. I guessed they were tracking the size and mood of the gathering, and seemed threatened by the teacher's growing influence.

Having watched them, I now recognized a core group. They came to each gathering, but separated and dispersed among the newer participants in an effort to blend into the crowd and learn what they could. They seemed to take careful notice of who was coming and who among us was closest to the man we followed. Maybe this had to do with the political aspirations of some of the followers. Perhaps they believed he shared these plans and was a revolutionary. In my mind, he was, but they did not know he held none of the worldly aspirations they attributed to the word. I wondered who they reported to, what they were telling, and why. I could not shake the feeling that they were plotting against him.

I watched these men through Gaius' analytical eyes, and I knew he, too, would have suspected them. Recognizing how I had absorbed so much of his soldier's mind by living with him, I saw the role Gaius played in my development. He was now a part of who I was. It caused me to wonder, is everyone in our life for a reason? All of us threads woven into a larger tapestry, each playing a significant part in the others' lives? And are we the ones weaving, or are we all part of a grand pattern woven together in some master design?

I felt these men recognized me from other gatherings and had became suspicious, maybe because I was observing them. The more I studied them, the more they watched me. I told myself I would interest no one, but I could not stop the mounting fear running through me. I stood up, acted busy, and walked away.

Lost in my disruptive thought, I felt a hand touch my shoulder. I jumped with such fright I almost screamed, and I threw my arms up, twisting to see who or what was behind me. When I looked up, I could not believe my eyes.

It was Seth, thin and worn, but still as handsome as ever. Several days' dust clung to him, so I knew he had walked a distance. On seeing my reaction, he let out a loud, throaty laugh.

"Are you guilty of some crime, Sister, to have such a reaction?"

"Seth!" I screamed, and I threw myself into his arms, once again letting out the flood of tears I had been holding back.

He grinned his charming, lopsided grin and hugged me. "How have I come to find you here? Where is your gallant soldier?" He stretched out his arms, still holding on to my shoulders and taking me in as he spoke. "You look different," he said, cocking his head. "Still a beauty without equal, but something has changed." He squinted his eyes and stared at me. "Are these tears of joy at seeing me, or are you unhappy?"

"Oh, Seth, this story is long. Come with me, and I will tell you everything."

He wiped my tears with his sleeve, a loving gesture I had sorely missed, and we walked to the side of the crowd and rested on a flat stone shaded by a massive tree. I shared with him the full story of the past year. I left none of it out, including my journey to the pyramids and my guide, someone only I saw, as perplexing as it all sounded.

It was comforting to tell my strange journey, even the details that had no explanation. I knew only Seth would listen with an open mind and I had kept my opinions hidden from everyone, including Gaius, since leaving the tent. No one would have understood, would have considered there was merit to anything I said or felt, and this only contributed to my feeling of isolation. How lonely life is when we have no one with whom to share our deepest inner thoughts, whether they are valid, folly or truth. In telling Seth about my experiences, I realized how little I had shared with Gaius, how false the relationship had been. I gave him my power and never showed him my truth. Seth was not surprised by Gaius, but was moved by the news of Lucius, and even more impressed by the visions I had been given. He found it fascinating that somehow, in the strangest of ways, some unseen force led to something of promise. He had great curiosity about Mary and the teacher. He wanted to hear everything I knew about them.

I told Seth about my experience with the boarder several nights before. He stiffened with anger. "You will no longer be alone," he vowed. "I am with you now."

Seeing Seth again after believing he was out of my life forever brought a joy that is difficult to describe. Since leaving him, I had been confused. I had given my will over to Gaius until the very end, and lost any sense of who I was. Through those many months, to stay sane and to keep them alive in my heart, I spoke to Seth and Mother endlessly, describing all I saw and telling them every new thought that came into my mind. I asked their advice and pretended I was not alone. They became ghosts in whom I took refuge, the only ones who knew my truth and understood me. In seeing Seth alive again, I realized the depth of pain, separation, and loneliness I had been carrying with me all this while, despite my exceptional talent for denial.

Seth had also changed. He seemed open in a new way and wiser, but then we were both lifetimes older.

"What great luck I have found you," Seth said, at last.

"I wonder if there is such a thing as luck," I muttered. "Maybe Mother was right, perhaps there is destiny."

He looked at me curiously, but I could tell he also felt this might be true, especially now that we had been reunited. We paused for a moment and sat without speaking, absorbing our thoughts. He placed his arm around me as an affectionate older brother might, and then told me how he came to be there.

Makas was dead. He passed in his sleep shortly after I left. A good death for a good man, I thought, remembering Mother's words. Seth kept the tent going for the girls, but his heart was no longer in it without Makas or me. He grieved the loss and felt the only stable forces in his life were gone.

He had been hurt in another doomed attempt at love and decided he needed a different path. He heard of a teacher who traveled the land giving sermons and changing people's lives. Seth went to hear the man speak and was curious enough to follow him to another gathering. When he saw him heal a lame beggar, he was not sure what to think.

Maybe this was some form of magic trick, for magic doers seemed to roam the countryside. Seth found it unconvincing and suspicious. But the preacher did not look for credit, glorification, or any payment for his acts. He said he only did the work of his father, not his own. He spoke only of loving one another, a message that resonated in a person like Seth. After following the crowds for weeks, he thought this teacher might be good for him. Seth felt great comfort in knowing he would not be judged by such a man, and that he had regard for the weakest and the least significant among us. And he had nowhere else to go.

Seth sold the tent to one of the musicians for very little coin and gave up that life for good. He brought Anna with him, for he knew she would never survive without him. Once I took off, she lost all interest in dancing, and any small income she once commanded was gone, along with her health. He doubted the others would keep her with them, most likely abandoning her in the first town they came across. I dropped my head in shame at hearing his words. I had left Anna behind to fend for herself with a few coins to assuage my guilt. My only concern at the time was for my heart and being with Gaius. Only what I wanted. These were not the actions of a devoted sister.

Anna knew she was a fallen girl with few choices in her life, and none of them were desirable. Men would use her or she would die, and I know she would have greatly preferred death. Seth felt the only right thing to do was to take her with him and pretend they were siblings orphaned from a young age. With his disarming manner, Seth made friends wherever they went.

He came to the aid of an older couple at one gathering, and they offered him and Anna a meal in thanks. The supper turned into a night's stay, and that turned into many days, and then weeks. Seth and Anna helped the couple around their house, for it was in considerable disrepair. Their sons were grown with families of their own, and their only daughter had died of fever many years before. Their children fed and clothed them, but they had no one to keep a close watch over them and help with daily care. They took to Anna at first sight, as she reminded them of the child they lost.

Seth and Anna stayed and helped the couple, making their house feel like a home again. Their natural warmth and charm brought light to the aged couple, and they felt renewed, offering a longer stay. There was much that needed to be done. Seth filled holes and cracks in the worn building to block the winter cold, and Anna beat the dirt from the carpets and cleaned the floor until it almost shone. She gathered wild-flowers and put them in cups to bring a smile to the elderly woman's face when she woke and sat for tea.

Anna loved caring for a house again, even if it was not her own. This was what she believed she was born to do, what she always expected for her life.

Seth, sensing they longed to have her stay, sat at the table one morning and sighed into his tea. "I am tired of dragging this sister with me everywhere I go. How is a young man my age to make his way with such a girl at his heels?"

The husband winked at Seth, for they had already spoken.

"If you do not want her, perhaps I should just have her as my own," the wife snapped.

Anna smiled down at her with pure love, and the old woman understood what Seth was up to. Was it possible? Could they keep Anna as their own? In tears, she said it would be the greatest comfort to have a daughter in her home again, and Seth noticed that even the little man sitting across from her had to wipe his eye.

Relief washed over Anna. Was this possible? She had hoped and prayed for a solution that would not eventually destroy her. She was only fourteen years and already felt her life was over. But she would not dishonor them with blind deceit and keep her history from them. Through her many tears, she told them of her uncle, of the man she intended to marry, and of her family turning her out into the wilderness to die. Her story ended with Seth finding her and helping her survive. She left out any mention of the tent, for she hoped that time in her life could fade from memory as if it had been a long, trying dream.

Having lost their only daughter, and living years with the regrets one always feels at the death of a cherished one—love not given, forgiveness not shared, or harsh words not taken back, the couple could not bear to lose another. Recognizing Anna's good nature, they already cared for her as their own. They wanted to protect her, something her own family refused to do. And they needed her care.

All Anna ever wanted was a family of her own. Perhaps that dream was dead, but at least she could belong to good and decent people.

"Do you like children?" the old woman asked, as Anna combed the elder's hair.

"Of course, Mother," Anna answered. "They are the joy in this world."

The old wife grinned and winked at her husband, who was stooped over in the chair opposite her. He smiled back with a knowing look in his cloudy eyes.

"What is so funny?" Anna asked, sensing she was being played. Seth laughed, and it made her more curious.

"I have a son who lost his wife but one year ago. It is difficult for him to care for his five children. Perhaps he can bring them here some days, and we can watch them together."

Anna lit up, delighted by the idea of caring for young ones. The old woman winked at her husband. They had already decided Anna would be a good match for their eldest son.

"I believe you two are cooking up some scheme at my expense," Anna said, but with a smile, knowing a joke was being shared.

"Never mind," the old woman replied, and she and Seth chuckled. "That can wait."

Anna wept when Seth took his leave, but both felt she and the couple were now happier than they had been in years. As Seth told the story, his voice choked with emotion. At last, he knew Anna was safe and had a chance at a decent life.

Losing Makas made Seth an orphan once again, without home or family, and with little hope for a future. He felt positive about Anna, proud that he had done at least one good turn for a girl who never had a chance. But Seth was born a motherless child, and that and his differences haunted him with renewed strength. His feelings of worthlessness and shame caused him to wonder if he only followed the crowds because he could hide within them, making his loneliness less unbearable. He had nothing else to do and nowhere to go. In time, however, he found the teacher's words comforted him, and he hoped he could somehow figure out his place in life. He recognized the man's compassion and understanding for people like himself and Anna and all the others the world condemned.

"This man seems different from other preachers. He asks for nothing in return," Seth said, impressed that the rich and their lavish sacrifices held no favor with him.

"He judges no one as unworthy," I answered. "He respects men and women alike, rich or poor. But it pains me to see he threatens some. I am uncertain why I think this, but I fear some are wishing him harm."

Seth gave my words some thought, but little weight. He could not fathom the threat these teachings posed to those who sought power.

"I feel he would judge no one, not even me," Seth finally said, his face falling. He still felt burdened by his differences and the hatred so many held without knowing him. His pain pierced my soul as it always did when I saw that familiar far-away look in his eyes.

"I know he would see you as I do," I whispered, "as the wonderful, good person you are. Seth, no one has a better heart than you."

Seth took a deep breath, wanting to believe my words. A long silence followed as we sat with our thoughts.

"How is it I have not seen you sooner?" he asked.

"The crowds are so big, it is fortunate you recognized me at all," I answered.

"I would know you from any distance," he said. "Any doubts I had are gone at finding you." And I smiled, feeling the same.

Seeing Seth again and knowing Anna's story brought a modicum of peace to the part of me that never rested, that deep hole in my soul that never filled. We held each other through the sermon, brother and sister, eternal friends, two people who never fit, except with each other.

From then on, Seth and I claimed to be related. I felt no lie was told, for he was more family to me than anyone besides Mother. No one questioned our story, and Mary's cousins naturally took to Seth and his disarming nature on first meeting. They planned to travel with Mary and the close inner group on a section of their journey across the countryside. They invited us to join them and we agreed, having nowhere else to go. But it was more than that. We wished to be with these people and needed some direction in our lives. They never asked about my relationship with Seth, which was a relief. Because I knew Mary, they trusted my word and were satisfied with my lie. I was still ashamed of my past, unsure how I fit in, or if my truth would be accepted.

We set out early and met the cousins who were joining a small caravan. A growing number of followers made these short pilgrimages to the sites where the teacher spoke, stayed a while to hear his words, and then returned to their lives. We were not in the innermost circle, but we were close, and I always kept my eye on Mary. She fascinated me for more reasons than I understood. The more I listened to the teachings and stories, the calmer I became, and the less I worried about myself. What a great relief to not take myself so seriously, although shame still haunted me. Seth, too, was more serene than I had known him to be. We were no longer plagued by things we felt we lacked, desires not met or wishes unfulfilled, but we had not let go of feeling we were at odds with the rest of the world. We were slowly stumbling into inner peace.

As we neared the city of my birth, I ignored my fear of being recognized. My former life was just that; over and behind me. No trace of the merchant's miserable young wife still clung to my renewed spirit, I assured myself. That Magdalena was dead, and I and all the world needed to be glad it was so.

Seth and I rented a room in a family's home when we returned. These people showed us acceptance and kindness, having more to do with their goodness than any help we gave in return. I was treated better by near strangers than I had been by my father and Abigail. These were individuals my mother should have known. Had the world allowed her a different path, she might have. I understood how it might feel to be part of a good and loving family, something I had always longed for. Life had not granted my mother or me such a gift.

* * *

The day began simply enough, with no foreshadowing of what would soon unfold. A light, cheery mood rested on the tradespeople, the warm morning sun promising an early Spring. We were staying at the cousins' home, helping with the household and caring for the children. Seth stayed back to help the men with heavy work, and I set out to buy food to cook for the evening meal. I had many coins left in my pouch, and I still owned many fine pieces of jewelry. I felt rich in ways I never knew as Tobias' wife, as successful as he was. When I was with him, I owned nothing, least of all my safety, dignity, or freedom. I had to wait for his permission to buy the food I fed him. Now that I had none of his riches, my life appeared more abundant than I could have dreamed possible, and for reasons I was not yet understanding. I would give what I had and trust my needs would be met, for my attachment to this world was diminishing by the day.

I wandered around for several hours, delighting in the rich colors of market life. Almost overwhelmed by recollections, my senses took in the sights and sounds of my childhood. These were the experiences that were real and precious to me, not the unspeakable nightmare of living with Tobias or the wretched days in my father's house when I no longer belonged. I moved about aimlessly, lost in rich, sensate memories.

Amid this walking daydream, I detected a rare but familiar scent. I looked up to see a woman selling precious oils remarkably similar to those Mother had made so long ago. But who could re-create these treasures? Not knowing if I was angry or pleased, I pushed forward, needing to know.

A woman, older than me but younger than my mother would have been, stood in a tented stall displaying clay jars of varying sizes. I approached her apprehensively, as a thief approaches her victim, and I opened a small crock. The fragrance filled my soul, and I swayed with the emotional impact.

"Do you care to try my oils?" she asked, in a merchant's way.

I struggled to recover my voice. I opened more jars and inspected her work with a keen eye, and each blend seemed a meticulous copy of Mother's own. But how was this possible? I stood motionless, and the woman stared at me.

"How have you come to make such oils?" I asked. "I have only known one person who could do this."

"Years ago, I bought a jar when I was not much older than you are now," she answered, still suspicious of me. But as she told the story, she softened with the memory. "The oils and perfumes were magnificent and I became obsessed with the artist and her wares. I looked for her every chance I could to inquire about them. She was such a kind woman, and I fell under the spell of her unique beauty. I tried, as often as possible, to be around her and ask her questions. She always took the time to tell me exactly how she made her precious oils. Sensing how badly I cared to know, she answered all of my questions. She held nothing back, even though it was her livelihood. It was obvious everyone prized her private blends, and they respected her. I am sure I would not be as unselfish and unguarded as she was to me. I went home and tried, over and over, to come up with something of like quality, but I never could. When I brought my blends to her, she instructed me on how to improve the scent or the consistency. She never failed to encourage or help me, never caused me to feel I was a bother, or that I was a thief to want her secrets. Even now, I do not understand why. Finally, I felt I had made something that would impress her and I hurried to show her. When I tried to find her, I heard they had stoned her to death for some deed I was sure she did not commit. I still cannot believe that a woman of such grace and kindness could meet such an end."

Memories came back to me, vague recollections of conversations I ignored when I was so young. I was too busy looking for children my age or filling my senses with the vibrant colors and sounds of the market. Boring talk of trade and business were of no importance to me then, so it was disregarded. It was the ever revelatory gossip I craved to hear. I stared at the woman in disbelief, tears burning my eyes. It seemed a lifetime passed before I could find my voice.

"She was my mother," I told her. "And it was a wrongful death, a deceitful act."

My throat tightened. It seemed words would never come to me again. I stared at nothing for the longest moment, and the poor woman looked at me with such grief and regret, I felt compelled to console her.

"I am so sorry. I should not have said all of this," she said, with deep concern.

"I am glad you are making her oils, that you knew her, and that her artistry lives through you. She would be pleased, I know." My words were clumsy and faint.

"I remember now. She had a small child with her," she answered, remembering back. "But the girl could not speak, so I hardly noticed her. Why did I not see it sooner? You look just like her. Please take a jar of my finest. It is nothing compared to what she gave me."

She handed me a colorful crock. Opening it carefully, I took in the deep, familiar scent, and it transported me back to those innocent days before Mother's stoning. And a great sorrow overwhelmed me until I could only weep. Seeing my pain, the woman also fell to tears, and we embraced each other as if lifelong friends who were afraid to let go.

How was I led to the very trader who sold these oils? It brought me comfort to know Mother lived in some memory apart from my own. Was this a message, some sign that I was on the right path? I clutched the jar close to my heart, where I wished with everything in me, I could hold my mother. I composed myself enough to take my leave, and I thanked the woman, and she acknowledged me back. Stepping away from those jars of oil, I felt I was, once again, walking away from the mother I would never stop missing.

Overwhelmed and confused, lost in memories both good and heartbreaking, I stumbled through the crowds barely noticing what was around me. The noise of the market felt distant and cacophonous. I ached for life to be different.

A man I barely recognized broke my stupor. He pushed me and said, "I know you!"

He had an unpleasant face and a soft, round belly. Recognizing his fine, showy robe, I vaguely remembered him as a merchant who had visited Tobias' tent on occasion.

"Pardon me, good sir, but I think not," I said, and tried to extricate myself as gracefully as I could. I recognized some men who worried me at the gatherings, and I sensed trouble coming toward me.

"Not so fast," he shouted, "I know you. You are that girl who was married to Tobias the merchant. The soldier who killed him was your lover."

His story was convoluted, but it hardly mattered, for he knew Tobias' death had something to do with a Roman and with me. He was with men who worried me at the gatherings, and I saw them coming toward me, ready to incite as much violence as possible. No one in the market bore anything but contempt for the occupiers, and they had a special hatred for any woman who shared the soldiers' beds, so it was easy to stir their passion.

"Her mother was no better," one shouted. "As the mother goes, so goes the child. They stoned her for adultery, and with a Roman soldier at that. I was there."

"She is possessed and has been since childhood. I remember hearing people speak. She was mute in her youth until that preacher cast devils from her. I heard she drove her mother to it," another man shouted, one I did not recognize.

"She supports that magician they claim drives demons from the possessed. That is why she serves him. She is unclean," he said, spitting at my feet.

I was both frightened and confused. It had been a great while since Tobias accused me of possession. He made up that story to cover his actions in his tent. Did anyone remember his lies from so long ago? Had this man been a part of my childhood, or was this something Tobias told again after my disappearance? A way to save face after his bride left him? A wife who would prefer death over a cliff to another night under him. Possession was the only way he could explain my actions and maintain his pride. It would be true to his nature; Tobias, who cared only for his image and himself.

I stood without reacting, confused and disoriented within the growing, choleric crowd tightening around me. The men shoved and pushed me, charging the air with their hatred and anger, and I struggled to stay on my feet.

"Let her follow her mother whore then," said another man, eager in his violence. He picked up a large rock and aimed it at me; the loathing in his eyes was so chilling, my stomach tightened. How could a person so hate a girl he did not even know? "Stone the adulteress. Stone that murdering prostitute. She took one of our own!" he repeated, spitting on me again.

The men were chanting, "Stone her, stone her," and gathering what rocks they could find. They dragged me to a clearing at the edge of the market, kicking up a storm of dust around me. The intensity of their hatred shocked me, their unquenchable desire for my blood a mystery. How, when I was finally finding peace, could life turn so violently against me?

Was this my destiny, as it had been my mother's? I struggled to find her somewhere within me. I had to be like her, to remain calm and dignified, but fear overtook me. The largest man in the group threw me roughly to the ground. Shaking, I stumbled and fell to my knees, trying not to drop the jar.

"Stone her! Stone her!" they called, hungry for my blood.

Another man shoved me harder until I fell on my face, placing me in a perfect position to take their stones. The clay jar cracked, and the oil leaked onto the ground.

"Stone the whore," they shouted, Mother's scent filling my soul as I tried to surrender to the inevitable.

A shadow then fell across my body, and I looked up to see what stood above me. A man spoke, his voice possessing such rare strength and resonance, it stilled the angry crowd. The men stepped back and stopped their shouting.

"Are we all so free of sin that we can condemn another?" It was our teacher.

This was the first time I had been close enough to see his features. I gazed at his face, into his deep eyes that held a kindness I had never known, and I fell to tears. At that moment, I did not fear death or have regret for any of my actions. I cried because of what I saw. It was more comforting and assuring than I could have imagined with my young, limited mind. I felt the power I witnessed in Ptahhotep's tomb and again in the high chamber of the Pyramid, all of which confused and overwhelmed me. Was it power or a knowing I could not yet comprehend? But if I had died at that moment, I would have no longer cared.

He possessed a love so strong and unconditional; I was a stronger human for receiving it. He not only understood me as no one ever had, he knew me as I did not yet recognize myself. To be seen as the individual you perceive and hope yourself to be is the greatest gift one can receive. But this teacher looked beyond that to a better me than I could have imagined. I saw in his eyes, at that moment, that if every person alive held some version of this love and truth, the world would be without war or strife. Living in this place of acceptance and loving forgiveness, we could exist without deception or cruelty. We could give up fear.

If anyone in the angry crowd understood what I saw, I do not know, and I highly doubt. I suspect most could not look past their hatred and violent nature to consider beyond those limitations. But they trembled under his gaze, even if they did not understand why. They knew he could see right through them, and I could tell they were afraid of what he saw. He could read the evil intentions, the dishonesty, and darkness in their hearts, their pleasure in violence, and their fear of others. If only they knew he could see beyond those illusions, that he recognized the part of them that was born good. If they only perceived how he said his Father saw them, they would be transformed. But hatred and fear blinded them.

"If you are free of any wrongdoing, throw the first stone," he said, and watched the men with a full knowing of each. They seemed to shrink under his gaze and dropped their stones, walking away as they muttered to themselves, or to no one in particular. The group that concerned me at the gatherings looked disappointed and angry. The experience did not change them; they held a determination for another day. His interference only strengthened their resolve against him.

"Magdalena," the teacher spoke, and I was surprised he knew my name. "It looks as though no one accuses you. Gather your things and go home. We will all move in the morning."

"Master," I replied, and I stayed on my knees before him. The oil clutched close to my heart spilled onto his feet, and I wiped them with my hair and tears. "Let me serve you in any way I can. Let me devote my life to you."

"You serve with your honest heart, Magdalena, and in ways you do not yet know. Go to safety and join us in the morning."

I accepted his outstretched hand, and he lifted me to my feet, just as I always imagined a loving father would. I do not exaggerate when I say, on taking it, I felt a strength I had never known before. Only now do I realize it was the power of pure love. I walked off, stunned, perplexed, and expanded in every way.

I ran back to the room I shared with Seth and told him what had happened, letting down my guard. I wept at the memory of Mother's stoning and how close I came to my own. More than that, I shook from the immensity of the entire experience, for all it had been, but I could not find words to explain that to Seth. He held me in his arms and stroked my hair.

"Magdalena," he pleaded. "We should go back to Egypt. This place is not safe for you."

"How could I leave them now?" I cried. "I would feel as if I lost a limb if I severed my ties to him and Mary."

"I fear you will lose more than a limb," Seth answered, with deep sadness. Dear Seth, who always held such love and concern for me, my dearest friend.

✶ FOURTEEN ✶

A SLEEPY, UNHURRIED mood lay over the crowd of travelers gathered at the edge of town the following morning. Some packed food in pouches and laid blankets across the backs of small donkeys while young children ran about in the growing light of dawn.

I felt like I was walking in two separate worlds. In one, I did not belong and never did, trapped in a body that carried endless grief, shame and uncertainty. But I felt I now had access to a lighter reality, one of happiness and love. How I could straddle them, I did not know. To which I belonged, I could only hope. No one in the crowd seemed aware of my experience from the previous day, a relief to me but a source of great agitation for Seth.

"How can everyone be so complacent? Why is no one worried about your safety? Does no one understand the weight of what has happened?" he muttered, as we began our pilgrimage.

"Seth, no one here knows of the incident. No one here wishes me harm," I answered, trying to reassure him. "We were called to this journey. That is enough." But Seth would have none of it. He wanted someone to assure my protection.

We ended up in the middle of a small group of travelers far from Mary and the teacher, who walked ahead, surrounded by his inner circle.

"What measures are being taken to make sure this never happens again?" Seth continued, unable to drop his anger.

"No one here caused what happened. It had everything to do with me, with my past. He saved me and I am grateful. I follow him not for safety, but for my heart."

My voice was soft and distracted for I felt altered in every way, a considerable weight having been lifted from my soul. So many times in my short, trying existence, I feared my mind had forsaken me. No longer. My perception of life had changed.

There was little justice in the world into which I was born, especially for women. I was abused, abandoned, and tortured in so many ways, and yet given visions and experiences suggesting a realm separate from the one that hurt me. In failing to make sense of what I saw, I thought I had been driven crazy by the circumstances of my life. Many would consider my visions pure fantasy, for they did not align with or serve the world's ideology. What many think of as insanity might just be a unique vision. Perhaps it is the world that is mad.

So, I walked on, feeling expanded and reborn. Had I remained practical, I would have realized forces were gathering that intended to do us all harm. I was not the target; I was kindling for the fire. The day before was a warning, but all I cared about at that moment was the change occurring within me.

By mid-day, Seth could stand it no longer. His anxiety had become unbearable, and as soon as he saw Mary standing alone, he approached her and unburdened his heart.

"Mary, do you know what happened to Magdalena yesterday?" he almost shouted.

Mary laid her hand on Seth's shoulder, and I watched him melt as I had on first meeting her.

"Yes, Seth," she responded. She met his eyes with her gentle and steady gaze, and I watched and smiled as his worry washed away. Just being in Mary's comforting presence quieted him. An orphan from birth, Seth was a man who never knew a mother. She was gone before he took his first breath. With Mary, he felt a mother's protective embrace at last. "We will all watch out for each other," she told him, her calm manner and quiet wisdom settling his soul. "There are those who do not understand our teachings, but we hope, in time, they will see the benefit of nonviolence and of caring for each other."

They spoke a few moments longer, and Seth returned, relaxed and at ease.

"I suppose there is no other place for the likes of us," he teased, and I smiled.

Making camp late in the day, we ate bread and dried fish and settled in for the night. I watched from a distance as our teacher and Mary walked off together. He held her arm with affection, and it was apparent she was the one closest to him, the one who understood him the best and in all ways. They sat in silence as the sun went down. Seth and I also rested in the evenings with our thoughts, as did the others, in quiet reflection of the day's sermon. There was joyful laughter in the group. Our teacher, although serious in his beliefs and convictions, was playful and laughed at every opportunity. He seemed to embody a sense of joy, and it spread to everyone around him. What a change from my old life filled with priests who wanted blood and sacrifice, all served with a large measure of judgement and downcast devotion. Our teacher told a story of a shepherd who would not rest until he found his lost lamb. I thought of the sacrificed animals at the altars of my youth that so disgusted me. Those priests wanted people debased and small and groveling for salvation, so they would be easier to control and lead. And I am sure they profited from the sale of the lambs they slaughtered. How I wished Mother could have known this world existed. I hoped a part of her did, and that she saw I was among them. This teacher preferred to elevate people to better thought. He had no desire or need to control anyone. He wished to bring light into the dark thoughts and hearts of men.

Being with Seth again helped me to feel more complete. He was the only genuine family I had known since Mother's death. But being with him also made me reflect, often, on our lives in the tent. At first, I had difficulty, even residual shame, trying to reconcile that life with my recent one, as nomadic as it still was. I never spoke of it, fearing others would see me as Gaius had. Seth never discussed it either, feeling the same. What would our current people think of us if they knew? They were kind, and they spoke of forgiveness and love, but beliefs run deep.

Gaius' judgements still haunted me. My lingering memories of dancing in the tent, when separated from my doubts and shame, were of the colors, the light, and sound, and the purest parts of my childhood. I was expressing what I loved most—movement and gratitude for the natural world. And those experiences brought me to some of the most important revelations of my life, as if art had gifted me with visions because of the creative force of dance.

In my heart, I realized this teacher would not judge me, for he knew my truth better than I did. I saw it in his eyes. He loved and accepted his father's children; his brothers and sisters. He would know how and why I was there and how it saved me. Dance gifted me the most revelatory vision of my time, that of the crystal jewels. The experience taught me more about existence and afterlife than any of those angry, hypocritical priests ever did. I thought it led me to Gaius, but it ended in his disavowing me because of it. It led me to understand life in a way I would not have known otherwise.

Seeing through this prism, I knew there was no shame in what I did. Tobias, who bought the approval of the priests by paying for extravagant sacrifices, was called a pious man. He paid to flaunt his devotion. I had no way of buying my redemption in the clerics' eyes, and no place in their sanctuary. Tobias was free to treat me as he wished, for I was just another of his possessions. I always felt this was wrong and political, a law made by men. I recognized that my new teacher accepted this truth, that he considered the intentions of my heart and the value of women. He would not judge me; he delivered me from those who did. The others in the tent were there because man's law allowed them no other choice. Seth gave only love. Was he to be condemned if this was his motivation? He protected Anna, a good and righteous girl who was wronged many times over. And he saved me. Are these the actions of a sinner? What would the priests have done with him? Stone him as an abomination? And what of Anna? Condemn her as unworthy and allow her to perish? Are these the actions of a father who loves his children? A loving God?

With each day and every sermon, I felt I understood myself better. Hearing words of forgiveness and love awakened my heart and the hearts of his many followers. But it also brought me closer to the truths I witnessed through my visions. I saw he was not dictating our beliefs; he was only trying to open a door to more loving thought. He was giving us a way to find our road to peace. For if we truly held love, how could we ever harm another?

But those watchers on the fringes of the crowds had gathered again, and my body sickened at seeing them. The fear of coming so close to the stones had seeped into my flesh, and it stirred at the sight of them. It seemed a battle was raging within the community. I listened as some followers spoke of dissent and overthrowing the occupiers that held our people down. They believed our teacher would deliver us from Roman rule. His miracles would empower us and make us invincible. These raging conversations confused me. Could they not see the true nature of this man? He had no violence in him. But they had the experience of endless occupation and could not rid themselves of their anger. They lived with fear, and I understood, all too well, that those who live in fear often do frightening things. Danger was brewing.

*   *   *

Seth and I returned to Mary's cousins' home, while the much smaller group continued traveling. The family invited us to remain for several weeks to provide care for their children while the wife gave birth to a new baby.

Toward the end of our stay, the small group returned. A large, joyous crowd celebrated our teacher as he entered the city, all seemingly passionate about his presence and his words. Seeing that, I felt happy, as if things were right in the world. But as I listened to Mary speak with her cousins, I became concerned.

"He has become grave and serious," Mary told us. "His laughter is missing. He talks of how things will be when he is gone," she said, her face drawn.

"What does that mean?" her male cousin demanded, shaken by the thought.

"I am uncertain," she answered. "He has not shared his thoughts further, even with me," she responded.

These words froze my heart. How could our teacher no longer be with us? Where would he go? What would become of us? Oh, how self-concerned I remained, worrying about my own future first.

"He is uncommonly serious despite the welcoming crowds. He stays to himself more and more, praying and thinking…as if preparing himself for some ominous event from which he hopes to save us." That was all Mary would say on the subject. She then told inspiring parables from recent gatherings to lighten the mood.

I see now, from where I sit, he understood the disappointing truth of humans. We are happy when things work in our favor, and angry, or of little faith, when they do not. It is easy to love those who give to us, but we turn against those who disappoint. We have no patience, wanting our desires met immediately, while having the audacity to question a gift that comes in different form than we thought we wanted. Hearing her speak, I sensed there was a growing confusion among his closest followers, all but Mary.

I cannot describe all that came next, for I was not close enough to see with my own eyes. History will no doubt tell and retell the stories and shape them to fit the version that best suits the teller and his day. Each retelling will come from the limitations or intentions of the mind that told it, and some will conflate my life with Mary's. What I can say is that it was a time of great sadness, confusion, and fear. And then, for those who understood, it was not.

We did not see Mary the following day. We were concerned but went about life as usual. Two days later, a messenger came in the dark of night and warned us not to leave the house. Someone had taken our teacher while he was praying. The young follower did not know who or why, but he was certain we were not safe in the streets.

As was my curse and habit, I would not do as told. I wrapped myself in my outer robe and veil and rushed out. Knowing there was nothing he could do to stop me, Seth followed. In the streets, people moved about like frightened, unpredictable animals. I saw one man from the inner circle, his robe held high to hide his face, and I hastened after him. He looked at me as if we had never crossed paths and ran into the crowd. I recognized others from the gatherings, and they seemed confused and angry. Seth was unhappy with me as I pushed through the crowd, fearing I would bring too much attention to myself. He stayed at my side, holding onto me to prevent being separated.

I spotted Mary with two other women far ahead of us. They were questioned and then given entrance to the Romans' inner courtyard. The gates shut behind them. I pushed my way through the thick crowd, with Seth following close behind me. By the time we reached the barricaded doors, even more foot soldiers with spears had gathered.

We strained to hear the conversations around us, trying to find out anything we could. Some said the preacher had been taken by Roman soldiers and would be tried as a heretic. As impossible as this seemed, I heard it repeated throughout the crowd.

I had no concept of time, for nothing felt real or normal. It could have been minutes; it could have been days. A small group of men, those who had been shadowing the gatherings, approached the gate surrounding and protecting the local priests. The sight of them infuriated me. Arrogant and righteous, they walked toward the soldiers as if expected. The guards opened the gates and allowed them entry. I rushed forward, trying to get through behind them, but I was met with the sharp end of a spear. Seth held me back, fearing I would try to push through.

I recognized one man who lurked in the shadows of our gatherings. He pulled on my robe and cried, "There she is, the one who follows him. Mary, they call her the Magdalene."

The guard who had his blade pointed at my chest, then shouted, "What is your name, Woman?" And he lifted his spear and pressed it toward the center of my throat.

Seth tried to insinuate himself between me and the spear, but the men in the crowd held him back. They handled him roughly, pushing and shoving him until I feared for his safety. The guard again shouted, "What is your name, Woman?"

"Magdalena," I answered.

"See," the shadow man continued, "She is a part of his heresy."

Seth became so angry he pulled away from the men holding him and prepared to strike the man, but I then held him back. "She is Magdalena, not the Magdalene," he shouted, his face strained.

Another guard brought his spear to Seth's throat, and I realized what I risked with my impulsivity.

The guard stared at me. I looked into his eyes, hoping I could find a place of kindness in him.

"Do you support this heretic, then?" the guard asked, and I saw his heart soften beneath my gaze.

I answered before Seth could deny the best thing to come into our lives. "Yes, I follow him."

"Then go, for it is not safe," the guard answered, to my surprise and Seth's great relief. I stood, stunned, not wanting to leave, hating to think of Mary in that courtyard without protection, especially with those I knew meant them harm. But Seth pulled on me, and I conceded, feeling I could not risk his safety any more than I had.

We wandered through the crowd so no one could follow us, not knowing what to do or where to go. We hoped Mary would return and tell us everything, so when we sensed it was safe, we went back to the house. Mary's cousins were eager to hear what we found, and we sat up for hours, terrified and anxious.

We waited through the next day, anxious and confused. We could not relax or eat. No one dared to speak our fears aloud. At last, I fell into an empty sleep that brought no rest, even my tortured dreams lost to me.

Somehow, piercing that unavailing sleep, I felt a brilliant light enter my soul and expand my spirit as it had at the pyramids, in the tomb, and again in the sandstorm. Was this a gateway to another world, or another dream from a broken heart? Perhaps simply the imaginings of a still grieving girl? It did not matter. I was uplifted. I opened my eyes, thinking I had slept far past the rising of the sun, but it was not yet dawn. Everyone in the house was asleep and the room was dark.

*   *   *

We spent so many days huddled together in the house waiting for some kind of news, we ran out of food and drinking water. Seth, wanting to help, offered to venture out for provisions. I left with him and took to the well to collect water and gossip. Seth and I knew we needed to leave and strike out on our own. Under the circumstances, we would only be a strain on the cousins. We planned to bring them supplies and then make our own way. I looked everywhere for Mary, but could not find her or any of the others. We returned with food and water, but little news. People were tense, we confided. The Roman presence was strong and vigilant.

After we left the cousins' home, we moved from place to place. They had offered us shelter if needed, but we felt to burden them would be unfair. We spent many nights sleeping on the ground in an area outside the city. Perhaps it was weeks. It was hard to know, for life seemed unreal and undone.

If I crept out at night, unable to contain my unease, I waited until Seth was asleep so he would not follow or worry. I required information, needed to know what happened to Mary. I was agitated and fearful, having no patience left to me. There were rumors that our friend had been executed. I could not perceive what was true and what was not. Who would do such a thing, and for what possible reason? And yet, even in my confused state, I could see the faces of his enemies in my mind.

But who might be imperiled by his message of peace, of caring for the poor, and the promise of a better existence beyond the hardships of this one? And then it became clear, and I understood—those who profit from this life and from having power over those who do not. He threatened their order. Perhaps there is no greater sin to those who seek sovereignty over others.

None of us knew anything for certain. Word spread that crowds were turning on everyone connected to our teacher or his followers. We were no longer safe, but did not know where to go or what to do. The Romans were on edge, looking to eradicate anyone who might be trouble. Each day seemed a year.

Concerned for our friends, Seth and I traded two of my rings for a great deal of food and wine and brought it to the house of Mary's cousins. We knew they would be afraid to leave their home, especially with the newborn. They were grateful for our kindness, the children hungry and worried. In gratitude, they offered us shelter for the next few days, so we could rest. Late into the evening of the second night, a knock came on the door.

One cousin answered, and hearing the hushed cries of relief, I ran to see who was there. It was Mary.

"Oh, Mary, I thought we had lost you," I cried, speaking out of turn.

"Much has happened," she answered, to all of us. "We need to move."

We gathered at the table, sharing the meager fare that remained, while Mary told a short, abbreviated version of all she had witnessed. She appeared older, as if she had been through an unspeakable ordeal, and she kept her narrative concise, with little detail. She brought no food to her mouth and looked as if she had not eaten for days. I felt there was much more to the story than she dared to share.

Turning to her cousins, she said, "Go, and stay with Martha for now. I know she will welcome you. Her sister is coming with me. I will need someone to accompany us as well. None of the others are willing."

"Seth and I can go," I offered, looking at Seth, who nodded in immediate agreement. He was eager to get me as far from there as possible. "Seth can protect us."

Mary looked at us with an almost vacant expression. "We need to leave as soon as possible," she said. "Perhaps before first light. Things have become too dangerous here. Seth, do you think you can arrange for a boat to take us across the sea?"

"I can try," he answered.

"Remember," she said. "Be cautious. Everyone is suspicious, and many wish us harm."

Seth nodded and I gave him the few coins left in my pouch and the last of my bracelets to barter for boat passage, provisions, and someone to guide us. Mary spoke with her cousins for a while longer, helping them with their plans, caring for them as she always did. We agreed to meet early the next morning.

I felt desperate watching Mary leave. She looked different; older, as if she had aged through a great trial. Seth returned several hours later, a worried look on his face.

"It is dangerous out there. It was hard to find someone who was not suspicious. I found one fellow, but he is greedy. He knows a man with a small boat that can carry the five of us, so I agreed to meet him before first light."

"Good," I said, "We can rest a while and then go."

After a brief and fitful break, we gathered our few belongings and trekked to the outer edge of the city. The fellow Seth hired met us as arranged, but I saw a second man dart away on our approach. Seth, focused on finalizing preparations, did not notice him. The observational instincts I had honed so well from my time with Gaius warned me the guide had betrayed us. I rushed around the corner to find a man lurking in the shadows, straining to hear what was being said. Seeing me, he fled into a nearby structure.

I was, again, struck by a physical sensation that had now become familiar to me. Impressions from the sandstorm flooded my mind. They appeared at rapid speed, one after the other, scene after arresting scene. My body shook with the impact, but then the images slowed, almost to a stop, until two pictures came into view. One seemed shallow, lonely and without merit, while the other felt more right to me than I could have imagined; a satisfying conclusion to the illusory narrative of my life. I rejected the first and embraced the one I knew to be what I wanted with all of my soul. It made beautiful sense, as if everything I had ever struggled and fought for would now be rested upon me. As if I, myself, had written the story.

In that instant, I saw that this world does not ultimately matter. It is but a dream within a dream. What a curious life I had lived, and yet every step had the purpose of bringing me where I wanted to be. I had prepared this last picture, molded it of my free will, created it as my choice.

The image passed as quickly as it came, and I walked back to Seth and took his arm.

"Seth," I said, whispering to him, "Go to meet Mary and let her know of our plans. I will follow with this man and be but moments behind you. I think it is better if we leave in smaller groups to avoid suspicion."

Seth frowned but did not question my word, and he hurried on. I stared at the man standing next to his donkey.

"I know you have betrayed us," I said, directly.

The sturdy man's mouth twisted, showing his stained, crooked teeth, and he looked at first frightened, then guilty, and then angry. The deep creases of his brow sank deeper into his forehead, burying the small slits of his eyes. Another moment passed, and he scowled at me.

"How do I know what crimes you have committed?" he almost shouted. "I am only making my living with what comes my way. Helping you could put my life in danger."

"You betray more than you know," I answered. "But since you care so much for money, I will give you even more if you forget the others and inform your men I am the only one they want. Tell them you think it best to separate me from my family, to avoid trouble. Then you can turn them on me."

I took out the one necklace I had left, the one that meant the most to me. It was the first gift from Gaius, his token of our love. Holding on to it until the very end made me aware of my remaining attachment to Gaius and what we had once shared. I smiled at the thought of it, for it was a lifetime ago, and this confused the gritty man, and he seemed to take notice of me in a much different way. When he saw the brilliant green stones, his eyes lit up.

"This is worth much more than anything they will offer you," I continued. "Inform them you will meet me at the water's edge while I wait for other companions. This must be after my friends have departed and are well on their way. Your co-conspirators will not want a commotion close to the city. The Romans will react to any violence that breaks out, and each one of you will be taken, in if not brought down on the spot." I said this as a reasonable threat, and I could tell it frightened the man as he considered its meaning.

"Tell the fellow hiding around the corner," I said, and I could see my acuity surprised him. My steady nerve impressed me. My resolve was so strong, the man dared not cross me. "You get this necklace when the others are gone."

Because of my strong conviction and the value of my necklace, the man assessed me as a person of importance. He would not complicate the situation more than he already had and risk retribution. He left to complete his plan and came back moments later. We hurried to catch up with Mary, Seth and the other women.

On seeing me, Mary sensed something had changed. My bearing was different. Seth spoke with the man and made sure we had water and provisions for the boat, while Mary took me aside.

"Magdalena, what are you thinking?" she asked, and I knew she wanted to stop me, even though I doubted she realized what I was planning. "You have helped enough. You need not do more. I am not afraid to risk my safety."

"Mary, you must continue the work. You know and understand this better than anyone. It is why you came into this life. If they suspect you have fled, they will not stop until they find you," I said. It was apparent there was no changing my mind. "If they think you are still here," I went on, "they will stop looking and keep their eye on me."

"But we do not know what they will do to you," she cried. Mary could not reconcile this in her mind, but she had been through an ordeal much bigger than I could imagine. She looked sad at that moment,

"Magdalena, you must come with us for your safety," she said.

"Mary, please, there are more lives at risk than your own, and you must continue teaching. I can easily pass as you and say I need to remain to join with family. Thinking you are still here, where they can monitor you, they will wait to see who gathers. I am more than capable. They will eventually recognize that I am not you, and lose interest. I can travel to Martha's when it is safe. They will not know where to look for you by then. We can confuse them."

I knew I sounded convincing, even though I believed not a word of what I said. I ripped my last coin, the one from Mother, from the hem of my robe in case I needed it before the day was over.

"I have one more coin and can buy passage when the time comes," I declared, showing her the piece of gold. "Perhaps Martha will travel with me if it feels unsafe for her in Bethany. At the least, she will find someone to accompany me. You know how capable she is."

Seth then approached, not knowing what had been said or discussed. "Come, Magdalena, we must get going. Everything is ready," he said.

Saying nothing of my plan, I took Seth's hand, and we hurried down the long stretch to the Great Sea. I sensed the men who sought us would arrive as the sun rose, and the sailboat would need to be well on its way before then.

"Mary tells me Martha will join us soon," I said, lying to Seth for the first time. "I offered to wait for her with Mary's cousins. I have a necklace that can pay for the second boat. Take Mary and get her away from here as quickly as possible. They mean to do her harm. I will be along tomorrow or the day after."

"I will not leave you here alone, Magdalena," Seth shouted. "Have you lost your mind? We will wait here together."

"Martha is not far behind. It will be but a day at most. We have paid this guide enough to get me back. Please, Seth, do not waste time. You know I can take care of myself. The sooner you are on the water, the better I will feel." I felt guilty about my lie, but there was no other way. "We cannot all fit in the one boat, and these women should not travel without a man to accompany them," I continued.

Seth struggled to make peace with what I was saying. "But this makes no sense, Magdalena. Why not wait until they arrive? Yes, you have taken care of yourself in remarkable ways, but these are danger-ous times. Another day will not matter, and we can all be together."

"That is my worry, Seth. If we take off in two boats, it will be more suspicious. This man probably thinks we are a household. Let this be. If too many of us move at once, they will suspect who we are, follow, and harm us all. This seems the only way. If I seem unhurried, if I leave with Martha and the others, we will also look like a family traveling together. I am the obvious one to stay."

I saw my lie was making sense to Seth, but he disliked all of it. "This does not sit well with me, Magdalena. I fear you are taking too big a risk. Your love for Mary is blinding you." Seth spoke with such concern it broke my heart, but I could not allow him to put her in more danger.

"Seth, this feels right to me. Please appreciate this." He could not resist me, so strong was my conviction. "I beg you not to argue. I value your love and concern more than anything, but you must listen to me and know what I am saying is right. Take Mary quickly. She is the one they want. She needs to leave here as soon as possible."

"Magdalena, I cannot…"

"Seth, you must. Please. Make sure she leaves now and arrives safely. No one here knows me, and I will join with Martha and the others and be safe in their company. They will think me a sister or cousin they must take with them. No one will suspect, and I will have a man by my side until I get there."

Seth argued again, but my stern expression convinced him he would not win. I was committed, and it showed. With hesitation, he supported Mary and the others into the vessel, and with a grave look on his face, he helped the boatman shove the craft out to sea and jumped in. He was not happy as I waved him off, smiling and pretending all was right in the world. I was the most convincing liar; I am not proud to say. Seth turned and looked in my direction one more time, anxious about leaving me with the questionable guide.

When the boat appeared small on the horizon, I turned to the stocky man. "Where are those who want me?" I asked.

He whistled, and four burly men soon emerged from the small crowd working on the boats. The sky was turning toward first light, and Mary's boat was now too far away to be noticed.

Looking into his confused eyes, I understood that he, too, mistook me for Mary the moment he learned who we were. I was the one who had the money to pay him and, therefore, in his mind, the one of importance. Any unobservant person could mistake us, and they rarely saw women for who they were. I was sure he had little knowledge of our teacher or his gatherings.

"There she is," one of them said, as he came toward me. The one he saved from stoning, the prostitute."

Another of them shouted to draw attention, "The one whose Roman lover killed one of our own."

Perhaps they confused me with Mary. Most likely, they did not care. Bent on doing their heinous job and getting paid, they surrounded me. The distracted guide, now eager to escape what was coming, pulled me close and demanded my necklace. In the loud confusion, I slipped it to him without notice. He then turned to the men and insisted on full payment for delivering me, feeling vindicated for saying I was alone the entire time. He saw the truth of the situation now and had some regret for being a part of it, meaning only to point the men in our direction and further the chase. He did not want blood on his hands, for he was greedy but not murderous. When I approached him with my necklace, he could not refuse, but he felt guilty about the violence that seemed inevitable.

The roughest of the men threw a pouch of coins at his feet. This threw the man off balance, and he grabbed at the scattered coins while trying to pull his donkey away. He craved every piece of silver, but he also wanted to extricate himself as expeditiously as possible. He stumbled and fell over his feet while the men crushed him in their rush to reach me. His animal pushed back, and he righted himself before disappearing into the gathering crowd.

"That heretic is no longer alive to save her," one of the men yelled out, and several of them laughed. "They took care of him."

These were ignorant, crass men paid to do cruel work they did not understand. Harming me meant nothing to them. It was a way to fill their pockets.

"Finish this," another man spoke up, this one more thoughtful than the others. "We were told to silence her before she spread her lies and made a martyr of that preacher. If his followers rise up, it could be bad for all of us." He was in an obvious hurry to be done with it and away from the crowd.

I said nothing as I watched the boat getting smaller in the distance. The scene seemed familiar to me, as if I had lived it before.

The men shouted as they pushed me about, hoping to attract the attention of the villagers and fishermen. They needed witnesses to their act as long as they were not Roman. The crowd closed around me. The angry smell and rancid heat of their bodies felt suffocating. These were ignorant hired brutes, but they were shrewd enough to recognize the danger of attacking Mary near her closest followers. In the Romans' sight, it would be riskier still. In this small fishing village at the edge of the sea, they felt they would have witnesses to her undoing and still be able to escape without harm or recognition.

They became rougher, pushing me about with increasing hostility. I fumbled in my pocket and found the rock from my mother. I unconsciously rubbed it in times of stress, but this time, as I stroked the smooth, worn edges, a faint light seemed to glow from within it. Mesmerized, I stared at the men who raged around me and then looked down at the mystery of this simple stone.

"Mother?" I called, quietly. "Mary?"

"Heretic's whore! Here is the prostitute he saved from just punishment," the leader shouted, drowning out my soft voice. "And she is possessed. Has been since birth."

Some in the crowd had knowledge of our teacher and found it difficult to trust these strangers without proof. They argued the issue, some dissenting and taking my side. Others knew nothing of Mary, so it was easy to believe these damning accusations against her, and a woman's word carried little weight with most of them.

I felt myself separating from everything around me, and I was no longer afraid. This was my decision. The images came to me again, and I now understood them. I saw into the future, and in it, I would be used to discredit Mary by men of influence who needed to disavow her and invalidate her wisdom and position. If I was a whore, then so was she. These men in power, seeking to hold and increase it, lusting for more, had no place for women in their hierarchy and no inclination to share. They needed to be seen as superior. They would validate their positions by manipulating the truth. Mary would be called a prostitute and whore, and this would come long after she and I were both dead and gone.

The largest brute yanked my arm, and I felt it dislocate with a sharp and violent snap, but I made not a sound. I was beyond the pain of human flesh, my spirit stepping out of this world and into another. My arm dropped to my side. It could no longer defend me even if I had the will, for its use was over. Another of them pulled my other arm, ripping my skin and forcing my stone from my hand. The worn rock rolled to the feet of an older woman who seemed upset by the violence around her. I felt my mother's grace, stored within the stone, embrace the woman who would remain in this tired world.

I turned and looked across the water. The boat, appearing so small to my eye, brought a clear memory to mind. I recognized the scene from a dream I had as a young girl. I was, at once, the child having the dream and the woman living it. Time within time. Which was real, and who was the dreamer, or had they now converged? Does all time happen at once? Or, is it all but an illusion, all just a dream?

The old woman, my worn rock before her, yelled in disgust. "Why do you torture the girl? Do you think the law is being followed?"

The people from the village, on hearing her words, asked more questions. The loudest of the hired men, the roughest and foulest of the four, led the shout again, "Stone her. Stone her and let justice be served."

The slighter man, in a quieter voice, muttered, "Let us finish this, collect our payment, and be done with all of it. There is too much notice now."

The old woman overheard him. "So, it is money you are after, not justice," she shouted, knowing truth was not being served. "What nature of men are you?" And the people of the village questioned them further.

"She is a Roman's whore. Her lover killed many of our own," the leader lied, adding excitement to the story, dragging me by my hair as my arms were no longer of use. "Who knows what she will unleash on all of you if we do not stop her, for she is known to be possessed? She whored with the heretic they crucified. She is vile. Evil." And with this, he spat on me for effect. "The Romans will kill every one of you if they find her here."

The villagers shouted among themselves, fear heightened, and many joined in the call to have me stoned. The sins they ascribed to me and the devil within seemed cause enough to concern them. Adding the Roman threat convinced them I was a liability they dared not risk. With political tensions so high, they could take no chances.

The frenzy grew fiercer, and I searched the angry and distorted faces, thinking of my mother and the fate that had fallen to us both. As the moment slowed in time, and as I gazed into the eyes of the men,

I saw only their fear. I could not hate them. They were concerned for their safety, misguided by ignorance. Sympathy filled me and soothed my spirit, my mother's great wisdom guiding me once again. With these thoughts, I looked up and there I saw him. In the back of the crowd, behind the anger, almost hidden by the mob shouting for my blood, stood my guide from the pyramids.

He smiled, seeing only me and not the surrounding cruelty. A gentle light surrounded him, a light so soft I barely saw the form of his body. And that light covered me, and lifted me from the anger and violence. Had he come to me, or had I already left and found him in the space between worlds?

Feeling his presence, I knew I was in the hands of something bigger than the world I was leaving. Perceptions and insights offered to me from a source beyond my imagination had always instructed and guided me. Rather than honor these gifts, I believed I had gone mad. I questioned them and myself. Even at that moment, I wondered, why me? Why was I, among so many, given these visions and guidance? And immediately the answer came to me.

Because I thought to ask.

I always thought I was in a fight against a force stronger than myself, a force against which I could not win. In my now elevated state, I understood I feared my own power; the latent potential to which, and with which, we are all born and need only to realize. I had wished for death so many times because I did not own my life.

As it came, I knew death was only the end of a dream. I smiled back at my guide, finally understanding.

One of the men threw me onto the ground, and I heard voices again calling for my stoning. I no longer cared. I had stepped into a better world.

The shouts seemed far away. I smiled and looked at the old woman. She understood these men were wrong. And as a female, she also knew my fate was in their hands. Nothing she could do would save me. I felt sad for her despair, but happy to know what ultimately awaited her.

With the one arm that still functioned, I held the coin Mother had once given to save me should I have need. It symbolized our first meeting of Lucius, her great love and concern for me, and my undying attachment to her. I needed it no longer. I was where I wanted to be. With all the shouting and anger, I was able to slip it into the old woman's hand without notice. Mother would have smiled.

The rocks flew, cracking the skull, letting the blood, crushing the bones until the body emptied its life force into the crust of the beautiful earth I so cherished. But I was looking down on it, separated from the violence. The heart that had loved and been broken many times over, that had cried and anguished but also laughed and wondered, was stilled. Its use was over. But I remained.

The old woman fell to her knees and prayed. "You have done wrong to an innocent girl," she cried, but no one listened, and they pushed her aside without concern for her age or safety.

Once released, I saw how my physical body had only separated me from what was real. It held me apart from others, caused me to feel alienated, different and alone. I was foolish and misguided. We are not these bodies we hold so dear. We are a force beyond the flesh, unequivocally joined, each a thread in the divine tapestry of life; none greater than the other, our differences bestowing great beauty on the whole and completing the intricate design. My story has not been tragic, or my death a sacrifice. It has been a success; an ancient agreement met, my part played as I willed it to be. Life does not end. The circumstances of the soul's journey merely change.

I, what is real beyond the physical, rose above the scene, no longer holding sadness for the cruelty and ignorance below. What could I care for that useless, ruined body now that it set me free? This was all I had ever hoped to find—freedom from pain, personal struggle, and the separation I feared I would always know.

All of this, everything I have told you, has passed by me as images in but an instant. How deceptive is time, that an entire life can pass in the blink of an eye? Every action, every journey, every transgression has delivered me to this place of wonder.

I was born under stars that summoned me to dance, but it was life's dance, not mine, and it led me to the wisdom I came to learn. My journey is, now and forever, a part of the collective experience. I am written on the scroll of time, as you will be, in good time.

Mother, Lucius, Gaius, Makas, Anna, and dear Seth, you have taught me love. Too many people walk this earth afraid to share this gift. Father, Abigail, even Tobias, poor ignorant souls lost within the limitations of your thoughts, I bear no animosity for your acts against me. And I ask forgiveness for any wrongs I have committed against you, for in my own ways, I have. We have all lived our part in this dream of time. I ask only for your awakening.

In the story of man, I will be used to discredit Mary. They will manipulate truth to serve their desire for control and power. They will hold the accusations of my life against her, labeling her prostitute, the lowest order they ascribe to a woman, just as they did me and my mother before us. With her grace and wisdom and her refusal to be less than they would allow, they will view her as a threat and will try to limit her influence. But snow always melts and what is beneath will be revealed. Truth will be known, at least by those with open minds and hearts. I have served my part in this dream, and I have lived my story.

I take one last glance at the scene below, the empty, torn corpse in my robe, the crowd that must realize they witnessed a wrongdoing if for no other reason than my ability to transcend the act with grace. I see Mary watching me, seeing me still, and I know her strength and knowledge will comfort Seth.

I look down the scroll of time and see Mary growing old and teaching to loving crowds, living a life of devotion and service to others. She serves the man she will always love and will someday join. Seth will watch over her and live his last days in peace, an orphan no longer.

Crystal jewels fill the heavens. I move without effort, for I am one of them, each facet reflecting a part of my story. Each living image dissipating into the source of illumination that holds it—crystal jewels of the universe—stories that merge together in perfect unity. I am more than the sum of these parts and I am them no longer. Light and sound are all that remain.

I move within the transcendent dance.

A fleeting vision of Gaius comes to me, and I know he senses my passing. He was present for my first revelation of the beads, and a part of him is now aware. He is looking up at the sky knowing I am no longer a part of his world, and for the briefest moment, I feel his anguish and guilt, and I am sorry for it, but then all sorrow leaves me, as do the memories of my physical existence. Love and joy remain.

If we think we know love on earth, we know it as a drop of water understands the power of the sea.

I am incandescence floating without form. The dreams I lived within time, the prisms of my life, join the stars and become the light of inspiration.

A heavenly choir echoes through the celestial jewels; voices of angels so exquisite they would stop a human heart. My soul, born for movement, flows to a song I have known forever; a last dance to a voice I will know for eternity. Time stops. Its insignificance made clear. I look up and see her; more beautiful and loving than I even remembered. Her love envelops me.

"Yes, Mother, it is I, Magdalena."

✶ EPILOGUE ✶

THIS BOOK IS a work of fiction, and not intended to be taken as dogma or historical fact. Inspiration for the story was born from a lecture given by a biblical scholar many years ago. His research showed that an unknown council had inserted the parable of the prostitute saved from stoning into the bible hundreds of years after the life of Christ, as many passages were. Beginning his research as a dutiful Christian, he became agnostic as his research continued. This brought up many questions regarding the purpose of the account. Why was it added, and by whom? This is the obvious question, but one might wonder further. Who was this girl, if she existed? Was she a real, but insignificant, character used to illustrate a narrative, or was the story fictional? Throughout the ages, women have been victims with few options in patriarchal societies; judged, with little sympathy, for not conforming to the roles dictated by men. Who they were; their hopes, dreams and accomplishments were largely unheralded and hardly considered. This book explores the life of a female who would not fit into the mold set before her. It is fiction, but the desire and ability to look without judgment at another's exploration is not.

Another aim of this book is to underscore that there is no evidence verifying that Mary Magdalene was a prostitute, and many scholars deny this altogether. There is research, as well as theory, that she was the closest and most learned of the disciples. There are temples and churches built in the South of France claiming to be the site where Mary landed when she fled persecution. The mystery continues with much speculation, some conflating the two women, as was sometimes taught in parochial schools the author attended. After all, a prostitute in these circumstances is but a one-dimensional figure representing a fallen, and therefore undeserving, woman. Patriarchal hierarchies' regard for women as Madonnas or whores, allows them to exploit females and allow their subjugation. Under these conditions, labeling a woman prostitute was enough to silence her and erase her legacy.

This book imagines the life of a creative, independent artist who endures great hardships on her road to physical and spiritual awakening. She follows a course we all must take in time, though the circumstances vastly differ; the road of self-discovery and inner peace. Magdalena illustrates that every life has multiple dimensions to it, and to judge another's life is not only meritless, but futile as well.